CHIMERA

C. J. Singh

First paperback edition February 2022

ISBN 978-1-7366354-3-8 (paperback)
ISBN 978-1-7366354-4-5 (ebook)
ISBN 978-1-7366354-5-2 (hardcover)

www.worldofcjsingh.com

To Ash, my paper eating, ear massage loving, loyal boy.

Chapter 1

Eden

The crisp, cool breeze brushed off my skin, but it didn't bring the shivering chill that it did to Tate and Old Bob. They both tugged their jackets up to their chins, trying to keep every bit of warmth in. Over the past two weeks, the air has become much cooler, causing our breaths to look like billowing clouds during our hike south.

We worked our way down an abandoned, broken concrete road that Old Bob said had once been called a freeway. I was thankful for the ease of just following a road instead of tracking our way through the wilderness, but this caused Jace, Ash, and I to keep a fast pace. It's a good thing Tate and Old Bob were in good shape.

I'm not sure what I expected to see as we worked our way south, but abandoned cars, homes, and even small towns were not it. It was hard imagining life within the abandoned buildings since all I knew was the cabin and then what I had seen of the city. We rarely came upon anyone, and the few people we did see from a distance hurried away from us in fear. At least I told myself it was from us and not my claws or the elongated fangs that popped out at the most harmless smiles.

"Sun's going down. We should find shelter," Old Bob called from behind. Glancing back, I noted the sadness still in his eyes since Ellie's death that I knew would never fade. We all missed her, but he most of all. That sadness and the grey flecks in his facial hair made him seem older.

"There. The car." Tate pointed to a large grey van parked on the side of the road, and I groaned. He looked at me. "What? You would rather sleep in the cold, letting the frost freeze to your eyelashes?"

"Doesn't bother me." I winked at him, giving his shoulder a light shove. "But if it makes you feel any better, we can all cozy up in the van."

"I'm not cozying up to Tate," Jace said as he peeked into the windows. We had already experienced a few mishaps of opening car doors just to be attacked by animals. A few even had decaying dead bodies. The smell was almost unbearable.

You're such a baby, I projected to Jace's mind.

He raised an eyebrow at me. *I never said I wouldn't cozy up to you.*

My cheeks warmed, and I looked away.

Tate rolled his eyes. "Are you guys doing your mind talk thing again?"

"Shut up," I snapped. "This looks OK." I slowly opened one of the front doors. Musty air hit me, and I coughed. "Let's air it out a little. I don't know if I can stand that smell all night." I moved around the van opening all the doors and checking for anything useful. Under the back seat, I found a few wool blankets that I shook out and laid on the ground to try and get the mustiness out.

"Tate, get a fire started. Eden, you and Jace hunt something we can eat," Old Bob said as he slowly sat down in the front seat and closed his eyes. "I'm going to rest here a bit."

Ash didn't miss a beat as he curled up on one of the long back seats. I gave his ears a little scratch.

"Sure thing," Jace said.

Old Bob may have been in good shape, but he was still the oldest and needed more rest.

I followed Jace closely, walking past Tate, who was swearing as he worked at sparking a fire. I kicked a twig at him as we passed and received a vulgar hand gesture in return. Chuckling, I caught up to Jace. "So, what should we try and get today?"

He gave me his best side-glance smirk. The one that showed off his dimple on his right cheek. The one that always made my heart speed up just a tiny bit. He pulled me out of my reverie when he said, "I've never met someone so excited to hunt."

"That's because you've never met anyone as good at hunting as I am."

"Sure. That *must* be it."

We jogged in companionable silence. I slowed and let Jace move to my side, and he gently put his hand in mine. I didn't look at him, but I felt his eyes on my face gauging my reaction. Always careful not to scare me off, he treated me like a scared bunny, but I couldn't blame him. He was letting me lead our relationship, never pushing me too far.

When the sweet smell of berries filled my nose, I stopped. "Do you smell that?"

Jace moved his face in different directions, nose in the air, trying to catch the scent. "Faintly."

"This way." I tugged his arm, careful not to slice it with my claws, and charged forward, following my nose. It wasn't long before we were standing in front of the largest wild blueberry patch I had ever seen. "OK. Let's get to work." I pulled off my jacket and laid it on the ground. "Start piling the berries on this."

"Eden, you'll freeze. Put it back on. We can get enough in our pockets."

"I'm fine. The emptiness of my stomach will not be satisfied by a pocketful of blueberries. Trust me. Plus, I don't feel the cold." Ignoring his narrowing eyes, I started to pluck the plump berries from the bushes—only half of what I picked made it onto my jacket. They had to be the juiciest and sweetest I had ever tasted.

We worked quickly in silence, but Jace never missed a chance to brush up against me, nor I to him. I bumped my shoulder into his, and he fell to the side laughing.

A twig snapped, and I whipped around with a growl already in my throat, but it was stifled by the two beady black eyes of a large brown bear. With my heart slamming in my chest, I slowly curled my claws and stepped between Jace and the bear.

"Eden," Jace warned as he rose to his feet.

"Stay back, Jace."

The bear was still, watching us, watching me.

Just back up, Eden. We can slowly move away.

The tension in my body released a little at his words. He was right. The bear, watching us with more interest than aggression, would let us leave. I was almost positive about that. Almost.

But the berries.

Jace laughed, and I knew how ridiculous that sounded, but my growling stomach wasn't laughing.

As the bear started toward us, my tension spiked again, but I didn't move. Neither did Jace. We stood, frozen, watching the bear move past us to the bushes. It picked berries and popped them in its big mouth, its teeth making a loud snapping sound. After a moment of watching, I took small steps back toward the bush.

Eden.

It's fine. It won't hurt us. Just keep picking.

Just keep pic—are you crazy?

Jace grabbed my arm to stop me, and the bear stilled, watching his hand tighten on my arm.

"Let go," I said quietly, not taking my eyes off the bear.

"Not a chance."

"Jace—"

The bear's growl silenced us both. Its eyes stayed fixed on Jace's hand until he finally dropped it. The bear looked back at me a moment before going back to the berries.

"OK," Jace said. "I'm not going to lie. This is creeping me out."

"Yeah." I watched the bear as I folded up my jacket. We had a nice pile that would have to be enough.

We slowly backed away, the bear not giving us a second glance as it filled its mouth with berries, some blue smeared on its snout. When we were finally out of sight of the bush, we turned and jogged back to the van. Neither of us dared to speak.

Chapter 2

Jace

I barely heard Tate's exciting story of Ash stalking and killing the rabbit. My mind was too consumed with Eden and the bear. She begged me not to tell the others what happened, and I reluctantly agreed. I could understand her fear; they would never let her away from them again, but a part of me agreed. Don't get me wrong; Eden can take care of herself, but still, she tended to be a little impulsive at times, not caring what happened to her.

"Man, Jace, I wish you could've been there. It was awesome," Tate said, grinning down at his charred piece of meat.

"I bet it was."

"Nice berries you found. Juicy and sweet," Old Bob commented before popping one in his mouth.

"You should've seen the bushes. The biggest I've ever seen this late in the year," Eden said.

"Yeah. Didn't think you would have brought back a jacket full of them. It seems so late in the season for berries." Tate inspected one carefully before eating it. "Maybe we should go back in the morning and grab more for the road."

"No!" I yelled.

Eden's smile dropped, and she furrowed her brows at me.

I cleared my throat. "I mean... I think we took most of the good ones. Like you said, it is late in the season." I looked down at my untouched rabbit, avoiding everyone's burning eyes.

"Everything OK?" Old Bob asked carefully, looking between Eden and me.

I chuckled. "Yeah. Yeah. Sorry, just tired." I stood and stretched, knowing it was much more exaggerated than it needed to be. "I'm going to turn in. Have to be in tip-top shape for tomorrow." Passing all their quiet stares, I moved into the back of the van, lay down, and closed my eyes.

After a few moments, I could feel Eden's annoyance fill the air outside and soon the van. Opening one eye, I peered at her tense face. She stood, arms crossed, watching me from just outside the van.

I sat up only my elbows. "Yes?"

Her leg moved like she was tapping her foot, and I stifled a smile. I could smell the smoke from the fire and could hear Tate and Old Bob's quiet conversation, but I knew better. I'm sure they were curious about our little banter.

Just come in so we don't attract unwanted ears.

She huffed before stepping into the van and slamming the door behind her. If the others didn't know she was angry with me before, they sure did now.

"Well, you didn't have to slam the door."

"If we don't want those unwanted ears to hear, then yes, I did."

"All right then. Have at it."

Her eyebrows went up. "Have at what?"

"Me. Have at me."

She blinked. "I don't understand."

"Jeepers. Yell at me!"

She smiled. "Why would I yell at you? I just wanted to make sure you were OK. You were acting... weird."

"Seriously? You're not mad?"

She laughed. "Honestly, Jace, sometimes I don't get you."

"Right. You don't get *me*." I chuckled softly. We sat in silence a moment. She wrung her hands together nervously, examining her claws. "Look, Eden. What happened today... it wasn't normal. Wild animals don't act like that."

"Ash does."

"All right, but you have had him since he was a pup. That's different from a full-grown bear. I mean, the bear seemed like it was... defending you, Eden."

"I wouldn't have let him hurt you." She tilted her head at me in that very animal way she does. It reminded me of our days in the city, locked away in the labs. She had changed from the old Eden and emerged as the Eden who sat before me now. Guilt still welled within me that I had told her about the city and hoped that she could make a positive difference. All it did was get her tortured.

"I know, but again, it's not normal that a bear didn't outright just attack us. It should have. That would have been normal. It wasn't scared of you but protective."

She bristled, and I immediately regretted my words.

"So, you're saying, I'm not normal?"

The hurt in her voice had me reaching out to her, but she automatically snapped away from my touch. "No. That's not what I'm saying."

"Then what are you saying?" Her voice held more steel, more fight, and a knot tightened within me.

"Look, I'm still trying to learn life like this as well—"

"Life like what, Jace? An animal? Not *normal?*"

"Eden."

"It's fine. Just drop it, all right? I've heard enough." She crouched, opened the door, and jumped from the van.

"Eden—"

She slammed the door in my face. Groaning, I punched my fist into the seat cushion with a scream. Why did I open my big mouth?

~

Eden, please.

I tried for the millionth time to talk to her, but she kept the walls of her mind strong, not even a little crumble. Every time I tried to catch up to her, she increased her pace. If it was just us, I would have stayed alongside her, but since we had Old Bob and Tate to worry about, I just let her take the lead and fell behind.

As we came to a small town, we all slowed, watching every direction as we walked down the main road.

"Stay alert," Old Bob said, quietly.

This town wasn't any different than any of the others that we had been through with abandoned homes, shops, and cars. But this one *felt* different. It was almost like we were being... watched.

"Stop." Eden held up her arm.

We all stopped abruptly. Her nose flared as she smelled the breeze, her eyes darting in all directions. Instinctively, I did the same, but I didn't smell anything, only felt it. Eyes on us.

Do you sense that?

I turned to her, startled at the invasion in my mind. I didn't expect her to drop her walls so abruptly. *Yes.*

"We aren't alone," Eden said, quietly.

"What do you mean? I don't see anyone." Tate nervously searched the area.

"That's because they're hiding."

Old Bob started forward. "Let's just keep on walking. We don't need—"

"Hello? I know you're there. Come out!" Eden's voice bounced off the buildings, echoing around us.

I grabbed her arm, yanking her back toward me. "Eden, what are you doing?"

She pulled her arm from my grip. "We don't mean any harm. We're just passing through!"

"Shut up, Eden," Old Bob yelled, facing her. "What are you trying to prove?"

Eden ignored all of us, pushing toward the small store. "Hello? I know you're there. Just come out! I promise we won't hurt you."

A loud chuckle echoed between the seemingly empty buildings, and a prickle moved up my spine. A man, flanked by one man and one woman both carrying guns, stepped into view. The man's clapping clanged so loudly I shook my head to try and clear my ears.

"Whooo! Well, aren't you gracious to not hurt *us*! Did you ever think about if we would hurt *you*?"

"Oh shit," I mumbled.

Chapter 3

Eden

"And who might you all be?" the man asked, stopping just before stepping onto the road. His eyes roamed over everyone but landed on mine. His mouth tightened as he took me in. He was trying to keep his face from giving away his alarm, but I caught it. That quick twitch of his eyebrows and cheek.

"We mean no harm. Just passing through," Old Bob said, stepping in front of me. "I'm Robert. This is Tate, Eden, and Jace." He motioned to us all.

"Eden," the man said quietly, looking me over again. "You have a very... unique look."

I smirked. "Likewise." Two can play the game of insults.

He chuckled again. "Careful. From where I'm standing, we're the ones with the weapons."

I snickered, pushing Old Bob to the side. Everyone was tense but smart enough not to interfere. I wasn't planning on being mean, but I don't take kindly to threats. "Well, you may have guns, but you don't know what I'm capable of." I moved my hand up dramatically, inspecting my claws.

I smiled at the hiss from the woman.

"She's a demon."

"Now, now, Clara, let's not overreact," the man said, the confidence in his voice wavering. He inspected my claws before moving back to my face. I gave him a large toothy grin, relishing the way his face paled at my fangs. Ash's warm body rubbed on my calf as he moved to my side. He was ready to act. All I had to do was ask.

Stop it, Eden.

You're no fun.

I'd rather not die today.

I turned to Jace, lifting an eyebrow before looking back to the man. "So, you're Clara." I nodded to the woman, whose gun was now shaking. "And you two are... ?"

"I'm Jimmy, and this is Dan."

"Nice to meet you," Old Bob said. "We are just passing through—"

"Passing through? And where might you be passing through to?" Jimmy asked.

"Kansas City," Tate said.

Jimmy barked out a laugh. "Kansas City!" He scratched the stubble on his chin. "Well, that isn't possible."

Old Bob stepped forward. "Not possible? What do you—"

"Rob, Cal," Jimmy hollered. Two more armed men stepped out from the buildings behind us. "Let's take our guests to their new living arrangements."

Rob and Cal started toward us. Every cell in my body tensed as a growl slowly erupted from my throat. Ash's snarl sounded along with mine, and they halted, quickly raising their guns to us when we took a slow step toward them.

"We aren't going anywhere," I growled.

"Eden." Jace kept his voice gentle as he moved to my side.

"I'm afraid you are. We never have visitors, so when four people and a... wolf come stumbling through, it piques my interest. If you don't want to be shot, then you will comply."

"Then just let us go through. We don't want anything from you," Old Bob said.

Jimmy shook his head. "I'm afraid that won't do. You know we're here."

I growled at the threat but relaxed slightly when Old Bob put a firm hand on my shoulder. "Eden, relax. If you fight, we will die. You're no match for four guns."

"I have Jace and Ash to help me." I clenched my jaw, keeping my eyes on Jimmy and his men.

"No." The firmness in Jace's voice had me turning to him. "Save it, Eden. Let's not show all our cards in one hand."

I bit my lip, hating that he was right.

Ash snarled, and I spun around. The butt of a gun pushed into my chest. I moved my hand up to grab it, but Jace snatched my hand away before I could push the gun away. I cursed. How did that guy, Cal or was it Rob, get so close to me?

Ash, baring his teeth, ambled between me and my attacker. The barrel of the gun quickly moved from me to Ash, and my instinct to protect skyrocketed.

"Don't. Point. That. Gun. At. My. Wolf." I kept my voice low and even as my eyes fixated on the man.

He smirked. "We don't allow live wild animals in our home. So, unless you want me to shoot him, he's gonna to have to skedaddle."

"Ash is with us. He's not wild," Old Bob said.

"He's a wolf, ain't he?" Jimmy asked.

"Well, yes—"

"Then he's a wild animal, and we don't allow them. So, like Cal said, unless I kill him, he has to leave."

Cal didn't waver his grip or aim as he flicked his gaze between me and Ash. Seeming to understand the conversation, Ash stopped baring his teeth and looked at me. His ears twitched, and he let out a little whine. I avoided the warmth from his golden stare on my cheeks. He would do as I asked, but what if we lose him? What if something happens to him? What if I never see him again?

I moved my hand to my butterfly necklace, clutching it for strength. I had this to remember Ellie, but I had nothing to remember Ash. I couldn't lose him. I have lost too much.

Thankfully, Tate moved up and crouched, scratching Ash's ears. "Hey, buddy. We're OK. Why don't you go hunt something for us, all right?" Ash whined, still watching me. He would wait for my command. As much as Tate tried to spare me from the anguish, it didn't matter.

I closed my eyes and sucked in a breath before looking down at my most loyal companion. He watched me, confusion and worry shone in his eyes. "It's all right. Just a few days. I promise." He whined again, giving my hand a little lick.

"Scat! Get outta here," Cal yelled, kicking at Ash.

Ash yipped as Cal's boot hit his side. I moved forward fast, pushing the gun away and grabbing the man by the neck, letting my claws poke into his skin just hard enough but careful not to break the skin. I touched my nose with his and snapped my teeth together in a very audible pop.

"Eden!" Jace and Old Bob yelled in unison.

I ignored them. "If you touch him ever again, I will end you."

Cal's face went white, but the click of a gun and the push of the barrel to my temple made me freeze.

"If you hurt him, I will shoot," one of the other men said.

"All I have to do is squeeze."

"All I have to do is pull the trigger. You choose."

I stood, frozen with my claws digging into Cal's neck, a small drop of blood trailing down his throat. He watched me with anticipation as I pondered my options.

"Eden"—Jace's gentle hand moved to my shoulder—"let go. It's all right. Ash is all right."

I glanced to the edge of the tree line and I saw Ash. He gave us one last look before he ran into the woods. Dropping my hand, I stepped back and turned. "You better be right about this."

"Get moving." One of the men pushed my back with the gun, and I tensed.

"If you touch me with that gun again, you won't live to see another sunrise," I said through a clenched jaw.

Old Bob moved to us and pushed the gun away. "There is no need for that. We'll cooperate."

"All right then, get moving." He motioned ahead.

With one man leading us and the other behind, we moved down the road. We arrived at a farm where we were led to the barn.

Once inside, we were brought to a horse stall and pushed inside. The smell of manure, dirt, and hay filled my nose.

Well, I can get us out of here tonight.

I looked at Jace to see if he had heard me, but he shook his head. Before I could ask what was wrong, cold metal wrapped around my wrist and clicked shut. The cuff was attached to a thick chain that was bolted to the wall.

"What the hell!" I yanked at it, but it didn't budge. Even with my strength.

"There isn't a need for this," Old Bob said.

"Not my orders. Jimmy's."

"Then let me talk to him. We don't need to be tied up like... animals."

The man snickered as he fastened the last of the chains on Old Bob's wrist. "Well, she sure looks like one."

I swiped out a claw so fast he didn't have time to react, but the chain kept me from making my mark. I only ripped his jacket, but the fear in his eyes was worth it. "Say that again, and I will make sure to show you how much animal I am."

"C-C-Clara was right. You are a demon." He moved to the edge of the stall and sidestepped to the door where his friend waited with a gun still pointed at us.

"There are a few blankets in the corner if you get too cold. The hay will also help. We will chat more in the morning."

We were silent as we listened to their retreating footsteps, then the closing of the barn door. Once it was closed, the only sound was our breathing and the jingling of our chains.

Chapter 4

Jace

None of us spoke for what felt like hours, but since we had no way of telling time, I am not sure exactly how long we were there. What I was sure of is that no one really understood how this all could have happened. How after everything—surviving Zane and the scourge, traveling south—we were now prisoners again, chained in a barn...like animals.

"You should have let me rip them to shreds," Eden said.

"They would have killed you," Old Bob said.

"I would have—"

"There were too many," I cut her off. "You may have gotten to one or two, but the others would have shot you. You're strong, but you're not indestructible."

"You would have gotten to them first," she said, watching me with so much trust it made my heart hurt.

"I would have tried." I smiled at her. "And probably would have died in the process."

"There are more of them. You wouldn't have survived," a female voice rang from the stall next to us.

We all stilled, slowly turning toward the thick wood wall between us. It blocked any view we may have had of who was there.

"Hello?" Old Bob said.

"Hello," the female voice replied.

"We didn't realize there was someone else here."

She laughed. "I'm sure you didn't. It's just me. A prisoner like yourself."

"And you are?" I asked.

"Lillyanne."

"Well, Lillyanne, why are you a prisoner?" Old Bob asked.

There was a short silence, then a long sigh. "I didn't follow Jimmy's *rules*."

"His rules? What rul—"

The barn door slid open with a loud rumbling, bringing in the late afternoon sun. Four men, two of whom we met before, stomped in holding guns.

"All right. You, blond boy. Let's go," the man Jimmy had called Cal said, pointing at Tate.

"Me? Why me?" Tate shifted farther back, looking to each of us for help.

"Because Jimmy said so. Stand up!" Cal moved toward him with a key. Before he stepped into the reach of Eden, he paused.

"No funny business, demon girl, or my friends will blow you all to bits." The cocking of two guns echoed his words.

"Where are you taking him?" she asked, curling her claws around her metal chains. I could feel the conflict within her. She wanted to yank them right out of the wall, but she didn't know if they would actually follow through with their threats, and she wouldn't test it when her brother was in harm's way.

"To the house. Jimmy wants to talk to him."

"I can talk to Jimmy. Just take me." Old Bob moved forward and raised his cuffs to Cal, who ignored him and continued to Tate.

"Nope. Sorry. Jimmy's orders." He yanked Tate's chains, pulling him to his feet. Tate wavered back and forth as Cal unlocked his cuffs, then pushed him toward the stall door.

"It will be all right, Tate," Old Bob said. "Just be strong and remember everything I taught you."

I turned to Eden's tight face as she watched her brother's back disappear out of the barn. We were again left in silence.

"Don't worry. He won't kill him," Lillyanne said.

"Kill him?" Eden's voice was deep, and her self-control was wavering.

"Yeah, no. They know if they kill him, you all won't cooperate."

"We won't cooperate anyway. But if they touch him, they're dead." Eden's knuckles were white as they gripped her chains.

Eden, he'll be all right. Old Bob taught him well. Like you.

She turned to me, and we locked eyes. *If they hurt him . . .*

Then I'll help you destroy them.

She visibly relaxed, and I reached for her hand. After a moment, she put her hand in mine, and I squeezed, sending her as much strength as I could muster.

Her free hand clutched the butterfly necklace around her neck, and I prayed that nothing really did happen to Tate because her frail heart couldn't lose another person she loved.

"He'll be all right," Old Bob said, still watching the barn door. His words seemed to be more to reassure himself than anyone else.

"He will. If he could survive escaping Zane when he was five with his baby sister, then he can survive this," I replied.

"Escaping Zane? Who's Zane?" Lillyanne asked.

We all turned to the wall. "Zane. The president," I responded.

"President?" She laughed. "There hasn't been a president in a long time. Since before the war."

"What do you mean? He is the current president." Eden pulled her hand gently from mine. I immediately missed her warmth but closed my hand over my propped knee to keep from reaching back to her.

"Ummm, no. We don't have a president." She paused a moment. "Wait. You don't mean that old kook up north?"

Eden and I looked at Old Bob. His face was white, and his eyes showed uncertainty. It was the first time I had seen him show any kind of vulnerability.

"Old kook?" Old Bob asked.

"Yeah. We rarely get visitors from the north. But a few years back a couple came through spoutin' some nonsense about a man playing president. We all just laughed it off."

"Playing president," Eden repeated, glancing between us. "So, Zane doesn't really have full control?"

"Is that even possible?" I asked.

Old Bob sighed. "Well, anything is possible, I guess. But that would mean—"

"That would mean the bastard is lying to everyone in the north," Eden said. "And they eat it up like it's cake."

"So, wait, you guys truly believe he is the president?" Lillyanne whistled. "And I thought all of Jimmy's followers were brainwashed."

"We aren't brainwashed," Old Bob said, sitting up straighter. "It's not brainwashing if you haven't been told differently. We were... misled."

"I guess. Where are you guys from anyway?"

I opened my mouth to respond, but Old Bob held up a hand to stop me and spoke instead. "Why?"

The jiggling of her chains rang through the barn. "Like I said, we don't see new people here. Like ever. So, you must be from somewhere far north, but if that's true, then I'm impressed you made it here."

Eden and I watched Old Bob as he thought through a reply. He slid his hand over the curves of the metal chain that linked him to the wall. "Yes, we are from up north. Been walking for a while now, and yes, it hasn't been easy, but we made it."

"Wish I could say welcome, but I'm sure you are regretting your walk through this town."

Old Bob's response was a grunt before he rested his head on the wall and closed his eyes. My stomach tightened as the faint smell of fear flowed toward me from him.

I turned to Eden as she slipped her hand back in mine. Squeezing gently, I gave her a smile, sensing she was on the brink of an explosion. I was honored she chose me to anchor her. Pulling her close, we sat in thick silence as we waited for Tate to return.

Chapter 5

Eden

The barn door rumbled open, and I jolted upward. I had fallen asleep on Jace's shoulder, with our arms linked. Giving his shoulder a quick glance, I let out my breath when I saw I hadn't drooled all over him.

"Rise and shine. Up, up, up! Everyone up," Cal hollered as he pushed open the stall door and walked in. Two men waited with guns at the entrance.

"Where's Tate?" I asked, taking Jace's hand to help me up.

Cal grabbed Old Bob's cuffs to unlock them. "He's waiting for you. Outside." Once Old Bob was unlocked, he pushed him toward the door of the stall. "Walk. They're waiting for you." Old Bob shuffled toward the barn door as Cal unlocked Jace then me. He motioned for us to walk out first, in mock politeness. "After you."

As we stepped outside, the cool, dewy air hit me. Old Bob bristled in the cold as we walked to the grassy area between the barn and the house. I pulled in a deep breath, thankful for the lack of manure smell.

Jimmy stood, flanked by four people on each side, all holding guns. Lillyanne was right: there were more people than we expected. Tate was sitting on the cool ground facing Jimmy, and when I stepped up to his side, the metallic smell of blood filled my nose.

"Tate?" He slowly turned his head and looked up at me. Or tried to at least. His face was so swollen and covered in blood I could barely make out his eyes. I dropped to my knees next to him and gently put my hands on his cheeks, careful not to scratch him with my claws "What did they do to you?"

He opened his mouth to speak. "I d-d-didn't—"

"He didn't want to give us information," Jimmy said, his eyes burning into my face.

Old Bob put his hand on Tate's shoulder, his jaw ticking. Although he was angry, he was more diplomatic than the rest of us. "There was no need for this. I would have told you anything you wanted to know."

"He was spouting lies. I couldn't let that slide."

I stood and faced Jimmy. "Lies? What lies did he say exactly?"

Jimmy watched me a moment, dropping his eyes to Jace's hand on my arm restraining me. "Chain the demon!"

"That won't be necessary," Jace growled.

I took a step forward, but Jace pulled me back.

"I'm not... a demon."

Cal moved toward me, but when I spoke, he stopped. Jimmy looked at him. "What are you waiting for? Chain her!"

Eden. Just go with it for now.

I clenched my hands, puncturing my palms with my claws. *Do you see Tate's face?*

I do, but right now we're outnumbered... please.

Cal reached me, and ever so slowly, put out a metal cuff and waited. He expected me to just put my hands in it. I looked into his eyes. He fought hard not to look away, not to flinch.

"What's the magic word?" I said.

"Put your damn hands in the cuffs, or I'll shoot your friend in the head. That magic enough for you?" Jimmy snarled as he whipped out a handgun, cocked it, and pointed it right at Jace.

"Now, now, let's all just relax." Old Bob took a step forward, but one of the men flanking Jimmy stepped to him, shoving him to the ground.

"Shut up, old man!" He shoved the muzzle of the gun into Old Bob's back.

My breath quickened and I ground my teeth together. I had to relax. I had to get control, but all I saw was red. Tate beaten, Old Bob with a gun to his back—it was all too much, but Jace was right. We were outnumbered, and if I acted prematurely, we would end up dead. I slowly put my hands out and let Cal lock silver cuffs around my wrists. When they were latched, he pushed Jace and me to our knees facing Jimmy.

At least they don't think you're as much a threat as me.

Jace's cheek twitched, giving me a peek of that dimple I so love. *Let's keep it that way. Until we need it.* He paused a heartbeat. *If we need it.*

"Tate here said something outrageous about a virus," Jimmy said with a laugh. "Then he said something about a president. So, I can either believe that you all have been living in an alternate universe for the past twenty years, or you're lying and trying to hide something."

"He wasn't lying," Jace said. "It's much... different up north."

Jimmy eyed Jace a little too closely for my comfort, and I stifled a growl, bringing his gaze to me. "Well, by the look of the demon, then I can agree it must be... different."

"Call me a demon one more time, and I'll show you what a demon can do."

"She's no demon." Jace motioned to the man that still had Old Bob on the ground with a gun to his back. "I think it's safe to let him up now."

Jimmy glanced down at Old Bob before nodding to his man. "Let him up."

The man stepped away but kept his gun at a ready aim. Old Bob stood, brushing himself off. "Thank you." He nodded to Jace, but his frown deepened when he took Tate in. "This really wasn't necessary."

"Maybe not," Jimmy said, nodding his head back and forth. "But it felt damn good."

Old Bob cleared his throat. "We've come to learn that some of what we've known in the north may not be common knowledge."

He swallowed again, scratching his jaw. "It seems that our president was just claiming to be so, but that claim has not drifted this far south."

Jimmy chuckled, but after a moment, it grew to a loud belly laugh. "Hold on. Are you talking about that man from a few years back who claimed to be the leader?"

Old Bob nodded. "I believe that would be the one."

Jimmy dropped his head back with another loud bark of laughter. "Well, I'll be. I can't believe he managed to control that many people for so long." He sighed. "He's the main reason no southerner went north, though. Nobody wanted to deal with a crazy."

"No. Of course not. Everyone here seems to be completely sane," Jace mumbled. Jimmy cut him a look but turned to me when I spoke.

"What's it you want?" My wrists ached, and I twisted them within the cuffs, which only made the cuffs tighten more. I locked eyes with Jimmy, and to my surprise, he didn't even flinch. The man gave me more of a pit in my stomach than Zane did.

"We're in the midst of a war, and I need all the help I can get, so you'll fight for me."

"And if we refuse?" Jace asked.

Jimmy laughed. "There is no refusal. You either fight for me or you die."

"And what's this war over?" Old Bob asked.

"Does it matter?" Cal said, with a snicker.

Old Bob glanced back at him. "Well, yes. What if there is a possibility of stopping it before it starts?"

"It's already started. How stupid are they in the north?" Cal said.

"Now, now, Cal. Don't insult the help." Jimmy took a step toward Old Bob. "We can get to details later. For now, I need to know if you are in, or are you... dead." He eyed us all, swinging his gun through the air.

I clenched my jaw, wanting to rip his smug face right off, but Jace's steadiness next to me kept me in check. He leaned over slightly so I could feel his shoulder against mine.

Tate struggled to stand. Old Bob grabbed his arm when he wavered, catching him before he fell. "We will... fight."

"Tate, we should discuss—"

"No," Tate yelled, which was followed by a fit of coughs.

"I agree with Tate," Jace said, stepping forward. "Fighting is better than... dead. We'll fight." He shared a look with Old Bob, and after a moment, Old Bob nodded.

"Well, at least some of you seem to have some brains." Jimmy tucked his gun away into the back of his pants. "Then we'll lead you back to the barn." He turned and walked back to the farmhouse.

"Wait! You're not going to give us more details?" Old Bob called after him, but Jimmy ignored him and continued toward the farmhouse.

"Move!" Cal yelled, pushing the gun into Old Bob's back, making him stumble forward.

Jace grabbed Tate's arm, and with Old Bob's help, they steadied him, and we walked back to the barn. When we arrived back at the stall, I put my hands out for the cuffs to be removed. Cal yanked me to the wall, and I stifled a grunt, grinding my teeth so tightly together I expected one to crack.

"Hey, hey. You don't have to be so rough," Jace said as he stepped to my side.

Cal pulled the chains from the wall and locked them onto my wrists. As he did the same to Jace, he said, "I'll be as rough as I want to be. You're at *our* mercy. Never forget that."

Jace chuckled, leaning closer to Cal. "And you never forget that you have no idea what we're capable of." He looked down at the chains on his wrists, then back up to Cal. "You think these chains can hold us? Well, let's see."

Cal's face blanched just slightly, his throat bobbing from a hard swallow. He glanced over to me but didn't meet my eyes before turning and storming out of the stall. The other men who had chained Old Bob and Tate followed him.

I thought you were going to keep your abilities secret.

Jace smirked at me. *I didn't show anything. Just put doubt in his mind.*

A smile crept along my face. I don't think I have ever been so proud of Jace than I was at that moment.

~

"You three, let's go," Cal said, pointing to Old Bob, Tate, and Jace.

"What about Eden?" Jace asked.

"The demon girl stays here."

I growled low, but Jace's hand on my shoulder calmed me. "She's no demon. If you call her that again, you'll deal with—"

Cal laughed. "Ahhh, isn't that sweet? Dan, you hear that? This guy is sweet on the... *demon*." He locked eyes with Jace. He was testing him, seeing how far he could push him before Jace actually did follow through or if he would at all.

Jace lunged with a snarl, but I moved faster. Stepping between Jace and Cal, I looked right into Jace's eyes. "It's all right. Not now." His eyes softened, and I could see surprise at my interference.

I thought you would've loved me tearing them apart.

I smiled. *Not sure what you did to me, but it seems I've gotten some sense.*

"Yeah, lover boy. It's all right," Cal goaded him, his voice bringing us back to our situation.

I whipped around and showed my fangs. Cal stepped back fast with wide eyes. "If you don't stop, next time I won't interfere. Trust me, you'll wish I had."

Cal didn't reply. He brushed off his shirt, a motion that reminded me of Zane, causing my whole body to tense. He looked at the others. "Let's go."

"You going to be all right?" Jace asked me.

I smiled at him. "Yeah. I'll catch up on some much-needed sleep."

After examining my face a moment, he turned and followed the others out of the stall. I sat down and listened as the barn became quiet again.

"Why do they call you demon?" Lillyanne asked. I had forgotten she was there.

Turning to look at the wall that sat between us, I weighed my words. I looked down at my claws, moving them in the air before me. How do you explain what I have become when you don't fully understand it yourself?

"Are you deformed?" she asked.

"Something like that."

Hearing the distance in my voice, she stayed quiet. I set my head back on the wall and closed my eyes.

∼

My eyes snapped open at the brushing sound of movement through the leaves outside the barn. My smile grew as they neared me enough that their scent consumed me. It was time, and I was ready. I tightly gripped my chains, pulled back, and with a loud grunt, pulled hard. The small metal plate in the barn wall pulled away slightly, cracking the wood around it.

Jace, I hope you can hear me. It's time. Be ready.

I adjusted my grip on the chains and pulled again.

Chapter 6

Jace

Despite the grumble of my empty belly, I fought the urge to rip into the chicken and potatoes that sat before me. All I could think about was Eden alone in the barn while we sat in the nest of the enemy. Tate and Old Bob must have felt the same since both of their plates sat untouched.

"Last I heard the cartel was in what used to be Oklahoma City. They have taken the southern lands and are working their way north. I won't live to see them take control of my town," Jimmy said around a mouthful of potato.

"The cartel?" I said.

"That's right." Jimmy stuffed a juicy piece of meat in his mouth. He eyed us as we watched him and his cronies eat around the large table. There were women in the kitchen, but they managed to stay hidden. "Not hungry?" He leaned over and stabbed a potato from my plate with his fork and ate it. "See. Not poisoned. You can eat it."

"I wasn't concerned it was poisoned."

Taking a drink from his cup, he wiped his mouth with a napkin and sat back. "No? Then why do you refuse my generous hospitality? You don't come by meals this good very often these days."

"This is very nice. Thank you," Old Bob said. "It's just—"

"Eden is still in the barn. We don't feel right eating without her," I interrupted.

Cal sneered. "Her. He called the demon a *her*." He shoved some chicken in his mouth but froze when the screech of my chair legs filled the room. Jimmy's hand raised to stop me. I froze a moment, every muscle in my body tight. I didn't want to follow Jimmy's command, but what would he do if I disobeyed him? Reluctantly, I sat, keeping my eyes on Cal's ashen face.

"Now, now, Cal," Jimmy said. "That's no way to treat our new allies."

I clenched my fists under the table, meeting Jimmy's eyes. "Jace, you have my word. We'll send a doggy bag of food for your friend." He watched me seriously for a heartbeat before bursting into a fit of laughter, which was echoed by his men around the table. "A doggy bag! For the demon dog!"

Letting a quiet growl escape, I moved to stand again, but Tate put his hand on my shoulder.

"Not worth it," Tate mumbled, his face still bloody and bruised. I looked at him and relaxed. He would be the first victim if I did anything rash, and how would Eden handle that?

Jace, I hope you can hear me. It's time. Be ready.

I sucked in a breath at the invasion of Eden's voice. How did she do that? We had never tried talking to each other from a distance. All the voices and laughter disappeared as her words echoed within me. It's time. Be ready.

Be ready for what?

My stomach knotted as I moved my chair back in toward the table.

I cleared my throat. "Why does the cartel want to take over all the land?" I asked, picking up my fork. If Eden was planning something, then she needed time. I could give her time, but my change in mood didn't go unnoticed.

Jimmy watched me as I ate a piece of chicken. I fought the urge to close my eyes and groan as the salty juices streamed down my throat.

Sitting forward, Jimmy started on his plate again, but I smelled wariness. "Why else? Resources. I'm sure you are aware that they are slim picking since the war."

"Yes," Old Bob said, following my lead and nibbling at his food. "Before the war, the cartel dealt in drugs. What are they dealing in now?"

Jimmy looked at him and smiled. "What everyone wants and needs in the southern heat. Water."

"Water? How can they do that? I mean, it's cruel," Tate said.

"Cruel." Jimmy smacked his hand onto the table. The only sound in the room was the clanking of our dishes. "The world is cruel, boy! You have to do what you gotta do to survive. If you can't do that, then this *partnership* isn't going to work out."

"Now, hold on," Old Bob said. "We've survived for twenty years just fine. I don't need you yelling at my son about survival."

Jimmy moved his gaze to Old Bob. "All right. I'll take that, but at the first sign of weakness, y'all are done. Ya hear me?"

"Understood," we said in unison.

I put another piece of chicken in my mouth, this time with a small bit of potato, and the two together tasted like heaven. I slowly chewed it as long as I could before swallowing.

Jimmy continued to explain the past twenty years, but my mind was distracted. My body itched with anticipation of what Eden was doing.

Eden?

She didn't respond, but my body tensed when I sensed her. Sensed them. The room's easy chatter quieted as the sounds of snarls outside floated into the room.

We're coming.

Gripping my fork tightly, I readied for a fight. The others hadn't heard the snarls yet, so I gauged everyone around the table. If I had to take on this whole room, I would die trying.

Two more snarls with an added howl rang outside, much closer than the last one.

"What the hell is going on?" Jimmy yelled and stood. The others mimicked him. "Cal! Dan! Go see what all the racket is."

Old Bob and Tate looked at me as we listened to barks and snarls outside. I gave them a slight shake of the head. "Not yet," I whispered.

Pulling in a large breath, I focused on my senses. I could feel her coming, with the others. There wasn't just one or two, but a dozen at least.

Dan and Cal grabbed their guns that had been leaning against the walls and stomped to the front door.

"Daddy?" A little blonde girl about eight stepped into the room, her big blue eyes wide with fear.

"It's all right, baby. You get your momma and the girls and head upstairs. We'll handle this."

The front door smashed open, filling the house with snarls, grunts, and thuds.

"Hello, Caaaaallll."

I stood and spun at Eden's voice in the doorway.

"I was hoping I'd get to see you again." She smiled down at Cal as he scooted backward toward us. Flashing her fangs and curling her claws, she slowly stalked him. He scooted into the dining room where the rest of the men had their guns aimed right at the door, now with Eden in it.

"Demon!" Jimmy said. His voice was firm, but I smelled fear. By the twitch of Eden's nose and the quirk of her smile, I knew she smelled it too.

"Jimmy," she said, taking another step into the room. She moved to my side, not giving any attention to the five guns aimed right at her. "I took offense at not being invited to dinner." She picked up a piece of my chicken and popped it in her mouth.

"We were going to send some back to you."

"Were you?"

I watched her carefully, but she avoided my stare.

What are you doing?

My whole body was tight. I was ready to attack, but I had to know her plan. She didn't glance at me or even acknowledge that she heard my words.

"So, what's it you want?" Jimmy asked, his eyes flicking quickly down at the wolves.

Eden smiled. "Well, you see. My family here, we were minding our own business when you decided to take us prisoner. You sent my best friend away, and now he's back—with new friends."

"Your best friend?" Jimmy asked, looking to Cal.

"H-her wolf," Cal said, trying to stand tough despite his stutter.

As if it had been rehearsed, Ash stepped into the room. His gold eyes glowed as his muzzle twitched just enough to show the tips of his fangs. But he wasn't alone. Flanking him were two more wolves, mirroring his posture.

Jimmy's eyes widened. "Her wolf?"

"Meet Ash," Eden said.

Old Bob stood slowly, with his hands raised. "Look. We don't want any trouble. We don't want to hurt you or your friends, but we aren't going to stay."

Jimmy growled. "What? Leaving is not an option."

Eden laughed. "Like you have a choice."

"I have the guns." Jimmy narrowed his eyes, and the room filled with the clicks of safeties being snapped off.

Tate slowly stood, sensing the impending fight, but his bruised and mangled body wouldn't last more than a minute.

Eden.

I didn't like being left in the dark. I needed to know what she was planning, or we would all be killed.

Eden licked her fingers after popping another piece of chicken in it. Then, without warning or any signal, she moved—no, floated— over the table and disarmed one of Jimmy's men, knocking him out. Ash and the other two wolves were at her side helping to disarm the others. Momentarily stunned at her actions, I barely noticed Cal's movement as he reached for his gun, but I was faster, snatching it from him and pushing it into his back, just like they had done to Old Bob.

The room quieted once they had all been disarmed. My heart hammered, and I was briefly shocked that there hadn't been one gunshot. No one had been injured.

Eden turned to Jimmy and smirked. "And now you don't."

Jimmy took a step back toward the doorway to the kitchen. His breath was rapid and he licked his lips. "We can... work something out."

"Can we?" Eden said, slowly moving toward him. Ash and the other wolves held two of the men by their throats. Their fangs digging just enough into their skin to keep them still, but not tight enough to puncture.

Eden had knocked the other two unconscious.

"Yes," Old Bob said, moving around the table to intercept Eden before she reached Jimmy. "We can just leave. Go on our way."

"You really think they'll just let us go?" She narrowed her eyes at Old Bob. Disgust showed on her face. "You trust that they won't follow us? Then try and kill us?"

He sighed. "What do you plan to do?"

"Kill them!"

Her voice filled the room, prickling every hair on my body. Ash and the other wolves growled louder around the throats of their victims. The aggression in the room was so thick I could hardly breathe. They were out for blood, and by the sounds of the barks and snarls outside, the other wolves were too.

"Kill them? Eden, you can't be serious." Tate limped before leaning on the table to stay upright.

She looked at him, her eyes softening slightly. "Look at you, Tate! After what they did to you, you really will let them live?"

"Yes! We're not killers." He paused, lowering his voice a little, then continued. "You're not a killer."

Jimmy's laugh filled the room. "I knew you were weak. That"— he pointed at Tate—"that's why he won't survive. But, you"—he looked at Eden—"I like you. You're tough."

Eden slowly turned her gaze back to Jimmy. "Do I look like I care what you think of me or my brother?" Her fists clenched, and I could smell her confliction. She wanted to kill. She wanted blood, but she knew her brother was partially right. The old Eden wasn't a killer, but the new one... the new one could be. Wanted to be.

Eden.

They need to die.

No. We can leave. Go on our way.

I knew she heard the desperation in my tone. I didn't want to see what happened when she slaughtered a house full of humans.

There are kids. In the back of the house. Lots of kids. You don't want them to see this.

Her mouth twitched at my words, and she pursed her lips. I saw her chest deflate as she let out a long breath, pondering her options.

"Eden." Old Bob took another step toward her. "Please."

If Jimmy was smart, he would have stayed put, but he wasn't. He ran. He made it as far as the kitchen door before Eden had a fist of his wavy salt-and-pepper hair. She yanked him back and grabbed his throat with her other hand, drawing blood from her claws. He let out a strangled cry but stilled under her grip.

I hit Cal on the back of the head with the gun, knocking him out, and rushed to Eden. "Eden!"

Old Bob and I stood near her, careful not to make any quick movements. "Eden, let him go. It's not worth it," Old Bob said.

"Not worth what?" Eden snarled. "He beat Tate. He imprisoned us. He was going to use us. How can you let this filth of a man live?"

Moving my hand to her shoulder, I gently squeezed. "You're right." She relaxed slightly, glancing to the side but not meeting my eyes. I continued, "He is filth. But, Eden, you don't want this. You don't want to become this."

She snapped her eyes to mine, and the knot in my stomach tightened. "Become *what*, Jace?"

"Demon," Jimmy forced out through her clenched hand. When she looked at him, his purple face smiled and he let out a winded laugh.

Closing my eyes at his idiocy, I shook my head, then moved fast to her back, grabbing her arms and yanking them back with my arms tightly around her, and put my mouth to her ear. "I'm sorry," I whispered, but to my surprise, she didn't fight me.

After shrugging from my arms, she stomped to the door with a low frustrated growl.

"Ash," she yelled. Ash and the other wolves dropped their holds on the men and followed her outside.

Jimmy was on his knees coughing between laughter. "I... like her."

"Shut up." I smashed his head into the wall. He dropped to the ground with a loud thud.

"What now?" Tate asked.

"Now, we run like hell." Old Bob moved to the door. He stopped and stared at the three men the wolves had on the ground. They sat stunned, watching us. "We will let you live now, but if you follow us, you're dead." He didn't wait for a response before he walked outside.

Tate and I followed, only to stop on the porch. In the yard, Eden, Ash, and the two other wolves stood with a group of ten wolves.

Ash brought a whole pack with him.

"Come on! Let's get a move on it," Eden said and started walking.

"Why don't we take their truck?" Tate asked.

We all froze and turned to where three trucks sat by the side of the house.

"Good thinking," Old Bob said.

I'd just opened the door to the blue truck when someone screamed, and I turned toward the barn. "Lillyanne."

"We can't take her," Eden said, sliding into the back seat of the extended cab.

"Why?"

"Because we don't know anything about her."

I looked at Eden. "Eden, that's not like you. What's going on?" I looked over at Old Bob, ignoring the pink tinge to Eden's cheeks. "She could have information we need. She is a prisoner, so I don't think she'll hold any loyalty to them."

Old Bob held my gaze before letting out a long breath. "Fine. Be quick."

"I just don't trust it, not after what we just went through," Eden protested, but he ignored her and got behind the wheel.

I ran to the barn, right to Lillyanne's stall. A blonde girl around Eden's age sat chained to the wall. The same way we had been.

"Oh, thank goodness. I thought you all were dead."

I moved to her side. "You had that much faith in us? I'm flattered." I grabbed the chain and pulled it taut with the wall, took in a few breaths, and yanked hard. It cracked and pulled right out of the wall.

She stared at the chain now fully on the ground. "You're tellin' me that y'all could do that this whole time, but you stayed? Why?" She turned her blue eyes to mine.

"We don't really have time for chit-chat. We have to go... now." I charged out of the stall.

"Wait." She stopped and ran back to the wall to grab a key. Quickly, she unlocked her cuffs so the chains fell to the ground.

My jaw dropped. "The keys were right there? Why didn't you just tell me?"

She smiled. "You didn't ask." She stopped when she reached my side. "Now where are the others?"

I cleared my throat. "In the car. Let's go."

We ran to the truck. I slid in the back next to Eden, and Lillyanne sat next to me. Before the door was even shut, Old Bob peeled out away from the house.

Chapter 7

Eden

It took all of two seconds before Lillyanne was freaking out at the sight of me. "I knew she was deformed, but what the *hell* is she?" she said, leaning as far into the side of the truck as she could. Away from me.

"Just relax, all right?" Jace held his hands up at her, motioning for her to calm down.

"How am I supposed to relax when she has... are those claws?"

Clenching my jaw, I pulled my claws into myself to hide them as best as I could. Old Bob didn't slow the car even through the commotion in the back seat. I met his eyes in the mirror, but when I saw the flash of pity, I turned my gaze to the trees moving by the window. It's not that I didn't want to help Lillyanne. I would never have left a prisoner behind before. But I just didn't want to deal with her response to me.

Jace turned his body toward Lillyanne. "They are... claws, but she won't hurt you."

I gave them a quick side glance only to see Jace had Lillyanne's hands in his. He was comforting her. Snapping my eyes back to the trees outside, I focused on the scenery, not the feeling of my heart being ripped out. How could he comfort her?

"All right," Lillyanne whispered.

Jace turned his body forward again. Our arms touched, bringing his warmth and security. Fighting the urge to grab his hand, I set my head back and closed my eyes. Maybe it was better if he found someone else.

Someone... normal.

~

"All I'm saying is I don't think it's a good idea. If we know there's going to be a war, why would we drive right into it?" Lillyanne said.

"Maybe we can help?" Old Bob rolled his head in circles, stretching his neck. "We need to find a place to rest. Maybe the next small town—"

"No," Lillyanne yelled.

A thick silence filled the car as Lillyanne's words echoed among us.

I glared at her, not trying to hide my annoyance. "Then maybe we should just drop you right here."

"Eden," Jace and Tate said in unison.

"What? She doesn't want to help, so what's her use?"

"I'm sorry." She glanced at me, careful not to look down at my hands, then turned back to Old Bob. "It's just if you thought

Jimmy was something, then you definitely won't like the people in the next town."

"All right. Then where should we go to rest?" Old Bob asked.

She bit her lip and let out a long breath. "Not many people have survived in the rural areas. I'm sure we can find an abandoned farm."

"An abandoned farm," I repeated, watching her cheeks turn pink. "And how do we know you aren't going to lead us into some kind of trap? I mean, really, we don't know her." I looked between the others in the truck.

Jace looked at me with his beautiful eyes, one blue and one gold, like mine. But instead of giving me his usual mischievous look, his eyes were pleading.

What's wrong?

I turned away from him, focusing on the open fields we passed. *Nothing. I just don't trust her.*

Fine, but you don't have to be so obvious about it.

I didn't look at him or respond. I wanted so badly to say that it was the way he cared what she thought and how she felt that had me all riled. Instead, I shrugged, keeping my eyes on the window.

"I can drive for a bit." Tate's voice filled the car.

Old Bob laughed. "Absolutely not! Since when do you know how to drive? Have you ever been in a car before this?"

"Well, no, but—"

"I'm fine. It's getting late anyway. We should rest, and since I tend to agree with Eden's wariness about trusting an abandoned farm, I think we should find somewhere else to rest."

A small flicker of hope warmed me at Old Bob's acknowledgment. He agreed with me. At least someone did.

"There is a patch of trees up ahead. Let's just stop there. We can build a fire, hunt, and sleep in the truck," Jace said.

"Ohhh like a camping trip!" Lillyanne giggled. "I read some books where they went camping in the woods. I've always wanted to try it."

"Well, it looks like it's your lucky day," Old Bob said.

Rolling my eyes, I set my head back with a groan.

~

I stepped quietly through the brush, tracking a smell. There was a rabbit, maybe two nearby. If I could catch them, we would eat well tonight. My mouth watered in anticipation.

"Oh my God! You're kidding." Lillyanne's voice echoed through the trees.

I ducked and stepped behind a group of trees. Peeking between the trunks, I watched Lillyanne skip and prance through the brush with Jace beside her. She had wanted to be useful, so Old Bob told her to go find anything we could eat. Well, she's not as resourceful as we all are, so Jace volunteered to go with her.

He volunteered.

My claws dug into the bark of the trees as I watched her face light up when she looked at him. Her hand gently touched his arm, and she giggled. Then he caught her when she so gracefully tripped on the root of a tree. I wanted to gag, but before I did that, I wanted to claw her eyes out. Literally.

A quick movement caught my eye. Moving my gaze to my right, I caught sight of a large rabbit. It sat, nose twitching as it smelled the air. I'm sure it could smell me, but it hadn't spotted me yet.

"You're so funny!" Lillyanne's voice echoed, and I clenched my jaw.

If she scared this rabbit away, I would kill her. But it didn't move. It sat, whiskers twitching. Jace and Lillyanne neared it. If I didn't act now, they would scare it away.

"Wait," Jace said, grabbing Lillyanne's arm. He gently moved her behind him. He must have sensed my hostility but hadn't spotted me.

Eden?

With a snarl that resounded off the trees, scaring birds into a frenzy of tweets, I launched forward and snatched the rabbit. With a swift flick of my wrist, its neck snapped.

Lillyanne screamed and fell back, landing on her back, eyes wide and filled with fear.

I stood watching her with disinterest, the dead rabbit dangling from my hand.

"Jesus, Eden!" Lillyanne shrieked.

"Eden,"—Jace knelt down to help Lillyanne up—"you didn't have to be so—"

"So what?"

Jace stood with his hands on Lillyanne's arm. My eyes dropped to them before meeting his gaze.

"She was so loud she was going to scare the rabbit away. I had to act, or we'd be going to sleep hungry."

"You had to snarl?" he asked.

I smirked. "Well, it completes the whole experience." I pushed past them through the trees. I could smell the fire Tate had started. "Come on, you two. Wouldn't want the bears to find you."

"Bears? There are bears?"

I smiled as I listened to Jace reassure her there were no bears nearby.

Chapter 8

Jace

"We have a quarter tank of gas left. Let's get as far as we can, then we'll have to finish on foot," Old Bob said as we sailed down the empty highway.

I don't know how Ash and his new pack had found us last night, but they did. Eden slept out by the fire with them, which had made me nervous, but I didn't insult her by questioning her judgment. Instead, I had tossed and turned, continuously peeking outside to make sure she was all right.

When we left this morning, Ash left again with his pack, but not before he and Eden seemed to have a silent conversation. She managed to avoid my gaze the whole day.

"How much farther to Kansas City?" Tate asked. His face had healed enough so he could now open both eyes.

Old Bob tossed his head back and forth. "About a four-hour drive, days walking."

"Man. It's freezing out. I'm not looking forward to walking in this for days." Lillyanne leaned into me, hooked her arm in mine, and squeezed it like we needed to hold the warmth right now. I shifted but was unable to free my arm.

Eden sat in the front with her eyes fixed forward. If she saw Lillyanne holding me, I'm sure I would have to intervene so no blood was shed.

I cleared my throat and narrowed my eyes on her face. She kept her gaze forward, focusing hard on everything except Lillyanne or me.

Eden.

Nothing. Not even a twitch of her cheek.

An involuntary growl escaped me. Why was she ignoring me?

"You OK?" Lillyanne asked, squeezing my arm.

Giving her a small smile, I slowly pulled my arm from her hold. "Yeah. Just not used to being in confined places for so long." I looked back at Eden, but she didn't flinch. Was she even listening?

"I feel you. I haven't driven a car since before the outbreak." Old Bob glanced back at us through the rearview mirror.

"Outbreak?" Lillyanne asked.

"Yeah. The Fever outbreak."

She tilted her head. "We didn't have a Fever outbreak."

The silence was deafening, then Eden chose that time to turn around and face us.

"So, no one was sick? Ever?"

Lillyanne shook her head. "Nope." We silently shared concerned glances. "Why? Is that bad?"

Ignoring her, Tate leaned forward. "Forgive me for being groggy, but how many days have we been with her?"

"With who? Me?" Lillyanne asked.

"Well, we left Jimmy's yesterday, but we were in the barn with her for a day before that. So, two?" Eden said.

"All right, so if it's going to happen, it would be soon," Old Bob said.

"What's going to happen? Oh my God. Am I going to die?"

I turned to her. "No, no—"

"Will you chill already?" Eden swung around and faced us again. "Yes. You may get sick. We aren't sure how the virus spreads, and we could have brought it to you, but we will know soon." She avoided my eyes, watching Lillyanne, whose eyes now shimmered with tears of terror. Eden turned forward as fast as she had turned around and sat silently.

"So . . ." Lillyanne sniffed. "I may get sick, but I may not?"

"Right," I said quietly.

She fisted her hands on her lap, and I could see her fighting to keep them to herself. She was a tactile person and needed touch. Pursing my lips, I moved my hand over one of her fists and squeezed. She looked up at me and smiled. Her eyes were green, almost iridescent. Keeping my hand on hers, I looked forward only to catch Eden's eyes on our clasped hands. Before I could pull my hand away, Lillyanne moved her other hand on top, squeezing them together. Eden slowly looked forward, bringing her arms into herself. Pushing out a feeling toward her, I searched to see if we were OK, but all I heard in return was the lock of her mind's doors securing into place.

~

"Stop the car," Lillyanne said. Everyone sat a little taller at her words, unsure of her plan.

"Stop the car? Why?" Old Bob said.

"You don't want to have to walk in the freezing weather the rest of the way, do you?"

"Well, no, but—"

Lillyanne leaned forward. "Then pull the car into this driveway and stop." Old Bob slowed the car but hesitated just before the driveway. "Come on, O.B. Trust me."

Eden growled in the front seat. "We barely know you."

"True, but you haven't survived around here, have you? I have. I know the ins and the outs. Just stop the damn car at this farm!"

Eden turned around so fast, leaning over the headrest of the front seat. Her claws punctured the leather with loud pops. "I haven't survived? You have *no* idea what I have survived, *Lillyanne.*"

Old Bob slammed the breaks, and Eden flew forward, her back hitting the dashboard. "Eden, relax!"

She snarled, whipped the door open, and stomped out.

"Eden," Old Bob and I called after her.

Lillyanne was shaking, her hands clutched onto mine so tightly her knuckles glowed white. I gently pulled from her grip.

"What is up with her?" Old Bob asked, watching Eden's back as she charged toward the farmhouse.

"I think I know. I'll go talk to her," I said, nudging Lillyanne to open the door and step out.

"No. Tate, you go. Jace, help Lillyanne with whatever it is she is going to do."

"But—"

"Tate, check for food, will you? It would be much easier than hunting. And be careful!"

Tate gave Old Bob a nod and wave of his hand before increasing to a jog to catch up with Eden.

"Are we sure this place is empty?" I asked.

"Yes," Lillyanne said, at the same time Old Bob said no.

He turned to Lillyanne with arched brows. "Yes? How do you know it's empty?"

She grabbed a bucket and hose from the bed of the truck. "The crops." She nodded her head toward the field.

I looked over at the empty field. "What crops?"

"Exactly." She winked and started out toward two trucks that sat near the barn. "If there were people here, there would be crops."

"And you know this how? I'm sure resources are short. How would people keep up crops?" Old Bob asked. He nudged me forward, and we walked after her.

"I grew up here, remember? Ever since the war, that's how we let people know if areas were vacant or"—she glanced back at us with a guilty look—"off limits."

Old Bob and I gave each other a worried look. A pit formed in my stomach, and I looked over to the farmhouse where Eden and Tate were. "What do you mean off limits?"

She stopped at the first truck. "I mean, everyone has their own property. We have learned over the years how to govern and police ourselves." She opened the gas tank on one of the trucks and stuck one end of the hose inside. "So, we all respect each other's areas, and the peace is kept." She put the other end of the hose in her mouth.

"What are you doing?" I pulled the hose from her mouth. She smiled at my disgusted face.

"Haven't you ever siphoned gas before?" She snatched the hose back from me.

"We have never had to," Old Bob said, continuing to look from the open area around us back to the farmhouse. He rubbed his hands together and bit his lip. "I'm going to go check on the others. Jace, stay with her." He turned and walked toward the farmhouse.

I turned back to Lillyanne. "A bucket and hose are a staple in every car these days. Stealing gas is the easiest way to get it." She put her mouth over the end of the hose and sucked on it. After a moment, she quickly moved away, spitting onto the ground. "Ew! That's the worst part." She moved the hose to the bucket and let the gasoline flow.

"Where did you learn to do this?"

"My brothers." She kept her eyes on the golden liquid as it filled the bucket.

"Where are your brothers now?"

Her eyes tightened at my question. I kept my gaze on her face, but she clenched her jaw and sighed. "At my farm. I'm sure they don't miss me though." I opened my mouth to respond, but she continued. "This bucket's getting full. Go grab the second one from the truck, will you?" She pursed her lips, never looking up from her work.

I turned, jogging back to our truck, watching the farmhouse for any sign of the others. I would have thought one of them would be back out by now.

When I leaned into the bed and grabbed the second bucket, I heard the cock of a gun and froze.

"Don't move." A woman pushed the butt of her gun into my back. "Raise your hands slowly, now."

I did as she asked, flicking my eyes toward the farmhouse, but she hit my face with the butt of the gun.

"Argh. Jesus, lady!" I moved my hand to my right temple where she had smacked me, but the lady pushed me hard and I fell to my knees.

I pushed out my consciousness, feeling for any sign of Eden. I really didn't want to start a fight without knowing who else we were up against.

Eden?

Silence.

My heart leaped and I growled.

"No fast movements."

There was a crack in the woman's voice that turned on the predator in me. My growl grew to a snarl, and I quickly turned, snatching the gun from her with a hard shove. She fell to the ground, and I took a step toward her. When she looked up at me, I didn't see the fear I expected, only defiance. She was tough. I asked, "Is there anyone else here?"

"I'm not saying shit to you."

Eden!

I gave the farmhouse a quick glance before I looked over to where Lillyanne was. She was partially hidden between the two trucks. I towered over the middle-aged woman. Her dark hair was tied tightly into a long ponytail. Her eyes glowed younger than what her sun-weathered face told.

"I asked if there is anyone else here."

She smirked. "Go to hell."

I raised the gun, only to stop at Lillyanne's scream.

"Jace, no!" She set the bucket down and ran toward us. "Don't shoot. That's my aunt!"

"Your aunt?" I lowered my gun, looking between the two of them.

The woman turned. "Lilly?"

I stepped back, letting her stand.

"Lilly! What are you doing here, you silly girl?"

Lillyanne reached her. Without a second hesitation, they embraced. "Aunt Bev! You're alive. Thank God."

I narrowed my eyes at Lillyanne. "So, you knew this farm? This wasn't just any farm to stop at?"

She shrugged. "I didn't think anyone was still . . ." She gave her aunt an apologetic look. "... alive."

"Alive." I pushed my hands through my hair. "You've got to be kidding." I pointed at the farmhouse and looked to Bev. "Is there anyone else here? Tell. Me. Now."

She looked to Lillyanne nervously before shaking her head. "No. It's only me now."

Lillyanne swallowed and closed her eyes a moment. When she opened them, they glistened but she sniffed and wiped away the tears before they could fall.

I let out a sigh of relief. "All right. I'm going to let Eden and Tate know so there aren't any misunderstandings." I looked down at the gun in my hand. "I'm keeping this with me."

Bev sputtered. "You—"

Lillyanne put her hand on her shoulder. "It's all right. I trust him." She gave me a nod. I watched her for a moment, and her cheeks grew pink before she looked away.

"This isn't going to go over well with the others. Why in the world would you bring us here? You do realize that Eden already doesn't trust you."

"So what, you think they would have stopped if I had told the truth?" She crossed her arms as she raised an eyebrow.

"It doesn't matter. What matters is that you had us stop at a seemingly unknown farm only to find your family is here. I'm warning you; they aren't going to like it." I looked behind me to the farmhouse. "Now, stay here."

"Yeah, whatever." Lillyanne turned away from me to face her aunt.

Bev watched us nervously. I shook my head before I jogged up to the house.

Chapter 9

Eden

I held the pillow sack with one hand, tossing the canned food in it with the other. The only sound in the house was the clanking of the cans hitting each other.

"You want to talk about it?" Tate asked as he handed me another can of beans.

"No."

Eden!

I growled. Why couldn't he just leave me alone? He had Lillyanne now. They would be good together.

After tying a knot at the top of the now-full pillowcase, I set it by the kitchen table. I picked up another one and tossed it at Tate's head playfully. He grunted, pulling it from his face. Narrowing his eyes at me with a grin, he leaned forward to grab my leg, but I bounced back with a giggle.

"You never were fast enough." I laughed, giving him a silly face. He chuckled and went back to work filling the pillowcase.

"I miss this side of you, Eden," Tate said, keeping his back to me.

My smile dropped as I watched his back as he worked. "Me too," I whispered.

Tate turned with wide eyes and an open mouth ready to speak, but Old Bob stepped into the kitchen. "It's odd. This place is in pretty good condition." He had scouted out the rest of the house as we pillaged the kitchen. "It's almost like someone still lives here."

My stomach sank. Lifting my nose to the air, I cursed myself that I didn't notice it sooner. My anger at Jace had masked my senses.

"Hide," I said, pushing Tate back into the pantry.

Tate pushed me back. "What? Why?"

Old Bob gave me a warning look. "Eden—"

"You're right. We aren't alone." I pushed past him to the kitchen window. Peering out, I looked at the two trucks Jace and Lillyanne were supposed to be at, but no one was there. My stomach tightened more. "Where are they?"

"What do you mean?" Old Bob said, peering out the window over my shoulder. "I left them at the trucks."

I spun around. "Well, they aren't there now!"

"Relax." Tate stepped toward me calmly. "Maybe they are back at our truck."

My breathing picked up as I looked at his bruised face. No one would do that to him again. I grabbed my butterfly necklace, fisting it for a moment. Rubbing my fingers over the curves and grooves, I closed my eyes and willed my emotions to level out.

The porch floor creaked, and I snapped my eyes open. When the door cracked open, I leaped over the counter with a snarl and grabbed the man by the throat.

No, not a man. Jace.

Jace clutched at my claws with wide eyes. I immediately dropped him. I should have smelled it was him. Why was I unable to focus?

"Jace, I'm so sorry! I thought you were . . ." I stepped back and bit my lip.

He was doubled over coughing. "It's... it's OK."

"Where's Lillyanne?" Old Bob asked. He looked out the door and froze. "Who is that?"

"What? Who's who?" Tate asked, moving next to him, but Old Bob slammed the door and pushed Jace against it.

"Who *is* that?"

"Relax." Jace coughed, pushing Old Bob back. "That happens to be Lillyanne's aunt. Apparently, this isn't just a random farm after all."

I growled. "I knew it. I knew we shouldn't have trusted her."

"It's fine," Jace said.

When I met his eyes, I looked away quickly. Ashamed I had attacked him. Ashamed I had ignored him. What was happening to us?

"Her name is Bev. This"—he held up a gun—"is her gun. She assured me that there is no one else here."

"And you believe her?" My stomach lurched at the red mark from my claws on his throat. Fisting my hands, I turned away. "Never mind. It doesn't matter."

"They're coming," Tate said as he peeked through the window on the door. "What do we do?"

Jace laughed. "What do you mean? We can't lock her out. It's her house." Old Bob and Tate both gave him a dry look. "What? No! This is crazy. She's fine. If we trust Lillyanne, then why can't we trust Bev?"

"I don't trust Lillyanne," I said as I plucked an apple from the counter and bit into it.

"Yeah, well, you don't trust anyone these days."

I stopped chewing at the sting of his words. When I looked at him, he had his eyes closed and was clenching his jaw. "I'm sorry Eden, I—"

"Hello?" The door opened. Lillyanne stepped in with Bev behind her. "Hey, guys." She gave everyone a guilty grin. "So, this is my Aunt Bev."

"Hello," Bev said, pushing a stray piece of dark hair from her face.

We all watched her in a tense silence, but just when I couldn't take it anymore, I bit into the apple. The crunch echoed throughout the kitchen, bringing all eyes to me. I gave a sheepish smile. "Sorry. It's just so good."

Everyone looked away but Bev. Her eyes widened as they fixed on me, and I watched the blood drain from her face. "W-w-wh-what . . ." She pointed a shaky finger at me.

"It's fine. She won't hurt you. I promise." Lillyanne gave me a pointed stare, which I returned with a raised eyebrow and a smirk. "They are from the north. Something happened to her, but she won't hurt you."

"S-s-she h-has . . ."

"Claws, fangs, amazing eyes, and a great sense of smell." I took another bite of my apple. "It's getting dark. We might as well stay here tonight and leave in the morning."

"Wait." Old Bob put up his hand to stop everyone. He stepped toward Lillyanne and her aunt. "You lied to us."

"I didn't lie. I omitted information."

"We trusted you."

"That's your fault."

Jace stepped forward. "We freed you. We could have left you behind, chained in the barn—"

"Chained in a barn?" Bev said.

"It was nothing," Lillyanne said, hastily. "Look. I'm thankful for everything y'all have done, but y'all to understand that I am alone here. There are four of you. If I'd told you the truth about the farm, would you have stopped?"

"Doesn't matter. You shouldn't have lied to us," I said, still working on my apple.

Lillyanne let out a frustrated breath, and Bev gently pulled her arm. "Who chained you to a barn?"

"It was nothing, Aunt Bev. Really."

Old Bob crossed his arms. "I guess you're right." Everyone turned to him. "Trust goes both ways. You trust us, and we trust you."

"She needs to earn our trust," I said. "I mean, look at Jimmy and his band of misfits. If the world outside of what we know is like that, we shouldn't trust anyone. Not if we want to live past winter."

Old Bob looked at me with a nod. "True, but we also need to earn others' trust. They will be thinking the same about us. It's not just about us anymore, Eden."

I pursed my lips together, fighting the string of curse words I wanted to spout, but deep down I knew Old Bob was right—and I hated it.

But there was still something about Lillyanne I didn't trust.

Bev cleared her throat. "Lillyanne, who chained you to a barn?"

"Jimmy."

"Jimmy? Well, what in the—"

"It's fine, Aunt Bev. Let's discuss this later?"

Bev watched her a moment.

Focusing on their faces, I watched Lillyanne's slight eye twitch and eyebrow raise. I fisted the apple core. She was lying again, but about what?

"The sun is setting. I think we should stay here the night," Old Bob said, looking at Bev. "That is, if you allow us to."

Bev smiled. "Of course. There is plenty of room."

"All right then. You all agree?" Old Bob looked between Tate, Jace, and me.

"Yeah," we said in unison.

Lillyanne said, "I agree."

I narrowed my eyes at her. "No one cares what you think. You aren't a part of this group. You are just a stray we picked up."

"Eden." Tate moved to my side.

"If I'm not a part of your group, then you can leave. Say bye-bye to this nice warm comfortable roof over your head. You can sleep in the barn." Lillyanne squared off in front of Bev.

"Come on, guys," Jace said, putting up his hands between us.

Tossing my apple core onto the floor, I stepped in front of Lillyanne. "Fine. By. Me." Bumping her with my shoulder, I pushed past her to the kitchen door.

"Now, Eden—" Old Bob said.

"I'll be fine. Ash should be showing up soon."

"Ash? There's more of you?" Bev asked.

"Ash is her wolf," Lillyanne said quietly.

"A wolf?" Bev's voice cracked.

I smiled and pranced down the porch steps toward the barn.

Ash and his pack showed up panting and happy a few hours later. Bev wouldn't come outside to greet them, but she did reluctantly say they could sleep in the barn. She watched through the kitchen window as she and Lillyanne made something to eat.

"You don't actually have to sleep in the barn with them," Old Bob said as he scratched Ash's ears. "I talked to Bev, and she said there are plenty of open rooms."

I looked up from picking at a piece of straw. "No. I'm fine. I would rather stay out here with them anyway. I can keep watch. We shouldn't be so trusting."

"You'll freeze!" Tate said.

I smiled at him. "I thank you for your concern, brother, but I assure you I'll be fine. I'm not fully human, remember?" I threw a few pieces of straw in his direction.

"I can stay with you," Jace said, sitting down next to me. Ash moved to Old Bob and rested his head on his lap.

I stilled.

"That's not a bad idea. I would feel better about that," Old Bob said. "I can grab some blankets for you—"

"That won't be necessary. Thank you, Jace, but I'll be fine out here on my own. You should get a good rest in a regular bed." I kept my eyes fixed on Ash's coat.

"Eden."

"I know how much you gripe and groan about your back since having to sleep on the ground. This will be good for you. Plus, I'll have the wolves."

Eden. What's going on with you? His voice was full of complete concern.

Seeming to sense our tension, Tate stood. "Well, I'm going to see if they need any help with the food." As he passed, he tossed a few pieces of straw back at me. "Lighten up a bit, sis."

"I'll go with you." Old Bob gave my shoulder a squeeze before following Tate into the house.

After a moment of silence, I sighed. "I'm sorry."

Jace tilted his head, examining me. I refused to look at him just yet, but I felt his eyes roaming my face. "For what?"

I finally turned to him. He showed no judgment as he listened. Really listened and my chest tightened. "For everything. I don't know what's going on with me. I'm so... edgy. It's like my emotions are taking control. I want to have fun and be silly, but I jump before I think. I don't know how to handle it. I don't know how to handle... this." I motioned a hand between us.

"Handle this?" he repeated. We watched each other a moment when it dawned on him what I was referring to, and he smiled. "Oh... this." He motioned between us. "Eden, we... well, you mostly, have been through so much. It's fine for you to have mixed emotions and outbursts."

"Why are you so... understanding? All the time. Nothing I say upsets you."

He chuckled. "Honestly, I don't know." Giving my shoulder a shove with his, he winked. "Maybe it's my winning personality."

"Oh, that must be it." I grinned back at him.

The house door slammed open, and Tate poked his head out. "Food!"

Jace jumped to a stand and offered me his hand. I stared at it a moment before slowly setting mine in his, careful of my claws. He gently curled his fingers around mine and squeezed. I stood, but neither of us dropped our hands. Instead, we stared at each other.

It's going to be all right. I'm always here.

I closed my eyes and smiled. "Thank you."

"Come on." He squeezed my hand again before dropping it and started toward the house, but I didn't move. Ash stood next to me, leaning on my leg.

Jace turned. "You coming?"

"You go. I'm not hungry."

"What?"

"It's fine really. I just need time." Without waiting for a response, I turned and walked into the barn.

～

Ash and I lay on a pile of straw that tucked into the back corner of the barn. The sun had set, but the bright light from the moon shone through the cracks of the wood and small windows. A crisp breeze howled along the rickety wood, leaking in through the wood panels and broken windows.

"Good thing there aren't any actual animals in here. They'd freeze when winter comes," I mumbled to Ash. He responded with a snort, snuggling in closer to me. His new pack members chose to snuggle on the hay pile opposite of us. They were a dark pile of fur that was hard to differentiate. All I could really distinguish were their noses, which had white puffs of air surrounding them.

The large barn door rumbled as it slid open. Sitting up, I watched the dark silhouette of Lillyanne step in, and I stifled a groan. She held a plate of steaming food.

Pulling her jacket closer to her body, she stepped inside and searched for me in the darkness. "It's freezing out. I feel the weather changing," she said, much more cheerful than someone should be with someone they just had an argument with an hour earlier.

"You sound like an old lady."

She turned toward my voice, straining her eyes until they adjusted to the dark. It didn't take long for her to spot me.

"I brought you a plate of food." She walked it over to me.

"How generous of you." I bit my cheek remembering Tate's words to lighten up. This wasn't a good start.

She stopped at the edge of the hay pile. "Well, I insisted you could just go out and find a rabbit to sink your fangs into, but Aunt Bev insisted I come and try to... make amends." She forced the last two words out.

I leaned forward and took the plate from her. "I'm sure you had no trouble telling her that someone like me doesn't make amends." I surveyed the selection of food on my plate. The green beans and pears had definitely come from cans, and the small piece of deer meat wasn't fresh.

"You really can't afford to be picky in a world like ours."

I picked up one of the green beans and popped it in my mouth. Not as fresh as ours from the cabin, but it would do. "You're right."

"Look"—she kept her eyes on the dirt floor—"I think we got off on the wrong foot. I'm sorry if I've been a little... rude."

"Are you"—I swallowed—"apologizing?"

She scoffed. "Well not because I *want* to, but because Aunt Bev said I should." I watched her, waiting until she continued. "It's not like we have a huge amount of people waiting to be friends or allies."

I laughed. "True." I put some more beans in my mouth. "So, what? You want to be friends now?"

"Friendly, at least."

Stuffing the last of the meat in my mouth, I nodded. "All right. Friendly."

"OK, great." She watched me pick the pear slice up and shove it in my mouth, licking my claws. "You know, I could paint those for you. Might make them look a little less... intimidating."

I froze, moving my eyes to hers. "Not that friendly."

"Yeah, right. Of course. That was a stupid idea."

"I'm done." I handed her the plate, and she quickly took it. Without a word, she moved to the barn door, but before she could shut it, I yelled after her. "Lillyanne?"

"Yeah?" He looked back at me.

"Thanks for the food."

She smiled, then left.

I sighed. I think Tate would be proud.

~

I tossed and turned on the poky straw, trying to get into any comfortable position. Letting out a groan, I gave up and stood. Ash lifted his head and watched me through tired slits of his eyes.

"It's all right. You sleep. I need some fresh air." He put his head back down at my reassurance.

I stretched out my back and arms and walked to the barn door, cracking it just enough for me to slip out into the freezing night. Each window of the house glowed with a warm light. Standing in the darkness, I tilted my head at the absence of longing. Before the city, I would have longed to be in the house with the others, but now... now I wanted to be alone.

Alone in nature with the animals.

"You can't say anything." Lillyanne's whisper reached me from the house.

Scanning the area, I saw her with Bev on the back porch, both tucked tightly into their sweaters.

"What's the big deal?" Bev asked.

"They already don't trust me. I have to be careful."

My stomach dropped, and I carefully stepped closer, staying in the shadows. I could see Lillyanne's eyes focused on her feet. Bev kept her gaze fixed on her face.

"He's your father, Lilly."

"I know. Just please. Trust me on this."

Bev let out a long sigh, pushing a hand through her hair. "All right. But I'll have no part in your lies anymore. This is it. Understand?"

"Understood. Thank you."

Bev quickly stepped back inside the house, leaving Lillyanne alone. She stood, leaning on the wooden porch rail, looking out into the night. Her eyes looked directly at me, and for a moment, I thought she spotted me, but then she dropped her head and let out a large puff of white air. She turned and stepped inside, locking the door behind her.

I fisted my hands. What was she hiding? I let out a small laugh at our conversation earlier that night.

Friendly. I don't have to trust to be friendly.

Yes, I can be friendly.

Chapter 10

Jace

I woke to the warm sun shining on my face. I cracked my eyes open but quickly buried my face in the pillow with a groan. My body felt like dead weight. Eden was right; I needed that sleep. It was the best sleep I had had in a long time. So good I didn't want to get up.

But clanking dishes and the smell of breakfast pulled me from the bed. Still yawning, I slowly made my way downstairs, following my nose to the table.

"Morning," Bev sang from the stove. "I hope you're hungry. I haven't had people to cook for in a long time, so I made a feast!"

I sat down at a table full of pan-fried meat, eggs, roasted potatoes, fruit, and bread. Tate, Old Bob, and Lillyanne all had full plates before them, eating eagerly.

"We told her it wasn't necessary, but I'm not going to complain. I haven't eaten this well in months," Tate said around a mouthful of eggs. His face looked better daily.

I spooned a heaping scoop of potatoes onto my plate as I scanned the kitchen. "Where's Eden?"

"She hasn't shown up yet," Bev said. "I hope your conversation went as well as you claim." She gave Lillyanne a raised eyebrow.

"It did. I swear!"

I looked at Lillyanne. "Conversation?"

"Yeah. Aunt Bev wanted me to... smooth things over."

I raised my eyebrows, pursing my lips to hide my smirk. "How'd that go?"

"Fine, until I offered to paint her claws."

I spit out my tea, quickly wiping up the damp table. "You what?"

Tate and Old Bob joined my laughter.

"Well, since you're sitting here unharmed, I'd say she likes you," Tate said.

"Who likes who?" Eden asked from the door.

I grinned at her. "Nothing. Lillyanne was just telling us about your conversation last night."

Eden pulled out the chair next to me, watching us all carefully. "And?"

I gently picked up her hand. "I think purple would suit you." The kitchen filled with laughter, and she snapped her hand back.

"Really?" She looked at Lillyanne.

"Sorry. I said you weren't into it, but they're all making it a *thing*."

"I'm sorry. I just had to see your face." I chuckled, letting my eyes roam over Eden. She looked well rested. Calmer than yesterday.

She piled food on her plate and didn't hesitate to eat. Bev finished cooking and joined us. We all ate our fill, chatting about our lives—sharing memories and dreams. It was the most relaxed I had been since leaving the camp.

"So, you're all headed to what used to be Kansas City?" Bev asked.

"That's the plan," Old Bob said. He had shaved and trimmed his hair with some items Bev gave him. He looked like I remember him when he beat me to a pulp before kidnapping me months ago. So much time has passed since then. I don't even hold any contempt against him.

"Well, you do know what's happening down there, don't you?"

"Yup. We are hoping we may be able to help in some way," Eden said as she finished the last of her potatoes.

"Help? It's a war."

She narrowed her eyes at Bev, who nervously looked away. I put my hand on her arm and smiled at Bev. "Yes. We heard about it, but I'm sure there is some way we can help."

"I guess, but it's suicide if you ask me."

Eden crossed her arms. "Well, we didn't, so—"

"Aren't you worried that if the people lose, then the cartel will just move their way here? They may take your farm," Tate said.

Bev set her cup down softly. "I suppose you're right, but I believe God will help protect me and my farm." She turned and smiled at Lillyanne. "And now Lilly."

Eden snorted. Old Bob gave her a pointed look, then turned to Bev. "Well, we thank you for your hospitality. It was a real treat sleeping in a bed."

"Of course. I'm sure Eden would enjoy washing up as well." She locked eyes with Eden and gave her a genuine smile. If I hadn't smelled her fear, she would have fooled me.

Eden nodded slowly. "Thank you."

Lillyanne's chair scraped along the kitchen floor and she stood. "I'll show you to the washroom."

Without a word, Eden stood and followed Lillyanne upstairs.

~

"I think that's the last of it," Old Bob said, patting the bed of the truck.

"You should have enough food and gas to get you to the Kansas City area, but you always have a place to stay here if needed." Bev pulled her sweater tightly around her, keeping the crisp breeze out. Her cheeks were rosy from the cold, and it made her look much younger than I originally thought.

"Thank you. Who knows where the road will lead us?" Old Bob smiled back at her.

"I don't know how it is in the north these days, but Kansas City isn't what it used to be. It's not even really a city anymore, it's—" Bev shook her head. "Well, you'll see."

Eden and Lillyanne emerged from the house. Eden had showered and wore a clean pair of pants and a plain shirt. Her long auburn hair was still damp, leaving small wet patches on her shirt. If she wasn't Chimera, she would have frozen from being so damp.

Ash met her halfway to the car. She crouched down to pet his head and whispered something in his ear before he ran off with his pack. I locked eyes with her after she stood.

What did you say?

She smiled. *He'll meet us in the city.*

I shook my head, letting out a small laugh. *Show off. I didn't know I was in the presence of a wolf whisperer.*

Her smile grew. *The one and only.*

"Oh, you'll freeze, Eden. Here, let me grab you a jacket. I have a spare one." Bev started toward her house.

"No, it's fine. I don't feel the cold like you."

Bev stopped, tilting her head at her. "You don't feel the cold... like me?"

"Yeah. Like humans." Eden opened the passenger door.

"Humans?" Bev's voice cracked, and she looked around at us with wide terrified eyes.

I chuckled, giving Eden's shoulder a shove so she landed inside the truck's front seat, squishing forward to accommodate for the rolling seat. "It's nothing. It's just a... northern thing."

Bev gaped at us, and I gave Old Bob a pleading look.

He nodded and smiled. "All right then! We better get on our way to save daylight."

Bev turned to Lillyanne, who held a small bag. "Wait. You're not going with them, are you? I thought you'd stay with me."

"You know I can't, Aunt Bev. I need to go."

"No. What you need to do is stay with me. Safe. Going with them is... suicide." She gave us all an embarrassed look.

"Let's not make this a thing, all right? I can't stay. I'm not meant to stay in one place. I need... more."

"But your father—"

"Don't. Mention. My. Father."

"But—"

"Bye, Aunt Bev." Lillyanne brushed off Bev's arm and pushed past me into the middle of the back seat, tucking in close to Tate. Bev pursed her lips as she watched Lillyanne.

"You stay safe then," Bev finally said, her voice wavering slightly.

"I will."

I smiled. "Thank you." Bev nodded at me, and I sat beside Lillyanne, sliding the seat back so Eden could shut the door.

Once we were all piled in the truck, Old Bob started out down the abandoned highway with Bev watching in the rearview mirror.

～

We drove almost nonstop. Old Bob played loud music from a tape that had been left in the car, but he seemed to take delight in hearing the familiar tunes. When we all started to complain, he told stories about his childhood and Eden and Tate's adventures as children. I don't know how long we had driven since the farm, but I do know we had used all the gas Lillyanne had siphoned, eaten half the food, and my butt hurt.

We arrived on the outskirts of Kansas City, or what used to be Kansas City, in the dark. A green sign had the name Kansas City crossed off and replaced with Dead Man's Land.

"That's reassuring," Lillyanne murmured.

The glow of small fires in cans scattered the roads in the distance. Old Bob pulled the car over. We hadn't met another car the entire drive, and it seemed that we were still the only one in the area.

"Turn off the lights," Eden said.

Old Bob complied. "I think we should wait until morning to... approach."

"That's probably a good idea," Tate said.

"So... we just sleep like this in the car?" Lillyanne shuffled side to side, bumping into both Tate and me.

Eden turned to face everyone. "I'll sleep outside. Jace, you can move to the front; it'll give you all more room."

I watched her avoid looking at how close Lillyanne and I sat. Luckily, Lillyanne hadn't grabbed me at all this entire drive. "I'll sleep outside as well. I need to stretch."

Eden furrowed her brow. "You'll freeze."

I laughed. "I'll wear a jacket and snuggle with Ash." She pursed her lips, and I raised an eyebrow. "I'll be fine."

I'm Chimera too, remember? I paused and gave her a quick wink. *I can snuggle with you if you prefer.*

Our eyes locked a moment, then she shrugged. "Suit yourself."

She stepped out of the car and walked into the darkness.

Chapter 11

Eden

The hard, scratchy tree trunk dug into my back. I rested my head on it with a loud sigh, glancing over at Jace who leaned on the neighboring tree. His knees were pulled up to his chest, and he tucked his arms as close to his body as he could. Keeping his eyes closed, his teeth chattered in rhythm with his trembling body.

"I told you it would be too cold."

He opened one eye. "I'm fine." His voice quavered.

"You definitely are not."

"I d-don't unders-s-stand why I don't s-s-stay warm like you."

"You have more tolerance than a human, but you're not as thick-skinned as me." I stood and moved next to him.

He looked up at me. "What are you doing?"

"I'm going to warm you up." I sat down and opened my arms. He stared at me before shaking his head. "Come on, Jace. You'll freeze!"

"I'm not snuggling into your lap like a... like a... dog."

I chuckled. "Then what would you have me do?"

"Nothing." He closed his eyes and rested his head back on the tree. My gaze moved down to his lips, which had turned a pale blue.

You're so stubborn!

After stomping over to the truck and shuffling through the items in the bed. Old Bob cracked the door. "Everything all right out there?"

"Yeah. Just Jace being Jace." I pulled out the last blanket we had and stomped back over to the tree and threw the blanket on Jace's head. "Here. At least put this around you."

He smiled. "You take such good care of me."

"Shut up."

Sleep tight, Golden Girl.

My cheek twitched at his words. He hadn't called me that in a long time. I didn't realize how much I missed it until he said it.

Night, Baby Face.

Ash had arrived with his pack a few hours after we slept. He realized Jace needed warmth more than anyone, so he snuggled tightly into him under the blanket. Jace's body tremors stopped shortly after.

The other wolves in his new pack slept near me, but not close enough for me to touch them. They were still working up their trust.

The sun peeked over the horizon and the birds' happy morning songs began. Smiling, I closed my eyes at the dewy smells and sounds of a new day.

"Ash, I could kiss you," Jace said, stretching out his back from a night on the ground. Ash sat up with a groan and looked at him. "But I won't because it may make Eden jealous." He scratched Ash's ears, giving me a wink.

I rolled my eyes and smiled. "Go ahead. I'd love to see it."

Our eyes locked a moment, and my smile faltered. A knot in my stomach formed. He wasn't for me. I thought he was, I wanted him to be, but then I saw how he was with Lillyanne and how much I'm not like her. He deserves to be with a girl like her.

I ripped my eyes from his and stood. He reached for my hand, but quickly pulled back when the car doors opened. Everyone got out to stretch out their cramped limbs, their echoing groans masking the sweet chirps of the birds.

"So what's the plan?" Tate asked.

"I don't know. We could just take a chance and drive right in," Old Bob said.

"Uh, guys? I don't think we have a choice." Lillyanne was looking down the road toward the city where three vehicles were moving toward us.

Tate looked at the vehicles and asked, "What are the chances that they don't see us?"

"None," I replied.

The exhaust billowed in large clouds behind them from the freezing air. I slowly walked in front of everyone, squaring off. Jace moved to my right, Ash and his pack to my left.

"Eden, let's not get ahead of ourselves. We don't even know what they want," Tate said as he stood behind the open car door.

Old Bob pulled out one gun from the trunk and cocked it. "That's where you're wrong, Tate. Look at it the other way. They won't know what *we* want."

The three cars, with windows so dark we couldn't see inside, stopped in front of us. They sat idling a moment before their engines stopped. A man stepped out from the driver's side of the middle car. He didn't seem fazed by our defensive state.

"Morning." The man leaned on his front bumper and crossed his arms.

"Morning," Old Bob replied.

"You all must have traveled from far. We haven't had anyone new arrive in... well I don't remember when since it rarely happens." The man dropped his arms, setting his hands on the car and leaning back.

"Seriously?" Lillyanne said from behind me. I clenched my jaw at her impulsivity and stupidity.

The man nodded. "Seriously. So where are you all from?"

Old Bob held up his hand to silence Lillyanne before she said anything. "Up north." He didn't offer any other information.

"And you just decided to go on a family vacation?"

I stepped forward. "We heard about the cartel, and we're here to help."

The man's face hardened and he pushed off the car. "What do you know of the cartel?"

I smiled, making sure he could see my fangs. "Enough to know that you need our help."

His eyes dropped to my mouth, then down to my claws. All the confidence he had earlier was gone. His face paled and he looked back to Old Bob. "I'm listening."

Ash leaned on my leg, nervous at the man's eyes roaming over me, so I set a reassuring hand on his head. But that only drew the man's attention back to my claws and the fact that my hand was on a wolf's head. His eyes flicked to the wolves behind us, then back to mine.

"I don't mean to stare, but—"

Jace stepped forward. "Then don't." The man looked at Jace, with one eyebrow raised in surprise. Jace continued, "Let's get some things straight. We won't hurt you if you don't give us a reason to."

The man didn't move his gaze from Jace. Crossing his arms again, the man was willing his confidence back, not wanting to look weak on his own turf.

"Like I mentioned before, we're here to offer help," Old Bob added.

The man let out a long breath, pushing a hand through his thick brown hair. "How exactly did you hear about the cartel?"

"Oh, we were guests at a farm a few hundred miles back, and they happened to mention it," I said.

Two more people stepped out from the other cars. One man and a woman, both looking around the same age as the man.

"And how did they learn of the cartel? Like I mentioned before, people don't come and go—ever."

Unsure of how to answer, we stood silent only to turn when Lillyanne stepped forward. She gave a sheepish smile. "Hi. I'm

Lillyanne." She cleared her throat. "A man named Cal. He came from here, saying he was running to save himself since the cartel was coming, and he didn't want another war."

I cocked my head. Cal. The same Cal who seemed to do Jimmy's dirty work. The same Cal who helped beat my brother. I swallowed down a growl at the memory.

"Cal?" the man said.

Lillyanne nodded.

"That sneaky bastard," the woman said. "I knew he was up to no good. Running away," she said.

"You know him?" Old Bob asked.

"Unfortunately."

"But you said no one leaves and comes," Lillyanne said.

The three strangers shared a look, and the man pursed his lips together. "I did. And that was the truth until Cal stole much of our supplies and ran."

"To be honest, we thought he was dead. He isn't the most resourceful, so we figured he wouldn't survive going off on his own," the woman said.

Lillyanne shifted uncomfortably. "Well, he did survive. He's living at my... at a farm north of here. Making quite a name for himself."

"Figures." The woman looked right at Lillyanne. "And you know where this farm is?"

Lillyanne gave a hesitant nod.

The woman looked at the man. "Let me go. I'll bring the bastard back. Make him pay for stealing from us."

The man scratched his silver-dusted chin and looked at Old Bob. "You say you want to help?"

"Yes. If that's something you need."

"Send the girl back with AJ here so she can bring Cal back. Then we will house and feed the rest of you until you prove your worth."

Lillyanne shook her head, wide eyed. "What? No! I'm not going back!"

"Well, you know where Cal is," AJ said.

"I'm not leaving my group!"

Jace put up his hands. "All right, all right, let's talk this through. We all know where Cal is."

The man paused. "Then you choose who goes. I don't care, but someone takes AJ to get Cal, or you all can turn around and leave."

I growled. "You really would turn away help? You're about to have a war!"

The man sneered at me. "You don't know anything about war, girl. Why do you think they call me Bomber?"

I stepped forward, baring my fangs.

Jace grabbed my arm, gently pulling me back to him.

"Let's just relax a moment," Old Bob said, narrowing his eyes at me.

Yanking my arm from Jace's grip, I backed down.

"Look. I can't in good conscience let Lillyanne go off with your people. You must understand that. Plus, like Jace said, we all know where Cal is," Old Bob said.

"Well, you must understand I can't just let you all in my city. I know nothing about you, where you came from, or . . ."—he looked right at me from head to toe—"or *what* you are."

I snarled at him, echoed by Ash and his pack. Bomber at least had the good sense to jump. He recovered quickly, but that ounce of fear he showed gave me some satisfaction.

Relax.

I bit down and closed my eyes. *Did you not just hear what he said?*

I did, but you know the truth. I know the truth. It doesn't matter what he or anyone thinks.

I pulled in a long deep breath and let it out. When I opened my eyes, I was met with Jace's handsome face. He gave me a small smile and nodded.

Do you trust me?

I raised my eyebrows at him, but my stomach dropped a little at his words. He's never asked me that before, but I'm pretty sure he already knows my answer.

I nodded.

Jace turned back to Bomber and Old Bob. "I'll go. I'll go with Lillyanne and AJ."

I could hear my heartbeat in my ears, and my stomach dropped to my feet.

He volunteered to go with Lillyanne. To split up from me. To leave me.

Old Bob shook his head. "Jace, you don't—"

Jace put his hand on his shoulder. "I know I don't have to, but it's the only way. This way everyone will be safe." He looked back at Bomber. "So if Lillyanne and I go, you'll house and feed the others?"

Bomber studied him a moment and nodded. "That's the deal."

I focused on staying standing, on keeping myself put together. Blood pulsing through my head drowned out the rest of the conversation. Jace was my rock. How was I supposed to contain my animal with him gone?

I blinked at Jace, standing before me, repeating my name.

"Eden, are you all right?"

I swallowed, giving my head a small shake. "Yeah," I rasped out. "I'm fine."

"Follow us close. If you get lost, you're on your own." Bomber hollered from his car. His companions had already started back toward the rundown buildings of what remained of the city. White smoke billowed up from their exhaust pipes.

I crouched and petted Ash. "All right, buddy—"

"Oh! And if you don't want your… pets to be shot, they should stay out here," Bomber yelled at me.

My heart froze. "I can't just leave them!"

Bomber shrugged. "Don't say I didn't warn you, then. Just saying what I would do." He slammed his car door, revving his engine. Our signal to hurry up and get in the truck.

I looked back at Ash. "I'm sorry." He whined quietly, pushing his head into my chest. I pulled him close, lowering my nose to his fur, and breathed in the smell of evergreen. The woods. He smelled like the woods. "Just stay out of sight. I'll find you when I can." I pulled back and looked into his gold eyes and knew he understood. Giving me a quick lick on my nose, he leaped into the trees with his pack close behind him.

Chapter 12

Jace

Old Bob raced in the wake of wafting dust that Bomber's car kicked up as we drove into the city. The tension rolling off Eden was thick. Of course, I had tried to talk to her, but she put up her stubborn walls to keep me out. She had said she trusted me, but when I said I would go, her face dropped. No, not just her face, her whole body.

"You don't have to do this, Jace. We can find another way. I could go," Old Bob said for the fifth time in the last five minutes.

"I appreciate your concern, but it's already done."

"We can always figure something out."

Eden kept her eyes forward and mouth shut from the front seat, holding her hands tightly on her lap, her knuckles white.

Eden.

My words reverberated back into my own head, and I ground my teeth. I had to get her alone before I left. We couldn't part like this.

Tate leaned over, murmuring softly in my ear. "Everything all right with you and Eden?"

I shrugged. "I thought so, but—"

"This is how they live?" Lillyanne asked.

Her nose touched the window as we passed crumbled buildings and streets lined with metal barrels filled with fire. They seemed to be used both for warmth and cooking. Some buildings had windows showing occupants inside, but many people lived in shelters built on the sides of the roads or in small alleyways between buildings. "How do they survive? It's too cold to live on the streets."

"I don't think they have much of a choice," Tate said, giving a small boy a hesitant wave as we passed.

People had stopped what they were doing and lined the streets at our approach. Watching us, the new arrivals, with keen interest, the people radiated a smell of distrust and concern that flowed in a thick sheet around us.

Bomber's car pulled behind a metal gate outside a tall brick building. We parked next to him and slowly got out, meeting him, AJ, and the other man behind the cars. Large groups of people stepped out onto the road and peeked past the gate to get a glimpse of us.

"This is how the whole city is?" Lillyanne asked.

Bomber looked at her. "What do you mean?"

She nodded her head at the people on the street. "I mean, like them. Living in the streets, with a fire in cans. I always thought this was a large city."

AJ chuckled. "It used to be. A long, long, time ago. With the war, then limited resources, this is what our city has become. Not much different than the other cities that survived the bombs."

"How many people live here?" Old Bob asked.

"Few hundred."

"A few hundred? There should be thousands," Lillyanne said.

"Thousands?" Eden said, widening her eyes at Lillyanne before glancing back at the others. "This is the most people I have seen gathered in one place in my life."

AJ and Bomber looked at her with raised eyebrows. "Your whole life?" Bomber shook his head.

"There should be thousands," AJ said, "but again, the war and limited resources. You can fill in the blanks on what happened to the people."

I stepped up next to Eden, so close our arms touched. She bristled but didn't move away. I could smell her feelings of betrayal. I had to let her know that I volunteered to keep her safe and to give her a chance to help others. That has always been her goal, even before her change. To help.

Moving slowly, I brushed my pinky against the back of her hand. She flinched, but again, she didn't move and eventually sighed. My heart flipped with a small bit of relief.

"AJ and the others will leave in the morning. Right now, I'll show you where you'll sleep," Bomber said, leading us into the building.

Eden pulled away quickly, being the first to follow Bomber. "When do we plan?" she asked him.

Bomber hesitated a moment, looking over his shoulder into her intense eyes. "Plan?"

"Yes, plan. Looking around"—she put her hands out, motioning to the people scattered about the street—"it doesn't seem like you have much of an army. So the more planning you have, the better."

He stopped, turned, and fixed his eyes on her claws before moving back to her face. "You may want to keep those hidden. Some people . . ." he hesitated. "Well, most or all the people may not be as... accepting to your... kind."

She smirked. "My kind? And what kind am I?"

Their eyes locked. I was impressed. He didn't back down or even flinch at the intensity of her stare. "I don't know. Why don't you tell me what you are?"

Old Bob stepped up and put his hand on Eden's shoulder. "All right. I think we should get to our resting spot."

Bomber peeled his eyes from Eden's and gave Old Bob a smile. "Right." He turned and continued through the building.

~

"Well at least there isn't the biting, cold wind," Lillyanne said, sitting on a pile of blankets in the corner.

Bomber had brought us to a small room that had piles of blankets and pillows scattered along the walls. Ollie, the man who was with Bomber and AJ, was assigned to our door. We weren't prisoners, of course, but he would be there just in case we needed something.

"I'm not going to lie. I may take a nap. It's warmer in here than it was in the car, and I can stretch out at least," Tate said, burrowing himself under one of the piles of blankets.

Lillyanne looked at me. "Should we find AJ and plan out our return?"

I opened my mouth to respond but turned when Eden flung the door open and stormed out. I met Old Bob and Tate's concerned faces, then looked at Lillyanne. "I'm sorry. I have to go."

I didn't respond to her objection and jogged out after Eden.

Chapter 13

Eden

I couldn't stay and listen to Lillyanne talk to Jace like they were friends. Like they have known each other forever and were planning a getaway—even if they were going away together.

I jumped down the steps, skipping two at a time, and had just stepped outside when I heard Jace call my name. Ignoring him, I jogged to the metal gate surrounding the building, but I was stopped by a man.

"Hey! You shouldn't go out there. You're new, and they don't always like new."

I flashed him a grin, reveling at the glimpse of fear in his eyes. "You don't need to worry about me. I can handle myself." I continued out onto the busy road.

"Eden." Jace's voice echoed among the buildings. Many of the citizens looked from him, then to me, studying our every move.

When they saw my more unique characteristics, many bolted back into their shelters, pulling behind them the curious eyes of their young. But some... some narrowed their eyes and watched me as if I was something to be hunted. And many of them didn't seem new to the idea of hunting other humans. Even if I wasn't fully human, they didn't know that.

I turned down a less-inhabited alleyway, hoping to lose Jace. I didn't know what to say. He chose to go with Lillyanne. He deserved to be with a girl like her. Looking down at my claws, I growled. How could he like me?

"Eden, stop!" Jace followed me into the alleyway. "Could you not hear me, or did you choose not to?"

I stopped, keeping my back to him, and fisted my claws with a sigh. "What do you think?"

I heard him take a step closer. "Well, since I know you have hyper senses, I'm pretty sure you were choosing not to, but what I don't know is why."

I took a deep breath. I didn't know how to do this. That's why he chose her in the first place, wasn't it?

"I think it's best if you and I don't talk anymore, other than what's needed to be said."

He coughed. "What? What are you talking about?"

I turned, keeping my eyes on the ground. He was only a few steps from me; his presence was powerful. I was definitely the dominant one, but he had an effect on me.

I cleared my throat and said, "I'm talking about us. About how it's not a good idea. You deserve better—"

"I deserve better? Eden. Stop. You don't know what you're talking about."

Now I did look at him. His eyes were calm. Caring. No anger or disgust. I continued, "Lillyanne is a nice girl. You two—"

"Lillyanne?"

"Yeah. I think you two are good together."

He pushed a hand through his black hair. "Thank God you brought this up." He let out a relieved chuckle. "You have nothing to worry about. I don't like Lillyanne."

I blinked at him, unbelieving, and he blinked back.

After a moment, he sighed in frustration. "Eden—"

"No, no. It's fine. I understand. I wouldn't like me either." I stepped back. "I mean, look at me." I held up my claws between us. We both stared at them, and when unexpected tears welled in my eyes, I pulled them back into myself and turned around.

"Eden." He stepped behind me, his broad chest flush with my back, warming me. "Look at me." His voice was quiet, reassuring.

I wiped away the one tear that escaped. "Just go, Jace. I understand."

"Look. At. Me."

He put his hands on my shoulders, giving me a gentle nudge to turn around. When I did, he put his finger under my chin and tilted my face up to his. "I don't like Lillyanne. Not in the way you're thinking."

"But you—"

"Was being nice. Polite. Understanding."

I scanned his face; he was being sincere. "But I... I've been so horrible."

He chuckled. "You're adjusting and confused. I get that, and I don't hold it against you."

I closed my eyes. "I'm sorry. So sorry I've been edgy and—"

His mouth covered mine, warm and soft. I stilled for a moment before I let myself melt into him. He slipped an arm around the back of my neck and the other around my waist. His firm hand on the small of my back made me shiver. Going to my toes, I reached up and gently pushed my claws into his hair. The growl that escaped from deep in his throat made my knees weak. Thankfully, he pushed me back to the brick wall before they gave out.

All I felt was him. His warmth and security filled me, filled every cell in my body. I have never felt so... whole.

When he finally pulled away, we were breathless as he rested his forehead on mine. My heart thumped so loudly that I had to pull in a deep breath to slow it. He smoothed his thumb along my cheek.

"I like you, Eden. Always have, always will. No one will change that."

I wasn't sure I could speak. My whole body was on fire. When I did finally say something, I was thankful my voice didn't crack. "You sure?"

He smiled. "I'm sure."

"All right." I smiled. We watched each other in silence a moment, then I giggled.

"What?"

"That was my first kiss."

His smile grew, lighting up his face. "You don't say." I giggled again. The dimple on his right cheek made my stomach flutter, and I looked down. He leaned closer to me and whispered, "So, how was I?"

Letting out a loud laugh, I rolled my eyes. "From *my* experience, you weren't bad."

"Not bad? You were as pink as a rose when I looked at you. I think I deserve more than not bad." He picked up my hands and squeezed.

"If you say so." I curled my hands around his and squeezed back.

"We should get back."

Smiling, I stepped forward, and hand in hand, we walked back to the building.

Chapter 14

Jace

We sat around a table in a large dining room. It was filled with at least ten other tables, mostly full of people eating quietly. Bomber brought us here, explaining it's where all food was served two times a day. They used to have three meals, but due to lack of resources, they had to ration everything, dropping meals to two a day. In addition to food rationing, they have people on only three bottles of water a day.

Next to me, Eden picked at her plate of potatoes, a small piece of chicken, and half an apple. Tate and Old Bob ate quietly, observing our surroundings.

Don't be rude. It's obvious they don't have much.

She raised an eyebrow at me. *Maybe I should help them hunt.*

Not the worst idea.

"So, everyone comes here to eat?" Tate asked.

Bomber nodded. "It was the easiest way to keep the peace. Some people hoarded food, then others attacked them to get it. This way, everyone gets an equal share."

"Who hunts the food?" Eden asked around a bite of apple.

I cut a small piece of the chicken and ate it. It wasn't horrible but definitely lacked flavor.

Bomber sipped his tea, watching Eden inspect the apple. "Everyone has a job. We have hunters, farmers, cooks, teachers—"

"Teachers?" Eden said, looking up at him. "You have that many kids here?"

Bomber smiled. "Yes. Enough that we have to teach them." He carefully watched Eden as she played with the potatoes. "Did you go to school? You don't seem that old."

She stilled, moving her eyes up to meet Tate and Old Bob's. "Why?"

"Just curious where our new members come from. What their history is." His eyes dropped to her claws. The way he watched her made my stomach uneasy. I set my fork down and cleared my throat. Leaning back in my chair, I set my arm along the back of Eden's chair. It was a possessive move, but I didn't care.

"We don't have much of a history really," I said, meeting Bomber's eyes.

He smirked. "You two together?" He moved a finger between Eden and me.

Eden glanced over at me, but I kept my eyes on Bomber. "Yes."

"Wait. Really?" Lillyanne asked, snapping her head toward us.

I gave her a quick nod.

Bomber scratched his chin. "You have the same eyes. Related?"

I snorted. "What? No! We... we just have the same—"

"Genetic feature," Eden said quickly.

I looked at her a moment with wide eyes before turning back to Bomber. "Yeah, that."

He glanced between Eden and me while taking another sip. When he put it down, he cleared his throat. "Contagious?"

"What?" Old Bob said, putting his fork down.

Bomber looked at him and shrugged. "Is it contagious? Whatever"—he waved a hand at Eden and me—"whatever these two have. This *genetic feature*."

"Genetic features aren't contagious," I said flatly.

"But the virus is," Lillyanne said, then stuffed a piece of chicken into her mouth. Everyone slowly looked at her, and I nudged her arm with my elbow. She shrugged. "What? You guys said that. There is a virus."

"What virus?" Bomber asked, now leaning forward, much more invested in the conversation.

"It doesn't seem to have traveled south," Old Bob said, narrowing his eyes at Lillyanne.

"But—" Lillyanne put her fork on her plate.

I elbowed her again. "But nothing. You don't know what you're saying. So stop talking."

As she clenched her fists, she set her mouth into a firm line. The skin from her neck to her cheeks turned red. "All I know, *Jace*, is what you all told me. You even said I may get it."

"But you haven't," Eden snapped. She leaned so far across me toward Lillyanne I had to gently push her back. If this conversation didn't end soon, blood could be shed.

Bomber put up his hands to stop everyone. "Now, hold on here. What virus are you talking about, and did I just risk everyone's lives by letting you all in my city?"

"No," Old Bob said. "There was a virus outbreak in the north. It was... manmade and very... deadly. We're still unsure of how it spreads, so when we took Lillyanne with us, we were concerned she may contract it. So far, she's fine, and it is past the usual infection time period, so you and your people should be fine."

"Should be." Bomber met Old Bob's eyes. For two minutes, it was tense, then Bomber spoke again. "How does it spread then?"

Old Bob cleared his throat again. "We aren't positive. We thought maybe airborne, maybe it was in the soil, the animals may have carried it. There are still so many unknowns."

"You all"—Bomber scanned us all landing back on Eden—"had it?"

"Yes," Old Bob said.

"And if you contract this virus, you become like... her?"

"You wish," Eden mumbled, and I grabbed her hand under the table to stop her from continuing. The situation was already fragile.

What? I'm way better than him.

I squeezed her hand. *I'm glad you got your confidence back, but this is not the time.*

"No. Eden and Jace are both exceptional cases."

I felt Lillyanne's inquisitive eyes scanning my face, then moving to Eden. "Exceptional how? I mean Eden looks different, but Jace doesn't. "

Eden growled. "That is none of your business. I'm not being dissected by any of you." She pulled her hand from my grip and stood. Her chair scraped along the floor, bringing every pair of eyes in the dining hall to us. Looking around the room, she smiled large and menacing. "What? You all want a show?"

"Eden," I said, slowly standing. Tears were building in her eyes. She kept her face fierce, the picture of uncaring, but I saw through it. I felt the terror within her of what others really thought of her. "Let's go." Gripping her hand firmly, I gently tugged her back to our room.

Chapter 15

Eden

The others arrived shortly after we returned to the room. I sat tucked into a corner with my knees pulled to my chest. I brought a pile of blankets, pulling them around and over me. It wasn't my den, but it was close enough.

"You're to leave at first light, Jace," Old Bob said, sitting on another pile of blankets. "Bomber is sending another man along with AJ. There'll be four of you."

"Understood." Jace sat next to me but kept his hands in his lap.

"I don't know how they expect us to take on Jimmy and his gang." Lillyanne paced the room, wringing her hands. "I mean, they outnumber us and have the resources."

I growled. "Then maybe you should learn to keep your big mouth shut." I pushed the blanket off my head and narrowed my eyes at her. "It's because of you that Jace has to go and save your ass, and now it's because of you that they know about the virus and will have a harder time trusting us. *You...* are the problem."

Lillyanne stopped, mouth open. "Well, that's not fair," she said, crossing her arms and cocking a hip. "It's not my fault that you all want to lie, and I want to be honest."

"Oh, get off your high horse." I stood.

Jace stood quickly beside me. "Eden."

"My high horse. You think your... your *deformities* make you better than everyone, but really you're just...just deformed!"

Standing still, I curled my hands into tight fists. "You better run, Lillyanne."

"No. Do *not* run, Lillyanne." Jace stepped closer to me. "Eden."

I shoved him away and took a slow step toward Lillyanne. She stepped back, eyes wide looking between Jace and me. "I said, you better run."

"Jace?" Lillyanne said.

Jace held up a hand to her. "Look, Lillyanne. Just stop antagonizing her!" He stepped in front of me, bracing my face with his hands. "Eden, stop threatening her." Looking away from Lillyanne's terrified face, I focused on Jace. He didn't smile. His eyes were intense and focused on mine, willing me to calm myself. "This isn't you. Let it go."

Tate and Old Bob slowly stepped in front of Lillyanne. Old Bob turned to her. "Leave. Just leave for a bit. She needs to cool down."

"This is so unfair."

Old Bob turned to her. "If you don't want to be maimed, then *get out!*"

"Whatever." She turned and stormed out of the room.

I focused on Jace's eyes. One blue, one gold, always understanding.

"Breathe," he whispered. I matched his breathing, and after a moment, I stepped back.

Old Bob cleared his throat. "I understand why you're so upset, but you're going to have to get over all this sensitivity if you want people to trust and work with you."

"I know." I closed my eyes and sighed. "But she said I had deformities. How did you expect me to respond?"

"I get it. I do. What she said wasn't right, but it's not just her." Old Bob put his hand on my shoulder and squeezed. "Jace is leaving. He won't be here to bring you down when you are worked up. Bomber is already wary about us—"

"Then, let's leave," I said.

"You're kidding." Tate stared at me. "You're not kidding. Wow. Eden, you're the one who is all about helping and bringing people together, and now when we get to the largest population we have seen, you want to just leave?"

"Yeah, well. I guess I didn't realize how much of an issue... an issue I would be." I looked down at my claws. "I mean, will I ever be fully accepted?"

"It doesn't matter," Jace said quickly.

"You say that now, but when it really matters, who I am—what I am—will make a difference."

"You're right," Old Bob said. "But I don't think you understand how much you, I mean the real *you*, can do." I blinked at him. "What happened up north, what is probably happening now, it's not going away. What you are, what Jace is, Derek, Brian, and hundreds of others by now, that is the new world. You"—he squeezed my shoulder, lowering his face so our eyes were level— "you can be the link between the chimera and humans. You can have a lot of power, but you have to learn to control that temper of yours and use your head logically."

I watched him smile at me. My father, in every sense other than blood, smiled at me like he was proud. No, not like he was, but is. He is proud of who I am.

"I don't know how."

"I'll help you."

"We all will," Jace said and gently grabbed my hand.

I looked at them all. They were all ready to follow me. I clenched my teeth and took a deep breath. "All right. Let's do this."

～

The sun peeked over the crumbled brick buildings as AJ, Sam, and Lillyanne loaded the car. I watched them while holding Jace's hand. "Don't do anything stupid, all right?"

Jace chuckled. "Since when do I do anything stupid?"

I looked at him. "Remember when I went to the city walls and you came running after me? That... that was stupid."

He put his hand on my cheek and took a step closer. "I will *always* go after you, Eden."

My neck and face warmed. I pushed my cheek into his hand and gave it a little lick. "Just promise me you'll come back in one piece."

He put his forehead on mine. "I promise."

Before I could speak, he kissed me. Firm, yet gentle. I put my hands around him, pulling him close, keeping him with me as long as I could. I wanted to keep his smell of cedar with me forever.

"All right, lovebirds! Jace, let's get going," AJ yelled from the car.

Jace and I parted, but I held tightly onto his hand. He gave me a smile and poked my nose. "See you around, Golden Girl." I laughed as he got into the car. AJ started driving before he even had the door shut.

I stood, watching the taillights of the car disappear around the corner. When I turned to walk back inside, I was met with Tate's pale face.

He swallowed hard. "When... when did that happen?"

"What?" I looked between him and Old Bob, whose face held an amused smirk.

"That! You and Jace. That!" Tate was pointing at the empty space next to me where Jace and I had stood.

My cheeks warmed again. "Like you didn't know?"

"Well, I didn't know it had evolved."

Old Bob laughed, squeezing Tate's shoulder, who was shaking his head.

"I'm failing as a brother."

"You can't keep them protected forever," Old Bob said, giving me a wink. "At least we like Jace."

"I'm right here." I pushed past them into the building. Old Bob's laugh followed me up the stairs.

Chapter 16

Jace

I managed to keep to myself for the first hour of driving. AJ and Sam talked from the front quietly about everything they planned to do once they were rid of the cartel. I didn't feel like being the one to tell them they probably had no chance of winning.

Lillyanne sat next to me, giving me continuous side glances that I ignored by keeping my eyes fixed on the passing fields and trees. The scenery was calming. Felt like home.

"Keep your eyes out for a place to crash tonight," AJ said.

Lillyanne leaned forward, between the seats. "Well, my aunt has a farm a few hours away. We stayed there on our way to the city. I'm sure she would let us stay the night."

AJ and Sam gave each other a look, then AJ met my eyes in the rearview mirror.

I shrugged. "She's telling the truth. We did stay there."

Taking my words as approval, she continued on, a bit more chipper. "Aunt Bev loves having company. I'm sure she'll love cooking for you all. She—"

"We aren't staying at your aunt's farm," AJ said.

Lillyanne sat back, giving me a confused look. "What? Why?"

Sam scoffed. "You think we're going to trust you? We barely know you. I'm not going to stay at your family farm."

"But... I swear. It's safe."

They both laughed.

"You swear?" AJ looked at her through the mirror. "And what does your word mean to me?"

"Well—" Lillyanne turned to me. "You tell them, Jace. It's safe."

AJ glanced at me, and our eyes met for a brief moment. I sighed. "All I can say is that it was fine when we stayed there, but I don't know if there have been any changes."

"Really?" Lillyanne whined, narrowing her eyes at me.

"You can't blame them for being careful."

She crossed her arms and sat back. "Whatever. At least I'm not the one who's dating an animal."

Snapping my head at her, I let out a growl. "I'm sorry? What are you, twelve?"

"What? I just don't get how you can like... be with *her*. I mean, have you looked at her?"

I clenched my fist. "Again, you know nothing about what you're talking about. I suggest you stop now."

"Well—"

"Stop! Now!" My voice filled the car. The tension was so thick, I'm positive no one took a breath in fear of what I might do. My eyes burned into Lillyanne's face. I don't know why I've been so nice to her. She really is annoying.

"Right there! Let's stay there," Sam said, pointing at a small wooded area on the side of the road. He flicked his eyes back at me. I'm not sure if he really thought it was a good place to stay or if he just wanted out of the car before I erupted.

"Sounds good to me." AJ cranked the wheel and pulled the car to the side of the road.

I opened the door and jumped out before it had fully stopped. Letting out a loud snarl, I stormed into the woods. If Lillyanne was going to make it out of this excursion alive, she better learn to shut her mouth.

I stopped by a large tree and leaned on the bark, letting the fresh smell of dirt and sap fill my nose. Letting my eyes close, I focused on steadying my emotions. I had to learn how to stay in control when people talked about Eden. I'm sure she will be the topic of many conversations.

Some leaves rustled, and I snapped my head deeper into the brush. I smelled him; no, I smelled all of them. Ash's gold eyes glowed through the thick leaves of some bushes. He pushed his head through upon seeing me but looked over my shoulder and growled.

"Don't move," AJ whispered.

Glancing over my shoulder at her, I froze. She had a gun aimed and ready.

"No!"

Her brow furrowed at me, but she didn't lower the gun. "What? They're wolves, Jace!"

"Yes. I know." I put my hands up and stepped toward her carefully, making sure I was in the path of the shot. "They are friends."

"Friends?" She lowered her gun a fraction but brought it back up when Ash stepped out a little farther.

I gave him a quick glance. "Ash, stay." He whined, moving back into the bush. "Remember? He was with us when you found us. Bomber didn't allow him in the city."

"That's the same one?" AJ shook her head in confusion, squinting her eyes at Ash to see if she remembered what he looked like. I was sure that to humans all wolves looked similar.

"Yes. That's Ash, Eden's wolf. The others are his pack." Lillyanne and Sam moved up slowly to flank AJ. I took another step toward her. "I promise, if he's not threatened, he won't hurt you."

"What about the others?" Sam asked, slowly raising his gun. His eyes fixed on a few sets of glowing eyes in a neighboring bush.

I looked at him. "They do as Ash says. Follow his lead."

AJ scoffed. "You speak of them like they can have a conversation with you. Like... like they understand."

I tossed my head side to side pondering her words. "Well, actually—"

"You should see the way Eden talks to Ash. It's like he's human, or she's an animal." Lillyanne cocked a hip and crossed her arms.

"Like I said before, you better drop your Eden bashing. Ash and I won't hear it."

AJ finally lowered her gun. "Shut up. Both of you." She turned to Lillyanne. "But especially you." She looked back at me. "All right, but I'm keeping my gun close, and if any of them makes one wrong move, I won't hesitate to shoot. Got it?"

"Perfectly," I said, lowering my arms and letting out a long breath. I turned back and faced Ash with a smile. He was so hunched down in the bushes it took a moment for me to spot his eyes. "Hey, buddy. It's all right." I moved closer and crouched, holding out my hand. "Eden will be so happy when I tell her I saw you."

Ash stood and slowly emerged. As he took a few hesitant steps toward me, his eyes stayed on the others. I could sense his tension and apprehension, but when he reached me, a wave of relief and happiness hit me. His mouth turned to a smile as he pushed his head into my chest, urging me to scratch his ears.

AJ shook her head. "That's... that's . . ."

"Crazy? Idiotic?" Lillyanne mused.

"Amazing."

I smiled back at AJ. "He's really friendly and would do anything for the ones he loves." Ash pushed into my chest so hard I fell back onto the ground, letting out a laugh. His tail wagged faster, and he gave my cheeks a few licks. Managing to push his head to the side, I looked at AJ and Sam. "You can pet him if you want. I promise he won't hurt you."

They both stood hesitantly, watching me interact with a wolf. Lillyanne turned and headed back toward the car.

AJ's mouth twitched, but she shook her head. "Maybe another time. Let's make a fire and get set up for the night."

"Suit yourself." My ear scratch pulled a deep moan from Ash's throat, and I laughed. "I didn't realize you liked me this much, buddy." He looked up at me with calm and content eyes, but I could feel a hint of loss. I frowned at him. "I know, buddy. She misses you too."

Chapter 17

Eden

"I'm not a little kid, Old Bob. I'm not talking like that." I turned my back to him, grunting as I tugged the small brush through my thick hair. It had grown to the middle of my back since leaving the cabin. Ellie had always brushed my hair for me, and I relished it, but now I did it as quickly as possible because I thought it a waste of time. But both Old Bob and Tate insisted that if I looked more presentable, it would help me make friends.

"I know you're not a kid, but you do have some . . ."

I turned to him and raised an eyebrow.

He smiled. "Communication problems."

Tate snorted from his spot on the floor, leaning against the wall with one arm on a propped knee. I shot him a glare. "I don't have a communication problem. It's not my fault people aren't open minded."

"You're right. I wish people were, but the fact is they aren't. Because of this, unfortunately, you're the one that has to change."

Slamming the brush onto the floor next to my blanket, I spun around and scowled at him. "How is that fair? I won't do it."

"Eden."

"Whatever happened to Ellie's lessons?"

Old Bob tensed at her name. It was a low blow, but I had to make a point. "She always said to never change for anyone. If they are worth it, then they'll accept you for who you are."

Old Bob stared at me, then let out a sigh, wiping his rough hand over his scruffy face. "How can I argue with that?" He smiled at me. "All right, you win. Just promise me one thing."

"What?"

He stepped next to me and rested his warm gentle hands on my shoulders. "You don't have to change who you are, but you do need to try your best not to lose your temper."

"Yes. No one wants to be friends with the crabby girl," Tate said. He stood with a large hop, then bent back to stretch, his back cracking in the process.

"Fine."

Old Bob smiled, giving my shoulders a squeeze.

"Good. And remember, if you need help with what you should say or—"

"Stop! I've talked to other people before. I'll be fine."

There was a knock on the door, and Bomber stepped in. "Morning. I thought I'd take you all on a tour."

I gave him my most convincing smile. "That would be just lovely, Bomber."

"Are you feeling, OK?"

My smile dropped. "Yeah. Why wouldn't I be?"

"I don't know. You're just... acting weird." He quickly turned. "Well, let's get a move on it. Don't have all day."

Tate held a hand over his mouth, hiding his obvious smirk. "Maybe you should have Old Bob and I help you out."

"Shut up." I slammed into his shoulder as I passed him following Bomber.

～

Bomber led us through the city, and he wasn't lying when he told us there were only a few hundred people. Half the city was uninhabitable, which caused people to either move to the center, where Bomber and his people had set up, or to the outskirts, which posed its own problems.

The compound was protected by a metal fence. The four brick buildings housed most of the city members, a school, cafeteria, hospital, and the few offices that Bomber worked from.

After the tour, we sat in the cafeteria eating our first meal of the day: bland oatmeal and a fruit medley that came from a can. I gagged it down, avoiding sharp looks from Tate.

"How much do you know of the cartel?" Old Bob asked.

Bomber let out a huff. "That they're violent bastards who want to control everything."

I pushed my half-eaten oatmeal away and looked at Bomber. "How violent?"

Holding his tea up to his mouth, he paused for a minute. "So, the cartel is divided."

"Divided?"

Bomber nodded. "Yeah. Juan Martin, their original leader, died, so now both his kids are fighting for control, stating they are the rightful leader. Unfortunately, as they try and take over our lands, they also fight amongst each other, putting innocent civilians in the crossfire."

I popped a squishy grape into my mouth. "Which one is the rightful leader?" Old Bob and Tate furrowed their brows at me, and Bomber took a long sip of tea. I shrugged. "What? I mean, one has to be, right?"

"That's beside the point. The point is they are trying to take everything over and people are dying," Tate said.

I looked at him. "I disagree. I mean, if one is the rightful leader, then maybe we can work with them."

Looking annoyed, Bomber set his tea down. "We hardly have the manpower to attempt anything like that."

I opened my mouth, but Old Bob spoke before I could. "What are they controlling? Don't the people fight back?"

"Of course, but they are untrained and many are too old or have children, so they don't want to risk leaving them orphans. There are a few militia groups, but the cartel deals in water. As you know, in the south, water is a necessity for survival. Many people are giving up in order to make deals with them."

I swallowed down a thick, bland glob of oatmeal before setting my spoon down and meeting Bomber's eyes. "You never told us before, why do they call you Bomber?"

His eye twitched and he sat back. "In the war, I was our expert bomber. Flew a B52 and hold the record for most bombs dropped of anyone who survived." His voice cracked on his last words as a shadow of pain passed over his eyes. That same shadow sometimes passed over Old Bob's eyes. It's the look of someone who has seen horrible things.

"Can't we use your expertise to our advantage?"

His mouth created a thin long line, not quite a smile, and he shook his head. "You think we haven't thought of that already? If we had the resources, we would have, but like I have mentioned many times before, resources are sparse."

A commotion outside brought frightened murmurs into the cafeteria. People moved quickly to the windows; some ran outside.

"Bomber, come," a man yelled from the door.

Bomber jumped up and ran after him. As we followed, I strained to glance at what was outside, but too many people blocked the windows. Old Bob, Tate, and I jogged down the stairs, only to halt at the large crowd of people in the doorway. I could see Bomber's thick black hair, and I gently pushed through the people to follow him. The metallic smell of blood filled my nose and every cell in my body went on alert.

When I reached the open area outside, three cars were idling. Screams and cries echoed against the buildings. Children were crying, some standing, some being carried; and there was blood, lots and lots of blood.

My mouth twitched as a quiet growl escaped me. Tate gently grabbed my arm, and I looked at him. "Who would do this?"

Bomber stepped in front of us. "Looks like the cartel is closer than we thought. They bombed a schoolhouse just a hundred or so miles from here."

My hands fisted, and I felt my claws puncture my palms. Old Bob grabbed my other arm. I may not be fully human, but I would never hurt the young of any creature. Whoever did this was evil.

Very, very evil.

Chapter 18

Jace

Ash and his pack stayed with us all night. I was thankful for his warm coat and body heat, which kept me comfortable as we slept outside. His pack didn't sleep near me, but I sensed their presence, keeping AJ and Sam on their toes.

"We should have just stayed at Aunt Bev's farm. At least we would have one comfortable night." Lillyanne grumbled. She twisted and stretched after she stepped out of the car.

I crouched near the small fire I had built at dawn, roasting rabbit. That was one nice thing about having a wolf pack stay with us: they hunted.

"What's that amazing smell?" Sam said. His smile almost reached both ears as he walked toward me. "Didn't you sleep?"

I laughed. "I'm an early riser, but as much as I'd love to take credit for our breakfast, I can't. The wolves must have figured we should have full bellies."

"Well, they figured right." Sam rubbed his stomach in anticipation.

AJ nudged him as she sat down. "All you think about is food."

"Because food is life." He winked, and she snorted.

Lillyanne sat down next to me. "I thought water was life." Everyone turned to her, staying silent. Raising her eyebrows, she shrugged. "Whatever."

I checked the rabbit and was confident it was done. Taking the sharp stick I fashioned into a knife, I cut it up, passing pieces to everyone, including Ash and his pack. No one spoke as they ate, but Lillyanne inspected the meat carefully. When I looked at her, she took a small nibble, and I laughed.

"Something wrong?"

"No," she said, taking another small nibble. Her face reflected uncertainty. "It's just, if we stayed at my Aunt Bev's, she would've—"

"Will you shut up about your Aunt Bev," Sam yelled. "Just deal with it. We aren't staying there. We aren't even stopping there!"

Lillyanne's cheeks reddened, and she dropped her hands to her lap. The rabbit meat left a greasy mark on her pants. "We aren't even going to stop there? But—"

AJ stood abruptly. "Let's go. We have to stay moving. Who knows who's around these parts?"

AJ walked back to the car, with Sam following, still licking his fingers. I was still crouched near the fire when I turned and looked at Lillyanne. Her jaw clenched and she kept her eyes on the fire. I extended another piece of meat toward her. "Want this?"

She looked at it, avoiding my eyes, and shook her head.

I sighed. "Look. You need to remember this isn't a road trip to visit family. It's a mission. They only care about getting Cal and bringing him back. They don't care about your family or situation."

Her misty eyes met mine and she sniffed. "I know. I just thought it would be nice to be hospitable."

Watching her fight back tears, my stomach seized for her. No matter how annoying she was, she meant well. "I know you did, but they live a different kind of life. It's survival."

"I guess."

I stood and offered her a hand. She looked at it a moment before taking it and standing. "Thanks for the food. You did... good with what you had."

I laughed. "I'm going to take that as a compliment."

"Come on!" AJ yelled from the car door.

I quickly covered the fire with dirt and leaned down to Ash, scratching him behind his ears. "We're headed north to the farm we escaped. I'm sure you can follow our scent. Your help would be much appreciated." I smiled at him, and he licked my hand. Whether it was in acknowledgment of my words or because of the remnants of the rabbit on my hands, I don't know, but as he ran into the woods toward his pack, I swear I heard a voice in my head say "got it."

~

The rest of the drive I dozed on and off, listening to the mundane conversations among the others. Every time we stopped so AJ and Sam could change drivers, I would get out for a quick pee and stretch. Lillyanne didn't say much, but I could feel her. She was calmer, more understanding since our little talk.

We arrived near a familiar tree line, and I cracked my window, taking a whiff of the air. Flashes of the manure smell from the barn hit me. Leaning forward between the front seats, I pointed to the farm. "I think this is it. Slow down."

Lillyanne nodded. "He's right. That's the farm."

"Stop here. We don't want to just drive in. They aren't very... welcoming."

"They probably already know we are here," Lillyanne said, stepping out of the stopped car. "They don't miss much."

I watched her slowly start toward the farm. Her face didn't show anxiety or fear as I would have expected. After all, they did have her chained in the barn.

"Grab the guns," AJ said to Sam. All the fun from the morning was gone, replaced with focus—preparing for a fight.

I stepped out of the car, feeling the cool breeze blow over me. I would have savored it if I didn't have a pit in my stomach. Something didn't feel right. Scanning the trees and fields around us, I noticed nothing out of the ordinary.

Sam and AJ flanked me, both holding guns at the ready. Lillyanne was already to the driveway, slowly making her way closer to the farmhouse. Another breeze hit me, and the smell was unmistakable.

Death.

"Lillyanne, stop!" I sprinted up beside her. She turned to me wide-eyed. "Something isn't right."

AJ's and Sam's feet crunched on the sand and stones behind me as they jogged to meet us. "What's going on, Jace?" AJ's voice held warning.

"I don't know, but something isn't right."

Lillyanne sighed dramatically. "I think you're overreacting."

I narrowed my eyes at her. "Really? Do you? Then why haven't they come out to meet us yet? Do you really think Jimmy would let people get this close to the farm?"

She opened her mouth to say something but closed it when she realized I was right. She looked back at the farm, her face going white.

"Mom!" She took off so fast the dust from the dirt road kicked up into my face.

"Mom? What the hell is going on?" AJ said.

"I don't know." I watched her run toward the house.

We jogged behind her, my eyes moving continuously in search of an attack. Jimmy wasn't one to be easily taken down, so whoever did it had to be bad. Very, very bad.

"Lillyanne!" I grabbed her arm before she stepped onto the porch. "Shut up!"

She pulled from me, but I held her tightly. I'm sure my fingers bruised her skin, but it didn't faze her. "Let me go. I have to check on my mom and sisters!"

I watched her. "Your mom? Sisters?" Then it dawned on me. The little girl that came to Jimmy the night we escaped. That was Lillyanne's sister. After yanking her back harder so she looked at me, I leveled my eyes with hers and growled. "What do you *mean* your mom and sisters?"

Her eyes locked with mine and fear flicked through them. She swallowed.

"Lilly?" a small voice said through the screen door. "Lilly? Is th-th-that you?"

"Marybeth?" Lilly's eyes widened and relief washed over her face. My hold lightened, and she yanked free of me, falling to her knees on the porch. "Marybeth!" The little blonde girl I saw before came running out directly into Lillyanne's arms. Her face was blotchy and her eyes were swollen.

I sucked in a breath and stepped back. That wasn't the only thing wrong. Marybeth looked up at me over Lillyanne's shoulder, and I wasn't met with the two big blue eyes I had seen before, but only one. The other was gold.

Chapter 19

Eden

People rushed bed to bed, yelling stats and demands as they worked on the victims. Twelve children and four adults. The smell of blood was so overwhelming I pushed myself back into the corner near a little girl, no older than six. She was unconscious, her face reflecting peace despite the cuts and bruises that covered her body.

The noise in the room increased to a humming. I focused on the girl's chest, rising and falling with each breath, and worked to match mine with hers. The smells and sounds were too much. Clenching my teeth, I squeezed my eyes shut.

"Can you help?" a distant voice said.

I pulled my knees up, wrapped my arms around them, and continued to squeeze my eyes shut. Someone kicked my leg.

"Hey, new girl! Can you help?"

Letting out a snarl, I whipped my head up to face a boy my age. He didn't balk at my display, only repeated himself. This time the humming of the room returned to the original sounds of screams and moans.

"Is that a yes?" he asked. "You know what? Never mind, I don't have time." He threw a damp rag at me, hitting me directly on my face. "If you're going to help, clean her up." He nodded toward the sleeping girl. "We need to make sure she doesn't have any open wounds."

I clenched the rag and opened my mouth to snap at the boy's audacity when Old Bob caught my eye. He was cleaning off another patient; Tate was doing the same behind him. Old Bob gave me the slightest shake of his head before going back to his work.

Letting out a rough breath, I nodded. "Sure."

The boy focused on examining the girl's legs. He moved gently, wiping away blood and dirt, looking closely for any deep wounds. I moved to her face and did the same.

Every breath I took, her blood filled my nose, and I clenched down the urge to lick her. If I could just lick her, it would make everything better.

Her skin was surprisingly clear after it was cleaned. The bucket of water next to me was so dark with blood that you couldn't see the bottom.

"Find anything?" the boy asked.

I cleared my throat. "No."

"Good."

I moved down her arms, only finding small scratches. I moved closer to her and sniffed deep. I could smell her and... others.

"I don't think this blood is hers."

The boy looked at me. "What?"

"The blood. It's not hers."

We locked eyes a moment, and I could see the question in his eyes, but he was wise enough not to ask. He just nodded. "Fine. Finish cleaning her up. I'll move to this one." He stood and moved to another child who unfortunately was not asleep. His voice rasped from his cries.

I finished wiping the girl down just as she started to stir. I slowly petted her matted dark hair back and smiled as her eyes cracked. "It's all right. You're safe now."

She stared at me a moment, letting her brain register, then her brown eyes went wide as she inspected me: my claws, then back to my mouth. My smile faded, and I stepped back.

"Hey there." The boy turned back to me and crouched next to her. "Can you tell me your name?"

The girl blinked and looked at the boy. He smiled at her, and she whispered, "Ana."

"Ana. That's a pretty name." He sat next to her. "Can you tell me if anything hurts, Ana, or if you can't move anything?"

She shook her head as tears filled her eyes. "Where's my sister?"

"Your sister?" The boy glanced at me, then squeezed her arm. "We'll find her, all right? We're just making sure everyone is all right."

Ana sniffed and swallowed. With more strength than I ever thought a little girl could have, she nodded. Then she looked at me, and I tensed. I waited for her scream or her words deeming me a monster, but they never came. Instead, she smiled and said, "Can she stay with me?"

I released a breath and my shoulders relaxed. The boy glanced at me again. "Of course. She won't leave your side." He gave me a pointed look that had me nodding before he moved to check on others.

I pulled up a chair and smiled. "I'm Eden."

She grinned back at me then grabbed my hand.

∽

Ana didn't let go of my hand for the next four hours as we watched people shuffle around, cleaning and bandaging wounds. Four people died, two of them children, and several were injured, with very beat up, broken bodies.

Tate and Old Bob approached us, their eyes on our hands. Ana mindlessly played with my claws as she watched all the commotion.

"Hello there," Old Bob said. He smiled down at Ana.

"Have you seen my sister?"

He furrowed his brow giving me a questioning look. "Sister? I—"

I leaned forward. "We don't know who everyone is yet. I'm sure we'll find her after things calm down more and we learn people's names."

She nodded, squeezing my hand tighter. "All right. Her name is Kat."

"Kat. We'll remember that." Old Bob gave her small shoulder a pat. He looked at me. "How are you doing?"

I cleared my throat. "Fine." He watched me skeptically but didn't argue. With most of the blood having been cleaned up and removed and Ana distracting me by clutching my hand, I wasn't as uncomfortable as I had been before.

"She did well. Made a friend, it looks like," the boy from before said, stepping up beside me. He smiled a perfect smile at Old Bob and Tate, holding out his hand. "I'm Jay." Old Bob and Tate took turns shaking it. When he extended it to me, I hesitated, shooting Old Bob a look. Jay chuckled. "It's fine. I already saw your hands."

I met his eyes and cocked my head. "And you're not scared?"

"Scared? No. Not much scares me anymore." He glanced down at his hand, held out in front of him. After a long moment, I slowly shook it, and he sighed. "Thank God. I was hoping you wouldn't leave me hanging while all my friends are watching." He shrugged toward the doorway where a group of kids stood, working hard not to stare. I quickly pulled my hand away, and Ana snatched it back up.

Bomber walked to us and slapped Jay on the shoulder. "I see you've met my nephew."

"We have." Old Bob crossed his arms and positioned himself in a more serious stance. "Did you learn any more about what happened?"

Bomber's smile faded, and he gave a little nod. "I did. It would seem that Izan, the brother and leader of half of the cartel, has begun showing up his sister. He wants to portray her as weak, but in doing so, he is killing and injuring innocent people. Lucia has yet to show herself after this display. Who knows if she will or if she will concede."

"Concede? And what, leave the control to this psychopath?" I asked. Thinking of how Zane controlled the people of the city and how so many innocent people died, I couldn't let that happen again if I could help it.

"I don't know. I have never spoken to them. All I know are rumors and what they've done."

"Maybe someone should talk to them."

Everyone looked at me like I grew a third eye.

Tate laughed. "Don't mind my sister. Sometimes she says things that don't make sense."

"Apparently," Jay muttered.

I opened my mouth, but Old Bob stopped me with a look. He looked at Bomber, who slowly peeled his eyes away from me. "It's been a long day. I think we could discuss this after some rest and food"—he glanced down at a sleeping Ana—"away from young ears."

"Agreed," Bomber said. "Clean up, and we can meet in the cafeteria."

Bomber and Jay walked out without another word. Old Bob and Tate just watched me as I gently set Ana's hand down. I didn't want to wake her. Quietly we walked through the room of injured bodies to our room to rest.

Chapter 20

Jace

I sucked in a breath and stepped back, urgently scanning the area. She didn't have a gold eye before. She had had two blue eyes. My breath increased to a pant as my heart pounded in my chest. She was a Chimera, but how?

I slowly backed up.

"Jace?" AJ asked, looking between me and Lillyanne, who still embraced her sister.

"We need to go," I said, a few paces away from her and Sam.

"What?" Lillyanne turned around, keeping her sister under the crook of her arm.

"Now. We need to go now!"

"No, Lilly! You can't go. They're all dead." Marybeth sobbed, and I halted, turning back toward them. She clutched Lillyanne, burying her face in her chest. I could see the vacant look in Lillyanne's eyes as she stared straight ahead.

I cleared my throat. "What do you mean they're all dead?"

Lillyanne snapped her eyes to me. "Seriously? Do you have no respect?"

"I'm sorry, all right, but... there's much more at play here than you understand."

"What's going on?" Sam said, glancing between us all. "AJ, this isn't going to plan."

"It rarely does," she mumbled.

"We should leave." Sam stepped back toward me.

I put my hand on his shoulder. "Wait—"

"No one is going anywhere." A firm male voice sounded from inside the house. It was familiar, but I wasn't able to place him. Squinting, I let my eyes focus on the darkness behind the screen door and was met with another gold eye. "Hello again... Jace, is it?" Jimmy slowly opened the porch door, letting its creaky springs echo around us.

I stood up straight and set my jaw. "Jimmy."

A smile snaked along his face, but his gaze quickly turned to Lillyanne and Marybeth. "Daddy," Lillyanne yelled, wrapping her arms around his neck. "I never thought I'd be so happy to see you."

Jimmy stood rigid as both his girls hugged him. He was the picture of a man who was uncomfortable with any sort of affection, which surprised me since Lillyanne was the opposite. He cleared his throat, gently pushing them both away. "Lilly, you're in big trouble."

"Hold on. You're Lillyanne's father?" I met Jimmy's eyes.

"That's right."

I looked at Lillyanne, who at least had the decency to look ashamed. "Jimmy is your father, and you didn't say anything? What the hell, Lillyanne. I don't think we can trust you at all!"

Her cheeks grew a deep tinge of pink. "What did you expect me to do? Tell you? No way you would've let me come."

"Damn right. What kind of father locks his daughter up in the barn?"

"One that's really good at discipline," Jimmy replied, not ashamed at the disgust in my voice.

AJ raised her gun at Jimmy. "Look. I don't give a shit about any of this. I'm here for Cal. Give him to me, and then you all can figure out your drama."

Jimmy looked AJ up and down like she was nothing but a kid with a toy gun. No worry or concern anywhere on his face. "And who the hell might you two be?"

"I'm—" Sam started to talk, but AJ gave him a hard kick.

"It doesn't matter. What matters is we want Cal, and we have the guns, so do us a favor and just give him to us. I've had a long few days and don't have time for song and dance."

Jimmy chuckled. "I like you." He glanced at me, then at Lillyanne. "You bring them here, sweetheart?"

Lillyanne wrung her hands, stepping back a few steps. "I-I didn't have a ch-ch-choice."

"You didn't have a choice?" Jimmy paused, watching Lillyanne before he leaned forward and gave her a swift slap. "There's always a choice!" Lillyanne moved a shaking hand to her pink cheek, silent tears streaming down her face. Marybeth continued to clutch her around the waist.

I stepped forward. "That's enough."

Jimmy scowled at me, and I took another step forward. "She didn't say anything. I did. She's just collateral."

Jimmy watched me carefully, giving Lillyanne a few glances. He stepped down the steps toward me. "You sweet on my little girl, Jace?"

"What? No. I'm—"

"I think you are." He took another step toward me. "See, my girls never lie to me. So if what you say is true, then this would be the first time and she'd need to be punished. And if what she says is true, then well"—he sniffed, wiping his nose—"then she'd need to be punished. So, either way… She. Will. Be. Punished." He was so close to me now our noses almost touched. I clenched my fists and held in the growl that fought to erupt from within me.

"What the hell kind of place is this?" AJ said.

I sniffed Jimmy dramatically. "Where is he?"

"Where is who?"

"The one who changed you."

Jimmy scratched the back of his neck, letting out a little chuckle. "I don't know what you're talking about."

"Don't play games with me, Jimmy. I know what you are." I looked at Marybeth. "I know what she is." I poked his chest hard enough I'm sure it will leave a bruise. "So, tell me where the person who changed you is."

AJ and Sam were slowly moving behind me. "What the hell is going on?"

I didn't look at them. I kept my eyes fixed on Jimmy and his face, which was now dropping with the realization that I knew more than he wanted. "There aren't many people in this world who know what we are or how to make us, so tell me."

"Daddy?" Lillyanne said quietly, sniffing. She pulled Marybeth closer to her.

Jimmy sighed. "He's inside."

We stared at each other in silence, then AJ and Sam started to move toward the house. "Stop," I said.

"What?" AJ said.

"I don't trust him."

"Well then, what do you expect us to do?"

I hated myself for what I was about to do, but I had no other choice. I looked at Lillyanne, then down to Marybeth. "Marybeth, come here."

Jimmy held up his hand. "You don't move anywhere, Marybeth." He eyed me. "What are you playing at?"

"She won't get hurt if we all stay alive and well. So, if you have nothing to hide, then everything will be fine." I held out my hand to Marybeth, who watched me with wide, wet eyes. "Come here. It's all right." She took a hesitant step toward me, but Lillyanne grabbed her arm. I looked at her, giving my head a warning shake. When I looked back at Marybeth, I smiled softly.

Come. It's all right.

Her eyes widened at the sound of my voice in her head and I nodded, holding out my hand. Slowly she stepped toward me, and I put my hand on her shoulders. "Now. Let's go inside."

Jimmy's mouth became a thin line as he watched my hands on his young daughter's shoulders. I'd never hurt her, but he didn't have to know that. He was a father who hit his kids, so I can only imagine what he thought I'd do. He went to the porch door and opened it.

I looked at AJ and Sam. "Be ready." They both nodded and followed me inside.

Blinking, I became accustomed to the dimmer light and leaned down to whisper into Marybeth's ear. "You said everyone died?"

Her swallow was audible as she looked back at me. "Well, no. Not everyone."

"Hello, Jace."

I whipped around, but before I could react, I was knocked on my ass. I slid across the floor; my back hit the wall with crunching force. Coughing, I looked up at my smug attacker. "Brian?"

"I see you have been keeping up on your training. Well done."

Chapter 21

Eden

I picked at my bland oatmeal, listening to Old Bob and Bomber talk. Jay joined us for breakfast, but he was too busy stuffing his face to have a conversation. I wondered if he had ever had a savory breakfast, with sausage and potatoes. My mouth began to water at the thought, but Tate's elbow nudge reminded me to take a bite. I gagged down the bland food, wondering if Bomber would let me hunt. Then I could show them all what flavor really is.

Jay finished his plate and downed his glass of water before looking at me. "So, you both did well yesterday in the clinic. We'd really appreciate the help if you're free."

Shifting my gaze to his, I gave him a small smile. "Thank you." I bit my cheek at the lie. I wasn't thankful; the whole experience of watching screaming and bloody people had me up all night. I could feel Old Bob's silent urge to say more, to try and build relationships. I cleared my throat. "So are you a doctor?"

Jay laughed. "What? No. I'm just a kid, but"—he paused, glancing at his uncle—"I'm hoping I'll be able to train under the medical professionals here. I'd like to be a doctor."

Bomber gave him a firm pat on the shoulder. "You will be. And a great one at that. He's a natural."

I watched the exchange, feeling the loving bond flowing between them. Bomber was more than just an uncle, and I'm willing to bet the war was to blame for that. His face beamed with pride, and Jay's reflected the same back at him. Bomber turned to me and his smile faded slightly. He furrowed his brow at my large grin, which turned to a hiss when Tate kicked me under the table.

"You're freaking people out. Act normal," Tate whispered into my ear.

I coughed, elbowing Tate back, then said to Bomber, "So, no one has spoken with either side of the cartel?"

His face hardened and he looked at Old Bob. "She's a persistent, nosy little thing, isn't she?"

Gripping my spoon tightly, I leaned forward over my plate. "Nosy?" Bomber watched me, unaffected by my aggression.

"She is curious, yes. But she is very smart and a great fighter," Old Bob said, gently setting a hand over mine.

"I only ask because if no one has talked to them, then how do we know if there is a possible way for peace? I mean... haven't you all heard of negotiation?"

Bomber crossed his arms. "I suppose you think you know how? How many *wars* have you negotiated?"

I clenched my jaw, ignoring Old Bob's pleading eyes burning into the side of my face. "To be honest? None." Bomber snorted, and I continued, "But I have read a lot of military books, and I have been through more than most people will ever go through in their entire life."

"Military books? Really? That's where you get your brilliant ideas? Why don't you let Bob and I do the planning? If we need your"—he gave me a once over before meeting my eyes again— "muscle, we will let you know."

I growled deep in my chest at the condescending tone in his voice and opened my mouth to speak when Jay slammed his hand on the table. "Oh! I almost forgot. My friends and I are having a party tonight. Tate, Eden, why don't you join us?"

My eyebrows shot up in surprise. "A party?" He nodded. I glanced at Tate and Old Bob. "Well, I don't—"

"That sounds great," Tate said.

"Great! Meet me out front at six." Jay rushed off toward his group of friends, not waiting for a reply.

"Really?" I said, watching the side of Tate's face as he conveniently avoided my glare.

"I think it could be good," Old Bob said. "You can make friends." His voice had that edge in it when his suggestion was actually an order. He wanted me to become likable.

I let out a breath. "Fine, but I'm only staying an hour."

"That should be enough time," Old Bob said.

Bomber brought his water glass to his mouth and right before he took a sip, he winked at me. "Have fun."

Tate stood, pulling me with him. "Come on. There are some things I wanted to do today. You can help." I glared at his obvious distraction, but he tugged me away before I could bite anyone's head off.

∾

Any other time I would have despised Tate hovering so close to me, squishing me into a corner, but today, today I was thankful. My heart beat loudly and steadily in my ears as I focused on relaxing my shoulders and claws.

Multiple conversations, filled with shouts and laughter, echoed around the room, but they were mostly drowned out by the thumping of music in the background. Someone bumped into Tate, causing him to shove me tighter into the corner. Multiple eyes flicked our way. I clenched my jaw and pushed a hand through my hair, letting out a curse when a claw caught a thick tangle. I told myself everyone around me was just curious about the new kids, but my heart knew the truth: they were staring at the animal girl, the girl with fangs, claws, and messy hair.

"Here!" Jay yelled over the noise. He held a cup out to me. When I hesitated, he laughed, shoving it at me. "Come on. Just take it!" I slowly took it, pushing more hair from my face with my free hand. My eyes flicked around the room, scanning the curious gazes that monitored my every move.

Tate leaned toward us. "What is it?"

"Berry juice," Jay yelled at him. He looked behind him giving another boy a head nod. The boy quickly filled a cup and brought it over to Tate.

I brought the cup up to my nose and sniffed, quickly turning away with a cough. "It smells horrible!"

Jay laughed and put a hand on my shoulder. "You get used to it." I stiffened at his touch and fought the urge to shrug him off. I had to remain friendly.

"So, is this all you do?" Tate leaned in again, yelling toward Jay.

"After the drinks kick in, it'll get more interesting." Jay motioned us to follow him. "Come. Have a seat."

Leaning into Tate, I spoke into his ear, just loud enough where only he could hear it. "What did he mean when the drinks kick in?" Tate shrugged and led me after Jay. We sat on a large couch and watched the others drink, laugh, and talk.

Chapter 22

Jace

Water dripped down my chin as I gulped the glass of water. Inhaling some, I slammed the cup down onto the table with a cough, meeting Brian's smirking face. I hadn't been able to say much since he knocked me down—both from the shock of seeing him and the shock of seeing that everyone at the farm were now Chimera.

"How's Little One?" Brian asked, leaning back in his chair, crossing his arms.

I wiped my mouth with the back of my hand. I could feel everyone's eyes on me, but I kept mine focused on Brian. The room was silent besides the clicking of the large wooden clock in the corner. "She's good. She's in Kansas City. Well, what's left of it, with the others."

Brian nodded.

"I hate to interrupt this sweet reunion, but we came here for a reason, and I don't intend on staying here much longer. We have a war to plan," AJ said, setting her gun on the table but keeping one hand steady on it.

Brian raised his eyebrows. "War? What war?"

"The cartel from the south is moving north, invading and taking over cities and lands," I said, ignoring the groans from AJ.

AJ leaned forward. "We're here for Cal."

Jimmy sat forward. His new gold eye burned into AJ, almost twinkling with rejuvenation. "And what do you need with Cal?" His eyes slid over to his right where Cal sat, completely unfazed by the threat or even from seeing AJ and Sam.

"We are bringing him back to the city so he can pay for his crimes."

Jimmy's bark of laughter was followed by chuckles from Cal. "Pay for his crimes? What crimes did he commit?"

"He stole from us. Supplies and food," Sam said. He sat next to AJ, still leaning back in his chair. His body signaled relaxation, but his hazel eyes showed nothing but aggression.

"I had every right. I worked my ass off there, so I earned those supplies."

I turned to AJ, who flexed her jaw. Brian raised his eyebrows at me as he watched the argument. How could this be the first argument they bring up?

Shaking my head, I put up my hands to stop everyone. "I'm sorry. Can we talk about the elephant in the room first?"

Lillyanne looked at me. "What elephant?"

"Are you serious?" I sputtered with a quick laugh, looking between everyone in the room, then back at her. "Did you not look at their eyes?"

Lillyanne gulped, looking down at her hand clasped to her sister's. "I did."

"You did."

"Yes. But I was just going to ignore it."

"Ignore it?" I looked at Brian. He watched me, relaxed and completely fine with me taking on the role of news breaker. "Well, Lillyanne, I hate to be the one to tell you this, but they are all Chimera."

"Chimera?" AJ said. "What in the world is that?"

I cleared my throat. "It's when one organism shares two different DNA."

Jimmy chuckled. "And it's amazing."

I widened my eyes, a knot forming in my stomach at his words. The last thing we needed was another psycho, power-hungry Chimera.

"Yes. Well, there is much you have to learn," Brian said to Jimmy carefully. "I found them mostly dead. Sick with the Fever."

I swallowed, remembering the weakness and pain of being sick. I wouldn't wish that on anyone, not even Jimmy.

"We lost most of us." Jimmy's face dropped. "My wife and most of my girls." His eyes met Lillyanne and Marybeth holding each other tightly, both with silent tears streaming down their cheeks.

"I'm sorry," I whispered.

Jimmy looked at me, and after a moment, he gave me a slight nod.

"So how did they become this... Chimera? And what is the Fever?" Sam asked.

I gave Brian a pleading look to take over the conversation. He sighed and leaned forward. "The Fever wiped out most of the population in the north. It took us many years to find a cure, which happens to be becoming a Chimera. It's the only sure way to survive it if you are infected, though some survive without it."

"And how do you do that?" AJ asked warily.

"Inject animal blood into the sick person."

Both AJ and Sam's faces paled. Lillyanne sniffed, blinking away tears. "So, all of you... put animal blood inside you?"

"That's right," Jimmy said to her. "It was that or die."

"But I don't understand," I said, shaking my head. "How'd they get sick?"

"You all had to have carried it here." Brian scratched his rough jaw.

"No"—I looked at Lillyanne—"if that were true, then she'd have gotten sick. The people in the city as well, but none have." I paused before turning to look at Jimmy. "Who got sick first?"

Jimmy sighed, pushing his light salt-and-pepper hair back. "Tim and Steve. Then my wife and the girls." He paused. "They were caring for the men. After them, it was all of us."

"They were almost gone when I arrived," Brian said.

"The fang marks weren't even healed on Tim's throat before they got sick," Cal growled.

"Fang marks?" I cocked my head at him.

"That's right. From your *wolves*," Jimmy snapped. "I should have shot them when I could."

Clenching my jaw, I looked at Brian.

It's the wolves.

The skin around his eyes tightened. *I don't think it's just the wolves. I think it may be all the animals.*

A loud howling bark floated in from outside, and my stomach dropped. Not the best timing for Ash and his pack to show up. If the people learned of this, the wolves would be slaughtered.

"And will y'all get... claws and fangs, like Eden?" Lillyanne asked.

"No." I looked at her. "Eden is a special case."

"Special?" Her eyes widened. "Special how?"

Brian sat forward. "That is a story for another time."

Lillyanne studied him a moment before nodding and looking back down at Marybeth.

Jimmy sighed gleefully. "I can hear better, smell better, see better, and even move faster!" He leaned forward over the table. "It's almost like we have been blessed by the Holy Spirit, baby girl."

I gaped and looked at Lillyanne. She was watching her father with mesmerized eyes, soaking up his words. AJ and Sam chuckled next to me, and a wave of relief hit me. At least not all of them believed that crap.

I looked back at Brian. "So, why did you come? Why are you here?"

"I came for help."

"Help?"

"Yeah. Zane is out of control."

My stomach lurched. I put a hand over my mouth, swallowing down the excess water that threatened to come out. That name would forever be a trigger. I never wanted to see that man again, but that didn't seem possible. "What kind of help are you needing?"

Brian sighed, leaning forward. "Any really. The more numbers, the better." His eyes moved over the others in the room.

AJ scoffed. "Sorry, but we have our own issues to deal with. They're a little more pertinent than a crazy man."

Brian's jaw ticked. "With all due respect, this man is your president—"

"President?" AJ scoffed. "What're you talking about? We haven't had a true president since before the war."

I swallowed and leaned forward, meeting Brian's confused gaze. "Apparently Zane has been manipulating the city. Since no one travels, it was never known that he isn't the true president."

Jimmy laughed. "If I remember right, Zane was just a senator before the war. How'd he become 'president'?"

Brian's tense face looked at Jimmy. "Everyone else was killed."

"Yes, well, he had you all fooled." AJ snickered. "For what, twenty years?"

I put my hands up, feeling the tension in the room rise. "All right. Now we know; Zane is a conman. But our bigger issue is we now have two threats working their way toward each other. Everyone in the middle is going to be affected. We need to figure out how to protect the people." I sighed and looked at Brian, whose face was still tense, but his body had visibly relaxed. "You can come back with us, but I don't know how we'll convince the others to help."

Sam leaned forward. "Whoa, whoa, who gave you the authority to just let others into our city?"

I leaned toward him just a hair, which caused him to flinch back. "I did. Just now. Because I know what's at stake. I know what will happen to all of you if Zane succeeds in gaining full control, and it won't matter if a million cartels come knocking on your door because he'll just take them all down with you."

The silence that filled the room was thick with fear. I could smell the salt in Marybeth's tears, which gave me a tinge of guilt at scaring her, but she was growing up in a world where fighting for your life is the only way.

Jimmy cleared his throat. "That does it then." He turned to Cal. "Load the truck with all the food you can carry." He turned to the rest of us. "We leave in an hour."

"I don't—" Sam started.

"This is more than revenge now. If we don't band together for survival, then we won't survive. It's that simple," Brian said.

AJ scanned the group. Seeing no other option, she pursed her lips and nodded. "We leave in an hour."

Chapter 23

Eden

I blinked. My eyes squinted at the brightness shining on me. No, blazing on me. I let out a groan, which only made the throb in my head beat more. Nausea boiled inside me, and I brought a hand over my mouth quickly to help hold it in.

"She's alive," a male voice said, followed by hoots and hollers.

"Eden?" Tate's voice wavered.

I turned my head toward him, blinking to focus my eyes, but the room spun and my stomach lurched.

I gagged. I don't think I can hold it in much longer.

"Someone, grab a bucket! I think she's going to hurl," the male voice yelled again, his voice rattling with laughter.

Tate gently took my hand. "Eden, what do you need?"

Squeezing my eyes shut, I batted him away. I wanted to say that I needed him to leave me alone, that whoever was yelling needed to shut up, but if I spoke, I would throw up. What would come up would only be bile since my stomach was completely empty.

"All right, all right," a woman said as she moved up beside my bed. "Why don't you all get out of here and let the poor girl rest?"

My mouth twitched as I tried to nod in agreement, but she gently put her hands on my shoulder. "Relax, Eden. You need lots of fluids and rest. Just lie back." She messed with an IV that was poking into the crook of my arm. "Are you nauseous?" I cracked an eye and looked at her blurry face. She watched me, waiting, and I managed a slight nod. "All right. I'll give you something for that in your IV. Now rest."

Tate leaned forward again, but the woman stopped him. "Let her sleep. She's fine."

"She's slept for almost twelve hours already."

"And she still needs rest," the woman said firmly. "So, you can let her sleep, or I'll send you away."

If Tate stayed or left, I don't know because I drifted off into a deep sleep.

~

"What exactly were you thinking, Tate?" Old Bob's clipped voice woke me from my deep slumber. "You say you went with her to protect her and yet she has been lying in this hospital bed all night."

"I know." Tate's voice cracked. "I didn't realize that the berry juice would do this."

"Sir, I take full responsibility." I blinked to see Jay standing rigidly next to Tate. He kept his head high, but his eyes pinned on Old Bob's chest.

Old Bob narrowed his gaze at Jay. I could let Old Bob rip into Jay, but for some reason, I liked him. He was genuine and didn't seem to be scared of me, so I cleared my throat, which had them all looking at me. Old Bob's face immediately softened.

"It's no one's fault," I rasped. My voice was gravelly, but I was thankful the nausea had passed. "I was the one who chose to drink it."

Old Bob's cheek twitched as his eyes moved over my face. "So then, it's *your* fault."

I swallowed and nudged my shoulders up in a pathetic attempt to shrug. "I guess it is, then."

"And don't worry." Bomber stepped up behind Jay, slapping a hard hand on his shoulder, "There will be consequences." Jay's face grew red, but he kept his eyes on the ground in front of him. "We can start with you pouring all of that berry *juice* out, with me watching."

Jay nodded. "Yes, sir." He followed Bomber out of the room. His head hung like Ash's always did when he was a pup, when he knew he'd done something bad.

The nurse stepped to the side of my bed and checked the fluids. When I looked up at her, she gave me a soft smile that started an ache in my chest. She reminded me of Sarah and everyone we left behind. Were they even still alive?

"You're a very lucky young lady. If you had drunk any more, I don't know what would have happened. That berry juice seemed to affect you more than it should have."

My eyes widened. "Seriously?"

"Yes," Old Bob said. His voice was firm, but the relief was etched on his face. "You're not like the others, Eden. Your body doesn't process things the same—especially not alcohol."

I scooted my body up, grunting at the tightness in my shoulders and the throbbing in my head. "Alcohol? But he said it was juice."

The nurse laughed. "That's just what the kids call it. It's fermented berries, also known as berry alcohol."

Tate shifted side to side behind Old Bob. "I'm so sorry, Eden. I should have known." He groaned, wiping a hand down his tired face. My nose twitched at the tang in the air, and I dropped my gaze from his face to his clothes. They were splattered with dark purple. The same dark purple as the berry juice. Warmth filled my cheeks as I looked back at his face.

"Did I do that?"

He dropped his gaze down to his clothes. "It's not a big deal—"

"Not a big deal!" I squawked. Glancing around the room to make sure others couldn't hear me, I lowered my voice. "Did everyone see?" His eyes met mine, but he didn't have to say anything for me to know the answer. My stomach dropped. "Great. Now I'll never make friends."

Old Bob barked a laugh. "That's what you're worried about? If you think this is why you won't make friends, we need to chat more."

Bomber stepped back into the room. "So the others returned."

My heart flipped, and I craned my neck to see around Old Bob and Bomber. Jace's eyes were dark and serious. Something was wrong, but my attention slid to the tall man next to him. The crinkles at the corners of Brian's eyes creased as he cocked a grin.

"Now, now, Eden. I don't remember teaching drinking in our training."

Chapter 24

Jace

Eden's squeal after seeing Brian still rang in my ears. Old Bob had to catch her when she tried to leap off the bed only to fall forward. Everyone had a smile as they watched her hug the stranger.

Bomber cleared his throat, and Eden stepped back, still grinning ear to ear. "I'm not sure what happened on this trip to capture Cal, but it looks like we have taken in many more new people. A lot more."

Eden's eyes snapped past Brian to see who he was referring to but saw no one except me. Our eyes locked, and she immediately turned red, looking down at her feet.

Why the rosy cheeks?

She looked back at me. *Don't be mad.*

I smiled. *Why would I be mad, exactly?*

She just stared at me, her cheeks turning a deeper burgundy.

Bomber cleared his throat. "Sometimes when they do that long stare, I think they are talking to each other." Everyone looked at him before erupting in laughter. His eyebrows rose. "What?"

Old Bob stepped to his side with a smile. "Nothing." His body was so relaxed, showing more contentment than I had seen in him for a long time. My stomach knotted at the knowledge that it would all disappear once Brian explained why he was here.

Bomber shrugged it off and looked to Eden. "Are you well enough to meet? We have a lot to discuss."

Eden stood taller, focusing on staying upright. "Of course. Lead the way." Brian gently took her arm before she tipped over.

The nurse cleared her throat. "You're not leaving until I check you and take that IV out, young lady."

Eden froze, turning back to the nurse. My jaw dropped at the large toothy smile she gave her. "Oh. Right, sorry." I tilted my head at her before looking at Old Bob. Was she being pleasant?

He patted my shoulder, leaning in closer. "She has been working on being more approachable."

"I see that."

"She even made some friends."

I looked at him. "And look where that got her."

He shrugged. "Yes, the party was unfortunate, but what do you expect from a girl who hasn't been able to be a kid?"

I pursed my lips. He was right: she grew up in seclusion, with no other young people other than Tate and Tristan. But that's why I liked her. She was raw and real. She didn't try to please anyone; she just was... Eden.

I stepped up beside Brian. "I'll stay with her. We'll join you when she's ready."

"All right." Bomber led the others out of the room. I wasn't sure Eden would let go of Brian, but when he set her hand in mine, she released him.

I held her steady as she walked back to her bed and sat. The nurse immediately went to work checking her vitals. I kept my eyes on her fidgeting body as she conveniently avoided my stare.

So, I heard you made some friends.

Her throat bobbed as she swallowed. *I wouldn't call them friends exactly, but yeah, I met some other kids.*

They the ones who got you drunk?

She looked at me wide eyed. *It's not like they forced me.*

No, I get that, but they would've given you the drink.

The nurse now moved to her IV. "All right, I'm going to pull the needle out now. Hold still." Eden didn't even acknowledge that the nurse had spoken; she just sat frozen with her eyes locked with mine. The nurse pulled out the needle and put a bandage on the spot. "There you go. Now, make sure you stay hydrated and don't hesitate to come back if you feel ill."

Eden finally looked at her with a small smile. "Of course, thank you." She stood and took one step, but threw her hands out and swayed. I jumped forward and grabbed her arm, keeping her upright.

She stilled at my touch, and I felt the tension between us. I let out a long breath and leaned into her. "I'm sorry." She lifted her gaze to mine, opening her mouth, but I spoke before her. "I'm sorry I wasn't here to make sure nothing happened. I know Tate was there, but he's about as innocent as you are when it comes to... parties." She cocked her head at me, and I smiled. "You happen to be looking at a world-class party guy. If you could have seen me . . ." I paused at my words, letting my memories fade to my younger life. Life with friends, sneaking out, and stealing drinks from our parents. My smile faded.

"I bet you were magnificent." She squeezed my arm, and I looked back at her. Her eyes told me she could feel it. Feel my loss.

Clearing my throat, I tugged her forward gently. "Let's get out of here."

"I wonder why Brian is here. Did he tell you?"

I clenched my jaw, keeping my eyes forward. "I think he should be the one to tell you. He knows more." She watched me a moment, thankfully not pushing the topic.

We walked in silence to Bomber's meeting room. I savored the warmth from her touch as she leaned into me. I opened the door and guided Eden in before me, but ran into her back. She stood frozen, looking at the row of new Chimera sitting at the table.

What is this?

I didn't have time to respond to her before Jimmy did. "Hello again, Eden." His gold eye twinkled at her, not with genuine happiness to see her, but with a slyness that made my skin crawl. He would taunt her until her control broke.

"Jimmy," she growled. Her whole body was taut, but when I gently took her hand, she released some of the tightness in her shoulders. Her eyes drifted to Brian. "Why"—she paused, composing herself with a deep breath—"are Jimmy and his friends here? And why are they Chimera?"

Brian sucked in a breath to respond, but Bomber jumped in. "I think the first thing we need to clear up is, what is a Chimera?" All eyes drifted to him, but he showed no fear. He crossed his arms and set his feet. "When you all said there was a virus, you never mentioned any side effects or that others had been infected with it. Others so close to this city."

"We didn't know," Old Bob said. "And this isn't a side effect. It's more what happens when you have the cure."

"The cure?"

Brian sat forward from his seat at the end of the table. "Yes. It's either this"—he motioned to the others, himself, then Eden and I—"or... death. Which would you choose?"

Bomber let out a low grumble and sat down. "How did they get sick? Should I be quarantining you all?"

"No. If anyone was going to get sick from us, they would have already," Old Bob said.

Jimmy cleared his throat. "Well, I believe Brian said it was—"

"We aren't sure how they got sick." Old Bob interrupted, glancing quickly to Eden before looking back to Bomber.

Brian gave Jimmy a rough pat on the back to silence him when he opened his mouth to speak again.

The air in the room thickened. Everyone knew about the animals. Everyone but Eden. When she learned that Ash and his pack were carriers, who knew what she would do to protect them?

We can't tell her here. We need to tread carefully. Brian's voice rang in my head. I locked eyes with him, giving a nod ever so slightly.

Agreed.

Tightening my grip on Eden's hand, I stepped forward. "I know this may seem like the most important discussion at the moment, but I am going to kindly disagree. No one is in danger of being infected at the moment, I promise." I met Bomber's eyes. He reluctantly gave me a nod. "What we really need to figure out is what we are going to do with the two threats that we all face."

Bomber pinched the bridge of his nose. "Two threats?"

"Unfortunately, the cartel is not the only danger to the people," Brian said. "In the north, we have a self-made leader who has misled the people for over twenty years. He's using the Fever and the effects of the cure to claim and keep control of the people."

"And how is he doing that?" Bomber asked.

Brian paused, looking at Eden before turning back to Bomber. "After Eden and the others left, he sent a small army farther north. We weren't sure if there were any people there, just like we weren't sure you all existed down here."

"And were there?" Eden whispered.

"There were." Brian nodded. "Zane secretly infected the people with the Fever. He then marched in with the cure, gaining their trust and loyalty."

Old Bob held up a hand and closed his eyes. "Wait. So Zane has gained more people to his army?"

"I'm afraid so."

Eden growled. "Great. That's just what we need. How many people does he have now under his control?"

Brian swallowed and sighed. "Around eight thousand."

Chapter 25

Eden

"What?" I said through a clenched jaw. Jace's hand dug into my forearm, but I didn't pull away. "How are we supposed to compete against eight thousand Chimera?"

"Easy," Brian cooed. "Why don't you sit down." He slowly motioned to a seat next to his.

Swallowing hard, I pulled in a deep breath and slowly released it. Jace led me to a chair and sat next to me.

"Am I missing something?" Bomber said. "So what if this crazy kook from the north has that many people. Why would that affect us?"

Brian narrowed his eyes at Bomber. "Do you like being conquered?"

"What?"

"Do you like being conquered?" Brian repeated. When Bomber shook his head incredulously, he continued. "I don't think anyone wants to be, but if Zane has already moved north, turned everyone there, and brought them onto his side, then I wouldn't put it past him to come to the south and do the same."

"He would make everyone this... Chimera?" Bomber asked.

"Yes," I replied for Brian. "Which isn't that horrible, but it would just be the beginning. Once he has conquered the remaining world and made his army, he will get bored."

Jace nodded and set a hand on my shoulder. "Conquering the whole world would only be the beginning."

A silence followed that was filled with a mixture of fear and hostility. I clutched Jace's hand tighter to keep from reacting instinctively.

Jimmy broke the silence, with the most thoughtful look on his face I have seen since I met him. "What is this Zane guy doin' that would be considered a threat? Maybe we should enlist him to help take down the cartel?"

"What?" I snapped.

"That's not a bad idea," AJ added. "I mean, if he has the numbers—"

"That is a horrible idea," I said.

"Why?" they both asked simultaneously.

I shook my head and let out a shocked breath. "Because... because he did this to me!" I held up my hands to show my claws. I felt tears build in my eyes, so I bit my cheek to keep them from escaping.

Jace put a gentle hand on my arm and pulled my back closer to him. Brian sat forward and squeezed my shoulder. "She's right. Zane may have the numbers and look like the best option at the moment, but once he's done helping, he'll turn on you."

"So, everyone becomes Chimera. So what? Like you said, it wouldn't be the worst thing." Jimmy snapped, looking over Brian's shoulder at me. "I don't know what you are. Why you're different, but you look healthy to me. Seems you have some badass skills as well."

I swallowed at his words. "You have no idea. Zane kept people—kids—in cages. He did indescribable things to them, killed them, then threw them out like a piece of trash."

Jimmy stepped back with a flash of wide eyes at my words. Old Bob held up a hand to keep him quiet and looked at Brian. "What's he doing now? Besides conquering, what is his crime?"

Brian cleared his throat, glancing at me before looking back at the others. "Anyone that defies him, he turns into a scourge."

A sound between a sob and a snarl escaped me. A floodgate of memories tortured me: from being back in the cage, to seeing all the horrible things Zane allowed to happen, to Tristan, to the moment I had to kill my best friend because being dead would be better than him living as a scourge.

I turned and buried my face in Jace's chest. He gently wrapped his arms around me and held me close.

"It's all right." He whispered into my hair, so softly no one else could hear.

"What the hell is a scourge?" Bomber asked.

It was Old Bob who spoke, his voice easy and calming. "A scourge is a Chimera who no longer has their mind. They are as close to death as someone can be with a beating heart." He paused and cleared his throat. "Do you remember the old zombie books and movies from before the war?"

"Of course," Bomber said. "But—"

"A scourge is as close to a zombie as we could get," Brian said.

A hiss echoed through the room, and I felt more fear thicken the air. I sniffed, momentarily embarrassed for my breakdown, then turned and faced everyone. Jimmy, Cal, AJ, Sam, and Bomber all had blanched faces, watching us with disbelieving gazes.

Brian sighed. "We learned through a mistake how to make a scourge. To cure the Fever, you give an infected person live animal blood. To make a scourge, you give them dead animal blood."

"It's that simple?" AJ whispered.

"It's that simple."

"This is why we need to figure out how to take Zane down. He won't just stop at conquering. He'll want complete power, and when he doesn't have that, he'll do whatever it takes to gain it," Jace spoke quietly. "Even if he kills every last living being to do so." His arm around my shoulder kept me steady.

Bomber let out a frustrated growl. "We don't have the people. The fighters." Pinching the bridge of his nose, he closed his eyes. "I'm at a loss. We can't fight two enemies from both sides with what we have. We won't last a day."

Tate met Bomber's eyes from beside Cal, shrugged, and sat forward. "Why don't we start training, then?"

"I'm sorry?" AJ said.

"What? Bomber is complaining that there aren't any fighters here. So why don't we at least give people a fighting chance? Train them. Prepare them."

"We don't have time—"

"Then why waste it here, wondering what to do?" Tate's voice was firm with authority. I wasn't the only one whose eyes grew at his words. "Look. I don't know anything about the cartel other than what I learned from Ellie... my mother. But I do know Zane and what the scourge are like. If you don't have fighters here, then we have to at least try and teach them. It's not right to just let them sit and wait, expecting someone to protect them. We don't live in that kind of world anymore."

AJ snickered. "Like you know. You who grew up in a secluded little home away from the real world."

"You're right." Tate shrugged. "I did grow up in a secluded home, but it definitely wasn't away from the real world. It was just a different world than here. That's the point. There are two worlds right now. The north and the south. Both have some extreme threats."

"And what, you're now going to say that if we train some weak, half-starving people and young children, we can beat them?" AJ's face was cringed up in disgust.

"No. What I'm saying is, we need to give people a fighting chance rather than leave them to be slaughtered." He paused before continuing, "And we should decide which side of the cartel is worse and use them against the other."

The room fell silent as they surveyed my brother, Tate, the quiet, sweet boy who wouldn't hurt a fly even if it bit him, who seemed to have some war strategy.

Old Bob sat forward, resting his arms on the table. He glanced at Tate with a smile. "He has a good point."

"He has a point all right. A point to get us all killed," AJ muttered. Sam grumbled in agreement next to her.

"No. It's a good plan," Old Bob countered.

"What?" Bomber said. "Getting in bed with one enemy to take down the other?"

"Well, yeah."

"Then what?" Jimmy asked. "We just go along with the surviving crazies?"

"No, we use our alliance with half the cartel to take down Zane," Brian said.

"I don't know what's in the water up north, but all of you are nuts," Jimmy said, waving a hand in the air at them as he sat back.

The room erupted in bickering, with everyone yelling their point, trying to be heard. I thought about what Bomber and the others had said about the cartel. They wanted control.

I sat forward, patting my hand on the table for attention. "What if we give the cartel what they want?"

The room turned silent with all eyes on me. Bomber tilted his head with raised eyebrows. "I'm sorry? Did you just say give the cartel what they want?"

I cleared my throat and sat up taller. This was the time I needed to show them I was more than just a girl with different genes. I was smart, and I could lead.

"I did." Almost everyone scoffed, and AJ rolled her eyes. I put up a clawed hand. "Just hear me out. The cartel wants control. Why don't we give the side we choose to work with control? We help them take out the other side, and in payment, they help us take down Zane."

"So, they would get control of what exactly?" Bomber asked.

I shrugged. "Well, the cartel for one thing—"

"And the other thing?"

I shrugged again. "Maybe some of the lands they are fighting over?"

Jimmy threw out a hand in disgust and slammed it on the table. "And there it is. The northerners are crazy."

The bickering began again, now about the morality of just giving land and people away. Jace leaned into me to speak, but I ignored him and put a hand up to get everyone's attention. "Wait!" They quieted and turned to me. "What if part of the deal is that they would rule without the name of the cartel. They would have to be a free leader."

Everyone blinked at me, and I bit my cheek to keep from smiling. I loved the feeling of power when others were scared of my claws and fangs, but I couldn't describe how elated I was at the astonished eyes looking back at me. They knew I had a point, and it made me feel empowered.

Bomber looked at Old Bob. "What did you teach these kids growing up?"

Tate laughed. "Most of our books dealt with war strategy."

Brian smiled, patting Tate on the shoulder. "Well, it paid off in the end."

"Did it?" Jimmy snapped. "I don't remember agreeing to this suicide mission."

Jace stiffened next to me at the growl in Jimmy's voice. The growl directed at me. I put a gentle hand on Jace's arm when he moved forward. "You're right. You haven't, but tell me, Jimmy. Do you have any better ideas? We are a little trapped here. We have two enemies, one closing in and one that soon will be, with no plans or even enough people to fight. What other options do we have?"

Jimmy's jaw ticked, watching me. He had nothing, and he knew I was right.

Bomber leaned forward, resting his arms on the table. "All right. Let's say we go along with this plan. Which side do we pick?"

I clicked my claws on the table in thought, bringing all gazes onto them. AJ and Cal quickly averted their eyes, looking anywhere but at me.

Jace cleared his throat. "I say we pick the lesser of the two evils."

"Makes sense. That way we take out the bigger evil and have less of a chance of getting screwed," Old Bob said. "But which one is the lesser evil?"

Bomber scratched his rough chin, watching me. He studied my eyes, dropping them to my claws. "Why should I listen to a kid?"

I bristled. It wasn't what I expected to hear, but it was a fair question. Why would someone listen to me? I was young and inexperienced.

"She's a lot smarter and tougher than you give her credit for," Brian said.

"I didn't ask you." Bomber's gaze never left mine. "I'm asking her." He grinned. "Think of it as a job interview."

Think carefully before you answer. Brian's voice was calming.

I sucked in a deep breath, letting it out slowly, ignoring Old Bob's encouraging face.

"It's true. I may be young, but I am no kid. My childhood ended years ago. If you would've put your faith in me a year ago, you probably wouldn't have survived, but now, now I have lived through things you can't imagine. I know what loss is, what evil is, and I know"—I paused, thinking of the right words—"I know how to do what needs to be done." I lifted my claws, looking down at them. "What was done to me was horrible, but it's done. I can't go back to the old me. I'll always have a piece of the old Eden inside me, but now I'm more. I have abilities—"

"So do I now," Jimmy snapped, interrupting my thoughts.

"No." I shook my head at him. "I started with your abilities, but mine have grown. I was a test subject. Just something to feed into the sadistic, power-hungry Zane's curiosity. I hope you are never put through what I was. I still struggle, but with help"—I glanced to my family—"with help, I can be better. Am better. I would never lead your people or mine knowingly into danger. I promise you that."

Everyone was quiet, watching Bomber study me. I could see him weigh my words for truth. After a long moment, he finally spoke. "All right. We'll go through you and your brother's ideas, but we all, everyone in this room, need to be in agreement to any changes and be a part of planning."

I smiled with relief. "Agreed."

Everyone else murmured in agreement, except for Jimmy. He pinned me with his eyes. I could feel him pushing all his dominance toward me, pushing me to lower my eyes. I didn't even blink as I leaned forward over the table toward him. "You, *old man*, don't want to push me." I let a wave of power leave me, and when it hit him and Cal, his eyes widened. Cal immediately lowered his gaze, and Jimmy did as well shortly after, his cheeks warming with embarrassment.

I sat back and looked between Bomber, Brian, and Old Bob. "So where should we start?"

"I think we do need to train. Let's get groups together based on knowledge and ability," Brian said.

"We can help with that." AJ nodded toward Sam.

"I'd like to learn more about the cartel and their abilities," I said.

"I'll help you get that information," Jace said.

Bomber nodded. "It would probably be best to talk to some of the survivors from the bombed city."

Old Bob nodded. "Good. Tate, you can help with that. Bomber, I think you and I should plan some strategies for protecting this city."

"All right then. Looks like we have a lot of work to do in a very short time. Let's get to work!" Bomber slapped his hand on the table.

Chapter 26

Jace

I followed Eden into the hospital hall. We'd just been here for her, but I didn't remember seeing the far-end rooms before, being so focused on getting to where Eden was.

As we stepped into the crowded room, I heard a happy giggle from the corner.

"Eden!" a little girl, no older than five, yelled. She had large brown eyes, with the longest eyelashes I'd ever seen. Her smile reached her ears as she watched Eden move toward her. "You came back."

"Of course I did. I had to see how my little warrior was doing." Eden smiled at the girl and sat on the side of her cot. "So, how are you feeling?"

I stepped quietly behind her, watching the exchange with curiosity. Who would have thought Eden would be good with kids?

The girl responded, "Good. This is Kat, my sister."

Eden smiled at Kat, the girl looked a few years older than her sister. "Hi. It's nice to meet you. I'm Eden."

"Yes. Ana talks about you nonstop. I heard the others mention you as well." She looked down at Eden's hands but immediately went right back to her eyes. Eden remained relaxed, unfazed by the small action.

"Oh, well. She was super strong. I don't think I could've been as strong as her." Eden smiled at Ana again before turning back to Kat. "Do you mind if we have a quick talk with you?"

Kat glanced up at me, the first acknowledgment that she had even noticed me. "Yeah, sure." She stood and followed Eden a little way from Ana's cot.

I moved to Eden's side, giving Kat a smile. "I'm Jace."

She gave a hesitant smile before nodding a greeting.

"Kat, we need to get all the information about the cartel that we can. What can you tell us about Lucia or Izan?"

Kat's eyes widened and she licked her lips. "Oh, wow. I don't know much. Just that Izan is brutal."

I widened my stance and crossed my arms. "How so?"

"He shoots anyone who gets in the way and bombs buildings to get the attention of his sister, Lucia. She has tried to stop him a few times. Her people are usually too late, but at least they try." She glanced between us a moment before continuing, "When Izan and his people attacked our town, Lucia sent a few men to try and get everyone out of the building before the bomb went off. If they hadn't tried to help, we would probably—" She couldn't finish the words. Her eyes filled with tears. She closed them and a tear streamed down her cheek.

"It's all right." Eden put a gentle hand on her arm. "That's good information. Thank you."

She wiped her cheek, giving us a nod before returning to Ana's side.

"So, looks like Lucia will make for a good ally," I said, watching Eden gaze at Kat and Ana. "I have to say"—I nudged her side—"I've never seen you so... gentle and caring."

She looked at me with a raised eyebrow. "What's that supposed to mean?"

"Nothing. It just surprised me. Never took you for a kid person."

She glanced back at Ana. "Honestly, I didn't either, but she saw me and wasn't scared away." Eden looked at me again with a look I have never seen on her face before. A look of need, need for acceptance and love.

"Eden," I said quietly and moved closer to her, leveling my eyes with hers. "You're not as scary as you think. I promise."

"Maybe not to you."

"Apparently not to a young child either." I winked and nudged her again. "They do say, children see the real person, no matter what they look like."

"Who says that?"

"People, lots of people... and me." I grinned, and she rolled her eyes.

"Come on, we need to figure out how to make contact with Lucia." She gave Ana and Kat a small goodbye wave. Ana returned a large grin and eager wave that brought a smile to my face. If only Eden could truly see how she looked through the eyes of a child.

~

Back in Bomber's meeting room, I shoveled the bland food in my mouth. I was so hungry I didn't care if the food tasted like dirt. I would eat it. We spent hours questioning people about everything they knew about the cartel. Most were willing, but some didn't want to say anything for fear of repercussions.

Everyone sat around the table in the same spots as earlier, with plates of food in front of them, but none of them ate as eagerly as I.

"What did you find out?" Bomber asked, watching me with wide eyes.

Eden glanced at me, then back at Bomber. "Basically, that Lucia is the better apple of the two. They can be difficult to distinguish, outside their colors."

"Their colors?" Tate said. He sat next to me, also watching me with surprise. I gave him a head shrug and returned to my food.

"Yes. Apparently, they have taken to wearing certain colors so others can distinguish whose side they are on. Lucia's people wear red, and Izan's, blue."

"Interesting." Bomber scratched his chin.

"So, we just go south wearing red and ask to talk to Lucia?" Tate asked.

My plate was now empty, but my stomach still grumbled. My eyes flicked to Eden's half-eaten plate. She looked at me with a grin, pushing it toward me. Giving her a grateful smile, I dug into that food too.

"Are you going to help out or just stuff your face?"

I froze with a piece of chicken halfway to my mouth and looked at Bomber. His eyes were annoyed, and his jaw ticked. I smiled and set my fork down. "Trust me, if I'm hungry, I'm of no help." He opened his mouth, but I put up my hand to silence him. "But if I were to put my two cents in, I would say we go south and start making some noise while wearing red. That way, she'll come to us." Without waiting for a response, I went back to my food.

"That's not a bad idea," Old Bob said. He sat next to Tate, sipping a cup of tea.

"I agree," Brian said.

"You really think they'll just come to us?" Bomber looked between everyone at the table.

I spoke around a bite of potato. "Wouldn't you go looking for a person that's impersonating your group? Especially if they are doing things you wouldn't normally do?"

Eden furrowed her brow at me. "What kind of things are you thinking?"

"Maybe we wear her colors but act like her brother."

"I'm not hurting anyone."

"No. We won't hurt anyone. This has to be done very carefully." Brian gave me a pointed gaze.

I sat back and shook my head. "I never said we hurt anyone, but if we don't do something impressive, she may not care." I shrugged and continued. "I'm just saying we act like him. We can find a building that she uses in some way, supplies maybe." I could see the hesitation in all their eyes. "We'll double, triple check the building to make sure it is empty, then destroy it. Trust me. It'll work."

Everyone watched me through an echoing silence. I'm sure at one time they never thought they would be in this situation. They probably had happy normal lives with families, but now they are strategizing to blow up buildings and make alliances with murderers.

"I hate to say this, but I agree with the kid," Jimmy said. Of all the people to agree with me, I didn't expect it to be him. "I know I'd go after someone if they did that to me."

"Right, but we don't want anyone to go after us. We just want to talk to her," Eden said.

"I doubt she's someone that'll just accept an offer to afternoon tea." I smirked and winked at her. "But if it makes you feel better, we can try talking first. If that doesn't work, then we turn to plan B."

Eden smiled and nodded.

"All right." Bomber turned to Brian, AJ, and Sam. "How did the training planning go?"

AJ nodded. "Fine. We've planned out groups and where to start. We can announce it and post the groups tonight to start in the morning."

"Good." Bomber nodded.

"So who's going to be the lucky few that get to go talk to Lucia?" Jimmy asked, looking between everyone.

"I'll go," I said without hesitation.

"I'll go with you." Eden gave me a smile.

"Well, that was expected, but it can't just be the two of you," Bomber said. "I would go, but I'm afraid if I leave, the people won't listen to newcomers. Brian, AJ, Sam, and Robert are needed for training groups."

"I'll go." Tate sat up as tall as he could.

"No," Brian said. Tate was going to protest when Brian continued. "You need to train. You have brains, but you need to learn better tactics."

"Well, I guess that leaves me and Cal," Jimmy said, smiling at Eden and me from across the table. Any other time I would've agreed with not trusting them, but if we were going into the belly of the beast, why not take the ones who acted most like beasts?

"All right then," I said. "I guess it's settled."

"You leave in the morning, then," Old Bob said, giving Jimmy and Cal a wary look.

Chapter 27

Eden

"Now, stick to the plan. Don't go off on your own trying to save the world," Brian said as we walked to the large truck. "Rely on the others to help; you don't have to do it all yourself."

I sighed. "All right, all right. I get it."

He stopped, narrowing his eyes at me. *Do you really?*

I met his gaze. *Yes.*

After watching me for a moment and feeling confident with my answer, he nodded and turned to talk to Jace. He probably would hammer in the same advice. Shaking my head, I smiled at Old Bob and Tate. "I'll be fine."

"Doesn't matter. We'll always worry." Old Bob pulled me into a warm hug. I reached around his broad chest and squeezed. "You be careful, and like Brian said, you don't have to be the hero."

"I know."

Tate leaned in, lowering his voice. "If you have to sacrifice anyone, sacrifice Jimmy or Cal."

I laughed, moving away from Old Bob. "Tate! I'm surprised you'd say that." I pulled him into a quick hug.

"Well, I want you and Jace coming back in one piece. I don't really care about those two."

Jimmy leaned out of the open driver's side window of the truck. "I heard that!" When we glanced at him, he winked. "Don't worry, Tate. Much to my surprise, I won't let anything happen to your sister. We're on the same side, and she seems useful."

"Right," Tate said, quietly. I pushed him back and gazed at the worry etched into his pale blue eyes.

"Tate, I'll be fine. I promise. I have Jace. Plus, you need to focus on training so you can be useful here."

"Yeah. I know." He glanced back at the growing crowd that came to watch the brave few who were going to confront the cartel. Lillyanne stood at the front of the crowd. Her cheeks grew pink when his eyes met hers.

"Looks like you have an admirer."

He quickly dropped his gaze with Lillyanne. "Yeah, well, she's too needy for me."

"Hmmm . . ." I pulled him into another quick hug. "I expect to see you taking down Brian when I return."

Tate laughed, but Brian called out from the bed of the truck, "Not likely!"

"Let's go. We'll just be gone a few days, no need for long heartfelt goodbyes," Jimmy yelled, banging his large hand on the side of the truck with a loud clang, causing birds to flee from the rafters of the building with angry squawks.

Rolling my eyes, I climbed into the back seat of the extended cab. Jace climbed in behind me, then Cal jumped in the front, closing the door. Gazing out of the small window, I watched and waved to the small crowd, but the hope in their eyes tightened a knot in my core. They had so much optimism, and I didn't want to let them down.

Jace looked at me. "OK?"

"Yeah, I just don't want to let them down."

Jimmy looked at us through the rearview mirror. "Don't worry, girl, it won't be just you letting them down. It would be all of us."

Meeting his eyes in the mirror, I gave him a small nod. The trees and fields passed in a whirl. I wanted to watch the woods float by us and soak in the beauty, but the anxiety of what we were about to do crippled my ability to do anything except close my eyes and breathe. My shoulders relaxed slightly when Jace put his hand on mine and squeezed.

~

We were only about an hour out when the familiar wave of love and loyalty hit me.

Eden.

I froze and held my breath. The voice that filled my head was not one I had heard before, yet I knew it. Jace's eyes warmed the side of my face as he watched my reaction.

Eden.

The voice filled me again, and I turned to Jace.

His brows were drawn together in concern. "What's wrong?"

"Did you hear that?" When he shook his head, I looked into the mirror and met Jimmy's eyes. "Was that you?"

"What are you talking about?" He turned and looked at Jace over his shoulder. "She going crazy? Because that's the last thing we need."

"No. I just thought I heard something." Looking outside, I pulled in a deep breath and let it out slowly. At least I hoped I wasn't going crazy.

We drove a few minutes more before a flash of dark grey between the trees had me pushing my face to the glass.

Eden!

"Stop," I yelled.

Everyone in the car startled, looking at me with wide eyes. "What are you yelling on about back there?" Jimmy snapped.

"Just stop the car!"

"What's wrong?" Jace asked.

I looked at him. "Look." I pointed to the edge of the trees. Ash stood in front of his pack, head held high, waiting for me. His eyes followed the car as we continued down the road. I turned my whole body to face out the back window so I wouldn't lose sight of my furry friend.

"Stop the car, Jimmy," Jace said.

Jimmy slowed the car. When Cal got out, I flew over the front seat, almost crawling out of the truck on my hands and knees. "What the hell?" He jumped back out of my way.

"Ash!" I sprinted into the trees, kicking up dirt behind me.

Ash bolted toward me; his muzzle formed a wide smile that showed the tips of his fangs. He hit me with so much force I fell onto my back. The impact of the hard ground took the air from my lungs, but I was so happy I didn't care. I coughed between laughs, pushing Ash's nose away when it tickled my neck as he nuzzled me.

"I missed you so much," I said. He let out a small groan.

"You made me stop for that damned wolf," Jimmy hollered. "Wait there, I'm getting the shotgun. Those things killed my friends and family."

Ash and I froze.

"Jimmy," Jace's voice held warning. "I wouldn't do that if I was you."

I kept my back to them all, my hands clenching in Ash's thick mane. I could hear Jimmy shuffling in the bed of the truck.

"Oh, you wouldn't? Well, those mangy things *killed* my family."

"You don't know that," Jace said, but his voice wavered ever so slightly.

Jace, what is he talking about? I slowly turned, meeting Jace's worried face. His shaggy jet-black hair curled wildly around his ears, but he didn't respond. He only held my gaze, willing me to stay calm.

Jimmy continued thumping in the bed of the truck, taking out half our bags until he found the gun. Cal shuffled his feet, nervously glancing between Jimmy and me. "Jimmy, you sure you want to do this?"

Jimmy pulled the box of bullets from a bag. "Damned right, I'm sure. I should've done this the first time I saw them!"

A growl grew in my chest as he started to pop the bullets into the shotgun. I looked down at Ash, his gold eyes watching me, waiting for instruction. "Go hide. Hide until I have this under control." Ash let out a soft whine, giving my chin a lick before running back into the tree line with his pack. When I couldn't see them anymore, I slowly stood and faced Jimmy.

Jace stepped in my path. "Eden, let's try talking first. Remember, we do need them."

Deep down I knew what he said was right, but I couldn't just let this threat go. Ash was my family. No one threatened my family.

I stepped closer to Jace, stopping when Jimmy jumped down from the bed of the truck. "What did he mean that Ash and the wolves killed his family?"

Jace looked at me with a pained expression and let out a long sigh. "When we escaped the farm, the wolves held two of his men by the throat."

"Right. But they didn't kill them."

He shook his head. "No. They infected them." His gaze was heavy on mine as I processed the words.

"Infected them," I repeated. Jace stood silent, watching me. "So the wolves have the Fever?"

"No, we think they carry it. Not only them but probably most or all animals."

My fists relaxed, and the trees swayed in my vision. If this was true and if it got out, all animals would be slaughtered.

"Where did they go?" Jimmy grunted, stomping to our side with the rifle ready in his hands.

Peeling my gaze from Jace's, I looked at Jimmy as he eagerly scanned our surroundings for the pack.

"I sent him away."

Jimmy stopped and looked at me, pursing his lips and lowering his gun. "Well, good."

I stood a little taller. "But they're coming with us, and if you try and hurt them, I'll kill you."

"Eden," Jace warned.

Ignoring him, I kept my gaze on Jimmy's.

Jimmy ground his teeth together. "There is no way I'm allowing them to come with us."

"Think about it. They could be good allies, good weapons when dealing with Lucia. Instead of just four against the cartel, it would be four of us with a pack of wolves."

Jimmy clutched the gun, his jaw ticking.

Cal stepped to his side. "She has a point, Jimmy. The more help we have, the better."

"They're unpredictable. They're animals!"

"Ash will listen to me, and they'll listen to him. I promise you."

I could see Jace from the side of my vision, tense with anticipation of what may happen. He took a slow shuffling step toward Jimmy with fisted hands, preparing for a fight.

"Fine," Jimmy grunted, lowering his gun. "But the first claw they step out of line, I'll kill them."

I smiled. "Then I'll kill you." I paused for effect. "But I assure you, they'll be on their best behavior where you are concerned."

Without a word, Jimmy turned and headed back to the truck. He helped Cal throw the bags in the bed before yelling at us. "Let's go, then!"

My smile grew and I called Ash and his pack back.

～

I nestled close to Ash's warm body. We had made it to the outside of the city and found an abandoned store. Ash and his pack had ridden in the bed of the truck to make sure they made it where we needed them. After having a quick meal of canned beans and vegetables, and raiding whatever was left in the store, we found a quiet corner to rest.

Rolling my stiff neck, I let the sound of Ash's beating heart soothe my nerves. Jace sat behind me resting his head on the wall.

You sleep. I will take first watch.

He set a gentle hand on my back. The warmth from his touch combined with Ash's body helped lull me into a content sleep.

Chapter 28

Jace

I stretched my tense shoulders as we walked down the road toward the city center. It was only a matter of time until someone came out and confronted us. We were pretty obvious, four humans and a pack of wolves, all marching with weapons in hand through the abandoned-looking city. I hadn't wanted to leave the storefront we slept in, feeling as if it was the only safety we'd have for a while.

Eden and Jimmy flanked each other at the front, Cal and I walked in the middle, with the wolves fanned out in the rear. My breaths puffed out in billowing clouds when they hit the crisp cool air. I didn't feel as nervous as I would have without Ash and his pack. Thankfully. Jimmy didn't put up a fight when Eden ordered them to come with us. We were safer with them.

"So, what, we just keep walking until we find them?" Cal said, adjusting the heavy pack on his back that carried half the fixings for our makeshift explosives for our plan B.

"Yeah." Eden scanned the road ahead. "I'm hoping we come across someone soon."

We walked in silence a few more blocks until the buildings became more condensed. I glanced back at Eden and opened my mouth to speak, but I froze at the quiet scuff of footsteps. I held up a hand to stop the others.

Someone is here.

I met Eden's eyes. She gave a slight nod before scanning our area. We moved slowly, focusing our senses so we could spot or hear anything. My head whipped to the right when another scuff echoed. White hair and blue eyes flashed down an alley before disappearing around the corner. A little boy.

I took off after him in a dead sprint.

"Jace!" Eden called after me, but I ignored her. If we caught this kid, he may be able to lead us to where Lucia is.

A warm body moved swiftly next to me. I glanced down and met Ash's gold eyes before turning the corner to follow the kid. The tail of his grey jacket flapped behind him as he disappeared around another corner. I kicked up my feet and pushed myself harder, my heart pumping in my ears.

As I rounded the corner, Ash and I slid to a stop. I threw my hands out beside me to keep from falling on the loose gravel under my feet. Sweat beaded on my forehead, and my breath came out in quick pants.

"Stop right there!" a brown-skinned man yelled, pointing a gun at me. His voice reverberated against the stone buildings around us.

Ash and I blinked at a group of twenty people, with three men in front pointing guns at us. The unmistakable red scarves around their necks flapped in the breeze.

I think I found them. They are armed, so stay where you are, Eden.

I slowly raised my hands. "I'm unarmed," I said, "I just want to talk."

The man sneered. "Talk to who?" His voice was laced with a slight accent. His hands tightened on his gun as he let his eyes drop down to Ash. I instinctively took a step to block him from the gun.

"Lucia."

The three men laughed, their guns never dropping from the target, Ash and me. The central one spoke. "No one comes and demands to speak to Lucia."

"I didn't demand. I asked."

The man shrugged. "Same difference." His eyes flicked over my shoulder to something behind me.

I held my breath as she slowly approached, unsure if the men would shoot or not.

I thought I told you to stay away.

Couldn't let you have all the fun.

"Hello," Eden said when she reached my side. "I'm Eden." She motioned to me. "This is Jace. We just want to speak to Lucia. We hav—"

"I already told him that it's not possible," the man said.

I tensed, waiting for Eden to snap, but to my surprise, she didn't. Glancing quickly to her face, she held a mask of relaxed pleasure.

"I really think she'd be interested in what we have to say," Eden said.

My eyes were drawn to the crowd behind the three men. They were a mixture of elderly people and young. The youngest was the white-haired, blue-eyed boy I had followed. He met my eyes and smiled. I gave him a smile and inclined my head.

"I hate having to repeat myself," the man snarled. "It won't happen. Go back where you came from, or I'll shoot you and remove our problem."

Eden opened her mouth, but I set a gentle hand on her arm to silence her. Unfortunately, my motion brought everyone's attention to her claws. The tension that was already in the air thickened, and one of the armed men stepped back.

"What is—"

I stepped forward. "Thank you. We'll go on our way." Tugging Eden's arm, I turned her and pulled her down the alleyway with me. Once we turned the corner, I let out a hiss of air and faced her. She met my gaze with a single arched brow and smirk.

"Protective much?"

"We don't know them. For all I know, they'd have just shot you outright." I stepped toward her and framed her face in my hands. "I won't risk you."

Her face flushed and she turned her cheek into my hand. Jimmy and Cal stepped out from a darkened doorway.

"So I take it we're moving to plan B?" Jimmy asked.

I dropped my hands and turned to them. "Looks like it."

"Come on, then. Let's get working." Eden nudged my shoulder and followed Jimmy and Cal back down the alleyway.

I looked back at the corner we came from to make sure we had no followers. The white hair and blue eyes of the young boy peered at me from around the corner, but the moment I met his eyes, he was gone. Rubbing my fingers together, I fought the urge to follow him to see if I could catch him for information, but Eden's call pulled me back to them. As we moved farther away to find a safe place to plan, I could feel warmth on my shoulder blades from watchful eyes.

～

We spent the afternoon into evening planning and scouting the area. After much argument and exploration, we found Lucia's and her people's location. We also found where most of the city citizens lived and worked—worked may be an understatement, as it was more like slavery.

We crouched on the third floor of an abandoned building, monitoring the grounds around Lucia's building.

"Did he say the blue cord connected with this part or the copper wire?" Cal asked as he worked on assembling our small bomb.

"I don't remember. Can't you read the diagram he drew?" Eden snapped. Her eyes never left the armed guards that congregated outside the building. The fires in the cans left a smoky smell in the cool air, but at least they lit up the area now that the sun was setting.

"I could, but I just figured I'd ask."

I gave Jimmy a pointed look. "You better be double-checking that thing when he's finished. Mishaps won't bode well for us."

"Yeah, yeah." Jimmy waved a hand at me before looking over Cal's shoulder.

I followed Eden's intense gaze as it moved from the guards to the group of residents that slowly made their way down the road toward their building. Their heads drooped and their feet dragged through the dirt, exhaustion radiating from them. A few of the men carried heavy sacks over their shoulders. As they neared Lucia's building, they dropped them on the ground in front of the guards, then turned and followed the rest of their group into their building.

"I think I'll be adding a few things to my negotiations," Eden said. She motioned to the group of people. "Making them work to provide the food is unfair."

"If they want protection, then I think it's fair," Jimmy grumbled. "I'd do the same thing."

I growled. "Then you're no better than the cartel." I motioned to the residents' building. "Most of those people are old and weak. It's not fair."

Jimmy shrugged and went back to inspecting the bomb with Cal.

I turned back to the window and scanned the area. The supply building sat across from the residents and next to Lucia's. "Have you given any thought to where we should place the bomb? We want to do our best not to have casualties, and we don't want to ruin all of the supplies."

Cal chuckled. "Should we bake Lucia some cookies as well? You're asking a lot." He sighed and sat back, resting his arms on his knees. "We're planting a bomb, Jace. There will probably be casualties—"

"We have to do our best to prevent them," I said.

Cal pursed his lips into a thin line and nodded. "I agree, but you need to be prepared." He moved his gaze to Eden, then to Jimmy. "We also have to be prepared for the fallout that'll happen from Lucia after we destroy her supplies."

Eden let out a long breath. "I know."

Jimmy sat forward. "We're vastly outnumbered. You both realize that this may go in a direction we didn't plan on, right?"

Eden narrowed her eyes at him. "Yes. But we do have the wolves."

"The wolves." Jimmy shook his head. "Even with the wolves, girl, we are outnumbered. What I need to know is are you able to do what is necessary to stay alive." He lowered his eyes to her level, giving her an intense gaze.

"I am."

Jimmy studied her a moment before looking away. "At least we have one thing going for us."

"What's that?" I asked.

A smile snaked across his face as he looked at me. "We're Chimera."

Eden nodded. "True." She glanced at me before looking to Jimmy and Cal. "With that being said, you two need to know the extent of our abilities." They blinked at her in confusion, so she continued with a sigh. "Besides being slightly faster and stronger and having heightened senses, we have the ability to talk to each other in our minds."

Both of their eyes widened, and Jimmy's smile grew so much the skin around his eyes tightened. He held up his hand to silence her, glancing between us. "You mean, like telepathically?"

Eden and I nodded.

"Why in tarnation did no one tell us?"

I cleared my throat. "We didn't really want to hear you chattering in our heads."

Eden gave me a pointed look and hissed at me. "Jace."

"What? It's the truth, isn't it?"

"It doesn't matter. What matters is that now it can be useful. We can communicate without speaking, so it'll keep us better hidden."

Jimmy rubbed his hands together in anticipation and grinned at Cal before looking back at Eden. "So how does it work?" He closed his eyes and put his fingers to his temples. "Do I just send words out?" His face strained in concentration.

"Oh, good lord," I mumbled. "Put your hands down. You look like an idiot."

He opened one eye. "What? Well, how do you do it then?"

Can you hear me?

I watched Jimmy's eyes widen. He swallowed and nodded. "How do I talk?"

"Say what you want to say in your head and focus on me."

Jimmy nodded and pursed his lips in concentration.

Yellow-bellied cockroaches.

I blinked and sighed. "Really?"

"What did he say?" Eden asked.

"Yellow-bellied cockroaches."

"Yes," Jimmy screamed.

"Shhhh!" Everyone hissed in unison at him.

"Shut up. Do you want them to find us?" Eden snapped.

"Sorry, sorry," Jimmy said, holding up his hands. "But this is just too darn neat."

We spent the next half hour practicing speaking telepathically with Jimmy and Cal, teaching them to focus on one person or multiple and also how to block others out. When the sun finally set and nothing but the moon and the canned fires lit the surrounding area, we packed up the small bomb and headed out to plant it in the supply building.

Keep your eyes and ears open. Eden's voice rang in all our heads.

We approached the building from the back alley, staying crouched in the shadows. Eden told Ash and his pack to stay behind unless we called for them, which at the moment, in the dark, I slightly wished she hadn't.

Jimmy and Cal moved in front, peeking around the corner.

Clear. Eden, you and Jace go inside and set the bomb.

Eden and I nodded without a word. I pulled out two small picks and picked the lock, letting the door click open. Staying to the side and preparing my gun, I slowly entered, scanning the room in the darkness.

There is nothing but supplies.

Eden nodded and stepped inside behind me. We carefully stepped around all the supplies. When we reached the front of the building at the locked front door, we spotted the shadows of two guards darkening the windows.

Eden clenched her hands, gazing at the guards' backs. *If we place the bomb here, it'll blow outwards and do less damage to the supplies. But—*

But it may kill the guards.

She looked at me and nodded. I sighed and stepped toward her. *We have to sacrifice something. I don't want to kill anyone either, but the more supplies we lose, the more people will be affected. Losing two guards won't be as detrimental.*

She gazed into my eyes. *It will be for their families.*

My heart sank, and I gave her a solemn nod. *It's up to you.*

She pursed her lips and closed her eyes. I watched her pretty face, etched with worry as she battled with her inner self. Finally, she opened her eyes and met mine. *I told the others I could do what needs to be done when the time comes. This needs to be done.*

I nodded and stepped closer to her, resting my forehead on hers. "This is not all on you. We handle this together and take responsibility together. Whatever happens, you'll not blame yourself. Understand?"

She swallowed and nodded.

After another thick moment of silence, she pulled the sack off her back and carefully pulled out the bomb. Setting it near the front door, she set the timer for eight hours. Before we snuck back through the building and out the back door, she glanced at the dark figures in the window. Pain and conflict swirling around her.

Maybe we can think of a way to lure them away from the doorway.

I smiled. *Good thinking. We have a few hours to decide.*

Careful not to step on anything again on our way out, we met Jimmy and Cal outside. They gave us a nod before we went back to the dark shadows and ran back to the vacant building. A sigh escaped me at having part of our mission set, but the unease in my stomach from the uncertainty overtook any feelings of relief.

~

I rubbed my eyes, trying to clear the bleary fog that filled them. Exhaustion set into my bones as Eden and I continued to monitor the supply building. The sun peeked out, leaving the sky a pinkish orange that reflected off the frosted ground and buildings.

Jimmy sat up from his resting place and stretched. "Anything exciting?"

"No," Eden said, keeping her eyes on the guards. "The bomb will detonate in thirty minutes." She stood and leaned back. Her back cracked, and she sighed, rolling her head in circles to stretch her neck.

Jimmy stood and kicked Cal's leg. "Get up."

Cal grumbled and turned over, giving Jimmy his back. Jimmy growled and kicked him again. "I said, get up."

Cal swiped a dirty hand over his scruffy face and sat up. Blinking a few times, he watched us. "I just fell asleep."

"Sorry, princess, but this isn't a relaxing vacation. We have work to do." Jimmy put on his pack and glanced between Eden and me. "Cal and I will be the distraction, like we discussed." He paused, then focused on Eden. "Don't waste our efforts."

"Never."

Jimmy turned to Cal, who now stood, ready to leave. "Let's go." He grumbled, and they walked through our abandoned building until they disappeared through the front door.

I looked at Eden, who kept her focus on the guards in front of the storage building. I could see the worry etched around her eyes and mouth. She bit her bottom lip and clutched her claws together.

I scooted closer to her, so our knees touched. "It's going to be all right. Jimmy and Cal's distraction will work."

She blinked and looked at me. "Right," she whispered and looked back at the guards.

My stomach sank slightly at the thought of Jimmy and Cal not succeeding. Eden would then carry the guilt that she planted the bomb. She was the one who hurt people. I could think of no words of consolation, so instead, I set my hand on hers and squeezed.

Chapter 29

Eden

"Let's go," I said to Jace and stood. Without a word, he stood and put on his pack. I paused and looked at him. "No heroics, all right?"

He smiled and winked before leaning closer. "You mean to tell me that you won't save me when I need rescuing?"

I chuckled and sighed. "You know what I mean." I met his eyes, letting my face turn serious. "I'm serious, Jace. Don't risk yourself to save me for any reason. All right?"

"Eden, you know I won't be able to watch you get hurt if I can help it."

"You will if helping me puts you in danger." I gently took his hands and stepped closer. "If something happens to you on top of what may happen to others"—I swallowed and closed my eyes—"I think I would truly lose myself." I let out a breath and met his gaze again. "Please, promise me."

"All right. But the same goes for you."

I smiled and nodded. "Deal."

He squeezed my hands before turning toward the door. "We should probably get going. It's close to detonation time."

We quietly snuck outside and worked our way down the small road. Staying tucked in among that shadows was more difficult in the bright morning sun.

We can wait here. I looked back at Jace who nodded in response.

Pushed into the crook of a doorway, half a block down from the supplies building, we had a good view of the doorway and the guards that were adjacent outside near Lucia's building. I kept my eyes on the building straight across from the supplies building, where the civilians lived, hoping none of them decided to come out at the wrong time.

Where are Jimmy and Cal?

I shrugged, trying not to be nervous, but truly I was terrified. Terrified something was going to go wrong.

A flash of white sprinted by us, and I stepped back, bumping into Jace's broad chest. "What was that?"

"No." Jace pushed me behind him and peered around the corner. "The kid."

"What? What kid?" I whispered, my heart picking up in my chest. "The bomb is going to go off any minute."

Jace looked back at me, locking eyes. I gazed into his beautiful blue eye, such a contrast to his black hair.

"I'm sorry," he whispered.

I opened my mouth and reached out to him, but he was gone. "Jace!" I hissed, jumping forward to the road.

What the hell is he doing! Jimmy's voice sounded in my head.

Ignoring Jimmy, I crouched low and watched Jace sprint down the road toward the small boy. I held my breath when the two guards in front of the building turned toward him and pointed their guns.

"Watch out," Jace yelled.

The blast hit me with a force I didn't expect. I was pushed back, hitting the brick wall behind me. Dust and debris filled the air, and my ears rang. I coughed, rubbing my eyes. Looking where I last saw Jace, I could see nothing but smoke.

"Jace!" I yelled, but it came out as a dry croak.

I used the wall for support as I stumbled to a stand. Jimmy and Cal ran to my side, both yelling at me, but I couldn't register their words. Pushing by Cal, I moved to get to Jace, but Jimmy grabbed my arm. Ripping my arm from his, I turned and gave him a snarl, only he didn't back down like I expected him to. Instead, he lowered his face to mine and snarled back.

"Get your head on straight, girl. You can't go running in there!"

"Jace is there!" I pointed back to the clearing smoke. The supply building's front wall was blown wide open, with bricks scattered about. Three bodies lay motionless before it. "Oh, God!" I jerked forward again, only to be stopped by Cal. He positioned himself directly in front of me, so I was met with nothing but his chest.

"They may shoot you if you go there, Eden." He clasped his hands on my waist and moved his mouth to my ear. "We have to move. Get out of sight."

"I'm not leaving him." My vision blurred. I focused on the bodies, but I couldn't make them out. There was too much debris and dust.

Cal started walking, pushing me back. I stumbled backward, but his hold on me kept me from falling. "Please, we can't leave him."

"We aren't leaving him. We just have to let the situation calm down before we make an appearance," Cal whispered into my ear again.

"Get her in there," Jimmy said from behind me. I glanced over my shoulder to see him holding the door to a building. The cries and screams from the bomb site filled my ears, and I tried hard to pick out Jace's voice.

"I don't hear him." Once we were inside the building, Jimmy shut the door and the sound immediately dulled. "Wait. Open it!" I dove for the door handle to pull it back open. "I need to hear if he calls for help!"

Jimmy blocked my way. "Eden, calm down."

"No! It's Jace!" I punched his chest with a snarl.

He grabbed my wrists before I could scratch him with my claws and leveled his eyes with mine. "I know, but I'm keeping you from getting killed!" I blinked, hating the feeling of the tears running down my cheeks. I didn't want Jimmy and Cal to see me so vulnerable, but it was too late now.

I sniffed and snatched my hands away. Quickly wiping my hands over my eyes, I stepped back and let out a breath. "So, now what? We just watch to see if he survives?"

Jimmy let his shoulders relax slightly and leaned back against the door. "We're going to let the scene calm down. Then we'll approach them."

I blinked and scoffed. "And you think they won't shoot us then? What if they just shoot Jace?"

"They may, but I can't in good conscience let you rush out there and get shot as well."

I let out a snarky laugh. "In good conscience. That's good." He didn't respond, only watched me as I crossed my arms and narrowed my eyes at him. "Just know, if they shoot him, I'll never forgive you."

He gave me a single nod. "But at least you'll be alive to hate me."

"Why do you care anyway?" I dropped my hands and stepped toward him. "You don't even like me."

He leaned closer to me. "I may be an asshole, but I take care of my own."

"Your own? I'm not one of yours."

He smiled and glanced at Cal. "We're all together, whether you like it or not. I won't let you endanger yourself or anyone else because of your infatuation with a boy."

I pointed at the door again. "That *boy* is Jace. He's one of us! So why don't you take care of him?"

"He made his choice," Cal said.

I whipped my head toward him. "Yes, and where the hell were you two anyway? He wouldn't have had to make that choice if you two would've been the distraction in the first place!"

"We were on our way—"

"On your way? The bomb went off less than a minute after Jace went after that kid! Your distraction wouldn't have done anything!"

I fisted my hands, letting my claws dig into my palms. The pain kept me from erupting too much.

Jimmy cleared his throat and crossed his arms. "We weren't going to do the distraction."

My jaw dropped and I blinked. "What?"

He shrugged. "We needed to make an impact. If some of her people were injured, it would be more of an impact to her." I let a low rumbling start in my chest, and I took a step toward him, but he held up a hand, showing no fear at my anger. "You can do whatever you want to me, girl, but you'll need us. You won't get out of here alone, alive."

"I have the wolves." I sneered. "They're out there, and they'll come when called."

Cal stepped up beside me. "Both of you need to calm down. We can't fight among ourselves." He faced me, gently grabbing my arm. "Eden, be angry with us, but wait to fight about it until we are back at Bomber's."

I looked at him. When I dropped my eyes to his hand on my arm, he dropped his grip and stepped back. "Fine. But this isn't over." I glanced between them. "You both have lost my trust, and I don't know if you can earn it back."

Jimmy shrugged again. "Well, at least you're alive and our mission to get Lucia's attention was a success."

"We haven't completed it yet, so don't hold your breath." I pointed a claw at him, my hand shaking with anger. "But you better hope that Jace is alive because if he died, you won't have a chance against me when we return."

He didn't flinch at my words. He just blinked and watched me a moment before he looked away. "Cool off, Eden. When everything calms down outside, we'll do our best to save him."

I didn't reply. I didn't trust myself not to rip his smug face off. I moved to the wall, sat down, buried my face in my propped-up knees, and let the tears fall.

Chapter 30

Jace

I blinked, but I still couldn't focus. The ringing in my ears and burning in my lungs was almost unbearable. Something tickled my jaw, but when I tried to turn my head, it began to pound, causing everything to spin again.

"Kemp," a woman cried.

A body stirred at my side, and the tickling moved to my neck. I managed to turn my head and saw the flash of white hair on my shoulder. Images of moments before flashed in my mind. The boy running toward the building, me panicking. I couldn't let him get hurt. I reached him just when the blast happened, but I had managed to get my body between him and the flying rubble of the building.

"He's not moving. Oh, God! Kemp! Please," the woman screamed again.

I felt a rough hand on my shoulder, pulling me to the side. The soft hair and fresh smell of soap disappeared as the woman picked up the boy, Kemp.

I coughed. "Is he—"

"Shut up," a man snarled before pulling me to my feet.

Everything spun so fast I squeezed my eyes shut, but it didn't do anything to stop the extreme nausea that hit me. Without warning, my meager breakfast of a slice of bread and an apple emptied onto the ground at my feet.

"Careful with him," another woman said.

"He's from the group that came yesterday. He probably planted the bomb," the man yelled.

I dropped to my knees, too weak to stay upright. My eyes watered as I dry heaved. Once my stomach calmed, I blinked and looked up at a hazy woman staring down at me.

"That may be so, but he still tried to save the boy," she said, watching me with a passive expression.

I swallowed. "Lucia?" I croaked out, which ended in a fit of coughs.

She didn't flinch at my words, keeping her face neutral. "Take him to a bed." She turned and walked away, only to halt with a rigid back when the man called after her.

"Is he a prisoner or patient?" He grabbed my arm and yanked me back to my feet. I clenched my jaw to keep the rising nausea from erupting again.

The woman never turned around. "Patient. Don't touch him, Raul, unless you're caring for him." She continued to another guard who was now propped onto the side of the gate that surrounded her building.

The man, Raul, pulled me forward. His grasp was firm and the only thing that kept me on my feet. My feet dragged through the rubble, and I almost fell a few times when my foot hit something large, but Raul's hold on me kept me from hitting the ground.

He dragged me inside the building and right into a room lined with some beds. Raul pushed me forward onto the first bed, and I landed with a grunt. He didn't pay any mind to me when he marched over to the other beds where a few other guards and the small boy lay. The boy was motionless with his eyes closed, and my heart seized. I had tried to get to him in time.

When Raul returned with a glass of water, I took it and looked up at him. "Will he be OK?"

He sneered at me. "Why do you care?"

I took a large gulp, letting it soothe my gritty throat. "I tried to get to him before the blast."

"So you did plant the bomb."

I blinked at him, setting the empty cup on a small table next to the bed. "We didn't want to hurt anyone. We just wanted to talk to Lucia."

"You planted a bomb! If you didn't want anyone to get hurt, then that isn't something you'd do." Before I could respond, he marched out of the room, leaving me with the cries of a distraught woman over a young boy.

~

I don't know how long I slept, but my head was much less groggy as I sat in front of Lucia and Raul. Lucia was pretty, with long dark hair, bronze skin, and a plush, feminine face. She didn't smile as she studied me carefully; neither did Raul, only he held a cringed look of disgust as he looked over my scratched face.

I was pleasantly surprised at the lack of injury I received from the blast. A few bruises and scratches, that was it. The boy, Kemp, finally woke, much to my relief, and also only had a few bruises. He had watched me with curiosity from across the room, but the woman, too young to be his mother, probably his older sister, never left his side or allowed him to speak with me.

"What is it you wanted to talk to me about?" Lucia asked. She sat back casually in her chair with delicate fingers clasped in front of her.

I cleared my throat. "I would prefer to wait for the others of my group to be here in order to discuss everything."

"Or what, you'll bomb us again?" Raul snapped.

I glanced at him but looked right back at Lucia. "No. We only did that because no one would allow us to speak to Lucia. We hadn't planned on it, but desperate times call for desperate measures." I shrugged and sat back. I flinched at the anger that passed in both of their eyes and wondered if I should feel more afraid. Probably, but that wouldn't do me any good, so faking toughness it was.

"What could be so desperate that bombing us is the way to get our attention?" Raul asked.

I shrugged. "Like I said, I'd like to discuss this when the rest of my group is here."

Lucia let her eyes roam over me but didn't speak. Her cheek twitched slightly like she was hiding a smirk.

"You're in no position to bargain," Raul snarled.

I sighed and sat back. "You speak very good English. From my understanding, before the war, you spoke a different language."

"Shut your mouth," Raul snapped.

I widened my eyes and raised my hands in surrender. "Touchy, touchy."

"Oh, funny boy now?"

I smiled and winked. "I have been told that."

Lucia let out a long breath and sat forward, resting her clasped hands on the wooden table. "Enough." She glanced between Raul and me, pinning my gaze. "First thing I want to know is, where the hell did you get that weird eye?"

I opened my mouth and closed it, trying to school my face from the apparent surprise at her question. I cleared my throat. "It's a genetic thing."

"Genetic thing?"

"Yes. Only people with a certain genetic makeup are blessed with the beauty of the gold eye." I smiled and winked at her again. I only received a grumble and clenched jaw from Raul.

"So, everyone in your group has the same genetic makeup them? Since you all have the same gold eye?"

My smile faded slightly, and I sat forward. "You've seen them?"

She opened her mouth to respond, but the shot of a gun had us all turning to the door. I stood quickly and began for the door, only to be yanked back by Raul.

"Please, they won't hurt you," I said to Lucia as she walked past me and to the door.

"Well, my men wouldn't have fired a gun if they were no threat."

My heart pounded in my throat, and I shook my head. "I swear to you. They won't hurt you. Please!"

She paused at the door and looked back at me. After a moment, she glanced at Raul. "Let him go." She nodded her head toward the door. "Let's go, but if they try anything crazy, it's you who'll take the punishment since you vouched for them." She disappeared around the corner.

I let out a breath before Raul pushed me forward. "Let's go, then, funny boy."

I shoved him off and followed Lucia, praying that Eden didn't do anything too crazy.

Chapter 31

Eden

"Jimmy!" I screamed, diving over him. He clutched his leg and rolled back and forth, groaning in pain. I looked up at the wide-eyed guard who shot him. "What the hell! You shot him!"

"I was trying to shoot you!" His eyes dropped to my claws. "Wh-what are you?" He raised his gun again, pointing it at me, but I didn't miss the slight tremor that vibrated through the gun.

"No," Jimmy yelled, pushing me back.

I shoved him away and glanced at Cal, indicating he should grab him. Cal reluctantly lowered his gun and grabbed Jimmy's arm. Sucking in a deep breath, I steadied my emotions before I faced the guard, who was now surrounded by three others.

"What I am is of no concern at the moment. We need to speak with Lucia."

The guard on the right stepped forward. "I told you yesterday: no one demands to speak to Lucia."

I snarled.

Eden!

Jace? I let out a sigh of relief and dropped my shoulders.

I glanced over the guard's shoulder. The door opened. A beautiful woman I assumed was Lucia stepped out, followed by Jace's familiar messy black hair and dimpled smile.

Hey, Golden Girl.

I let out a laughed sob and grinned. *I was so worried.*

Same. He stood between Lucia and another man. His eyes dropped to Jimmy and his brow furrowed.

He took a bullet for me. Just in his leg, he'll live. Idiot.

He met my eyes. *Shouldn't you be more grateful?*

I shrugged. *Not my problem that he feels the manly instinct to protect the girl.* Jace's only response was to purse his lips. I'm sure it was to keep from smiling, but my gaze moved to Lucia.

She looked at her guards, then scanned me, Jimmy, and Cal. "Let them in." She nodded her head at a woman in the growing crowd around us. "Get him some medical attention."

I looked back at Jimmy and Cal. Jimmy shook his head. "You will not go in there alone."

I locked eyes with Cal. "Stay with him."

"Eden, don't walk away from me," Jimmy growled.

I paused and turned back to him. "I'll be fine. Jace is there."

His eyes widened. "He's alive?" He strained to look around the people blocking Jace from his view.

Cal put his hand on Jimmy's shoulder. "He is."

Jimmy nodded. "Fine. I'll allow it."

I snorted and shook my head, before turning back to Lucia. *You're lucky you're already injured. Otherwise, I wouldn't tolerate you talking to me like I work for you.*

You'll thank me later for it, girl.

I rolled my head and shook out my arms as I walked toward Jace, fighting the urge to run to him. Lucia waited until I passed, then followed me to the doorway.

"Eden," Jace said with a large grin on his face. He had minor scratches and a few bruises, but for the most part, he seemed unharmed. He moved his arm to touch me, but fisted his hand and pulled back.

"Jace." I clenched my jaw. I wanted to reach for him and bury my face in his neck, but we couldn't let the others know how much we meant to each other. We didn't want anything to be used against us.

The man next to Jace growled and motioned to the doorway. "Inside."

Jace and I followed him in, with Lucia behind us. I usually didn't like having a potential enemy at my back, but given our situation, I didn't have much of a choice.

We stepped into a nicely lit room that was scarcely furnished, except for the large table in the middle. Lucia walked to the opposite side and sat, always keeping her eyes on me. Her face was unreadable as she motioned to some chairs across from her. "Please. Sit."

I didn't move, so neither did Jace. "Thank you, but we'll stand."

She smirked. "Suit yourself." Her eyes roamed over me from the top of my head to my claws. "Are those real?"

I blinked. No one had ever thought they weren't real. "Yes."

"And you have this specific genetic makeup to give you a gold eye like Jace?"

"Yes," I said, cautiously, glancing at Jace. "Why would you think we have fake eyes, and I have fake hands?"

She chuckled, looking down at the table, moving her fingers over the grains of the wood. "You'd be surprised what people do to show strength. Some to try and scare me off, and some"—she looked up at me under long dark lashes—"some to try and make an alliance."

I clenched my jaw but held my gaze. "Understood. But I assure you, this is all me." I lifted my hands slightly at my sides. "I used to be normal, fully human—"

"You're not human?" Her eyes flicked to Jace. "Is he not human either?"

I cleared my throat. "Not fully, no. We are from the north, way north. A Fever spread there, killing most of the population. I was used for experiments to create a cure, which was found, but not without a cost." I looked down at my claws, then over at Jace "Jace was given the cure. Because of this, he shares some of the same characteristics as me." I motioned to his gold eye.

"So, in order to survive this Fever, people have to become like you?"

I met her eyes again, which held no judgment, only genuine curiosity. "No, not like me, but like Jace. One gold eye, heightened senses, but not the claws or... fangs." I opened my mouth to show my elongated canines.

Her face held a neutral stare, and she was silent for a long moment. Dropping her hand, she sat forward. "You said you wanted to talk to me. What about?"

I cleared my throat. "The people whom I've banded with a little south from here will help you take down your brother." I kept my back rigid, not showing the tension that currently flowed through my body.

She chuckled mockingly and sat back. "And I'm sure you want something in return?"

"Yes." I let out a slow breath. "Once your brother is taken care of, you'll help us take care of our problem up north."

She swiped a hand through her thick hair. "Aren't I your problem?"

"Well, not as big as our other problem, I'm afraid."

Her smile dropped. "Why do I care about all your problems? I can just take you all out, take what I want, and be done."

I tossed my head side to side. "You could, but you'd still be fighting with your brother. If we help you, then you won't have him as a problem. Plus, the man we need to take down will become your problem very soon if we don't do something about it."

She studied me for a long moment. The thick silence built between us. Jace finally took a step forward to one of the chairs and sat. "Sorry, my body is tired." He smirked at me, sheepishly, before looking back at Lucia. "The man in the north has already spread farther north and built a large army."

"How large?" Raul asked.

"Ten thousand, give or take," Jace replied.

Raul snorted, but Lucia put up her hand to silence him. "Why is he a threat to me?"

I sighed, biting down my frustration. "Can you take on ten thousand people and win?"

She pursed her lips. "So, you help me defeat my brother, then we help you defeat this mysterious man in the north."

My heart sped up hearing her say the words of the deal. It sounded as if she may agree. I nodded.

"There is still a problem for me."

My pounding heart clenched and my stomach dropped. "What?"

She stood and slowly moved around the table, trailing her fingers over the wood. Her nail made a quiet scratch as it slid, catching each groove under it. Stopping in front of me, she leaned back onto the table with crossed arms. "After we each help defeat each other's problems, I'll still have to take control of all the people to get what I want."

I focused on her face in order to keep my composure, but every ounce of blood rushed to my feet. We did foresee that she would still want control.

"So what exactly do you want?"

"After we take down each other's problems, give me control of the southern lands, then we have a deal."

I flexed my legs to stay upright and fisted my hands.

Jace glanced at me. *It's all right. We planned for this.*

His reassuring words calmed my nerves, and I nodded. "That would work." I paused, and she smiled, then I continued, "Under a few conditions."

Her smile faded. "Excuse me?" She dropped her arms and leaned forward. "Who the hell do you think you are to give me conditions?"

Jace stood slowly, holding his hands up in surrender. "Look, we want everything to work out, but we're all thinking of the future of the world. This is literally all that is left." He held out his hands. "Unless we want to kill off what's left of civilization, we have to learn how to live with one another."

Raul stood and moved to stand next to Lucia. "All right then, what are the terms?"

Jace nodded at me to continue. I cleared my throat and met Lucia's cold, dark eyes. "First, you'll need to drop the title of cartel and rule as a free leader. One that will negotiate and have a peaceful relationship with the north."

She cleared her throat and nodded. "That it?"

I shook my head and let out a breath. "You'll also not have slavery."

"Excuse me?" She sneered and stepped forward. Both Raul and Jace positioned themselves closer to us. "There are no slaves here."

"That's not what I've seen." I pointed at the door. "Those people who live here. Who you have come and taken advantage of, they're your slaves."

"Those people"—she mimicked my pointing—"are thankful I'm here protecting them from my brother."

"So you force them to work? Half of them can barely walk."

She stepped closer; the smell of flowered soap filled my nose. "Everyone works, or they leave."

I opened my mouth to speak, but Jace set a hand on my arm. "All right, that may work now, but after we take down the leader in the north and your brother, the world will change yet again. At least agree to have a process put into place where the elderly and sick are exempt from hard labor. People earn wages or are able to trade goods. Something."

Lucia studied Jace closely for a long moment. A possessive growl built in my throat, but I swallowed it down when she looked at me and sighed.

"Fine."

I let out a long breath. "Good."

She turned and walked back around the table. "Raul, take them to the others in the group." She looked at us. "I will have someone bring you here when I'm ready. Then we'll plan."

Without another word, Jace and I followed Raul out of the room, the tension in my shoulders slightly more relaxed than when we went in.

Chapter 32

Jace

Raul led us through the courtyard to the neighboring building. Lucia's guards watched us warily, but their eyes were mostly pinned on Eden. I didn't like the fact that she was being scrutinized too closely, and I could feel she didn't either, but she gave nothing away.

We entered the building, and the strong smell of disinfectant made me cough. Jimmy lay on the far bed, the same one I had been on after the bombing. He scowled at the woman who was bandaging his leg. Cal was sitting against the wall with one leg propped up on the wall. His smug face made me chuckle.

"He's enjoying himself," I said and jutted my chin out toward Cal.

Eden smiled. "I'm sure he is."

When we reached the bed, Jimmy's scowl turned toward us. "There you are. Did you get done what needed to happen?"

Eden frowned. "I don't know—"

Jimmy raised a hand silencing her. "Did you, or did you not, girl?"

My shoulders went rigid as I watched him confront Eden. I wasn't the only one who watched the interaction with curious eyes. Raul stood behind Eden, his legs wide and arms crossed.

Eden fisted her hands. "I did." Jimmy nodded in approval and looked back at the woman who worked on his leg, but Eden continued, taking a step so her chin met the bed, and she leaned over him. "If you talk to me like you're in charge one more time, I won't hesitate to show you who is in control. Understand?"

Jimmy scanned her face before looking down. "Understood."

"Good." Eden stepped back and turned to the woman, who kept her nervous eyes downward. "Is he all right?"

"Yes. We removed the bullet—"

"Hurt like the dickens too!" Jimmy interrupted.

The woman gave him a scared smile. "Yes, sorry. But it's out, and the wound is cleaned and stitched. He just needs time to rest."

"Good," Eden said.

Cal sat forward, and they began a quiet conversation as my eyes drifted to the bed across from Jimmy's. The white-haired boy lay watching me. His pale blue eyes twinkled when I met them, and his cheek twitched as he attempted to smile. I quietly stepped away and approached his bed. His sister sat on a chair next to it, with her body draped over him as she slept.

"How are you feeling?" I asked.

His cheek twitched again, and his throat bobbed as he swallowed. "Good. Tired."

I smiled and nodded. I shoved my hands in my pockets and looked at my feet before meeting his curious gaze. "What's your name?"

"Kemp."

"I'm Jace."

We stood in silence a moment before I nodded and turned to return to the others, but his small raspy voice followed me.

"Thank you, Jace."

I stilled, my back to him. Letting out a breath, I turned and smiled. "Anytime." His cheek twitched again just before his eyes fluttered shut. I watched him a moment, my shoulders relaxing when his chest rose in a steady rhythm from his breathing.

When I reached Eden's side, Raul stepped closer. "You all stay here, rest. I'll get you when Lucia is ready to plan." None of us spoke, but Eden gave him an acknowledging nod. After he left, I looked at the empty bed next to Jimmy. My head ached, and my muscles were tired. Without a word, I lay down and closed my eyes. The last thing I remember was a gentle hand brushing my wayward hair from my face.

～

The next morning, we walked behind Raul to the same building where Eden and I had negotiated with Lucia. Jimmy grumbled as he leaned onto Cal's shoulder and rested his other arm on a stick. He held his leg bent and back so as to not put any pressure on it. If he wasn't grumbling, he was wincing in pain, which then ended up with him snapping at Cal.

Eden and I had given them a quick overview of the negotiation with Lucia, which they seemed to approve of.

At the sound of the wolves howling in the distance, Eden jerked to a stop. She turned and scanned the roads and buildings around us, but there was no sign of Ash and his pack. She looked at me with a flash of worry. I set my hand on her shoulder and leaned in closer. "He's fine. You told him to stay hidden until we needed him."

She nodded and let out a breath. "Right. You're right."

Raul reached the doorway to the building and held it open for us to enter. We passed the group of guards outside the building. They still watched Eden carefully, but this time they also had eyes on Jimmy and Cal.

I looked back at Jimmy only to see him wink at an armed woman, then wince from the pain. The woman snickered and looked away. Letting out a quick laugh, I shook my head and continued forward. Eden waited at the door with a serious expression. She stood patiently for us, and when we all reached her, she met everyone's eyes with an intensity I hadn't seen in her before. She was all business. Raul was a few steps away, so she spoke softly to keep our conversation private.

"Lucia is smart, very smart. So, you need to think before you speak. Don't be hot heads." She paused, looking between Jimmy and Cal. "Better yet, it may be best if neither of you speaks much... or at all."

Cal watched her with a smug smirk on his face, but Jimmy dropped his chin and glared under furrowed eyebrows. His upper lip twitched. "Girl, I've grown to respect you, but let's get one thing straight: you don't ever tell me what to do. Ever."

Eden didn't flinch, only met his glare. There was a long, thick silence, and I caught many of Lucia's people watching us curiously, including Raul. I stepped forward, halfway between Eden and Jimmy, and spoke low.

"This is not the time or place. We need to have our heads on straight when we walk in there, and plus, we can't look divided in front of her people who are all watching us at this moment." I nodded my head toward the guards whose eyes were on us intently.

"Everything all right?" Raul asked.

Eden pulled her gaze from Jimmy's and turned to the door. "Yes." She pushed past him and into the building. I followed closely behind, with Jimmy and Cal grunting their way in.

The smell of roasted chicken filled my nose, and I immediately started salivating. I hadn't had a decent meal since we stayed at Lillyanne's aunt's farm.

Two angry-looking armed men inspected us from head to toe as we entered the room. I clenched my teeth so tightly when they frisked me that I thought I may have cracked one. Rubbing my tongue over my tooth, I could feel it wasn't broken but my jaw was sore.

"Is this necessary? They have been here all day, and I've been here since the blast. If we wanted to hurt you, we would've already," I said.

Lucia chuckled. "Just a formality. Can't be too careful." She waved her hand dismissively at the men. They stepped back, giving Raul a look. Raul's jaw ticked again, but he gave them a nod. The men exited the room.

The large table in the center of the room was set with plates full of meat and vegetables. I kept my body taut and willed my empty stomach to stay silent as I watched Lucia on the opposite side of the table.

She smiled large, showing full lips and perfect white teeth. Her long, thick hair draped over each shoulder, the lights in the ceiling giving the dark brown a gold hue. I had been so bleary eyed from the blast before that I didn't appreciate how pretty she was.

"Please, sit." She motioned to the table where she sat.

Raul sat in the seat at the end of the table, not waiting for anyone, and dug into his food. Following Eden's cue, we all sat. Jimmy's grunts and hisses filled the room as Cal eased him into a seat. Full plates sat in front of us.

Lucia moved her eyes over all of us, then back to Eden. "So you all have this genetic feature?"

Eden nodded. "Yes."

Lucia scanned us along the table, her gaze intent as she studied us. She was definitely dominant, and unlike before, I found myself fighting the urge to look away. If I could get rid of one of my new traits since becoming Chimera, it would be the biological need to submit to dominant beings. If I had to submit to anyone, it would only be Eden.

Lucia smiled. "Please, eat." She took a bite of her meat, moving her full attention now to her food.

Hesitantly, we all started on our food, eating mostly in silence. No one spoke until all our plates were empty and our bellies full. Lucia looked over at Raul, who sat hunched over his plate with a scowl on his face.

"Raul, would you please take their plates?"

His eyes snapped to hers, and I could see the argument in his eyes, but her passive, firm face made him freeze. They stared at each other a moment before he stood without a word and gathered up our plates. Lucia smiled back at us.

"Why is it you only speak English to your people? I thought Spanish would be your language of choice," Jimmy asked.

"Yes. Well, I find it important that my people are able to speak the language of the people we are to rule over, so I require English to be the only language spoken. Once we overtake Izan, then rules may change, but for now, English it is."

"Izan, your brother, correct?" I asked.

"Correct."

A loud crash of plates echoed in the next room. Lucia flinched and closed her eyes a moment but focused on keeping her face inert. When Raul stomped back into the room, she watched him with heated eyes all the way back to his seat.

"Everything all right?" she asked, her gaze never leaving his tense body.

He answered with a grunt as he crossed his arms and sat back in his chair.

"So what's the plan?" Eden asked, giving all of her focus to Lucia.

"How long will it take for you to return to your people?"

"Two or three days," Jimmy said but paused looking down at his leg. "Probably closer to three."

"All right. I have scouts monitoring Izan's movements." She looked from Jimmy to Eden, deciding they must be the two decision-makers. "How long will it take to get your people here? A week?"

"A week?" Cal scoffed. Lucia looked at him with one eyebrow raised. I coughed on the water I sipped, glancing at Eden. She kept her gaze on Lucia.

That's not enough time. They only began to train the others. I hoped Eden would listen to me. But all I got in response was a tick of her jaw. She pursed her lips and let out a breath. "Let's make it two."

Jimmy and Cal turned to her with wide eyes. Cal set a fist on the table and leaned toward Eden. "That's still not enough time."

Lucia looked between Cal and Eden. "Time for what? I thought your people would be waiting for you."

Cal scoffed. "Yeah, but they still need to train."

"Train? They aren't trained?" Raul snapped and looked to Lucia. "I thought they were going to help take down Izan. If they aren't trained, we have no chance."

Lucia narrowed her eyes at Eden, the skin tightening around the edges. "How many people do you have, Eden?"

Cal spoke again. "We have—"

"Cal, shut up!" Eden snarled. The animal sound echoed throughout the room, and Raul jumped. He grabbed his gun, which had been set on the table next to him. Lucia put up a hand to him. Eden looked at Lucia. "We have a little less than a hundred. But as Cal said, we need a little more time. Two weeks should be sufficient."

Raul sat forward again. "What kind of people do you have? If you say women and children, the deal is off."

"I don't remember giving you any authority to make or end deals," Lucia snapped.

He looked at her with an almost pained face. "Lucia, this is getting ridiculous. We can handle Izan ourselves. We don't need a bunch of farmers to fight with us and probably screw it up."

I grabbed Jimmy's arm when he sat forward to go at Raul. Jimmy looked at me, and I shook my head; this wasn't an argument to have.

"They are mostly farmers, yes." Eden looked between Raul and Lucia. "We have many women and children, but we won't allow children to fight. We do, however, have the best trainers working with them as we speak."

Raul sneered. "The best trainers. The best at what?"

Eden leaned forward toward him, sending him leaning back an inch. "I know they're the best because they trained me."

"That means nothing to me. All I know is you are all strangers with weird eyes. And you"—he looked at Eden—"you have creepy fangs and claws. Lucia said it was some weird genetic testing, but you look a lot like a demon to me, and I don't make deals with the devil."

Eden's throat rumbled with a low growl, and her eyes never left Raul's face. I put a gentle hand on her shoulder, which made her flinch back, but I kept my hand firm.

Eden, breathe.

She swallowed, closing her eyes. "Look. I know we may seem… different to you, but like I told Lucia, if we do nothing, you'll all be just like us or worse. And you won't have Lucia as your leader. You need our help, and we need yours." Her eyes snapped back to Lucia. "That was the deal."

Lucia gave a curt nod. "That's right. So, two weeks then."

Eden nodded. "Agreed."

Jimmy cleared his throat and leaned forward. "Just out of curiosity"—he paused when Eden slowly turned toward him with a daggered stare—"how many people do you have?" He glanced between Raul and Lucia. "From the looks of it here, it doesn't seem like a lot."

Lucia smiled, but it wasn't a friendly smile. "This is not my permanent residence. I have more people elsewhere."

Jimmy opened his mouth again, but Eden stood. Her chair legs scraped the ground with a deafening sound. "Thank you."

Lucia inclined her head but never moved. "You may stay here for another night, and leave in the morning."

"That's kind of you, but we should probably get on our way," Eden said, watching Jimmy pull himself to a stand, his face red with pain.

"Suit yourself."

I moved to Jimmy's other side to help Cal assist him, but he pushed his stick toward me. "Don't you dare. I'm fine with just Cal."

I held my hands up and followed Eden out of the building.

You sure you know what you're doing?

Eden's shoulders were tight as she walked in front of me, past the guards, and down the road back to the vacant building we had hidden out in.

I do.

I let out a small breath. *Two weeks isn't enough time.*

She was silent a few beats. I didn't think she would reply, but then a quiet, defeated voice rang in my head. *It has to be.*

Chapter 33

Eden

After making it to the vacant building, Cal and Jace ran to grab the truck. We managed to get a grumbling Jimmy inside so we could drive back to the vacant store. It was a much more comfortable place to sleep than the rundown building we sat watch in.

No one spoke much, and the tension was thick. Jimmy and Cal were upset about the timeline. Their glares created stabbing prickles along my skin. Although they didn't like my negotiation technique or the deal that was made, they knew I was right. We couldn't wait much longer than two weeks if we were to get the help we needed to take down Zane. We needed to act now for everyone's sake.

Jace was quiet and patient as usual, trusting me. We slept next to each other; his body warmth at my back called to me. I wanted to scoot closer and burrow myself into the safety of his arms, but there wasn't time for that.

When the first bird sang its morning song, I stood from my pile of blankets and stretched before making my way out to the crisp morning air.

A new car was parked behind the truck, and Raul leaned against it with crossed arms. White puffs of air floated from his mouth as he breathed. "Lucia felt it would be in our best interest for me to come with you. Make sure everything is conveyed correctly."

I watched him a moment, then nodded. Ash and his pack emerged from the tree line. With a smile, I crouched and gave him a good ear scratch. At the sight of him, a small coil of tension that had built in my gut slowly unwound. I was so focused on my reunion with Ash that I didn't see Raul approach, only heard his footsteps, soft and hesitant.

"Did you train them? Have them as babies?" he asked. His voice was gentle and didn't hold any of the disgust I usually heard.

"I have had Ash since he was a pup, yes. The others, he brought with him when we were forced to separate. They are skeptical, but we're building trust in each other. They trust him and he trusts me, so that helps."

Raul met my gaze, turning my words over in his head. Jace emerged from the store. "Morning." He looked at Raul and nodded. "Raul."

"He's coming with us. Lucia's orders."

Jace didn't respond, but Jimmy's voice echoed from the store door. Cal stood next to him so Jimmy could lean on his shoulder. "We're taking orders from Lucia now?"

Raul's jaw tightened, but I held up a hand. "No. But I respect the order she gave to Raul." I looked at Raul before looking back at Jimmy. "I probably would've done the same. Anyway, we have nothing to hide, so he's free to come." I could feel Raul's eyes burning into the side of my face.

Jimmy grunted and gimped to the truck, tugging Cal along with him. "Let's get going then. If we don't waste time, we could get back late tonight." Cal quickly tossed their bags into the bed of the truck as they passed before he helped Jimmy into the passenger side. I opened the back hatch to let the wolves in.

"I need someone to ride with me," Raul said. I froze and kept my back facing him. "For collateral. You understand, don't you?" I sucked in a deep breath. I did understand, but that didn't mean I liked it.

Jimmy and Cal both grumbled quietly. Cal continued around the truck to the driver's side. "That's right. You understand, don't you, Eden?" Jimmy snapped, glaring at me from the front seat.

I composed my face and closed the hatch after all the wolves were set. I turned and met Raul's eyes. "Of course—"

"I'll ride with him." Jace opened the passenger door to Raul's car.

Snapping my eyes to his, I clenched my hands. "Why don't you ride with Jimmy and Cal? I can go with Raul." The last thing I wanted was for Jace to be used against me. I was stronger than him, faster, more... predatorial. If I had to kill Raul, I could. Jace would die inside if he had to hurt anyone.

Jace smiled, seeming to read my mind. "I'll be fine. Plus, his car looks much more comfortable." I let my shoulders relax when he winked and sat in the front seat.

I looked at Raul and nodded. "Keep up. We don't want you getting lost."

Be careful, I sent to Jace as I crawled behind Cal into the truck. *Always.*

~

We rolled into the courtyard between the buildings after dark. The glow from small fires in tin cans on the side of the road led the way. Bomber, Old Bob, Brian, and Tate were in the front of the small crowd that emerged from the building as we stepped out of the truck. Bomber's eyes were tight as he watched Raul's car park behind us, inspecting the new face carefully.

"Who's this?"

I stretched as I walked up to them. "Raul. He's one of Lucia's men."

When Jimmy hopped out of the truck with his stick, all eyes moved to him. Bomber's eyes narrowed. "What happened?"

"They shot me. That's what happened,"

I quickly put up my hands to stop the eruption of rage that wafted through the courtyard. "It was a misunderstanding. He's fine. They got the bullet out and stitched up the wound." I glared at Jimmy, and he only shrugged. A few women moved to his side to help him inside the building, and his demeanor immediately softened as he spoke to them with twinkling eyes.

Bomber's shoulders relaxed slightly and his eyes widened. "The deal went through?"

"It went through. We meet her in two weeks."

Their faces dropped, and Brian sighed. "I'm sure you know that's not enough time to get people war-ready."

"I understand, but we don't have much choice. She's ready to be rid of her brother, and to be honest, we shouldn't let Zane do more damage than he already has."

"Agreed, but Eden, you haven't been here to see the training."

Bomber looked at him. "I warned you all; we don't have fighters."

"You don't have fighters?" Raul's voice was loud, his accent barely there. Lucia's English practice really did help them.

He narrowed his eyes on mine. "We were told you'd fight with us. That was the deal."

"We will. What he's saying is our people are just a little rusty."

"Eden, can I speak with you a moment?" Old Bob said.

When I looked at him, his face seemed more tired than when we left a few days ago. I'm sure from worry over me. I stepped to his side far enough away from others' ears. I knew Brian and Jace could still hear, though.

"What did you tell them?"

"I told them what we decided on. That we'll help them defeat Izan if they help us take Zane down. She wanted more, so that's when I brought up giving her the southern land. She accepted the conditions, so here we are."

"Did you tell them we have an army? What exactly did you say?" He crossed his arms as his gaze intensified on my face.

"I said we have people that can fight. I never said army."

He let out a long breath, his eyes flicking to Raul's commanding presence. "Well, let's hope we can live up to their standards. I'd hate to learn what will happen if we're unable to keep our end of the bargain."

Turning, I met Raul's eyes as he watched us talk. His face was intense and angry. He already didn't trust me, and this was causing that small amount of trust he did have to dissipate. The knot inside me tightened.

"I hope so too," I mumbled, and we walked back to the group.

~

I stared up at the ceiling in our dark room listening to the steady breaths of the others sleeping. Surprisingly Brian, Old Bob, and Raul hit it off. They had a mutual understanding that I don't think many people would understand. It came from being in battle, fighting for survival, and taking lives.

Raul was given his own room to rest in. Although he was to assist Brian in training tomorrow, I'm sure he'll be inspecting the fighters rather than helping.

Closing my eyes, I let out a long breath, but it didn't release the knot that was still in my belly. I moved my hand over the butterfly around my neck, wishing Ellie and Tristan were here. I missed them. Missed the cabin, and the life we had before all of this. I can't help but wonder if I'd never left with Jace that day, would we all still be happy at the cabin together. Tate and Ellie still alive.

A tear slipped down the side of my cheek, and I moved my hand to wipe it away, but Jace's warm gentle fingers were there first. I turned to look at him. He watched me with soft eyes, his hand still warm on my cheek.

What are you thinking about that would make you so sad?

Ellie. Tristan.

He was silent a moment before gently wiping his thumb over my cheek again. *I'm sorry. I'm sure it's hard.*

I'm scared.

He studied me, pulling his hand away. *Of what?*

Of failing. Everyone is counting on me. If we can't help take Izan down, I fail. If we can't take Zane down, I fail. It's just... I paused and swallowed. He waited patiently for me to collect my words and finish. I met his eyes again. *It's just so much. Sometimes I want to just run. Run away with Ash and his pack. Live with them, away from it all.* I watched him for any sign of disgust or betrayal, but I am only met with kindness, love, and understanding.

He sets his hand over mine, giving me a little smile that showed the dimple I so love. *I hope you'd let me come with you.*

You would want to?

I want to be with you. So, where you go, I go.

I felt my face warm, and by the way he smiled and squeezed my hand, I knew he could see how red I was.

He leaned in and let his lips hover over mine, his eyes intensely watching me, waiting. I moved forward, closing the space between us, and met his mouth in a warm and gentle kiss. His hand slid into my hair to the nape of my neck, holding me close to him. When we finally pulled away, he kissed my nose and smiled. His fingers gently trailed down the length of my neck, setting my skin on fire.

Sleep, we have a long few days ahead of us.

I didn't reply but turned my body to rest on his shoulder, sinking into his warmth and safety. He stiffened a moment before wrapping his arm around my shoulders.

Night, Babyface.

Night, Golden Girl.

Chapter 34

Jace

I stretched my body from side to side and shook my legs and arms out, getting ready for the early morning training. Stifling a yawn, I rubbed my eyes. Eden's confession had me up most of the night trying to think of a way to help her. I had pulled her close, wrapping her in the safety of my arms. It had felt right. If she would let me, I would escape with her like she said, but I knew she'd never abandon everything now.

Ash walked up to me, and I crouched to pet him. He panted happily with affection, his breath blowing white smoke into the crisp air. "Your coat is getting thick," I mumbled to him as he rubbed his head onto my knee with a groan.

"He lets you pet him too?" Raul asked.

I turned and saw him watching us. Giving Ash one last ear squeeze, I stood. "Yeah."

"I thought it was only her because she's . . ."

Clenching my teeth, I tilted my head. "She's?"

He watched me a moment before shaking his head. "Nothing." I didn't respond, only watched him scan the small courtyard where the training would take place. Some people had emerged, and Raul was inspecting them carefully, his face in a scowl. "How did she think we could win with help like this?"

"Well, I suspect she figured it was help like this or no help, which would you rather have?"

He met my eyes. "I didn't realize how many of you had the special genetic trait."

I smiled. "Yes, well, that's another reason for joining forces. We help you, then you help us." I watched his jaw tick. "Unless you want pretty eyes like mine."

"Right, because of the crazy leader in the north. Right?" He looked back at the growing group of people.

"That's right." I shrugged. "I will say it's not the worst thing in the world to be Chimera, but I don't think it should ever be forced on anyone."

He blinked at me without a word before walking away, toward Bomber who approached the crowd.

A golden light shone on the side of my vision, and I turned. Eden was approaching, the sun hitting her long auburn hair, making it glow a deeper red.

"Hey," she said, smiling as she stood next to me.

"Hey." I smiled and stepped toward her. Her cheeks warmed, and I leaned in close and kissed her cheek. I let my nose trail to her ear, and I breathed in her woodsy smell.

She giggled and pulled back. "Aren't you affectionate today?"

I grinned and pulled her closer, wrapping my arms around her waist. "I don't think I'm affectionate enough."

She laughed. "Oh, really?"

"Really." I blinked at her with a serious face. She pursed her lips to keep from smiling and leaned in again and pushed my lips to the throat below her ear. It wasn't a kiss, but an act of fondness. Her sigh made my chest warm.

Brian stepped up to the front of the crowd and stood on a few boxes to make himself slightly taller. Eden and I untangled ourselves and turned toward him, our hands twined together. Beside him stood Old Bob and Bomber. "All right, I know we've started our training already, but we are going to do some reworking of our groups. Everyone will be broken into groups and trained by Robert, Bomber, AJ, and Sam."

A man in the front stepped forward. "Who's this guy?" He motioned to Raul.

Bomber looked at the man. "He's an ally." Not giving anyone the chance to ask any more questions, he clapped and said, "Now let's get to work! We don't have a lot of time so we need you to give us a hundred and ten percent every day, all day."

Old Bob and the others started calling out names of people to their groups and people moved to their trainers.

Brian approached us. "I'll be working with all the Chimera. There is a room in the next building that we'll be training in. Jimmy and Cal are already there."

"How is Jimmy supposed to train?" I asked.

Brian shrugged. "He can at least watch for now. He still has to learn what to do." He turned to Raul. "You can work with whomever you want to or just observe. It's up to you."

"Thank you. I'll observe out here today."

"Very well." Brian gave him a nod and led Eden and me to a building I thought had been abandoned. "There's a large, empty room in there that is perfect for our training."

"We going to work on hand-to-hand?" Eden asked, shaking out her arms. I could see she craved the physical exercise. It had been a long time since she had had it.

"Yes, but we also need to teach them our other abilities."

I smiled. "We already taught Jimmy and Cal about the telepathy on our trip."

Brian looked at me. "And he hasn't been grumbling in your heads?"

I laughed. "To my surprise, no."

He led us up a few flights of stairs into a large open room where Jimmy and Cal rested on the far wall. Two of Jimmy's other men, Tim and Lou, waited next to them, stretching out their bodies.

"About time y'all showed up. I was just about to call it a day." Jimmy wiggled against the wall with a grunt. Cal smirked down at him and shook his head.

"Watch this," Brian mumbled to Eden and me.

Lou scrunched his brow and looked at Brian. "Watch what? I'm get—" He froze. His eyes widened and all the blood drained from his face. "What... did you hear that?"

I bit my cheek to keep from laughing. Eden and Brian did the same.

"Hear what?" Tim asked. "I didn't—" He then froze, looking between Lou and Brian. "Why is your voice in my head?"

Jimmy and Cal laughed, knowing they weren't being left out of the joke. Eden and I burst out laughing, and I slapped Brian on the shoulder, who had a large grin on his face as he watched both Tim and Lou.

"What's going on?" Lou asked.

"You haven't learned all your new abilities, it seems," Brian said. "As Chimera, we are able to speak to each other telepathically."

"I think it's my favorite superpower," Jimmy chimed in. He had a large grin on his face that made him look slightly less rough.

"How?" Lou croaked. Tim's color had returned to his face, but Lou looked like he was going to be sick.

"Who knows?" Brian shrugged his shoulders. "I mean, do we truly know how animals communicate? No. They may be able to communicate telepathically, and that is why we are able to."

A wave of insecurity hit me, and I looked over at Eden. She didn't look at me, keeping her eyes forward on the other men. Her eyes held something. Something I couldn't make out, then she looked at me and swallowed.

"I think they do," she said quietly. The others stopped talking and turned to her.

"What?" Brian asked.

"I think they do. The animals. I think—" She paused, searching for the words or building courage, I don't know. She let out a breath. "I think Ash has spoken to me." She didn't breathe, as if she was waiting for us to attack her.

Brian cocked his head at her and scratched his rough chin. "When?"

She let out the air she held. "When we were heading to see Lucia. I heard him... call to me."

I remember her looking out of the truck into the trees, screaming for AJ to stop. "You heard him, and that's how you knew he was there."

She looked at me and nodded. "Yes, but it was just my name. I don't even know if it was real or if it was... my imagination." She looked down and twisted her claws together.

"It's possible." Brian looked from her face to the claws she had clasped together. "You were... changed more than us. So maybe some of your other abilities were heightened."

"Why don't we get him in here and try it out?" Cal said.

I shook my head. "No. It's too risky. They're waiting away from the other humans. If something was to happen, it could blow this whole deal. We have to keep them away unless there's war."

"Jace's right," Eden said. "We'll figure it out later, next time I see him."

"All right," Tim said. "Why don't you explain and show us how to do that?"

Brian nodded and started the lesson.

Eden and I, drenched in sweat and exhausted, slowly walked up the steps toward our room. It felt so good to work until enervation. To work out our stress and concerns.

We practiced schooling our thoughts, building walls in our mind, and only sharing with select people. Then we moved into some stretches and yoga poses, which progressed into one-on-one combat and ended again with yoga and stretching.

"I call first dibs on the shower," Eden said as we reached our room. No one else was back when we entered, and she went right for a change of clothes.

"Please, yes, I can't take how stinky you are."

She gasped, and I smirked and winked at her. Putting her hands on her hips, she looked at me. "And you think you smell like roses?"

"Don't I always?"

She shook her head with a chuckle and moved to pass me.

I closed the door but didn't let her by. She stopped in front of me with her eyebrows raised. "Don't tell me, you want to fight over who gets to go first." She leaned in and sniffed my neck, trying to keep her face from scrunching. "But you smell like roses, so not sure why you need to go first." She smirked, but I still didn't move. I just watched her until her cheeks went rosy and her eyes dropped.

I moved my hand gently along her cheek. "Remember when you said you were thinking about just running away?"

She looked up at me and swallowed. "Yes."

"I would go with you. No questions. If that's truly what you wanted."

Her eyes mapped my face, and she let out a sigh. "You know I can't."

I shrugged. "Why not?" I moved my other hand to her face, holding her cheeks in my palms. "The fate of the world is not on your shoulders, Eden. If you want to leave, you can. And I'll go with you."

Although my heart knew that she never would, I wanted her to know she had the choice. Part of me hoped she would take it, and we could slip away into the wilderness together.

She rested her forehead on mine. "I can't." Her voice was a cracked whisper.

I sighed and kissed her forehead, resting my nose in her hair. "All right." I pulled back and leaned down, leveling our eyes. "Promise me, though, that when all this is over, you'll stop trying to save the world?"

She smiled. "When Zane is gone, I'm all yours."

I grinned and pulled her into a hug. "Deal." After giving her a squeeze, I pushed her back and scrunched my nose dramatically. "All right, yeah, you need a shower." I opened the door and gently shoved her out of the room.

She chuckled and headed down the hall toward the showers. Her quiet laughter brought a smile to my face.

Chapter 35

Eden

I moved through the early morning exercises with focus and ease. A small weight was lifted after Jace's conversation the night before. He knew I'd never leave the fight to the others, but he wanted me to know I had a choice.

Pausing my actions, I watched him move. He was graceful yet powerful with his muscular body. He had become more built since I first met him. Since he became Chimera, his hair had grown shaggy and flopped over his eyes with his movements. He shook his head to toss it to the side. I'm sure if I asked him to cut it again, he would refuse. I remember how upset he was when they cut it after we were captured.

"Eden, back to work!" Brian's voice echoed throughout the room.

Jace glanced at me, and his mouth twitched to show his dimple. My cheeks warmed, and I looked away.

Like what you see?

I giggled and shook my head, not giving him the satisfaction of responding. Brian moved to my side and watched me like a hawk as I moved through poses to work on balance and strength. His eyes burned into every move I made, causing my balance to slip. I tilted to the side and had to drop my other foot to catch myself.

"You're not focusing," Brian said, and crossed his arms.

"I'm sorry. I just—"

Everyone stopped their movements when Raul walked into the room.

Brian leaned closer to me. "Get it together. You have to be able to focus in all situations. Stop ogling your boyfriend."

I opened my mouth to talk back, but closed it when I thought of nothing to say. My cheeks warmed again and I looked away. He turned and walked over to the others.

Yeah, stop ogling me.

Shut up.

I looked at Jace. He winked. I rolled my eyes.

Raul stepped to my side, watching Brian show new combat techniques to the others.

"I've been watching the other groups," Raul spoke softly and kept his eyes on Brian's movements. "I don't think we're going to be ready."

I turned to him with raised eyebrows, and my heart skipped a beat at his words. "What makes you think that?"

"Have you seen them?"

"No." It was true, I hadn't. But going from what I knew of the people, I'm sure they weren't the fighters Raul expected.

He leaned closer to me, his nose almost touching mine. "If your people aren't able to hold up their end of the bargain, then you and I"—he moved a finger between us—"will have a problem."

At the echo of Raul's voice, Brian stopped going through movements with the others and turned to us.

"Everything all right?" he asked, slowly stepping toward us.

Jace followed his lead, staying a step behind him. His eyes focused on me, with concern etched in the corners. *You all right?*

I nodded and looked back at Raul. "Yes, Brian. Everything is fine."

Raul sneered and looked at Brian. "I was just telling Eden that it doesn't seem like your people will be ready in time."

Jimmy snickered from his position against the wall. "I could've told you that before you came here."

"Shut up." Jace snarled at Jimmy.

Crossing his arms, Brian said, "Well, Raul, we don't really have a choice, do we?"

"I don't care. She"—he pointed at me, and I stiffened—"told us that there were people able to fight."

"There are people able to fight," Jace said, stopping between Brian and me.

"No," Raul said, stepping back. He obviously felt the threat of all of us near him. "No, what you have are people. Fighters? No, they aren't fighters."

"In these times, we can't be picky. We have to make do with what we got," I said.

Raul clenched his jaw when he met my eyes. Letting out a huff of air, he turned and stormed out of the building. We stood silently and watched his retreat.

After a moment, Brian patted my shoulder and turned back to the others. "All right, no time to waste. Let's get back to work."

I let out a long breath and looked at Jace, who watched me. Despite the cool air, his skin glistened with sweat. He took my hand and ran his fingers gently over mine. "Just let it go for now."

"But he—"

"Let it go." He leaned down and faced me.

"Get your chatty asses over here and to work," Brian bellowed at us.

Jace leaned back and tugged my hand, pulling me with him. For the next few hours, my focus was divided between my training and wondering if Raul was right. That the people we had wouldn't be enough. That we won't succeed. My stomach dropped, heavy like it was filled with stones, at the thought.

We had to succeed.

∾

The following eleven days were all the same. We woke, had a quick bland breakfast, and got to work. Just from the few days of consistent work, I felt my body growing stronger, more precise. I felt clearheaded and focused.

Old Bob and Bomber seemed pleased with the progress the other groups were making as well, even the people with no formal fighting background. They were all becoming stronger, quicker, and surer-footed. Since we didn't have enough guns for everyone, Sam and Bomber taught a select few how to shoot. They said the progress was slow but promising.

Raul continued to monitor each group and nightly he would complain and argue with us about it. Even though Brian, Old Bob, and Bomber did most of the discussing with him, his threat toward me still hung heavy in the air.

The night before we were set to leave, a group of us ate in Bomber's office. Raul sat between Bomber and Old Bob, quietly sharing old war stories. I ate between Brian and Jace, who picked at his food. I felt his nerves at the impending battle. AJ and Sam sat squished between Brian and Old Bob, not saying much as they shoved food in their faces. Cal and Jimmy had decided to sleep rather than eat. The training had taken its toll on Cal, but Jimmy was just tired from his healing body.

Tate had shyly expressed wanting to eat with his training group, which coincidentally included Lillyanne. Although I was happy he was making friends, I felt a little wary he and Lillyanne were becoming so close. After all, he was my brother, and I didn't want to see him hurt.

"We have all the vehicles we could get up and running ready. We'll put the older and weaker people in them to follow you, Raul. The others will go on foot." Bomber wiped his mouth after his last bite and sat back in his chair.

"You do realize it'll take days for them to walk to my camp," Raul said, pushing the half-eaten meat around on his plate.

"Yes, but we don't have a choice."

Raul didn't respond. He looked at his chicken, dropping his face to look closer to it. "I just have to say, I've never in my life tasted such bland food. Have you all never heard of spices?"

I burst out laughing but stopped when I realized I was the only one who found his words amusing. "What? I have been waiting until someone said it." I looked down and poked my own chicken when Old Bob gave me a pointed glare.

Bomber scowled and said, "I'm very sorry that you all are unhappy with our *bland* food, but as you can see, we're short on supplies here."

Raul sighed. "Yes. So I've been told. Still, all you need are a few herbs. When we get to my camp, I'll show you."

"We'll need a few days to rest and plan when we arrive. I hope that'll be taken into consideration," Brian said, pushing our conversation forward. He pushed his empty plate away and sat back in his chair.

"Yes. We'll plan. Izan is smart and ruthless. We'll need to prepare."

Jace rolled his fork between his fingers, keeping his eyes down. Feeling him thinking, planning something, I looked over at him when he spoke. "Do we really need everyone to go?"

Raul met his gaze. "What's your meaning?"

"I mean, how many people does Izan have? Do we really need everyone from here to go, or could a select few of our best fighters go? That way we can take him down with strategy over quantity. This will be less risk for us, and then the less skilled will have more time to train for when we move north. We'll need numbers *and* skill to take down Zane."

Raul studied him. "Izan has between thirty and forty people. We've killed some, so I don't know the exact number at this time. Lucia has around forty-three people that follow her, including me. If we took a few skilled people, we may be able to take Izan down, but he is smart. It will not be easy."

Old Bob sat forward and leaned his forearms on the table with clasped hands. "No, I don't expect it to be, but Jace has a point. Zane will have numbers, many more than forty, and it'll be mostly hand-to-hand combat. Weapons are not as prevalent in the north. The more training people can get, the better."

Raul nodded and looked at Bomber when he spoke. "Who would we send? I need skilled people."

"I'll go," I said, giving Raul a nod.

"Me too," Jace said.

I looked at Brian, who met my eyes. He gave me a soft smile. "I'll stay, along with Jimmy, Cal, Tim, and Lou. The more training they all get the better. Plus Jimmy's leg needs to heal. We'll need strong Chimera when we move north."

"I'll go," Old Bob said. I opened my mouth to protest, but he stopped me and held up his hand. "I have skills in strategy. I led battles and fought in the wars. I'll be useful." Clenching my jaw, I stayed silent, knowing he was right.

Bomber sighed. "I'll go, but I'll leave AJ and Sam here to train the others. They are skilled, and the people have been responding to them. We don't want to lose momentum."

"Is four enough?" I asked. "Could we take some others who have caught on to training? The wolves will come, of course, but still."

Bomber nodded. "I think that would be smart. I'll talk to AJ and Sam to pick some people." He looked at Raul. "How many would be sufficient?"

"Twenty?"

Bomber pursed his lips and nodded. "I'll see what I can do." He looked directly at Old Bob. "It'll be good if we have a few with battle experience and strategy."

"All right then. We leave at first light. Everyone get rest," Bomber said, dismissing us all.

Chapter 36

Jace

I rolled my neck from the rough night of sleep. I stepped outside but grabbed the door quickly when my feet slid out from under me. After pulling up to a standing position, I grunted and steadied myself. The ground was covered in a sparkling sheen of crystal white that crunched under my feet.

"Careful. There was freezing rain last night," Eden called from one of the cars.

I raised an eyebrow. "You don't say?" I slid my feet carefully, putting my hands out for balance. "How are we supposed to drive in this?"

"Very carefully. But I'm guessing that you will not be driving." He threw a bag in the trunk of a car. Bomber smirked.

Raul stood next to the car and rubbed his hands, giving them a puff of warm breath every few minutes. "It's freezing. Why did it get so cold so quickly?"

"Happens this time of year. One day it can be warm; the next, winter is here." Bomber spoke through grunts while he tossed more bags into the cars.

"We need to work fast. It'll only be colder up north," I said.

"I already gave orders for people to gather warmer clothes, blankets, and jackets in preparation for our trip. We'll need to be prepared." Bomber looked back at the building when Old Bob emerged with a large group of others, including Tate.

Old Bob had his arm around Tate's shoulders as he spoke to him. Tate leaned in, soaking up every word that was said. A pang of jealousy hit me. I'd never had that bond with my father. We were cut from different cloths. When I saw how Old Bob was with Tate, I missed my father and the possibility of what we could have grown into—even if we were oil and water. A deeper pang of guilt hit me when I thought of the last time I saw him. Leaving him behind as Eden and I escaped into the woods. I was sure he was dead, or worse. Zane would never let helping us escape slide.

Tate slapped his hand on my shoulder. "Be careful and take care of my sister." His golden curls framed his blue eyes. He had grown more confident with the training, or maybe a certain someone's affections.

"Always." I furrowed my brow. "Why aren't you coming? You know how to fight."

Tate smiled. "Yes, but I volunteered to take over some of the training."

I looked back at the doorway and saw Lillyanne pulling her sweater tighter around herself. Her face held the same look of concern since we got back from her farm. "I'm sure that has nothing to do with it?"

He glanced quickly over his shoulder and pushed a hand through his hair, trying to hide his reddening cheeks. "No." He cleared his throat. "It was completely the training."

"How's that going anyway?"

He dropped his hand and shrugged, digging his foot into some frost on the ground. "It's going."

I watched him and bit back a smile. "She's nice."

He glanced up at me to see if I was joking. Confident I wasn't, he responded. "Yeah, she is. A little misunderstood, I think."

"I agree." We stood in companionable silence, watching as the others loaded the three vehicles.

"She can also be a pain." He smirked.

"I also agree."

He turned to me, and his smile faded. "I'm serious, though. Be careful and please take care of Eden."

"I promise." I squeezed his forearm and turned back to the group. "I better help." He didn't say anything when I walked toward the others, picked up a bag that was piled on the ground, and loaded it in the back of one of the cars. Who knew we'd have so many supplies.

The cars were loaded and warmed up. The crowd grew; some with tear-filled eyes mumbling farewells to loved ones. Tate hugged Eden and whispered something to her, which only made her squeeze him tighter.

"All right! Let's roll!" Bomber's voice echoed in the courtyard, puffy white air billowing from his mouth.

Eden called to the wolves, who had been waiting down the road, and helped them into the bed of one of the trucks. Two cars, two trucks, with the beds filled with wolves and some very bundled people, plus Raul's car slowly drove out of the courtyard and down the road, away from the crowd of silent onlookers. Twenty people. Everyone was unsure of who they'd see when we returned.

If we returned.

～

The drive went much slower than expected due to the icy roads. We took many breaks to switch drivers and the people in the truck beds, and to have quick meals. Everyone had a quietness about them, a knowing. A knowing that we were all walking into something we couldn't predict and that some might not walk out of at all.

The people Bomber found to come with us may have been the best fighters at the time, but their limited amount of training would definitely be a disadvantage. They trembled, and the two women among them were continuously fighting back tears. It was obvious that they had never been in any kind of battle before this.

After dark, we arrived at Lucia's. Immediately, her people perked up when they saw Raul's car leading ours. The looks between her people and ours were curious but careful as we slowly stepped out of our vehicles. A crowd of the city folk came out to see the people who came to help. I spotted the blond hair and blue eyes of Kemp, standing and huddling next to his sister. He grinned big and gave me a wave, which I returned with a smile, my heart lightening that he seemed to have healed well.

Lucia floated forward, her long dark hair pulled back into a braid that was swooped over her shoulder. She greeted Raul with a large smile, much larger than a leader would to a soldier. When he pulled her into a tight embrace and a deep kiss, Eden and I froze in surprise.

She turned to the rest of us, still tucked under Raul's arm with a large smile that brightened her pretty face. "Welcome. How many people have come?"

"Twenty," Raul said but continued quickly when she opened her mouth to speak. "But they are some of the best fighters, and we have some good strategists. Izan doesn't have numbers, so we figured this would be enough. We needed the others to continue training."

After watching him for a moment, she nodded, and I let out the breath I had been holding. She looked at everyone again with a smile plastered on her face. "Please come in. I have some warm drinks and food for you." She took Raul's hand and led everyone into her building. Eden and I were at the front of the group and Lucia smiled at us when we stepped in from the biting cold. "I wasn't sure if you'd be back tonight or tomorrow, but I wanted to make sure I had food ready for you." She hugged Raul again. She was much more relaxed this time, nothing like the leader we met before.

"Thank you," Eden said. She spied Old Bob and Bomber in the group and motioned them forward. "Lucia, these are two of our leaders, Bomber and Old"—she shook her head—"Robert."

Lucia stepped from Raul's arms and reached out her hand. "Very nice to meet you." Bomber and Old Bob smiled and took her hand firmly.

"You as well," Old Bob said, his eyes meeting Eden's in obvious confusion at Lucia's warmness.

Raul didn't miss it, and he laughed. "She's not always like this, Robert. She's just happy this will all be over soon, and she'll be the only rightful leader of the south."

Old Bob and Bomber nodded; the nervousness rolling off both of them was thick. They felt the same as Eden did: not wanting to fail; if we failed, we most likely would die.

Lucia motioned to the table. "Please help yourself. There isn't enough room for everyone to eat here, but I'm sure you're tired anyway. Take a plate, and I can show you to where you'll sleep."

Without pausing or talking at all, everyone loaded a plate and took a mug of warm tea. Lucia and Raul led us down a hall to a few rooms. They were empty but we were thankful they kept out the freezing cold air outside.

"I hope this will do. You all rest, and we'll get to planning first thing in the morning."

"This is fine," Bomber replied. "We'll get some of our bags after we eat."

"I can have them brought in if you'd like."

Bomber stiffened. "That won't be necessary." He met her gaze, and they locked eyes a moment. He didn't want anyone touching their things.

I stepped forward. "I'll just grab them now. I'm not very hungry and need to stretch my legs." Bomber looked at me with a nod.

"I'll help," Eden said, following me down the hall.

I hope we can keep everyone from killing each other.

Agreed.

The wolves waited for us in the bed of the truck. Lucia's people watched them warily, and I could see it made Eden uneasy. "Go find a place for the night, Ash. I'll call you in the morning." He gave her a quick lick on the nose and a yip before leading his pack down the road. Eden watched until they were out of sight.

"Let's get our stuff inside before I freeze." I rubbed my hands together. Since the cold didn't affect me like it did a human, I could only imagine how Lucia's people felt standing guard overnight. The fires in the cans didn't provide nearly enough warmth.

It only took three trips for us to grab all the bags. Everyone finished their meals, then piled up clothes, blankets, and bags to make small beds. Old Bob and Bomber created a rotation of who would take watch: two people at a time, but thankfully I wasn't first, because even though my body wasn't tired, my mind was, and it didn't take me long to drift off into a deep sleep.

Chapter 37

Eden

I woke early, while everyone was still sound asleep except for Bomber and one of the new recruits that came along. I stood and stretched before walking over to the window. The ground and rooftops sparkled with ice crystals as the glowing morning sun reflected off them. Ash and the wolves had been out in the cold all night. Although his coat had grown thicker to accommodate the change of weather, this would be his first winter not sleeping in a shelter. He always stayed in the cabin with me.

"I'm going for a walk. Need to stretch my legs," I said quietly to Bomber. He gave me a groggy-faced nod in reply.

I rolled my shoulders and headed out to get a good stretch. Sleeping on the ground didn't help after a day stuck in a car. When I stepped outside, the cold air hit me so hard it made my eyes sting and water, but I didn't pull my arms tightly around me like I would have before I became Chimera. My body now adjusted quickly.

As I slowly walked out to the courtyard, the ground crunched under my feet. Four of Lucia's guards turned to see who was approaching. They held their gloved hands under their arms, hunching their shoulders to keep their necks warm. At least they had hats. By the redness of their cheeks and chins, I wondered if they would've had ears left without them.

"Morning." I nodded my head as I passed. They watched me with curious gazes. "I'm just going to stretch my legs," I said to no one in particular and stepped out past the makeshift gate.

Once out, I started to hop up and down, feeling the traction under my feet. The ice had broken up mostly, so a run shouldn't be too difficult. It would be good practice to run on slippery ground anyway. Good for my leg strength and balance, Old Bob always said.

I increased to a jog, still shaking out my arms for the first few paces. The only people on the roads were a few who lit the fires in the cans. Small faces of children peeked out from the surrounding buildings, watching me jog past. I headed toward the area where we first drove in, where we had met Lucia's people. My speed increased as I got onto the straight road. My heart pumped, and my stiff legs finally started to stretch out. Though the cold air stung my face, I smiled at the feeling of freedom.

I approached the edge of the buildings and saw the tree line. My senses were piqued and I turned, half sliding down the ditch off the road before I made the small incline toward the trees. The familiar smell of pine and dirt filled my nose, and I increased my speed. Weaving between trees and over downed stumps, I felt like I was flying. The only sound was my quickened breaths and the snapping of twigs under my feet.

Eden!

I tripped at the invasion of the new voice in my head, and my pace slowed. Scanning my surroundings, I didn't see anyone at first, but then I saw the flash of grey.

Eden! Run! Home!

I smiled, letting out a small laugh. Ash leaped to my side and met my pace. "Hey, buddy," I said between pants. "Is that you I hear in my head?"

Eden!

His gold eyes twinkled, and a feeling of excitement and fear rushed through me. I could hear Ash in my head. Ever since I was young and he was a pup, I always wished I could communicate with him, but to actually be able to talk to him? Wow. I slowed my run and stopped at a huge tree, leaning on the trunk. Panting hard, I met his gold eyes. His tail wagged slowly, and he rubbed his head on my thigh.

I could hear Ash. Talk to him. A wolf. My stomach leaped and dropped all at once, making me nauseous. I dropped to the ground and sat against the tree. What does that make me? Am I now an animal?

A twig snapped. I snarled and whipped my head behind me. Jace stood with his hands up. "Whoa. It's just me." His chest rose and fell in quick motions, and I spotted a light sheen of sweat on his skin.

"What are you doing here?"

He shrugged and knelt down to pet Ash when he approached him. "I woke shortly after you, and the guards out front said you went for a run. I thought it was a good idea, so I followed."

I watched him conveniently avoid my gaze. "Liar." I stood and stepped toward him.

He gave me a mock look of surprise.

I laughed. "I think you just couldn't stay away from me." I poked his chest.

"You got me." He laughed and brushed some hair lightly from my face. The light touch of his fingers tingled along my skin. "I also didn't want you out here by yourself."

I stopped and stepped back. "I can take care of myself."

"I know you can—"

"Then why would you come out here as a bodyguard?"

"Eden, whether you can take care of yourself or not, there is no shame in taking precautions."

I turned away and moved back toward the tree. "I know." Gritting my teeth, I swallowed hard. "It's just... I heard him again. And this time I know it was him." I slowly moved my eyes to his.

Jace blinked and tilted his head. "You heard who? Ash?"

I nodded and waited for the look. I don't know what look exactly, but one not of admiration or love, more of disgust or fear. Only it never came. Instead, he smiled and took a step toward me. "Wow. That's pretty amazing."

I raised my eyebrows. "It is?"

"Of course, it is. Think about it, you are the only person in the world who can actually communicate with animals. That's amazing."

I watched him, smelled the air. He wasn't lying; he truly did think it was amazing.

"I guess. I just wasn't sure if it made me more of an animal—or worse, a monster."

He stepped even closer to me and rested his forehead on mine. I pulled in his musky scent and closed my eyes. "You're not a monster, Eden. You're special. There is no one like you, and you should be proud of that." His hands moved to my waist at the same time as he put his lips to mine. His grip on my waist tightened, and I reached my hands up, winding them around his neck to pull him closer. A small growl vibrated from his throat, and I pulled away with a giggle. He smiled and his cheeks turned a deep red.

A loud scream echoed through the trees, and we froze. All the fun between us disappeared, and I stepped away, looking into the distance through the trees. Focusing on the sounds, I heard engines, voices, and small whimpering cries.

"Something isn't right," I said and started forward, but Jace tugged me back.

"Wait. We have to go slowly. Use the wolves, and fan out."

I nodded, looked at Ash, and whispered, "Go see what's up." Ash dashed away between the trees, disappearing in the thick brush. I turned to Jace but didn't speak. I didn't want to risk the sound.

Go toward the tree line slowly. Watch every step.

Jace nodded, and we started out. The sound of the engines grew louder along with the smell of exhaust.

"Where is it?" a man growled.

I saw the road, now filled with the dark shapes of trucks. The beds of each truck were filled with gun-holding men and women.

"Which way?" the man yelled again.

"Th-there," another male voice stammered out.

The trucks turned down the main road. The road toward our buildings.

I hope that's not who I think it is.

I looked between the trees to my side for any sign of Ash.

Ash? What do you see?

There was a long pause before his voice filled my head. It was different, indescribable, but distinctly him. *Men. Trucks.*

How many? I paused after my words. Ash doesn't know how to count. How was I going to do this? *A big pack or small?*

Big.

My stomach dropped. I could see the few trucks through the trees, but if Ash said it was a big pack, that means a lot of people.

I looked at Jace. *We need to get back, now.*

Follow me.

Before I did, I scanned the woods for any sign of Ash. *Stay safe and out of sight.* I heard no response, so I only hoped that he heard it.

I followed Jace out of the woods. We stayed crouched, ready to drop down into the cover of the ground if we needed to, but by the time we reached the road, the trucks were gone. They probably made it to the gate by now. My body tensed, and I growled at the thought of Old Bob being there without me.

Jace turned and faced me. *Stop. You need to trust me right now. I have a way there, but I need you calm and collected.* I looked at him a moment before giving a curt nod.

He took my hand and led me across the road to the first building, and we slipped inside. We weaved through the halls and doors to another door. He peeked outside before leading us straight to the next building. We repeated this through four buildings, then in the fifth one, the hall we went through was lined with small groups of people. Their small homes were divided by sheets of fabric hanging from the ceiling. Belongings piled in their respective squares. We slowly moved down the middle, meeting the scared eyes of a few.

"Jace," a small voice shrieked and a young white-haired boy ran into Jace, giving him a tight hug. "They're here. They have my sister!" My jaw dropped at the sight of the child Jace saved from the bomb.

Jace crouched down. "It's all right, Kemp. Did you see how many there were?" He kept his voice low and calm.

Kemp looked at him; tears streamed down his dirt-smudged cheeks, faded bruises still covered part of his face. "There were a lot of trucks full with lots of guns. He's not happy."

"Who isn't happy?" I asked carefully.

Kemp looked at me. "Izan. He's here to kill us."

My stomach dropped, and I moved toward the window. Jace stood but held Kemp's hand. Looking down at the street in front of the gate, I paled. There were indeed many trucks. Eight. Most of the men and women stood on the beds with guns pointed at the fence. In front of the truck was a row of armed men with guns pointed at a group of civilians, who all huddled on the ground.

One man stood in front. He was tall, with the same thick dark hair and eyes as Lucia's. He rubbed his gloved hands together before yelling out, his voice echoing in the courtyard. "Lucia! Sister. Come out to play!"

Chapter 38

Jace

Kemp clutched me as we peered out the window and down at his sister, who had a gun pointed at her back. Silent tears wet his cheeks, and I squeezed his hand. I hadn't spoken with him since I saw him in the small medical center, but for some reason, he seemed to have taken me as someone he can trust. The thought warmed me, and I vowed to do whatever I could to be that person for him.

Eden watched with clenched fists, and when I looked at her face, her eyes glowed with rage.

"We have to do something." Her voice was low.

"There's only two of us. What can we do against all of them? They have guns."

She looked at me. "We have wolves."

"Still not enough."

Kemp sniffed and turned his face into my stomach. I put a gentle hand on the back of his head. "You have to help her, Jace. Please."

Letting out a sigh, I met Eden's eyes again but still gave a slight head shake. "It's too risky."

"We can't just leave them."

An old man stepped up to the window. "Just wait. Lucia won't let them down." His voice was weak but confident. My chest clenched in hope that he wasn't wrong.

Eden looked at him. "I hope you're right because if I have to go out there, things will get bloody."

"You're not going out there," I said through clenched teeth.

"We'll see." She kept her back to me. I could see the taut muscles through her shirt.

The number of guards behind the gates grew. Although they all pointed guns toward Izan and his army, he didn't seem the slightest concerned and didn't give them even a glance as he stepped past the gate. Instead of moving in on him, they all took a step back. You could see the fear in their eyes.

"Lucia, come out, come out!" Izan held his hands open and wide at his sides and took a few more steps forward. He stopped when Raul emerged from the door. "Raul. My former best friend. How good it is to see you. You wouldn't have happened to see my sister around, have you? We have some business to take care of."

"She's not coming out." Raul's voice was clipped. He stepped toward Izan empty handed. Why didn't he have a gun?

Izan dropped his hands and laughed. "You keeping her locked up, are you?" He paused to watch Raul, and delight sparked in his eyes when he saw Raul's jaw jump.

My eyes snapped to the side. Eden had slowly moved her way to the doorway. While the door wasn't fully open, only cracked, the few guards that were near it hadn't noticed her yet. If she made one wrong move, they would, and things would get ugly fast.

Eden. Don't.

She didn't look at me, but I felt the tension within her. *I can't just watch. I've already called Ash. He's here.*

They'll shoot you all.

She turned to look at me, her face vacant. She knew that was a possibility, and she didn't care.

Wait. I'm coming.

No. Stay with the boy.

I shook my head. *Where you go, I go. Remember?*

Even if it's to death?

I paused and we watched each other a moment before I nodded. *Even if.*

Crouching down, I took Kemp's shoulders. "All right. Eden and I are going to try something. Just stay here. Safe and out of sight. All right?" He nodded quickly before wrapping his arms around my neck. His tears wet my shirt, and I squeezed him close. If anything happened to his sister, he would have no one left. I couldn't let that happen.

I gently pushed him back and passed him off to the old man, who gave me an earnest nod.

I reached Eden's side and peered out. The door opened out behind the bulk of Izan's group, which could be good or bad. We had the element of surprise, but then they may spook and just start shooting, ending in many deaths, probably including our own.

"What's your plan?" I whispered into her ear. I fought the urge to pull her to me. If this was the last time we were together, I wanted to show her how much I cared for her.

"That." She jutted her chin toward something down the road.

Slowly moving in our direction was Ash and his pack, only it had grown. There were now closer to twenty wolves. Ash was central and a few paces ahead of the rest, who fanned out in a long line behind him. Their heads were low as they stalked toward Izan's people, eyes intent on their targets.

As they neared, one of the guards in the back spotted them and froze. She said something in Spanish, and the two guards near her turned. Their eyes widened, and they turned a few shaky guns toward the wolves.

"They are going to shoot them," I warned Eden.

The nervous commotion grew, and the other members of Izan's crew slowly turned back to see what was happening. Their focus was split.

"Izan," one of the men in the front called to him. "We have a... situation."

Izan stiffened, turning from Raul to look behind them. He spotted the wolves and his eyes widened. Scanning his people, he noted their tension. "You'll have guns, don't you? Shoot them!"

Before I could stop her, Eden stepped out of the door.

"I wouldn't if I were you." Her voice was loud and commanding but didn't hold the growl I knew it could. She was holding back.

Izan looked at her and furrowed his brow. His people shifted, now with three places to point their guns, unsure of which danger was the most imminent.

"Who are you?"

Eden slowly moved out to stand in front of Ash. He stepped up beside her. Her claws were curled and ready at her side, and she sneered to show her fangs. "My name is Eden. These are my wolves, and if you touch them, you will regret it."

"Izan," one of his soldiers said, stepping back from Eden. He said something fast and shaky in Spanish, but Izan didn't move. He kept his gaze locked on Eden.

I hesitated at the door, unsure if I should step out or not. If I did, I lost the element of surprise, but I would be closer to helping Eden if she needed me.

Stay. Protect the kid.

I let out a frustrated breath when her voice filled my head. She had a point, but I hated it.

Izan squared off with Eden, showing he wasn't frazzled by her. "What is it you want, Eden of the wolves?"

Eden smiled and started to take a few steps forward. Ash and the wolves followed. "I'd really like it if you left. Leave the people and drive away. If you do it nicely, then no one gets hurt."

Izan chuckled, watching her. His chuckle built to an echoing laugh. He turned and looked back at Raul, whose eyes were as wide as saucers. "Where did you find this one, Raul? She's "—he turned back to Eden—"entertaining."

"Well, I'm glad you find me amusing, but I'm very serious." Eden stopped just steps from the last group of Izan's soldiers. "Leave. Now." She dropped her chin, baring her teeth. The soldiers gasped and stepped back, mumbling what sounded like a prayer in

Spanish. I don't know Spanish, but I'm pretty sure they were saying the word *demon*.

My fists clenched into balls, and I lifted my foot to step outside, but everyone turned as Lucia's voice rang throughout the courtyard.

"Izan, how inconsiderate of you to show up unannounced."

Izan turned, obviously nervous to put Eden at his back. Lucia watched his hesitation and smiled. "I see you've met my new ally, Eden. She's a delight, isn't she?"

"Lucia. I'm happy to find you so well." His voice didn't have the confidence it did when he first arrived. The surprises of the day clearly rattled him.

"What do you want, Izan?"

He laughed. "For you to surrender, sister. You know that you don't have the strength to take me down."

"Don't I?" Her face was set in stone and Izan blinked.

"Well, your spy"—Izan held out a hand, keeping his eyes locked on Lucia. At his command, one of his men opened a door to a truck and dragged out a bruised and bloody man. Izan grabbed the man's jacket and tossed him forward onto the ice-covered ground. "Your spy didn't say anything about a wolf girl."

"That's because he's loyal. You should try that sometime, maybe today? Show your loyalty to your family. Kneel to me."

"So loyal he'd lead us right here?"

"Maybe I wanted him to. Maybe that was the plan." Lucia's response was so quick I almost thought she was telling the truth, but then I noticed a slight twitch on the edge of her eyes as she kept them locked on her brother. She was a good liar.

Izan chuckled again. "Lucia, you know you don't have the strength—"

"I'm the eldest!" Her voice rang so loudly that Izan took a small step back. "My right. I should rule. That is what father wanted, and you know this. You were just too greedy to accept it!"

His smile faded. "That's because you are weak! You don't have what it takes to lead."

"You can either kneel to me, Izan, or face my wrath." Her bluff may have worked if Raul's eyes hadn't snapped to her. He quickly turned back to Izan, but it was noticed.

"I don't think you have any wrath, Lucia, besides wolf girl, but we can take care of her and her wolves with a few pulls of a trigger." He paused, taking a few slow steps toward her. "I'll ask you again. Surrender and kneel to me and no one will get hurt. If you don't"—he looked to all the civilians, kneeling on the ground—"everyone will die."

Lucia stood silent and watched him. As everyone waited for her response, my stomach tightened and the air was thick with anticipation. She knew she'd lost; she didn't have the strength. That's why we needed to plan, to strategize, if we were going to beat him. But then he showed up unannounced.

I glanced at Eden and Ash, who patiently waited for what Lucia would do. I feared if Lucia did surrender, Eden would attack. I put a hand on the door preparing to bolt out and fight.

Lucia took a step forward, brushing off Raul's arm when he went to stop her. "I have a better deal."

"Oh?" A smile snaked across Izan's face. "What might that be?"

"We fight."

"Lucia, no," Raul said, but she ignored him.

"We fight for control."

Izan laughed. "You know that's not how it works. Tradition—"

"To hell with tradition!" Lucia screamed. Her cheeks were red with rage. "You always say that you can best me with knives, say I cheat whenever I win. Well, let us settle this once and for all. With knives."

"You sure you want to do this?" Izan's face was grave. He almost seemed like his original reason for being there was a game, and now that she was giving a real solution, he was unsure.

"I'm sure. The winner rules, and the loser's people must kneel."

I looked at Eden from the crack in the door.

Can she win?

Eden's eyes flicked toward me. *I sure hope so because I don't know what will happen if she doesn't.*

Raul stepped up to Lucia's side. "I'll fight in place of Lucia."

"No." She looked up at him. His lips were pursed to contain his anger. "This has to be done by me. There's no other choice."

Raul's eyes were pleading when he looked down at her. "Lucia, please."

"What about us?" Izan asked, already shrugging out of his jacket. He didn't even bristle at the freezing cold wind that whipped his hair around.

Lucia looked at him. "What about us? The fight is to the death, so whoever doesn't win won't have to worry about the other."

Izan stood rigid, two knives in each hand. "To the death it is, then."

I slowly opened the door wider and met Eden's eyes.

Shit.

Chapter 39

Eden

Once the deal was made, the rest of Lucia's people emerged from the building. They met Izan's group and formed a large circle in the courtyard. Lucia swung her arms, flipping her knives in the air to warm her body up. After taking off her jacket for easier movement, she pulled her hair into a high ponytail, defining her high cheekbones.

Raul spoke quietly to her, with pleading eyes, but she pushed him away hard enough that he stood at the edge of the circle, tight lipped and tense. His eyes burned into Izan. If she lost, Izan wouldn't survive long.

Jace and I weaved our way through the group. Most of Izan's people parted the way, too scared to be near me. The wolves stayed on the road near the building to keep from causing panic, but they were close enough to hear if they were needed. We reached where

Old Bob and Bomber had emerged from the building and stopped at their sides.

"Looks like we didn't have to go searching for him after all," Bomber said.

"Looks like it," I said.

Lucia and Izan warmed up their joints, rolling their shoulders and shaking out their legs, neither taking their eyes off the other.

"Any ideas what we do if she loses?" Jace asked, his voice was barely audible over the screaming crowd.

Raul turned his head back toward us and narrowed his eyes. "She won't lose."

Old Bob gave a quick shake of the head when Jace opened his mouth to respond.

"Who's to be referee? Make sure there isn't any... cheating." Izan's voice echoed over the crowd, and his people hollered in agreement.

"I've never cheated. Plus, how do you cheat in a knife fight?"

"Fair enough." He paused before letting his head fall back to holler, "Let's fight!"

Lucia nodded, and they started to circle each other, their knives ready in both hands. The crowd was a hum of cheers and screams that vibrated through my entire body.

This may just end up as a blood fight after all. Jace's eyes scanned the people.

If it does, we get our people and get out.

Agreed.

Izan made the first move, lunging in with a swipe of his knife, but Lucia easily evaded it. I was impressed with her quickness and skill. She smoothly maneuvered the knives in her hands for a strike in any direction.

They took turns, lunging and swiping, neither able to make contact with the other.

"You've been practicing, sister," Izan said right before he lunged again. Lucia jumped back but slipped on a piece of ice.

Raul took a quick step forward, but a man beside him grabbed his arm, keeping him in place. His jaw ticked as he snapped his arm from the other man's grip.

Lucia quickly stood, but not before Izan was able to move in and slice her arm. His people screamed louder, slapping each other on their backs. Lucia stood and hissed down at her cut arm. Shaking it out, she positioned her knives again.

"Ready to quit yet?" Izan goaded her.

"Just a scratch."

She charged him, but when he lunged for her, she dropped down and slid on the ice, positioning her knife just right to slice his left calf. He twisted with a scream and reached out to stab her, but she rolled away and jumped up. She stepped back and put distance between them.

"Ready to quit yet?" she mocked him.

Panting, he stood, favoring his left leg. "Just a scratch."

Something between them changed. It was no longer a fun family feud; now, it was real. Their attacks became quicker, harsher, and more deliberate. The crowd's cheers grew louder, and the air around us became more hostile.

My breaths quickened in response to all the tension in the air. Baring my teeth, I closed my eyes and clenched my jaw, focusing to control my breath. Warm fingers twined into my hand with a squeeze. Opening my eyes, I turned and saw Jace watching me carefully.

You all right?

Just all the hostility. It affects me.

He squeezed my hand again, and we turned back to the fight.

Both Lucia and Izan had bleeding cuts in different parts of their bodies, and despite the cold, sweat washed the dirt from their faces. Izan charged Lucia headfirst, wrapping his arms around her waist, taking her down. She fell onto her back with a loud grunt, dropping one of her knives. Izan pulled his hands out from behind her as he straddled her. With a quick flip of his knife, he stabbed it into her upper arm, the same arm she held her only knife. Lucia's scream rang in the courtyard, and the crowd quieted, with eager anticipation of a possible ending to an epic family feud.

Izan pinned her down, panting as he moved closer to gaze into her eyes, their noses almost touching. With one hand piercing the knife into her arm and the other going to her throat, he said, "Last chance, sister. Kneel before me."

Raul took a few steps forward, his fists clenched and eyes struggling between his love for Lucia and the rules the fight must go by. If he interfered, it may forfeit everything.

Izan looked at him and smirked. "Doesn't this look familiar, Raul? Only your lover is my sister, so I'm a little more lenient." His face turned to rage. "You didn't provide mine with that luxury, did you?"

"Raul"—Lucia gasped out, straining to look at him—"don't."
Raul's mouth tightened with his restraint.

The crowd was silent. The only sounds heard were the grunts and labored breaths between Lucia and Izan. He looked down at her, slowly twisting the knife in her arm, and she screamed.

I squeezed Jace's hand and looked at Raul. What would it feel like to be that helpless and watch the one you love be tortured and killed? I could feel the desperation and fear roll off him, and my breath caught in my throat. I envied his restraint. If this was one of my family, I wouldn't be standing here. Izan would be dead.

Lucia let out a loud scream before she leaned in as close to Izan's face as she could get, then she dropped back slightly before propelling forward again. After lifting her leg up, she hooked it around his head and pushed him back with her legs. He dropped the grip on the knife in her arm, and she used the chance to stab him in the thigh and push him off her. He screamed and grabbed at his leg. She swiftly sat up, twisted her legs around his body, pinning his arms under them, then grabbed his hair. She yanked his head back and placed her knife against his throat.

Setting her mouth against his ear, she said, "Last chance. Kneel or die."

My jaw dropped. I glanced around me to see a circle of stunned faces, including Raul.

Izan grunted. "I have to... say. I'm... impressed."

Lucia smiled. "Is that your answer?"

"If I kneel, what will happen to my people?"

A gasp moved through his people. They glanced at each other in disbelief that he would even think of surrendering.

Lucia's eyes widened. "If they kneel, they live. Otherwise, they'll be killed." When he didn't say anything for a moment, she added, "I'm not that horrible of a person, Izan. I'm your sister. We were raised by the same man."

Izan chuckled but winced when the skin of his throat cut into the knife from his movement. "You choose."

"What?" Lucia's grip was loosening.

"I said, you choose. You choose if I should live or die."

"What is this Izan? That's not part of the rules. You either kneel or die." Raul yelled, but Lucia ignored him. She was still, thinking on his words.

Finally, she dropped the knife. "Because you're my brother, I'll spare your life, but also because you're my younger brother, you'll kneel before me." She stood and quickly kicked the knives out of his reach.

Izan sat a moment to gain his bearings. He panted before he turned himself onto his knees to face his sister and looked up at her with a grin. "Lucia Rivera Mendez, I kneel before you to show my loyalty. I will fight for you, protect you with my life, and follow your commands. I will do all of these under penalty of death."

Raul stepped up to her side, towering down at Izan. "And I won't be so lenient."

Izan looked up at him with a cocky smile. "I'm sure you won't." He reached his hand up to Lucia, who hesitated, but then she took it and pulled him up. He turned to his people, who looked at him with wide eyes. "You will all pledge your allegiance to Lucia. If you don't, I'll kill you myself."

The crowd started to disperse, and Bomber and Old Bob turned to us and I said, "That was too easy."

Old Bob set his mouth into a thin line, looking over at Izan. "We'll need to watch him carefully."

"We'll need to watch all of his people," I said, trying to shake the feeling that Lucia was just played.

Chapter 40

Jace

Tensions were high at breakfast. It took an order from Lucia for Raul to get Izan's people set up. He still didn't trust Izan and his people, even though they had all knelt in front of a bleeding, dirty, and tired Lucia and pledged their loyalty—some more convincingly than others. She watched them all with the same stone-cold face.

A woman cleaned and bandaged Lucia's wound. Lucia sat at the end of the table, with her food untouched in front of her. Izan sat to her left, Eden on her right.

I took a bite of my eggs, then elbowed Eden gently in the side. She blinked and shook her head before focusing back down at her food. Old Bob and Bomber didn't touch their food, only sipped their tea.

Once her arm was bandaged, Lucia waved the woman away and leaned forward. "All right, so now that's settled, let's get to planning the next adventure." She picked up her fork and smiled at everyone before taking a bite of her eggs.

Izan looked at her. "What adventure?"

Lucia waved toward Eden with her fork, speaking around her food. "Eden, explain."

"We're all moving north to take down the leader, Zane."

"No, we're not."

Lucia stopped and glanced at him, but Eden spoke first, leaning forward over the table. "Well, good thing it's not your decision then. We made a deal with Lucia. Help take you down, then she helps us."

Izan's smile grew. "Well, that's easy to remedy. You didn't help her, so she doesn't have to help you."

Eden growled but stopped when I put my hand on hers and gave it a squeeze. "It's not your call."

Lucia put up a hand. "Quiet." She looked at Izan a moment, thinking. "He's right technically."

Old Bob and Bomber both set their cups down, and Eden snapped her gaze to Lucia's. "Not because we didn't want to."

Lucia waved her hand again. "No, no. I get that, but—"

"But if you don't help us, the threat of Zane won't go away. We can't take him down without you, and he'll come south. When that happens, he may be stronger and have more people. You could kiss your new leadership goodbye," Old Bob said. His voice was steady and held the authority of an experienced leader. One you could trust.

Izan looked at him. "We don't know if this Zane will come south. Why give up what we have on a guess?"

Old Bob let out a soft laugh and looked down at his mug. "You're right. It is a guess, but if that guess does come true"—he looked up and met Izan's eyes—"there will be no one left to help you."

"We have power and weapons. I don't think this Zane is anything we can't handle."

Eden snatched her hand from mine and slammed both of her claws onto the table, creating a clanking of dishes that rang through the room. Food spilled onto the table, and Izan jumped, pushing his chair back to give some distance. Eden leaned forward with a sneer, and a growl rumbled in her throat. "You have no idea what Zane is capable of." She glanced down at her claws. "I used to have regular nails." She smiled to show her fangs. "And teeth."

Izan's eyes widened, and he swallowed hard.

"It's not just strength and power that Zane deals in, Izan," Old Bob said gently. "It's biological warfare. Trust us when we tell you that if you try and defeat him on your own, you will fail. Just the same as if we try without you. We need each other, and forgive me for being dramatic, but the human race needs us to succeed." He gave Eden and me an apologetic look after the words left his mouth, but I only returned it with an understanding nod.

Izan looked back at Eden, then to me. Putting my hand on Eden's, I gently tugged her back into her seat. While I held her firmly, she matched her breath with mine, slowly calming her nerves.

Lucia cleared her throat. "All right"—she looked to Izan—"let's get one thing straight. You have no say in any of my decisions.

You can tell me your opinions, but I don't have to consider them. I made a deal with Eden and her people; we will abide by it." She looked at Old Bob and Bomber. "We need to plan how to move everyone north now that winter is here."

Izan sat back with a grumble and crossed his arms. He met Eden's stare again, but when her lip twitched, he quickly looked away and met my eyes. "You the same as her?"

"Almost." I smirked and looked at her. "But not as magnificent." Eden snorted and rolled her eyes. My smile grew at the effect I had on her.

Eden stood, pushing her half-eaten plate away. "I need some air."

I watched her tense back disappear through the door before I turned back to Izan and fixed him with a hard stare. "Don't underestimate her."

He smirked. "And you?"

I leaned forward, resting my forearms on the table. "Let me rephrase that. Don't underestimate any of us." I nodded toward Old Bob and Bomber. "None of us will hesitate to kill you." I looked at Lucia who evaluated my words. "I'm sure Raul thinks the same." She said nothing, only gave a single nod.

"Maybe I made the wrong decision," Izan mumbled.

Lucia turned to him with raised eyebrows. "You'd have rather died?"

"You wouldn't have killed me." Izan leaned back in his chair and gently tapped his fingers on the table as he said, "You always had this fantasy about our family."

"Fantasy!" Lucia narrowed her eyes. "I may have let you live because you're my brother. I did give you a second chance, but don't for one second think I wouldn't have killed you. You step one toe out of line, and you're dead."

He chuckled. "Ah, Lucia. It's all right. This temper is why I let you win."

She stood, grunting quietly as she held her arm carefully. "Let me win?" She clenched her jaw and looked down at the table. Izan watched her with twinkling eyes, loving the fact that he was under her skin. She finally let out a long breath and glanced at everyone in the room. "Give me an hour. We'll start planning, then."

Everyone nodded and watched her leave the room.

～

I stood and cracked my back with a groan. We had been planning for hours, and I was losing my patience. That says something since I'm the most patient person I know.

"There is no way to make it in one trip. We don't have the supplies or vehicles," Old Bob repeated again. We've been saying this over and over, but Lucia and Bomber have been trying to come up with any way to get everyone north in one trip.

Eden reached her arms up before pushing her claws through her thick, auburn hair. "I'm not affected by the cold. I can go on foot with the wolves."

I stiffened. "I'm not letting you go alone."

"I agree," Old Bob said.

"Fine. I'll take Brian."

My eyebrows rose and a twinge of rejection hit me. Why would she want Brian to go with her over me?

Her cheek twitched as she read my mind. "I need Brian to go with me so he can tell me what we're walking into, since we'll get there first, leaving a few days before the others." I opened my mouth, but she quickly continued, "I need you to stay with everyone to make sure they get to the camp safely."

And to watch Izan and Lucia. Our eyes were frozen together. No one but Old Bob knew she was talking to me. To the others, it was just an intimate look. *You're the only one I really trust. I need you with them, Jace.*

After a long moment of silence, I sighed and said, "Fine."

"All right. We'll start first thing in the morning. Pack everything we can carry, and we'll get moving in two days. It would be best if we are able to get north before the first heavy snowfall," Lucia said.

Everyone nodded and grumbled before retreating to their rooms for the night.

~

We took two days to pack and get organized. Six people and half a truck bed of supplies filled each of the trucks. The people outside would get the blankets and warm clothes, and every hour, we would shuffle, switching people from inside the car to take their turn in the truck beds.

Eden and I rode in the bed of one of the trucks, with five of the wolves including Ash. We hoped the other wolves would meet us back at Bomber's. Eden and I didn't talk much about her leaving. I kept myself busy with planning and work so as to not think about all the things that could happen to her while she was gone, but I also knew better than to insist she stay. She was strong and smart; plus, she would have Brian and the wolves.

It was way past dark when we arrived back at Bomber's. He was outside talking to his people before all the trucks were even parked. They quickly moved into action, showing Lucia's people their places to warm up and rest.

Jumping down from the bed of the truck, I smiled when I spotted messy white hair and blue eyes getting out of one of the cars in the front.

"Jace," Kemp yelled as he rushed at me, hitting me with a force I never thought possible in a child so small.

"Hey, buddy." I squeezed him before ruffled his hair. He grinned up at me but didn't let go. "You know you don't have to hug me every time we see each other. I just saw you an hour ago at the last stop."

"I know, but I want to. My sister always says to let the people you care about know before it's too late."

My smile softened, and I squeezed him again. "Wise words." I felt eyes on me, and I turned to see Eden sitting on the back of the truck bed, her feet dangling as she watched me with a smirk. "I never thought of you as a kid type."

"And?"

She jumped down, slowly making her way over to us. "Can't say I dislike it." Her eyes twinkled as she gave my shoulder a little shove with her own before she continued on into the building.

I swear she swished her hips a little more and a laugh resonated within my head.

I cleared my throat and looked back at Kemp. He watched me with a much-too-knowing smile for a child. I ruffled his hair again. "Let's get inside. I don't want you to freeze out here." Slinging my arm around his shoulder, I walked him inside.

Chapter 41

Eden

"We need to leave now if we are going to make any ground before dark," Brian said, slinging a pack onto his back. His chin had grown scruffier in the past few days. The sunlight hit small patches of grey, aging him much older than his eyes told. He looked at Cal. "We'll be moving hard, so your training will hopefully pay off. We don't have time to waste."

Bomber stepped up, wrapped in a thick jacket that bunched at his neck. "We hope to be on the road in the next few days with the first group."

Brian nodded. "It should take you two to three days to drive. We should be there in a week."

"A week?" I screeched. "It took us two weeks when we walked down here earlier, and it wasn't this cold. If we come across snow, that'll slow us down."

Brian fixed me with a stare. "That's why I said we'll move hard. I took a week to find you. We'll rest for short periods, not whole nights. We don't have time to waste. I can't imagine what has happened in the time I've been gone." His voice turned soft and quiet. He's concerned about the people, yes, but I know he's mostly concerned about Sarah.

"I'll be with the first group in case we make it there before you. People will know me," Old Bob said. He nodded at me; his cheeks and nose were as red as a ripe apple.

Jace leaned on the doorframe with crossed arms next to Tate and Lillyanne. He watched us with a grave, worried look. He hadn't spoken much to me since it was decided that he would stay instead of going with me. I knew it hurt him, but I truly did need him here. He was one of the only people I trusted.

I gave him a smile, but he moved inside without returning one. Tate watched him go in before giving me a remorseful look.

Jace! I was met with nothing but silence, but I could feel his mind open. He could hear me. *I'm sorry, but I need someone I trust here. I'll be fine, I promise.* Nothing again.

Sighing, I looked at the others. They watched me, waiting patiently. Pressing my lips together, I nodded and started forward. "Let's go." I don't wait for them as I charged down the road back toward home.

~

We jogged carefully on the frozen ground, fanned out in a row with some wolves in front and some behind us. We continued on the road, but we would soon be moving into the woods. Our quick breaths left a long path of white clouds behind us.

Eden!

I stopped, my feet sliding on the ground. Brian and Cal didn't notice and continued forward. Turning around, I squinted at the bright sun reflecting off the icy ground and saw a dark figure jogging toward us. Jace.

Eden, I'm sorry.

I smiled as a wave of relief flowed through me, and I ran back toward him. His shaggy dark hair blew wildly in the wind. We stopped, facing each other. "What are you doing here?"

He panted and looked down shyly. "I couldn't let us part like that. One thing I've learned over the past few months is to not let the people you care about go without telling them how you feel."

My heart skipped, and I focused hard to keep my feet right where they were and not throw my arms around his neck. Not yet at least. "And how do you feel?"

He looked up at me. "You know how I feel." He swallowed, his throat bobbing nervously. "It scares me how much I care for you. I don't understand it, but... I don't think we're supposed to, really. I'm still hurt—"

"I didn't mean to hurt you."

"I know." He took a small step toward me. "It's just hard for me. All the women I have known have always needed me. The girls in the city were helpless. Always wanting a guy to do this and that." He smirked. "It's great for the male ego." He paused, gently moving a stray hair from my brow. "But you're nothing like them. You are strong, smart, and independent. You don't *need* me."

My jaw dropped. "I do need you, Jace."

"You may need me emotionally, but you don't need me. You can handle yourself." I opened my mouth, but he put his thumb on my bottom lip to stop me. "It's not a bad thing. It's just an adjustment for the men in your life. That's all."

I felt my neck and cheeks warm, and I met his blue eyes. He gave me his lopsided grin, showing the dimple on his right cheek. My heart fluttered; I loved that dimple.

"So, we're good?"

"We're good." He paused, and I let out a breath, then he continued, "If you promise not to go rogue. Don't do anything to save the world or anything rash."

"I would never—"

"Promise me, Eden."

I bit my lip, keeping my gaze matched with his. "Fine."

He smiled, his shoulders slumping in relief. "Good. Now, may I kiss you goodbye?"

"You're asking me?" I laughed.

"Well, I don't want to assume. You can take me down, and the ground is rather cold—"

I moved forward and met his lips, silencing him. I reached up on my toes and melted into his strength and warmth, letting my arms snake around his neck. Putting his arms around my waist, he pulled me closer and held me firm. For that moment, we weren't standing on an icy, cold road with an unknown future. We just were. We were together. Together with no known threats or problems. It was everything I wanted. Jace and safety.

I slowly pulled from him. "I hope one day it can be like this, only I'm leaving for a fishing trip, not to save the world."

He laughed quietly. "Me too."

We stared at each other, neither of us moving away, but we both startled at the whistles and hollers that echoed from the others. I turned to see Brian and Cal watching us impatiently, but they had amused faces.

"If you two are done, we really should get moving!" Brian yelled.

I looked back at Jace. "Great. I won't hear the end of it for the next few days."

"Oh. It's all right. You are a strong, smart, indepen—"

"Oh, shut up!" I laughed, watching him slowly walk away.

"Be careful, all right?"

"You too."

With his smile and a wink, he turned and ran back to Bomber's.

We moved almost continuously, only taking short breaks for a few hours, taking turns keeping watch. The wolves stayed with us, but they were also helpful in hunting and bringing us food. I never thought my bond with Ash could get stronger than it was, but being able to communicate with him had made him even more real... or me more animal. Brian encouraged me to practice talking to him, so I did. Although he could only reply in one or two words, so it wasn't full conversations, it was more than anyone else could do.

We arrived back at the camp in a week's time. The camp was empty due to the weather. Brian led us farther into the trees to a group of small cabins clustered together. Smoke billowed from the chimneys and lines of clothes dried in the cold air. Work areas were set up outside for various tasks, such as cleaning animals from a kill.

Careful. We don't know what has happened in the time I was gone. Brian led us slowly toward the closest cabin.

No one was outside, but I heard voices. *People are here.*

Yes, but what people? That's what I'm concerned about.

My stomach dropped at the tension in his voice. Had it really gotten that bad in the short time after we left?

One of the cabin doors opened, and a petite woman stepped out, shrugging her jacket up to cover her neck, her long brown hair bunching in the back. Brian stopped and let out a long breath. Sarah.

I moved to call to her, but Brian grabbed my arm with a small shake of his head. Sarah stepped down the steps and turned, freezing at the sight of us. Her cheeks were already red from the cold, but they brightened and she smiled.

A squeal echoed out among the trees as she bounded forward, yelling, "Brian! Eden!"

Brian didn't hesitate and moved toward her. She was in his arms, burying her face in the crook of his neck. He held her so close and firm that I almost lost sight of where she started and he began.

"You all are really a sappy lot, aren't you?" Cal grumbled behind us.

Brian pulled away and looked down at Sarah, ignoring Cal's comment. Sarah looked over at me, and her eyes grew wider.

"Eden."

I held out my arms. "Hey."

She laughed and pulled me into a hug. A much stronger hug than expected. "He found you." She pushed me away, holding me out to get a good look. It was such a motherly action that my heart flickered with loss. It's what I would have expected Ellie to do, but now she wasn't here to do it. "Well. You look well. Come in. It's cold. LaRae just made some dinner."

"Oh, fantastic. I'm starving." Cal pushed past us toward the cabin. Sarah watched after him a moment, then looked back at Brian.

"You get used to him."

We entered the cabin, filled with the smells of roasted meat and firewood. LaRae gave us a greeting very similar to Sarah's, only her hug wasn't as firm. Dr. Hahn, frailer than I remembered, shook our hands with a large smile. I stood stunned to see them alive and well.

"You survived?"

"Yes, yes," Dr. Hahn said. "We were sick, very sick for some time. But we healed."

I looked at Brian. "I don't understand."

"Well, not everyone survived, but the majority did. Because they were Chimera, most healed quickly." I turned to see Jon leaning on the wall with crossed arms. He smiled. "Never thought I'd say this, but it's good to see you, Eden."

I grinned. "Likewise."

As we sat around a small table having a warm meal, my heart began to feel slightly more at home.

Chapter 42

Jace

"Good! Now try putting more strength behind that punch." I set my feet and held up my hands, waiting for Kemp to punch one. He held his fists up to protect his face, just like I taught him, and watched me carefully. With a swift movement, he punched his right fist out into my hand and brought it right back to his face.

"Careful!" Lacy, his sister, called out to him. I met her eyes, but she quickly looked away, a blush moving up her neck to her cheeks. She had opened up somewhat in the last week, but whatever happened to her after their parents were killed must have been traumatizing, and I wasn't going to pry. Kemp has mentioned a few things, but I didn't push. It's not my business.

Kemp and I continued working for the next hour. We practiced his punching, strength, and endurance. I had never seen a kid so young take to physical activity with such focus and dedication, especially after healing from a bomb blast. I smiled at him and rustled his hair. "All right. I think it's time for a break."

"Ahhh, come on. I can keep going. I swear!"

I headed toward the building his sister and he were staying in, along with many of the other folks. "I'm sure you can." I laughed. "Blame it on me. I need a break."

He giggled, hopping around me in a circle. "Are you telling me you're an old man?"

I gave him a funny face, and his laugh grew. Lacy handed me a cup of water, smiling down at Kemp's giggles.

"I can't remember the last time I heard him laugh like that." She watched him sadly as he grabbed his own glass and filled it. Water dribbled down his chin while he guzzled it down.

I studied her carefully. She was about Eden's age, maybe slightly younger, but her green eyes seemed older. They were the eyes of someone who had seen much more than someone their age should have. She caught me watching her and quickly fussed with her blonde hair, walking away.

"I can train you too," I said gently. She kept her back to me, making herself busy with putting items into the single bag they are allowed to bring north.

"I don't see what the point would be."

I stepped up next to her and set my empty cup on the table. "To defend yourself. You never know what could happen." I kept my voice soft and soothing, like I was talking to a scared rabbit.

She glanced at me, her eyes glistening with tears. "I... I—"

"It's all right. I won't make you do anything. If you don't want to train, you don't have to." She looked over at Kemp who skipped to her side. I smiled and said, "But it's a standing offer."

"Thank you."

"Standing offer for what?" Kemp asked, starting to punch my belly.

I moved and blocked him, giving him small jabs and pokes in his side. "An offer to learn how to take you down now that you think you're a hot shot." I picked him up and flipped him over my shoulder, smiling big when his laughter pulled small giggles and smiles from everyone in the large room. If anything could take the solemnness out of anything, it was a child's laughter.

"Jace."

I turned and saw Bomber standing in the doorway. I gently put Kemp down.

"We need you." His eyes skimmed over everyone in the room.

"Be right there."

He nodded and moved back to the main building.

I pulled Kemp's head into a headlock and rustled his hair again. "All right, Tiger, I'll see you later. Be good for your sister." I smiled at her watching us. "Think about my offer." She nodded quickly and looked back to her work.

"See you later, Jace."

"See you, buddy." I jogged outside after Bomber.

~

"So what are you saying?" Bomber growled at Lucia, raking his rough hands through his dark hair.

She sat in her usual seat, leaning back with her hands clasped in front of her. The perfect picture of relaxation. "I'm saying we're going to have to take a third trip. We just can't make it safely in two."

"That's going to push our timeline back."

"Would you rather our fighters freeze to death?" She narrowed her eyes at him.

I looked at Bomber. "It should be fine. Eden and the others should be there by now. Old Bob is there. Just take the second group tomorrow, and I'll follow with the last. No point in grumbling about it." He glared at me but didn't respond, other than to sit back in his chair.

Lucia looked at me. "I'll stay with you for the last trip."

"No. I think you need to go in the next round along with Izan. There will be too many of your people there; they'll need someone to give orders."

She watched me a moment. "What about the people left here?"

I rubbed my tired eyes. I needed sleep, but it didn't come easy lately, and if I did sleep, it didn't last long. "I say leave the ones that can help but can't fight."

Jimmy leaned forward, smirking. "Like the kid and his cute sister?" I snapped my eyes to him with a low growl. "I see you getting close to them. Wonder what Eden would think?"

"You know nothing of my relationship with them. I'm helping the kid learn to defend himself. It's more than what you do."

"What about the sister?" He raised one eyebrow and leaned to the side onto his walking stick. His leg was healing enough to where he could put a slight amount of weight on it, but he still gimped around with the stick.

I leaned forward and bared my teeth. "What about her?" My eyes never dropped from his, but he was not affected by my anger.

"Pretty defensive."

"All right. Will you two stop this peacock dance?" Lucia sat forward. "Jimmy, leave Jace alone. The kid likes him."

Jimmy snickered. "Looks like the sister does too."

I swung my fist fast and true, landing right on his jaw. His head snapped to the side, spraying blood onto the wood floor. When he looked back at me, his eyes held fire. "You shouldn't have done that, boy."

I leaned forward, not afraid in the slightest for him to retaliate. He knew he wouldn't win, especially with his current injury. "You talk about them or my relationship with them again, it'll be more than a punch." I shoved the chair out behind me with so much force it fell with a loud clanking, and I stormed from the room.

My body was tight with tension. I needed to run it out. I stomped outside and to the main road, with Jimmy's words moving through my mind on repeat. He was taunting me, I knew it, but not knowing where and how Eden was made me more agitated.

I thought of Eden and what she'd think about me helping them. As I passed the building where Kemp and Lacy stayed, I spotted her in the window. She glanced out at me, letting a small smile show before looking away. I shook my head and jolted into a run.

Chapter 43

Eden

Old Bob and Tate had arrived with the first round from Bomber's city several days before we got back to the camp. They were both visibly relieved when they saw us. Being back home was more comforting than I ever thought possible. Ash was even happy, going for daily runs with me through the trees. I loved seeing the dusting of the first snow cover the ground and tree branches.

I jogged toward the cabins but stopped behind a large birch tree when I heard Sarah and Brian arguing.

"I don't think it's smart to bring her," Sarah pleaded, not only with words but also with wide worried eyes. "If Zane sees her, he may decide to send some of his people out here. We've been lucky that he's left us alone this long."

"I understand where you're coming from, but she has to see for herself. They all have to see what we're up against."

"Are we able to get word to Derek first?"

Brian shook his head. "The gathering is tomorrow morning; there's no time. He's trained well. He'll be able to school his emotions and improvise if he spots her."

The gathering? I pursed my lips and stepped out from behind the tree, with Ash following me. We slowly walked toward them, but I stopped when Brian gave me an accusatory side glance.

You do know that we can't really spy on each other, right?

I scrunched up my nose at him, and he laughed. "So what is this I hear about a gathering?"

Sarah looked at me warily before excusing herself back into the cabin to make food. Brian turned to me. "We have been invited to the city for a gathering."

I arched a brow. "Invited? By whom?"

"Derek."

I watched Brian's serious gaze as he studied me. "So is he working for Zane now?"

"Not exactly, though Zane may think so."

I didn't like the sound of that. I pursed my lips and sighed. "Interesting." I wanted to say more, but I had a feeling Brian wouldn't tell me anything I truly wanted to know at this time.

"Yes, well, like I said, lots of things have changed. We need you all to see for yourselves, but I also need you to stay hidden."

I bit my lip and crossed my arms. "What if I don't want to?"

He rolled his eyes. "I know you have more control and brains than that, Eden. I am surprised how quickly you've learned to be honest, so I know that you understand why it's important Zane shouldn't see you now."

I groaned. "I know, but I just want to get this done with."

"I know. I do too, but you know we can't rush it. We have to be prepared. We need more people."

I sighed, knowing deep down that he was right. We wouldn't survive without the others. We needed all the strength we could get. "Fine." I walked past him toward the cabin. His eyes were warm on my back as I walked away. He was nervous. My stomach sank at the thought of what could make someone like Brian nervous.

$\backsim$

"Stay out of sight." Brian spoke close to my ear, so quiet I'm sure the others couldn't hear him. His body was on edge, and he smelled of nervousness.

The whole camp came, except a few fighters who stayed behind. Raul, who came along with the first round of fighters, picked a few of Lucia's group to come so they could witness Zane and what we're up against.

"So what is this gathering?" I asked.

"You'll see," Brian replied before taking Sarah's hand in his. He blocked himself off; he was done explaining. He wanted me to see for myself and make my own judgments, but I didn't know how I felt about that, especially when the smell of unease followed him. My stomach sank at the thought of what we may be walking into.

Old Bob, Tate, and Lillyanne walked quietly beside me. A light dusting of snow crunched under our feet, and despite the clear sunny skies, the air was freezing. They all had as many layers of clothes on as they could manage and still move. As we entered the open city gates, we merged with other groups of people, all walking toward the city center. No one spoke, and everyone held grim faces. This was not what I had expected when a cure had been found.

As we walked through the streets, I took in the tall metal structures erected in a circle in the central park, and the large empty field with a wooden stage. People stepped up and moved down the structures, finding empty spots before sitting. The echoes of footsteps on the metal resounded around us. It was filled with many more people than I remember there being, so I suspect some of the crowd were the new citizens from the north.

We positioned ourselves on a row of seats halfway to the top but all the way at the end, in case we needed to get away fast. Raul and his people sat in the row behind us, his eyes wide as he scanned the area. He hadn't realized how large the city was, with so many people, even though we told him. By the looks from some of the citizens, they spotted us as newbies.

Just keep your eyes forward.

Brian gave warm smiles to some of our onlookers as I tried to keep my eyes from them, but the urge to look was too strong. My gaze clashed with a few women watching us with wary eyes. Their bodies tensed when I smiled, and they quickly looked away, clutching each other as their gaze dropped to my hands. I closed my hands into fists before tucking them under my thighs. The last thing we needed was for me to start a riot.

Brian glanced at me, looking at my hands under my thighs, but he just gave a grim smile before looking back at the empty stage.

"Why is everyone so uninviting?" Lillyanne asked.

"I don't think we want to know, but I'm guessing we'll find out," Tate replied to her gently.

My heart warmed at seeing their relationship grow. After some time, she seemed to relax, and Tate was patient with her. At times he even laughed at her unbelievable comments, but she didn't take it personally from him. She would just blush and look away.

Just as I was about to tell Brian this was a waste of time, loudspeakers turned on with a few high-pitched rings. Instinctively I put my hands over my ears and was happy I had the wolves stay behind; the pitch of this sound would have deafened them.

The movement on the side of the field quieted the low murmurs from the crowd. Derek walked out onto the stage first. My heart jumped at the same time as my stomach dropped at the sight of him. He stood stoic and serious, with no emotion on his face, as he held a black case in one hand.

I knew he was working with Zane, but this almost looked like he was being controlled by him. My eyes flicked to Brian, but he kept his face forward, watching Derek carefully.

The unmistakable putrid smell of sweat and feces filled the air, and a low growl rumbled in my chest. I never thought I would smell them again; never wanted to smell them again. Two rows of ten men walked onto the field, each pulling a scourge behind them. They each held whips to jab and hit their scourge, keeping them in line. The men didn't bring the scourge onto the stage but separated at the edge of it, creating a circle around the stage.

I watched the scourge, straining my eyes to see if I could recognize any of them, but I was too far away for me to examine their faces. Everyone stood silently, and I looked around surprised. Slowly, I stood along with the rest of them, wringing my hands together in front of me.

Two figures walked onto the field, waving to the crowd with large smiles. When I recognized Zane in his impeccable suit, my lip twitched. He held his head high with confidence, not a hair out of place. The man next to him was shorter by almost a foot. He also wore an impeccable suit, but on top of it, draped over his shoulders, was a thick embroidered sash.

Reverend Peters. Brian's voice answered my question about the man before I could ask.

They made their way to the stage, and Derek gave them both firm handshakes. Zane raised his arms to the crowd, like he wanted to silence them, only there hadn't been a sound the whole time since they walked onto the field. He dropped his arms and everyone sat.

"Good morning, friends! I'm so happy so many people made it on this cold morning, but I knew people would choose belief over being a sinner." Zane paused, giving the circle of scourge a sad look before continuing, "As you can see, we had many sinners this week." He paused again, moving two fingers to pinch the bridge of his nose. Reverend Peters dropped his head, giving it a sad shake. "We have two more here with us, in hopes that they may repent. That our words may save them from this eternal damnation."

My jaw dropped, and I could barely breathe. I blinked and looked over to Brian, but he gave me a quick headshake, the muscles in his jaw jumping. People really believed this?

Looking back to the stage, I closed my mouth, ready to listen to whatever other monstrosities Zane had to say.

"Some of our sinners have been insistent they are not, that they live honest God-fearing lives, but I disagree. They'll be given the serum, and it will show the truth."

"I don't like this," Old Bob muttered, receiving the stern look of an older man in the row in front of us. Unable to resist, I set my hand on his and squeezed.

"Bring them in," Zane yelled.

A moment later two cuffed men were led into the arena and onto the stage. They both held their heads high to show confidence, only to be exposed by their red-rimmed Chimera eyes. A woman across the field let out a sob that echoed through the quietness. She buried her face into the shoulder of the woman next to her to muffle her cries. The taller, older man's chin quivered and tears streamed down his cheeks.

I don't understand. They're already Chimera. How can they become scourge?

He's used the virus and the knowledge of how the scourge are created to make his own injection. Brian's voice was grim, almost defeated sounding.

I widened my eyes at Brian and looked back at the stage. *Using the virus and dead animal blood?*

Yes.

Zane looked to Derek, his fake concern creating an itch of irritation within me. I wanted to slice his face to pieces. "The case, please." He held out his hand. Derek brought the case over to him, opened it, and positioned it in front of him. Reverend Peters stepped in front of the men with an open book in his hands. He began to read, holding out a hand a few inches from the head of the first man, the man the woman in the audience had cried for.

Zane plucked a pair of gloves from the case and slowly put them on. After making sure each finger was meticulously in, he looked back into the case. My heart thumped so fast I could feel it in my throat. I could feel the tension throughout the crowd as everyone waited. Waited for whatever sadistic action Zane was going to do.

Are you going to do something? We're just going to sit here?

Calm, Eden. Just watch.

But this man. His life.

Brian finally turned to me. His eyes were firm, but they reflected pain. *We have no choice.* Before he looked away, I could see a flash in his eyes. Something I couldn't fully read in the quick moment I saw it, but it almost looked like expectation.

I looked back at the stage. Zane pulled a syringe from the case and stepped behind the man. He was full-on crying now, his eyes squeezed shut and cheeks wet with tears. Zane held up the syringe, and Reverend Peters quieted his prayers. "Behold. Our serum of sins. If this man is free of sins like he says, nothing will happen. If not"—Zane looked out at the scourge—"he'll join them. The damned ones."

My hands curled around my kneecaps, and I leaned forward, moving my head to the side to get a better view. I watched Derek a moment; there was still no sign he cared. No sign he'd interfere. I tapped my foot, itching to run toward them and take Zane down. I continued to hold my ground since I told Brian I would stay put. But then doing something felt like the better choice. The confusion within me built steadily.

Zane held up the syringe, then so quickly I almost didn't see, he plunged it into the man's neck. The man let his head fall back with a cry. The woman across the stadium sobbed again.

"No! James!" Her words echoed.

Zane stepped back and bowed his head a moment before stepping to the side, behind the second man. Derek moved to Zane's side, holding out the case again. Zane grabbed the second syringe and plunged it into the second man's throat. When both people were injected, Zane, Reverend Peters, and the rest of the crowd bowed their heads. The mumbled words of prayer surrounded us like a blanket of lies. Did these people really believe this load of crock?

"What exactly is supposed to happen?" Raul whispered into my ear.

I shook my head and whispered, "I don't know."

The next two minutes felt like hours. Despite the cold, a light sheen of sweat covered my body from my pounding heart. Every single one of my muscles was taut and fatigued. Just when I shuffled my feet to stand, to leave due to the unbearable feeling of the unknown, the man shrieked.

The murmured prayers stopped, the woman sobbed louder, people made cross-motions in the air toward the man, and Zane gave a clucking noise into the microphone.

"Oh, James."

The man's head started to twitch, his shoulders rolled, his arms and hands flicked in every direction, and his shrieks grew, filling the air.

"You may have survived if you hadn't lied—if you'd come to me or Reverend Peters and repented."

James screamed, his skin dulling from his original peachy pink to a grey—the grey of a scourge.

I turned to Brian and didn't even bother talking to him in our minds. "Do something."

"Eden, we can't. There are too many."

I looked back at the stage where James continued to transform into a scourge, but next to him, the other man remained Chimera.

"Why is the other one not changing?" I whispered.

Brian shrugged. "We don't know. That's why Derek is there, playing the game of loyal servant. I haven't had a chance to speak with him."

James was now on his hands and knees, writhing in what looked like pain. My throat rumbled, and I scanned the area.

"All the guards are occupied with a scourge."

"Eden," both Brian and Old Bob said my name in warning. The rows of people around us flashed us nervous glances. They sensed my hostility and were probably subtly reacting to it.

Raul put his hand on my shoulder. "I'm with you, Eden."

Brian gave him a hard look. "No one is doing anything." His words came out in a whispered hiss, but he didn't radiate the same urgency as before The tapping of my foot on the metal stands became louder, matching the thumping of my heart. "Eden, no." Brian's hand grabbed mine, but not as tightly as I would've expected.

I looked at him and back to the stage. Old Bob leaned into my ear. "Brian's right. Let's not be rash. We need to plan."

I shook my head and ripped my hand from Brian's. In one rapid move, I jumped onto my seat with a loud clanking that reverberated through the crowd. A woman in front of us screamed. I stood tall and pointed a claw toward the stage.

"Zane!"

Zane froze, moving his gaze to the sound of my voice. He put his hands over his eyes, blocking the glare of the sun. When his eyes focused, his face transformed from confusion to almost glee.

"Well, well. She returns!"

All eyes moved toward me, and I met many of them. The feeling of being among so many of my kind felt different. Almost safer. But these Chimera were broken down and scared. They wouldn't be of any use to me, not now at least.

"Will none of you stand up to him?" I pleaded with the crowd members that actually met my eyes. They looked away quickly, regret and shame reflecting in their faces.

"Eden," Brian hissed and grabbed my arm again. But his grip wasn't nearly strong enough, not for me.

Pulling my arm from him, I started to step down on the seats toward the field. Zane watched me with twinkling eyes, tracking my every move. Reverend Peters moved to his side and leaned in to say something, but Zane waved him off.

Eden! Don't do this. You don't understand.

I looked at Derek as his voice filled my head, but I didn't slow my forward movement. People slid to the side, leaving a path for me to walk through. I heard footsteps behind me from Raul and the few fighters he brought. Knowing I had some backup, my confidence settled.

You aren't doing anything. Are you siding with him?

No, but he has everyone on his side. He has the weapons.

So?

Derek's mouth became a thin line, and he looked forward toward Zane and watched me curiously as I made my way closer to him.

"Eden, how was your vacation?" Zane asked, stepping to the edge of the stage. He dropped his shoulders and clasped his hands in front of him like we were old friends meeting after a long time.

I sneered. "It was great. I made some new friends."

Zane looked behind me at Raul and his men. "Interesting. And they haven't got the Fever yet, I see."

I almost tripped at his words. None of the people coming had had the Fever, so they would be vulnerable in a different kind of way. I wanted to slap myself for being so careless.

Jumping onto the grass from the last row of seats, I steadied my gaze. "It won't matter. We'll be rid of you soon enough."

A bark of laughter erupted from him. "I see. Pray tell me how you plan on doing that when I have"—he motioned to the crowd—"the people on my side."

"You think they'll follow you? After they learn what the scourge really are? After they learn how they are—"

"Release them." Zane waved his hand at the two rows of guards on the grass in front of me holding the scourge. The rest of my words were lost when the chains were released and all twenty scourge charged us.

Eden! Run! Derek's voice invaded my mind once again, but I ignored him.

The crowd screamed, and the people in the lower levels moved higher.

"What do we do?" Raul yelled. His men and he took up defensive stances.

I readied myself into a fighting stance and curled my claws. "You fight."

The first scourge reached me, a female not much older than me. It jumped toward me, but I ducked and moved under it. When it landed, I grabbed its head and twisted. The snap of its neck was washed out by the snarls and screams erupting around us. I took on another as Raul and his men fought beside me.

Movement on the grass caught my eye. Looking past the scourge I was fighting, I saw Zane, Reverend Peters, and Derek walking away. They were leaving the field as if they didn't care what was happening.

"Eden," Raul yelled with a strained voice.

I sliced through the chest of the scourge in front of me with my claws and turned. Raul and his men were outnumbered, struggling to fight with no weapons. I saw the blur of Brian, Old Bob, and Tate running down the stands toward us. They pushed through the chaotic, screaming crowd.

My heart pumped as the feeling of rage overcame me. With rapid breaths, I looked over all the scourge, stopping at one. He snarled and clawed at one of Raul's men. Even though his skin was now grey, the blackness of his hair was distinctive.

David, Jace's father.

"No," I whispered.

Raul's fighter readied himself. His eyes narrowed, and I knew it wouldn't take much for him to kill David.

Rage and power simmered low in my core, and with a few deep pants, I let it erupt. "Stop!" My voice was a distinct snarl that was so loud it sent the birds in the nearby trees squawking in fear.

Everyone froze. The crowd, the scourge, even Zane.

"Stop!" I repeated, holding out my hands. The scourge shook their heads, unsure if they should listen to me or follow their instinct to kill. I let a low growl rumble toward them and took a step forward. They returned with whimpers and took hesitant steps back. "Go!" I stepped toward them again, and they took another step back. I could control their pursuit.

I was power.

Zane slowly turned and watched me. I kept my eyes on the scourge, mostly David. His eyes flicked to mine but quickly lowered. I stepped toward him. "David," I said quietly. When the other scourge jumped toward us again, I snapped my hands up quickly. "Stop!" They stopped again, letting out small screams of frustration and confusion.

Zane stopped after taking a few steps toward us; the skin around his eyes tightened as he focused on me. I looked back to David, my hands still out in front of me, and I took another step forward. "David." His eyes met mine, and for a moment, I thought he understood. I thought he recognized me, but then he let out a deep snarl.

"Eden, let's go!" Brian pulled my arm.

I looked back at Zane only to see the back of his dark suit disappearing behind the stands. A moment later, another two dozen scourge came charging onto the field. I squeezed my eyes shut and screamed.

"I can't control them all!"

"Let's go." Brian pulled my arm. I looked behind me; everyone was already running. Just Brian and I remained. I looked back at the few scourge fighting my control, including David, before I dropped my hands and retreated with Brian back to the camp.

Chapter 44

Jace

Lacey's cheeks, nose, and the tips of her ears were a deep red. She slowly went through the motions I showed her. Her balance wasn't the greatest, and it was even worse on the icy ground. Kemp worked the same motions next to her, much nimbler and more balanced.

He stopped with a loud sigh. "Is that as fast as you can go?"

With cheeks turning a deeper red, Lacey set her foot down and relaxed her arms. "I'm sorry."

"Kemp!" I yelled, trying to give the best impression I could of Brian or Derek. They both startled a moment, but his eyes widened at the firmness of my voice. "We never, under any circumstance, comment on others' abilities. She's doing the best she can, and you should be happy that she's trying."

"It's really—"

I stopped her protest with a raised hand, not taking my eyes off Kemp. "No. He needs to learn. This is serious. We aren't just learning all of this for fun; this is life or death."

Kemp's smile disappeared, and he stood straighter, giving me a firm nod. "Understood."

"Good. Now, back to your positions."

Kemp was right there, but Lacey took a moment, watching us with wide eyes before raising her hands again and setting her feet into position.

We moved through balance positions to strengthen and stretch. Then Kemp and I worked on his hand-to-hand while Lacey watched, before we switched. She was hesitant, and it took a lot of coaxing to get her to actually put some muscle behind her punches, but by the end of her session, she was pretty good.

The cars from the second drop drove into the camp. Kemp ran to us, sliding on a patch of ice. "We get to go. We actually get to go and fight now!"

Lacey's eyes widened in fear as she took in her young brother. I put a hand on his shoulder. "Yes, we get to go, but you're getting nowhere near the fighting."

His mouth dropped open, and he started to protest, but his sister grabbed his hand, pulling him inside. She mumbled agreements and how he was too young to be thinking such things.

"Jace," Ryan, one of the drivers, called as he jumped from the truck.

"Everything go smoothly?"

"Yeah. Everyone is there safe and sound."

I nodded, biting my tongue to ask how Eden was, but I didn't really want to hear the chiding they would give me. I had already been nicknamed "lover boy" due to Jimmy's comments about Lacey, so I didn't need any more.

"How much time do you all need before we head out? Is tomorrow morning too early?"

Ryan shook his head. "No, tomorrow morning should be fine. We just need a meal and rest, and then we should be good to go."

"Great. Tomorrow morning it is." I gave his back a pat before he led the other drivers inside to rest.

The city was eerily quiet since the second group left for the north. Since most of the fighters were gone, except for a select few who stayed behind with me, I was always on edge. If we were attacked, I'm not sure we'd come out on top.

I walked back to Kemp and Lacey's building and let everyone know to be ready to leave by morning.

Thankfully, the drive was uneventful. We made it north in two long days of driving, with no attacks or bad weather. I could sense the half of the wolf pack that stayed behind moving alongside us. How they kept up, I don't know, but I was grateful for the extra protection.

The woods thickened as we drove through to the camp, and my body itched to get out and find Eden. Growing up, I was never fond of seeing the white-covered trees and ground, but the sense of home I felt made me regret never fully seeing the beauty in it.

The closer we got to the camp, the more I could sense Eden. I fought the urge to scream out to her in my mind. I wanted to see her face when she saw us arrive. Jimmy may have teased me about Lacey, but after the last few days of training her, it became clear that Eden was mine. I cared for Lacey and Kemp, but I don't think any other woman would come close to how I felt about Eden.

Ryan parked the truck at the tents. My eyes moved around the abandoned area when Ryan spoke. "We have to walk the rest of the way. They have cabins not too far from here."

I let out a breath. I remembered Derek mentioning the cabins before.

Everyone unloaded and put packs and supplies on their backs before following Ryan through the woods. The sun shone through the white-covered branches of the trees, reflecting off the icy ground. The crunch of the snow and ice under our feet kept everyone's attention as they maneuvered over the uneven terrain without falling. Kemp stayed close to me, eager to come into any kind of combat. No matter how many times I told him he wouldn't be fighting, his hopes stayed high.

The soft sound of voices, along with the musky smell of firewood, drifted toward us. Increasing my speed, I pushed past Ryan, whose chuckle followed me. Kemp moved to a jog next to me, puffing air as he worked to keep his pace with mine.

The cabins came into view. They were small, with smoke billowing out of chimneys. A few lit firepits were outside, surrounded by some log benches lined with fighters. They turned at our presence, quickly raising their guns until they saw who we were.

"Ryan! Finally made it," one of the men called.

"It's the last of them," Ryan said, dropping his pack on the ground. He warmed his hands over the fire.

I looked through the group, not seeing Eden or any of the others. "Where is—"

"Inside," one of the older fighters, Jose, said. He nodded his head toward the first cabin. I gave him a thankful nod and headed toward it, trying to keep the skip out of my step. Lacey put her hand on Kemp's shoulder to keep him from following me.

My feet made the few small clunks on the wooden stairs leading to the door, but it wasn't as loud as the door was when I pulled it open. The smell of firewood hit me just before a large squealing body did.

"Jace!"

I laughed. Wrapping my arms tightly around Eden, I breathed in her fresh deep-woods scent.

Yeah, there was no other girl for me.

"Did you all just arrive?" Old Bob asked, looking over my shoulder at the group finding rest near the fires.

I gently pushed Eden back but continued to hold her hand. "Yeah. No issues."

Jimmy sat back in his chair, giving me a smirk. "The kid and his sister... your new friend, they all right?"

I clenched my jaw and narrowed my eyes at him. "They're fine."

Jimmy looked at Eden. "You should've seen him. Training all the ladies. The way they batted their eyelashes at him."

Eden's smile faltered just as her hand's grip loosened in mine. I squeezed hers tighter, not letting her retreat. "No. I trained Kemp and his sister, Lacey. She did no batting of eyelashes." I growled.

"If you say so."

I turned to Eden. "You'll like her." She gave me a quick smile before looking back at the others. Her confidence slipped, but not completely.

I looked around the table that sat in the middle of the room until my gaze landed on LaRae and Dr. Hahn.

"You're both alive."

LaRae smiled. "Yes, we made it, along with most of the other people who had gotten sick. The virus didn't hit us as hard as it had before the cure."

"It's good to see you, Jace," Dr. Hahn said. "Yes, very, very good."

I gave them both a smile before turning back to Eden. She squeezed my hands and sighed.

"I'm so glad you're here and you're safe."

I grinned down at her. "Me too." As she gazed into my eyes, I suddenly felt the guilt that thickened the room.

I furrowed my brow. "What happened?" Her excitement at seeing me was replaced by a look of sorrow.

"I think you should sit down."

I looked around the table again. No one said anything as they watched her lead me to an empty chair.

I sat.

"What is it?" My stomach knotted tight.

Eden turned in her chair and faced me, gently taking my hands. "We saw Zane two days ago, and saw what he's doing."

"All right." I brought my brows together. "Isn't that what the plan was?"

She nodded, pursing her lips together, and looked down at our joined hands. "I think you all should leave." She didn't look up, but everyone in the room quietly dispersed, giving me solemn looks. When the room was empty, she met my eyes. "Zane isn't the only person I saw." I swallowed, realizing I may not want to hear what she had to say next. Before I could stop her, she continued, "Jace, I also saw your father."

I sucked in a breath. My heart was in my throat. "He's alive?"

Her eyes never left mine when she said the words that I never thought I would hear. That I never wanted to hear.

"He's a scourge."

The room spun, and I squeezed my eyes shut to steady myself. The threat of losing the contents of my stomach had me swallowing hard. I'd hoped that Zane would have just killed him, not make him a scourge.

When my vision blurred, Eden pulled me to her. I buried my face in her shoulder and cried.

～

I don't know how long I cried on Eden's shoulder. Time stopped and my memories of life with my father flowed through me. We didn't have the strongest bond, but he was my father. He was all I had known, since my mother died when I was born. When he helped us escape, I figured I'd never see him again, that he'd be killed. But to become a scourge? The thought pained me to the core. Did he know who he was? What he was doing, even though he had no control? Or was he as good as dead?

I sat numbly as the others returned into the cabin, including Lucia and Izan. He grumbled about the cold, which resulted in a smack in the arm from Lucia.

Once everyone was seated, Eden retold what had happened. Everyone listened in horror. Raul confirmed the severity of the situation when Lucia asked him about his perception.

I cleared my throat, still not sure of the strength my voice would hold. "The people are falling for this religious crap? Like they truly believe it?"

Brian sat forward. "I think some do, but I feel the majority don't. They know there's something not right, but the fear is too strong for them to go against it. Plus, like you witnessed, not all people he injects turn into a scourge. He is using a placebo we think, but Derek hasn't gotten enough information to confirm that. There is too much uncertainty, so the safest bet is to follow him." He pushed a hand into his hair. "Plus, they are loyal to him. He did give them the cure for the Fever."

Eden pursed her lips. "We can't not do anything, though. We have to fight him."

"I agree," Raul said quickly, before anyone could object.

Old Bob sighed. "You saw what happened when you attacked."

"Yes, but that was spontaneous and with fewer people. We're all here now. We can take them on. We have weapons!" Eden's cheeks grew red, and the ripple of her anger filled the room.

"Not that many weapons," Brian replied, with a frustrated growl. "We still need a plan, Eden."

"What if we do a full-frontal attack? We have some weapons and numbers. We may be able to breach them and take down Zane. Once he's gone, then we have control," Raul said.

Brian wiped a hand over his tired eyes. Old Bob shook his head. "It's too risky—"

"What about Derek?"

Brian looked at Eden. "What about him?"

"Is he with us or not? Couldn't he help from the inside?"

"It's not that easy. Zane isn't stupid. He watches everything carefully, and he has spies that report to him about everything. Derek is outnumbered, so if Zane gets one whiff he is disloyal, he'll be gone to us. No matter how much he fights."

She let out a frustrated growl, and I set a hand on her back that she leaned into. I looked at Brian and asked, "But would he fight if he needs to? If he sees we're there?"

"Of course, but—"

"Then why don't we take a vote?"

"A vote?" Eden asked, looking at me.

"Yeah. A vote for if we attack now or wait longer and plan." I avoided the daggered looks from Old Bob and Brian. "I mean, we'll still plan if we attack now, only it won't be as detailed."

"All right. I agree with that. Let's vote," Lucia said, sitting forward to rest her forearms on the table.

I smiled. "Good. All in favor of fighting now, raise your hand."

Eden's hand whipped up so fast I had to lean back to avoid getting swiped by her claws. She gave me an apologetic look that I shrugged off with a smile. I looked around the table and counted. Lucia, Raul, Izan, Bomber, and Eden. I slowly raised my hand. "Six for yes." I looked at Brian and Old Bob. "Two for no. Looks like we'll be attacking at dawn."

"This isn't how we usually do things," Brian said.

Lucia looked at him. "Change isn't always a bad thing."

"We need to plan."

"We have six hours to do so. We can plan through the night and fight at dawn," Eden said, squeezing my hand. Her excitement was infectious. I smiled at her but dread filled me at the possibility of seeing my father as a scourge.

Chapter 45

Eden

Despite being up most of the night planning, my body was in a hum of anticipation. I had one focus: kill Zane. Brian and Old Bob didn't hesitate to tell me how upset they were with my display at the church, but I just repeated that I'd rather look like a lunatic than let people be tortured and killed.

We moved as a large group, working our way through the woods toward the city walls. The knife in my boot jabbed my calf, and I fought the urge to stop and discard it, but I knew Jace would argue since he was the one who gave it to me. When I insisted I didn't need it because of my claws, he just said, "Humor me."

I watched our large group break off into three smaller groups. One group led by Jimmy and Old Bob moved around to the east entrance, and another group led by Tate and Cal moved to the west entrance. My group continued toward the main entrance.

Do you think we left enough people behind? Jace's voice invaded my thoughts.

Jace looked over his shoulder for the millionth time.

I stopped and turned toward him. "What's wrong?"

He pushed a hand through his hair. "I just can't shake this feeling." He looked at me, then back toward the cabins. "We're taking most, if not all, of the decent fighters. There are a lot of people back there."

"The kid has really gotten under your skin."

"He's a good kid. He deserves a childhood."

I watched his eyes and saw his lost childhood. The childhood he wanted to give Kemp. Losing his mother so young and not having a strong relationship with his father, he hoped to change Kemp's outcome. I also saw pleading, a pleading I guessed was to not make him face his father.

"You want to go back?"

Brian had continued to lead the group on, leaving us alone among the trees.

"I can't let him get hurt. I know Zane, and I don't trust this."

I pursed my lips, watching him. "And your father?"

He sucked in a shaky breath. His voice was a quiet rasp when he said, "Put him out of his misery." He swallowed hard, letting a breath out slowly.

I took a step toward him and wound my hand in his. The blue in his eyes shimmered when he looked at me. "You sure?"

He gave me a single nod.

While he composed himself, we clutched each other in silence a moment. Touching his forehead to mine and squeezing my hands, he smiled and said, "Please don't do anything crazy. I'm begging you, Eden."

I laughed. "Begging me?"

"Well, the last time I asked you, you ignored it. You could have been killed the other day."

I stifled a groan at his words and pulled back from him. I had been hearing that enough from the others, and I really didn't want to hear it from him, but I could see in his eyes he wasn't mad, just concerned. I wondered what he would do if he knew the full plan Brian and I had created earlier this morning. Deciding not to tell him because I was sure he would try and talk me out of it, I pursed my lips and nodded.

"I promise."

He sighed. "Good."

Eden.

I glanced over and saw Brian waiting impatiently. He wasn't happy about the attack, so he'd been extra edgy all morning. His plan with me was the only reason he seemed to have some interest in leading a group.

"I have to go." I gave his hands one last squeeze. "Be careful and watch over the kid."

He smiled. "You too."

I started to pull away, but he gripped my hands tight and pulled me back to him. A gentle hand smoothed along my cheek, and his lips met mine in a soft kiss. His warmth and love filled me, bringing me to my toes. I wrapped my arms around his neck and held him close. The impending battle disappeared, and all I wanted was this. Me and Jace.

He pulled away too soon. As he looked intently into my eyes, he let his thumb slide across my cheek, and I'm sure he could see into my soul. Without another word, he turned and ran back toward the cabins. After watching his strong back disappear, I turned and ran toward battle.

∽

"Have the others reached their locations?" I asked Brian. Jimmy and Cal were to touch base with him when they arrived. We had tested how far our telepathic abilities reached earlier today, and to our surprise, it was far.

"Jimmy has. I haven't heard from Cal yet."

Nodding, I looked at the wall from our vantage point in the woods. The wall was now partially torn down, but not a guard was in sight. This was unnatural to me after living my whole life with walls and guards.

Lucia and Izan crouched next to Brian and scanned the area intently. Their sibling similarities were more noticeable from the side angle. The slope of their nose and fullness of lips were identical.

"How many guards do you think he has?" Lucia asked.

"A lot. Don't know actual numbers, as there may be some new ones since he gained more people from the north, but he also has a small army of scourge," Brian replied. His eyes went distant a moment before turning to me. "Cal is in position."

Lucia and I nodded. A ripple of tension moved through every fighter in our group, including me. I had fought before but never in a real battle. My anticipation and nervousness flowed with every pump of my heart.

Brian looked at me. "You remember our plan?"

Lucia furrowed her brow at his words, and I nodded. She opened her mouth to ask him what he was talking about, but we both ignored her and started forward.

"Let's go," Brian said, loud enough for our group to hear but not loud enough to bring attention to us.

I gave Lucia a quick glance, but when she frowned at me, I took off after Brian. Out of the corner of my eye, I saw Izan give her arm a smack, and they followed us along with the others.

We moved silently through the door and toward the city center. I was to sneak into the lab building, find Zane, and take him out. The others will be focused on a fight, at least that's what Brian had claimed, so they shouldn't notice when I sneak away. The roads and buildings were eerily silent, making my skin crawl. Something wasn't right.

Brian stopped and scanned the emptiness around us. "Where is everyone?" He turned and looked at me. "Something isn't right."

I nodded, relieved someone else noticed the tension in the air. I started at a movement behind him. A flash of grey before I smelled it: scourge.

"Brian," I warned.

"What's that?" Izan pushed Lucia behind him, an action I was surprised at. Despite being enemies for so long, his first reaction was still to protect his sister.

"Scourge," I said before charging forward, edging past Brian's hand when he tried to grab me.

The only sound I heard was my breath and my heart pumping in my ears. A long line of dozens of scourge came toward us. Their screams and snarls echoed between the buildings. I met the first few with a strong impact that made them all fly back and skid onto the snowy ground, then I quickly ended them with a swipe of my claws.

Glancing back, I saw my group coming forward, aiming their guns and shooting.

"Don't waste bullets. We don't have enough," Izan screamed at some of the men.

Brian took on a few scourge easily. He blocked and moved between their claws and teeth, ending them with swift snaps of their necks.

Cal? Jimmy?

I called to them, needing to know if they were also being attacked, but I received no reply. I hoped Jimmy's leg was holding up. He insisted on coming even though he was still limping when he walked.

Three scourge came at me. I grabbed one on the upper arms and swung it into one of the others, knocking them to the ground. I jumped at the third, slashing it in its throat. As it drowned in its own thick dark blood, I turned back to the others. They stood and started back at me, only to be shot down.

I looked back and saw Lucia lowering her gun. She gave me a small nod before turning back to the fight.

Go! Now!

Brian's voice filled my head, and I jolted while I fought off two more scourge. My nose filled with the metallic smell of blood as my claws dug deep into the chest of one. It had been a female around my age. I blinked back the thought. I couldn't think of them as human right now.

There are too many. I don't want to leave you.

We'll be fine. You have to go. Now!

Looking back at Brian, I saw him fighting easily. The others were taking shots from their guns only if they could guarantee contact; otherwise, they fought using their knives. We were outnumbered, but we were in no way losing. Letting out a small breath, I turned and sprinted toward the lab building, taking down as many scourge as I could on the way.

My stomach dropped as I worked my way there. There were so many. How were there so many?

The door to the building was open. Pushing down any feelings of doubt, I ran right inside and stopped in the empty entryway, memories flashed in my mind from when I had been a prisoner here. I heard nothing inside, only the sounds of fighting outside. My skin prickled with unease, but I couldn't go back now. I had to find Zane. I had to end this. Remembering Jace's eyes when he begged me not to do anything dangerous made my chest tighten.

I'm sorry, Jace, I sent to him, no idea if he would hear, but I had to try.

I took the stairs up to the lab rooms, two at a time, but when I walked down the hallway, I found no one present. The labs and cells that once housed scared scientists and tortured people were all empty.

No one is here, Brian.

I spun around as the silence filled me.

Brian?

His lack of response sent my nerves on edge, so I started down the hall back toward the stairs. The screams and random gun shots echoed outside as I neared the top of the stairway, but a flicker of light farther down the hall caught my eye. I glanced back outside, weighing my options to go out and help my group fight or to stay and explore the open doors to the gym at the end of the hall. Screens reflected and flickered as they lined the walls. They showed the fight outside. Letting out a quiet growl, I headed toward the gym.

I stopped, cocking my head to focus on everything being shown. I saw Brian, fighting off a group of scourge. Old Bob and Tate were fighting another group near the gate where they came in, the same with Cal and his group. It was all being broadcasted on screens.

I slowly walked toward the doorway and kept my eyes fixed on the screens. All I saw were scourge.

Where were the guards?

My stomach suddenly felt rotten as I scanned the scourge from head to toe. They all wore similar white clothes, with the same insignia sewed into them. The scourge *were* the guards.

I should run. Just like Jace asked me to do if I got into trouble, but something pulled me forward. I continued down the hall toward the gym. Toward the screens.

As I stepped into the gym, I let my eyes roam over all the screens. They filled the walls in every direction, showing every section of the city. In the center of the room, Zane sat, flanked by Derek and Reverend Peters. Behind them was a large group of guards... not scourge, but actual guards.

"So, you do still have guards," I said, letting my eyes meet his. "I was wondering if you replaced them all with scourge."

Zane chuckled. "I do, not many, but I do. They're easier to control than the scourge, but less"—he let his eyes watch a few screens before looking back at me—"lethal."

I didn't respond, but I turned to Derek. He met my eyes. His face was void of emotion.

You going to help or just watch?

He didn't respond. His body tensed with anger, and I sensed the battle within him. If I could sense it, I'm sure Zane could as well. I shook my head and looked back at the screens. Speakers throughout the room brought in the screams, grunts, and hollers of the fighting outside.

I started to stalk toward Zane. He didn't flinch, but every guard behind him pointed their gun toward me.

Don't. Derek's voice filled my head, and the skin around his eyes tightened.

I flicked my eyes back to Zane quickly so as to not to give away Derek's warning. Zane clasped his hands together and set them on his crossed knees. "You should know by now, Eden, that you and your friends aren't strong enough to win."

I growled, letting my lips twitch to bare my fangs. "If you hadn't changed almost everyone into a scourge, it would be easier. I'll agree with that."

He smirked. "If only." He flicked his fingers and more guards filed in, lining the walls behind me and blocking the door. A loud click, followed by the screeching of a sound system, echoed outside and through the speakers in the gym. I saw scourge and fighters alike putting their hands over their ears. Outside of the lab building, in the field, a large screen came to life showing me standing before Zane. The guards behind me were visible with their guns pointed at my back.

Zane didn't need to speak loud for his voice to be heard throughout the entire city. "I find it a little degrading that you sent a child to try and kill me." He paused, watching my expression with amusement. "But we have her now. If you wish to join me, fall to your knees and surrender. Otherwise, I suggest you leave promptly before I release the third wave of my army."

My eyes snapped to the screens, and I searched for Brian, Old Bob, Tate, anyone who would give orders. I couldn't pick them out, but I could make out Brian's voice. "Retreat. Back to the woods!"

No! Don't!

Brian either ignored me, or he couldn't hear me. Derek's feet shuffled, which brought my eyes to him. My look of pleading wasn't lost on Zane.

"Oh, Derek won't be helping you. He works for me now."

After a moment of silence, Derek set his jaw and looked past me with a look of disinterest. A knot formed in my stomach.

"What do you want with me? You have everything. You have the cure. You created some kind of injection to make scourge, which is keeping the people under your control. What else do you want?"

Zane stood and took a few slow steps toward me. "You're the original, Eden. I wasn't finished with you before you escaped."

Our eyes were drawn to the screens by the sound of yelling, not in pain but in anger. Brian and Lucia faced off with Izan.

"I knew you would end up being weak," Izan said.

"This isn't the time." Brian pushed his shoulder back toward the woods. "Let's go, you can argue later." Izan tripped on a dead scourge and fell back. Most of our fighters had already retreated out of the city into the woods.

Lucia stepped in front of him. "My order is for you to fall back."

"Come on, Lucia. We can take them on with our people, and we can take control."

My fists clenched at his words. I knew he'd have trouble letting Lucia take the lead.

Zane's eyebrows rose, and his smile grew as he watched the argument.

Lucia stepped toward Izan, a bloody knife in her right hand. She reached down and offered Izan her left hand to help him up. He took it, and she pulled him up, but without hesitation, she buried the knife into his ribs. He dropped his jaw, and his eyes went wide as she pushed it in deeper, at an angle to pierce his heart.

"I told you, if you defied me again, I'd kill you." She moved back, pulling the knife from him, and gave him a shove to the ground. "I let you live before out of respect of our father, but I can't have you defying me at every serious moment." She stared down at him as he took his last audible breath, stilling on the red-stained, snowy ground.

Brian's jaw dropped slightly as he watched, but when Lucia looked at him, he steadied his face.

"Let's go" was all she said before stepping over her dead brother's body and jogging out of the city.

I blinked, watching all my people scatter back to the woods, killing any scourge that was in their path. My stomach sank when my eyes met Zane's again. He watched me, but before I could speak, three darts hit me in the neck and I was draped in darkness.

Chapter 46

Jace

I ran the whole way back, scanning the woods for any sign of an approaching attack. I was relieved when none appeared and more relieved when I saw Ash and his pack patrolling the perimeter of the cabins. Eden had pondered the idea of taking the pack with her but figured they'd be more use protecting the people at the camp.

"Good boy," I mumbled to him as I passed, stopping to give his ears a quick scratch.

Only five fighters had been left behind, and they weren't even the best. I just couldn't shake the sense that something was coming. Zane knows that Brian and Derek's people live out here, and now he knows Eden is back. He's not just going to let things slide.

I entered the largest cabin and was greeted by an excited Kemp.

"Jace, is it over?"

I smiled at him, trying to look reassuring. "No, bud, not yet."

"Why are you back then?"

I glanced from him to the others in the cabin. Besides him and his sister, there were seven other adults. They all watched me with a mixture of curiosity and nervousness. I smiled at them and said, "Just wanted to make sure you were safe."

After a few calming words to the others, I stepped back outside to talk with the fighters. They sat near a fire, rubbing their hands close to the flame, trying to keep warm. The smoke rose high in the trees, and my stomach knotted.

I moved right to the fire and started kicking snow over, watching the flames flicker out.

"Hey," one of the men yelled.

I narrowed my eyes at him. "This is like a beacon to anyone looking for us."

"We'll freeze!"

"Then I suggest you start moving to keep your blood pumping."

They grumbled as they stomped away. Watching them huddled together, I smirked at how much Brian had rubbed off on me.

"Break up. Go in two groups," I yelled at them and pushed my hands through my hair. How was it these idiots were the ones left to protect everyone?

Sarah stepped out of one of the cabins and walked over to me. "Is everything all right?"

"Yeah. I'm just being careful." She narrowed her eyes, and I sighed. "I just can't break this feeling—"

A wolf snarled. Then two more snarled. Then the rancid smell hit us. I whipped my head toward the trees where I saw Ash in a flash of grey limbs flying through the trees. Sarah's face went white, and I pushed her back toward the cabins. "Go! Get inside and barricade the doors!"

I ran to the largest cabin where Kemp was peeking outside and pushed him back inside, right into his sister's arms. "Stay inside, no matter what you hear. Barricade the doors."

Lacey nodded, tears building in her eyes. I looked at her a moment, keeping her gaze on mine. "You know what to do if you have to. Don't hesitate. All right?" She nodded again; her knuckles were white as she clutched Kemp's shoulders. The others in the cabin had already started moving furniture to block the entrances.

I closed the door but didn't dare leave until I heard them moving the table, followed by the thump onto the wood of the door.

I ran into the woods right toward the sounds and the smells of the fight. Swallowing down a gag, I thought of how I never wanted to smell a scourge again, but until this nightmare was over, I didn't have a choice.

"Jace," one of the fighters yelled as he pointed a shaking gun at an approaching scourge.

"Shoot it," I yelled at him and quickly looked away to take down two scourge coming at me. I needed to drive them away from the cabins.

I pulled the small dagger from my belt and sliced both scourge down their fronts. They shrieked in pain before falling in a puddle of their own blood. Stepping over them, I snapped their necks for good measure and turned to see a line of dozens more charging at me. Ash and his pack's snarls, mixed with the shrieks of the scourge, made my spine tingle.

I moved in quick movements, focused only on killing. Everything around me turned to a blur, except the scourge bodies that dropped one after another around me. My hands and clothes were covered in black blood, but that didn't stop me from charging another small group of scourge. I kept my mind cut off from the thought that they had once been people. People with loving families that missed them.

A terrified scream from the cabins pulled me from the barricade in my mind.

Kemp's scream.

My head snapped back to see several scourge scaling the walls of the cabins. One hung halfway out of a window, another pushing at its back to get inside.

"Fighters! Ash," I screamed and sprinted back toward the cabins. Where were the men with guns?

Ash met me at my side, along with two other wolves, their thick coats sloppy and caked in scourge blood.

I went right for the window and yanked one of the scourge back, but before I threw it to the ground, I let my knife slide across its throat. Ash and the wolves went for the other scourge at the cabin's walls.

"Lacey!" Kemp screamed.

I leaped through the broken window toward the three scourge attacking everyone in the cabin. How did three get inside so quickly?

Kemp hid in the far corner, with tears streaking his cheeks, as his sister fought off a scourge with a spoon. Jumping over a tipped chair, I moved toward them but was slammed back onto the table when a scourge hit me from the side. Startled, I pushed back at its yellow teeth snapping just an inch from my face.

Knives flew by me; one so close I had to quickly move the scourge in front of me, and the knife embedded into the scourge's back. It reeled its head back with a cry, trying to reach over its shoulder and pull the knife out. I used that opportunity to push my dagger deep into its chest, piercing its heart.

"Stop throwing knives," I yelled. The others in the cabin cringed back at me. Two scourge lay in front of them, covered in blood, along with two other humans.

"Argh!" Lacey's scream gave me a shot of adrenaline, and I pushed the dead scourge off me and slid across the floor toward her. The scourge had its clawed hands on her throat, and she gasped for breath. Her hands were firm on its shoulders to keep it from biting her.

I grabbed it from behind, snapping its neck in one swift movement. Lacey pulled in a gasp of air when the hands released their grip. Throwing the scourge to the side, I knelt down beside her. Her eyes watered as she gasped and coughed, slowly moving her hand to her upper side. My eyes drifted after her hand, and I saw blood. Lots of blood.

"Lacey?" Kemp said, moving to her side.

A scourge screamed at the entry of the window but was silenced by wolf snarls. Confident that the wolves had the entry, I moved Lacey's hand gently from the wound.

"Let me see."

She gasped, tears sliding from her eyes into her blonde hair. "It's pretty... deep."

Kemp clutched her arm as I tore her shirt away from the wound. Blood pulsed out, soaking the wood floor beneath her.

"I need some water! Something to bandage this," I yelled. Some of the others came to Lacey's side and put reassuring hands on Kemp's back. I could hear banging items in the small kitchen area.

The scourge's screams outside were dying down. A few more gunshots rang along with hollers from the fighters outside.

"I think they're all dead," a man said quietly.

I turned when a bowl of fresh water and some clothes were set beside me. I looked at the young woman. "I need you to be brave, all right?" Her eyes widened, and she gave a hesitant nod. "I need you to go to the next cabin and get Sarah. Can you do that?"

She nodded, but a man stepped up behind her. "I'll do it."

Giving him a curt nod, I turned back to Lacey, holding hard pressure on her wound. She was getting paler. "You're going to be all right. A healer is on her way."

"Jace... if—"

I leaned closer to her, cutting her off. "Stop. Don't waste your breath."

A few of the others helped the man move the furniture away from the doorway. Armed with random utensils and broken pieces of wood for weapons, they slowly opened the door, peeking outside first.

One of the fighters, covered in blood, stepped up to the doorway. "They're all dead. Everyone all right in here?"

The man moved him to the side. "I need to get Sarah." He pushed by the fighter and disappeared.

The fighter came inside, getting a glimpse of me kneeling next to Lacey, and swore under his breath. He dropped his gun and knelt on the other side of her.

I looked up at him. "I need you and the others to patrol the area. Make sure there are really no others and find out how many people we lost." I let my eyes drift to the two bodies that were pushed to the wall of the cabin. I hoped there hadn't been too many.

His face turned serious, but he stood and grabbed his gun before disappearing through the door.

Sarah charged into the cabin, almost knocking me to the side when she knelt next to Lacey. "All right, Jace, I need you to get the boy out of here. Kelly! I need Kelly! Sam, grab my bag." She looked at me, setting her hands over mine on the wound. "It's all right, Jace. I got it from here. Please take the boy. I don't want him to see this."

Slowly relinquishing my pressure on Lacey, I met her eyes. "Be strong, all right?" She nodded, her eyes full of tears. I took Kemp's arm, tugging him with me. He willingly came, burying his face in my chest.

Lacey watched me as I led Kemp away. I met her gaze before stepping outside, her brother under my arm. Her eyes said all I needed to know, and I gave her a nod. "I will. I promise you I will."

As I held Kemp outside, his tears wet my shirt. I vowed that I would always take care of him, no matter what happened. He was now mine.

~

Lacey died an hour later. I still held Kemp with my nose buried in his messy white hair as his face was buried in my shirt. His sleeping eyes were puffy from all the tears he spilled.

"We lost seven," Sarah said, quietly. Lacey was the only one whom she had a chance to attempt to save, but her wound was too deep.

I gently stroked Kemp's hair and sighed. If we lost seven, I wondered how many were lost in Eden's group.

"There is a bed in my cabin you could take him to. He may be more comfortable," Sarah said.

I shook my head. "No. He doesn't want to be left alone."

The others went to work moving the dead scourge from the ground. They created a large pile on the edge of camp.

"We can burn them," one of the fighters said.

I didn't respond. I was too tired, too broken. Lacey wasn't my family or even a close friend, but I felt a sort of responsibility toward her. I failed her. I failed Kemp because I couldn't protect her. I would never fail him again. I pulled him closer to me, and he let out a sleepy sigh, hugging my waist tighter.

My eyes shot open at the call from a fighter. I must've fallen asleep, but the blurriness of exhaustion faded quickly when I saw the large group of our people returning. Eagerly scanning them, I searched for the auburn locks I missed, but didn't see them.

Eden?

I called out to her, but there was only silence.

Examining them more carefully, I could see their cuts and bruises. Blood covered their faces and clothes. Some limped, being held up by friends. My heart seized, and I began to pant. I couldn't take any more loss. If Eden didn't make it back . . .

I spotted Brian and Jimmy in the crowd.

Brian!

He squinted as he searched the area. When he noticed the pile of scourge, he broke into a sprint toward us. The others that were in decent condition did the same.

What happened?

Scourge attacked.

His face and body relaxed when Sarah broke through the crowd toward him. He pulled her into a tight hug. I watched her mouth move, telling him what happened. His eyes snapped to mine, then dropped to Kemp clutching me. I knew she told him of Lacey's death.

Eden? Where is she?

Taking Sarah's hand in his, he worked his way toward us. Old Bob moved up next to him; his shoulders were hunched, and he avoided my gaze. Fear rippled through me, and I clutched Kemp tighter. He'd be crying if she were dead, right? But he wasn't and neither was Tate. She must be alive, but then where was she?

I knew the answer before they had to say it. I shook my head. "No, she said she'd be careful. She wouldn't do anything crazy."

"I'm sorry." Brian's voice was quiet. "We had a... plan."

I knit my eyebrows together. "A plan?"

Brian swallowed and rubbed the back of his neck. He looked anywhere he could other than my intent gaze. "Yeah. She was to break in and take out Zane. We didn't think it would be that difficult."

I stiffened. She promised me she wouldn't do anything dangerous, but she had already created this plan with Brian. She lied right to my face.

"Sarah, please take Kemp inside the cabin." I lifted him into her arms. The trauma of the day was so much he didn't even flinch when she carried him inside.

I stepped down the steps and leveled my stare with Brian's. We were the same height, almost the same size. He may have had more skills than me, but I had youth and speed.

"I'm sorry, but she can handle herself. You know how independent she is—"

"Yes. I do know," I snapped, and pushed my finger into his chest. "But that is also why she needs someone to help her see the dangerousness of her actions at times. She will always think of the endgame first, not what could happen before that." I let out an edgy laugh and stepped away, looking at Old Bob. "And you went along with this plan as well? She's your daughter!"

Old Bob swallowed and gave Brian a quick glance. "I didn't know. It was just her and Brian."

I blinked before turning around and fixing Brian with another hard stare. "All right. Since you seem to be so big on planning, what's the plan on getting her out?"

He scrubbed a bloody hand over his face, leaving streaks down his cheeks. I didn't flinch at the thought of what they went through. We had our own battle here and Lacey had died. Seven people died.

"It's not that easy. We'll need to plan—"

I growled. "Plan." Pinching the bridge of my nose, I sucked in a deep breath. "Then you better get planning, Brian. You're the one who created the plan that got her caught, so you figure it out. I've lost too many people already. I will not lose Eden too."

I pushed past him, knocking him off balance with my shoulder, and stormed into the woods. I only allowed the tears to come when the only one around me was an understanding wolf.

Chapter 47

Eden

I blinked and looked up at the familiar bright white ceiling. A pit formed in my stomach, and I squeezed my eyes shut, counting to ten before slowly opening them again. The same white ceiling stared back at me. My nose twitched at the smell of disinfectant and metal. Turning my head, I squinted at the glare from the glass windows that caged me in.

My cage.

A male scientist worked quietly at a desk. He was no one I had seen before, and my stomach dropped when I realized I wouldn't be seeing LaRae, Dr. Hahn, or David here.

When I sat up, the scientist looked up from his work, and we locked eyes, but his expression never changed. He looked down, picked up the phone, spoke a few quiet words, and went back to his work. A short time later, Zane strode in with his impeccable black suit and perfect hair, just the way he used to—the only difference now was his one gold eye.

"She's awake!"

I stood and stretched out my arms before walking to the glass. Crossing my arms, I leaned on the small table and stared. He watched me, his eyes twinkling with delight.

"I bet this brings back fond memories." He held his arms out to my cage. "Being back in the place where I created you. Where your best friend—died."

I clenched my jaw. I wouldn't give him the satisfaction of seeing any emotion from his words.

He glanced at the empty cage behind him. Jace's old cage. "How is Jace? I suppose he's still with you?"

I dropped my arms and pushed off the table back to the bed. I gave Zane my back as I sprawled on my side facing the wall. After a moment, he took the hint and left just as I fell asleep.

The clank of my cage door riled me from bed. I sat up with a snarl but froze when I looked directly down the muzzle of a gun.

"Get up," the scientist said. Three guards behind him held the guns pointed at me.

I didn't move. "What's your name?"

His jaw muscles ticked, and he repeated, "Get up. Let's go."

One of the guard's guns clicked, and I smiled. "Name."

"They'll shoot."

"No, they won't. Zane doesn't want me dead, not yet at least. Tell me your name, and I'll go."

He watched me, his lips smoothing into a thin line. "Eric."

I stood and walked toward him. "Nice to meet you, Eric."

He observed me carefully as I passed him and headed toward the guards. I said nothing as they all led me out of the lab and down the hall. Glancing through the windows, I was surprised to see them full. But this time instead of having deteriorating humans in the cages, there were scourge. I swallowed down a growl and focused my eyes forward.

The screens still lined the gym, but they were shut off. Zane and Derek stood in the middle of the large blue mats. More guards lined the wall behind them with guns in their hands, ready.

"Morning," I mused, looking between them.

Derek's face stayed stoic, not showing any expression. Zane flashed his best smile, but I cocked my head at him. There was something a little different. I pulled in a deep breath through my nose. He wasn't well.

"Feeling all right, Zane?"

He waved me off. "Oh, it's nothing I won't recover from. You did." He stepped toward me.

"I'm sorry?"

His smile grew and he tugged down the sleeves of his suit jacket. "Yes. See, after I saw the reaction the scourge had to you the other day, I knew I had to have that power. I couldn't just let you have it all." I watched him, dread pooling inside me. When I glanced at Derek, he refused to look at me.

What are you so afraid of? Why don't you try and stop him?

Derek didn't show any sign he even heard me. I looked back at Zane who watched me with a knowing look. What did he have on Derek?

"So you're infecting yourself?"

He sighed. "Yes. I was injected again for the second time today. The effects aren't as strong as the first, which I'm thankful for."

"Why?"

He chuckled again. "Like I said, I can't let you be the stronger one of us."

I raised my chin in disbelief. He was truly crazy. "Why am I here?"

"Right! Well, I need to dispose of some overflow, and I need you to do it."

"Overflow?"

He nodded and gave a quick motion with his hand. The doors on the side of the gym opened. Guards filed in, each holding a chained scourge. The room immediately filled with their putrid smell and shrieks.

I snapped my eyes to him. "What do you want me to do?" I swallowed the bile down that threatened to erupt.

"Dispose of them."

"Why don't you just shoot them yourself?" I asked, my heart pumping loudly in my ears.

A slimy smile spread across his face. "I could, but that wouldn't be as fun as watching you kill them. I can't wait to see the battle in your eyes as you try and justify having to kill. Even if they are just"—he raised an arm toward the line of scourge—"this."

He walked past me, stopping to lean close to my ear. He smelled of sickness and soap. "And be quick about it." He walked to the door of the gym.

Without turning around, I yelled at him. "Where're you going?"

"I feel like shit. I'm going to rest. Derek will inform me when you've completed the task."

"And if I don't?"

His steps halted, and I heard his intake of breath. "Then Derek has his orders. Get to work."

Derek finally looked at me. His eyes didn't hold the void they had before, but instead, he watched me with regret. Sorrow for what I had to do.

Letting out a snarl, I curled my claws and approached the first scourge. I wouldn't let Zane enjoy my suffering. What I was going to do was more humane than a life like theirs. That's what I told myself for each one that I killed.

～

It took me just short of an hour to kill all the scourge that were brought to me. The first few were the hardest, but once I erected the wall in my mind to block out the horrid fact that I was killing people, I got through it. I didn't think about it. I just killed. They were better off dead, after all.

Covered in blood and feeling empty, I followed Derek back to my cage. All I wanted to do was shower the smut off my skin and soul. I had worked so hard not to become a monster, but now was the first time I actually felt like one.

Derek said nothing to me. Nothing.

I curled my claws and fought the urge to slash his back.

I wouldn't.

I bristled at the invasion of his words. Being exhausted physically and mentally, I didn't realize my walls had come down. *Why? It's not like you're doing anything to help.*

He didn't respond until after I walked behind the doors of my cage. He dismissed the guards, who gave him wary looks, but assured them he'd be fine. When they left, it was just the two of us. He stood in the doorway of my cage.

"Your display the other day caused more issues than we were dealing with before." He met my eyes. He had no regret for abandoning his people and siding with Zane.

"You care why?"

"Because it's going to kill more of the people I'm trying to protect!"

I laughed. "Right. By the number of scourge I just killed, you've done a fine job protecting the people."

His face hardened, and he took a step forward, pointing a rough finger at me. "You left, Eden. You don't know what it was like when they all got sick. Once they learned they'd survive, Zane feared losing control so he went on a rampage. He moved north, infecting people, then saving them with the cure. As their savior, he gained thousands more followers. Some people began to see him for who he really is, but he got rid of them. Now using his new weapon and Reverend Peters's bogus religious claims, he threatens death by scourge." He paused and shook his head. "Our world here has retracted back twenty years. Instead of getting better, it's gotten worse. Far worse, and your display"—he dropped his finger and let out a mocking laugh—"your display just made Zane more power hungry. He's making himself *you*." He motioned to me from top to bottom with his hands and his face scrunched in disgust.

The dismissal and jab stung, but I couldn't let him know that. I bit my tongue to keep from snapping at him. He wasn't done yet, and a small part of me wanted to hear what he had to say.

"I had a plan. I had spies. Brian and I were working together, but Zane slowly picked out each spy, one by one, until there were none. I've had to stay quiet and loyal to stay alive until I can think of another way."

"Why don't you just fight? Or leave?"

He shook his head, and his anger subsided slightly. "You don't think people have tried that? It would be me against an army of scourge. I'd be dead in a second, if that. If I left, what do you think would happen to everyone in the camp? He'd just send his army after us. Too many, if not all, would die." He paused and watched me. "Do you even know how many of your people died yesterday?"

I swallowed and shook my head. I didn't and part of me didn't want to know, but I knew I should in order to respect their sacrifice.

"Thirty-two."

I sucked in a breath and closed my eyes. Thirty-two people gave their lives for my cause to take down Zane. That would leave the numbers much lower than Zane's large army and lessen the probability of success.

We stood silent until he sighed and pushed a hand through his salt-and-pepper hair. He may have been wearing a suit just like

Zane's and had greying hair, but he was still strong and fit. He could fight.

"There is one way we can do it, though, if you're willing." His eyes met mine. A prickle went through my skin, making me shudder.

"What?"

He stepped closer and lowered his voice. "Zane wants power. That's why he's making himself like you. He perceives you as powerful. So once he's done, he'll still have you to contend with."

My blood ran cold. "He'll kill me."

"Maybe, but you're good at antagonizing him. If you put in his head the threat you pose, maybe you can get him to fight you."

"Fight me."

"Yes. For control. Whoever wins will be the leader. Kind of like an... alpha wolf."

I shook my head rapidly. "I don't want to be a leader."

"That doesn't matter. Win first, and then we'll handle that. It's really our only choice. Will you fight him?"

I swallowed, hating the fact that he was right. The only way to stop Zane was to kill him, but he was so powerful that it wouldn't be easy to get close to him. A challenge, witnessed by all, was the only way.

"Yes."

He nodded with a sigh of relief. "Good. Start your antagonizing, and I'll work on my end." He stepped out of my cage but hesitated before shutting the door. "Be careful, Eden."

Not responding, I moved into the shower to scrub my body clean.

Chapter 48

Jace

The sun peeked through the small window of the cabin, lighting the side of my pillow. I rubbed my tired eyes carefully so as to not wake Kemp. He slept soundly next to me with puffy eyes, clutching my arm.

Beds clanked and the floor creaked as people started to rise for the day. I gently slid my arm from Kemp's grasp and stepped outside. A groan escaped me at the sight of a newly built fire. Brian and Old Bob agreed with me that the smoke exposed us, but the danger of the people on night watch freezing was apparently more important.

Sarah approached me with rosy cheeks and eyes at half-mast from exhaustion.

"Everything ready for today?"

She nodded. "How is he?"

"He won't say much. Just wants to be close to me. I keep telling him that I'll care for him, but I think the fear of being a stray child is too strong."

To my surprise, she reached out and grabbed my hand, giving it a squeeze. "You're a good man."

"I'm doing what anyone would do."

She dropped my hand when Brian came to her side. He panted from running patrol in the woods, but it didn't stop him from leaning down to give her a kiss on her cheek. Still angry with him, I turned and headed back into the cabin to check on Kemp. I could feel his eyes burning into my back.

"Jace," Kemp's tired voice hit me the moment I stepped through the door.

"Hey, bud." I sat on the bed and tousled his already messy hair. "Sleep good?"

He stretched with a nod.

"You want something to eat before we head to the site?"

Keeping his wet eyes on his twined hands, he shook his head.

"All right. Let's head out, then." I stood and held out my hand. He didn't hesitate to take it, staying so close to my body that our legs moved in unison.

A large group of people, including Lucia, Old Bob, Sarah, and Tate, walked to a small clearing within the woods. Seven large holes had been dug, and lying next to them were the bodies, wrapped in fabric. Kemp squeezed my arm tighter the closer we got to his sister's wrapped body. He watched her lifeless frame with anguish, torn between running to her and staying close to me.

The group created a large circle around the bodies with bowed heads. A woman named Karen led a prayer. I put my arm around Kemp's shoulders, pulling him to me so he could hide his face in my side. His muffled cries broke my heart and brought tears to my eyes. While I'd lost my mother young, it wasn't sudden or traumatic, and I didn't lose my entire family, parents and sister, in a short period. There were a few others letting soft sobs and tears shed around their friends' lifeless forms.

Karen finished the prayer, and her soft caring eyes moved to Kemp. Even though he wasn't the only one who lost someone, he was the youngest and probably the most impacted. "Did you want to say anything, Kemp?"

He sniffed and peeked out from my shirt to shake his head. I squeezed his shoulder and knelt next to him, keeping my voice so quiet only he could hear me. "Do you want some time alone with her? We can all leave."

His red eyes and blotchy face looked at me. With a sniff, he gave me a slow nod. I stood, looking at the crowd. "He would like a moment alone."

Everyone nodded, some giving him reassuring glances and pats on his back before slowly walking back to the cabins. I began to move away, but Kemp grabbed my hand to hold me back. "You stay."

I gave him a single nod but stepped back to give him space.

He took a few slow steps toward his sister's body and dropped to his knees onto the white snow. He whispered some things I couldn't make out over his sobs and sniffles. When he dropped his body onto hers, my heart cracked. I didn't even know I was crying until a single tear froze to my cheek. I quickly wiped it away and sucked in a shaky breath. I had to be strong for him. Kemp's sobs echoed through the trees and were joined by the howls of Ash's pack in the distance.

~

We sat around the table, planning our next move. My body shook from the fatigue of loss. Sarah had Kemp with her, keeping him busy with organizing items for winter. He had been reluctant to leave me, but Sarah's warm personality and promise of something sweet to eat lured him to her.

"We lost too many people. We need to get more on our side if we're going to try another attack," Brian said. He kept his gaze from mine in fear I'd snap at him again. We hadn't spoken since our argument the day before, and I'm sure he sensed I wasn't ready.

"Where will we get more people? We're pretty limited in that area," Lucia said. She stuck close to Raul, but the guilt I'd have expected from her killing her brother didn't show. That either made her very dangerous or a good actress.

I leaned forward, and everyone looked at me. "What about the people in the city?"

Brian shook his head. "They're too scared—"

"Because they don't know the truth. What if we send people out to tell them the truth?"

Brian opened his mouth to object, but closed it after a sigh. Raul put a gentle hand on Lucia's back with a nod. "That's not a bad idea."

"What exactly would we tell them?" Tate asked.

I shrugged. "What is their greatest fear right now?"

"The scourge," Brian said.

I nodded. "And we know how they're made, but Zane is lying. He's using superstition and religion to manipulate them. We need to tell them how they're really made."

"But he can still change them with just a quick stab of a needle, Jace." Brian strained to keep the frustration from his words, but it came through slightly.

"True, but they also believe that the injection will only work if they are sinners. They need to be told exactly how the scourge are made. The fear may slowly disappear."

"What will make them believe us?" Old Bob asked. He sat back in his chair with bulky arms crossed over his broad chest.

Everyone sat silently, thinking over the hardest part of the task. Tate broke the silence. "What if we don't really have to make them believe us? What if just by starting rumors, it could bring enough doubt that they start to see Zane in a different light."

Old Bob rubbed a rough hand over his greying stubble. "That may be what we'll have to do."

"Gossip has been an ally for centuries," I said with a smirk. "Let's pray it doesn't fail us now."

Raul looked at Brian. "Do you have enough people who know the city to be able to work their way around spreading this information?"

"I can find some."

"How much time do you think we need? I don't want to leave Eden in there too long. Who knows what he's doing to her?" This time I did look at Brian.

"We can't rush things. You know this."

I growled. "Maybe I can go and talk to him."

"And what? Get yourself caught? What good would that do?" Tate looked at me. I raised my eyebrows at the force in his voice. "Eden would want you to be smart. If you are captured, she'll want to save you and not think clearly." He softened his voice. "Plus, think of Kemp."

Letting my eyes close, I groaned. Kemp. I couldn't leave Kemp. He needed me, and I wouldn't abandon him.

"Let's send the first group out tomorrow to the city and gauge it from there," Old Bob said as he put a reassuring hand on my shoulder.

I nodded and stood. Without a word, I left the room to go find Kemp.

Chapter 49

Eden

Without Jace in the cage across from me, the past two weeks have been excruciatingly boring. I focused on staying strong, mentally and physically. I created a small area of my cage to do workouts, which I did multiple times a day in order to try and create faster days.

I spoke to Eric daily through the glass, even though he never responded and just kept his eyes focused on his work. I told him stories of my life in the woods, growing up, mixed with the stories of being captured by Zane before. He never showed any flicker of acknowledgment until I described how we learned how the scourge were made. How Zane used Tristan against me, and how I had to kill him. My best friend.

Zane finally came and spoke to me again, two weeks after our last encounter. My heart pounded in my ears as I watched him walk toward my cage with a smug look. I kept my eyes on him, not letting them drop to his newly grown claws. So he really did do it: he made himself like me. The urge to break through the glass of my cage and claw his gold eye out was strong, but I had to control my rage. I had to be smart.

"I hope you're well," he said smoothly, the tips of his fangs peeking out as he spoke.

"You really did this to yourself? By choice?"

He chuckled and started examining his claws a moment before he looked up at me and said, "Honestly, I don't know why you're so sore about it. We're the most powerful beings in the world."

Watching him with wide eyes, I slowly shook my head. "Well, the world isn't what it used to be."

"True, but nonetheless, we are powerful."

Cocking my head to the side, I examined the sparkle in his eyes, thinking of my conversation with Derek. He wants power, and he'll do almost anything to get and keep it.

"We're powerful, but I wonder"—I stepped closer to the glass, keeping my eyes on his—"will the people think we're partners then? I mean, you're the leader, but what am I? A rebel? I am in no way in alignment with you and your views, so what'll they think when we have the same abilities?"

He kept a smile plastered to his face, the only indications that my words hit home were the twitch of his cheek and tightening around his eyes. I didn't stop there; no, I had to have the last word.

"I'd hate for *your* people to think that I may be more powerful or influential than you."

He let out a bark of laughter. "Eden, you're in a... what is it you always call it? A cage? You're *my* prisoner. My people will know you for what you really are. *My* prisoner to control as *I* see fit."

"Control?" I raised my eyebrows. "How exactly are you going to control me, Zane? Tristan is already dead; Jace isn't here. What do you have against me?"

"You're right. I really don't have much to control you. When we attacked the cabins a few weeks ago, we only managed to kill seven people." He paused, watching me carefully. I stilled my face to try and keep him from seeing any emotion, but if his senses had become the same as mine, he could smell my drastic increase of panic. He smiled. "I heard Jace fought like a knight. So gallant and strong."

The blood rushed to my feet, and I set a hand on the glass to keep from dropping to the cold tile floor. The pounding in my ears increased, and I was unable to focus on anything but Jace.

"Who were the people that died?" My voice cracked. I didn't keep my emotion from my gaze this time, and it only gave Zane a more satisfied aura.

Turning on his heel, he walked to the door of the lab. "Have a good day."

"Zane! Who died?" I slammed my fist onto the glass so hard a small crack echoed. Zane froze and slowly turned. I let a predatorial smirk fill my face, and I narrowed my eyes. He now knew what I was capable of, so maybe he wouldn't push me. Maybe.

"Who. Died."

He took a few steps back toward me. "Like I said, Jace fought gallantly trying to protect the others."

A snarl escaped me, and I slammed the glass again. "I challenge you, Zane! I challenge you to a fight."

He laughed. "What time period do you think we live in?"

"I challenge you for leadership. To the death. Show your people how strong you really are. Show them how powerful you've become." I sneered, leaning into the glass as far as I could go. "Show them how no one, not even someone who is your equal, can beat you." I paused, watching his eyes weigh my words. "Or are you too scared you'll lose?"

His smile dropped as he surveyed me and sucked in a deep breath. Just when I thought he would respond and give me the chance I wanted to kill him, he turned and stormed out of the lab.

Another snarl ripped from deep within me and I saw red. I slammed my fists onto the glass over and over, another crack echoing.

I didn't hear the door to my cage click open or the release of the tranquilizer gun. I didn't even feel the sting of the three darts that hit my back. Not until my heart slowed, bringing fatigue.

I dropped to my knees, panting.

Jace! Please, Jace, hear me!

I fell onto my side, a tear slipping from my eye, then the familiar darkness took me.

～

When I woke, I was still lying on the ground, facing the glass wall. A small crack had formed in the top corner from my burst of anger, but a smearing of a substance over it bound it back together.

I blinked, meeting Derek's empty face. A small wave of relief passed over his eyes before the wall went back up.

"I don't know what you said, but it worked. You have one week."

I didn't move. "He said Jace died." I swallowed. "Did he?" The last two words came out in a whisper. I immediately swallowed down the bile that threatened to erupt.

Derek watched me. "I don't know."

I closed my eyes. Maybe it wasn't true. It had to be false.

One week, Eden. Be prepared. Physically and mentally. Then this all can be over.

I watched his back retreating. He reached the door before I responded. *Without Jace, what's the point?*

He froze, making a play at adjusting his jacket so as to not raise suspicion from Eric, who inconspicuously watched from his desk. *Just be ready.*

The door slammed behind him, and he disappeared down the hall. There was no sympathy in his voice. I'm just a weapon to him. A means to their end.

I let out a cry and buried my head in my arms. I had a day to mourn. A day to mourn Jace, then I would prepare. Zane had taken too much from me. My parents, Ellie, Tristan, and now Jace. He'll die for it. I will make sure of that.

Chapter 50

Jace

Over the next two weeks, pairs of people were sent into the city to spread the truth about the scourge. In the beginning, they tried to talk to people directly, but we underestimated how afraid people were. People fled from them, yelled, or even attacked when they spoke. So, we changed our tactic. Our people went in pairs, drank in coffee shops, and sat in the central park where the citizens walked daily or even just shopped. Instead of having conversations with the city folk, our people talked loudly amongst themselves, causing listening ears.

We knew this tactic was more successful when two of our informants said they heard a table of men discussing it in a pub. But we still didn't know how many people would actually fight when the time came. If the time came.

My days were filled with creating any possible plans to get Eden out and ending Zane. My blood boiled to end him.

Keeping Kemp busy was my second job. The grief within him had changed to a burning fire for revenge. We worked daily on his exercises to keep him ready, even though I would never let him near battle, but he didn't have to know that.

One day as we worked on the well-beaten snow, hoots and hollers echoed through the trees, stopping our routine. Everyone in the camp halted their work, looking into the trees in the direction of the city.

"Scourge?" Kemp asked, looking around us to grab anything for a weapon.

I put my hand on his shoulder. "No. I don't think so." Squinting through the trees toward a growing crowd, I spotted the familiar dark hair and stern face of the once leader of the camp.

Derek.

Skipping a step, I charged through the trees toward him. Brian and Old Bob shook his hand, but none of their faces reflected a happy reunion. Derek's face held a grave look as he watched everyone with tired, dark eyes.

I pushed through the crowd and stepped up beside Brian. "Where's Eden? Have you seen her?"

Derek looked at me, his eyes widening slightly before giving me a slight nod. "Yes. I have seen her, spoken to her, and she's fine."

"Why didn't you get her out?" I leaned toward him only to be pushed back by Brian.

"Jace, calm down. Let's hear what he has to say."

Derek watched me a moment, then let his eyes roam over the rest of the people. "I think we should talk inside—"

"Talk now," I growled, snapping my arm away from Brian's grip.

Derek narrowed his eyes at me. "Fine." He paused, running his tongue over his teeth before letting out a long sigh. "There is to be a fight."

"A fight?" Old Bob asked.

"Yes. Zane was... inspired by how Eden was after her display, so he's made himself like her."

I stepped back closer to the murmuring crowd.

"What does that mean?" a man called from the back, fear radiating from his voice.

Derek looked at him, then moved his eyes over the rest of the crowd. "It means that we have two powerful Chimera who'll fight for dominance."

Lucia let out a laugh. She leaned on a tree at the edge of the crowd, with Raul next to her. "Looks like our little fighter is going to get what she wants."

Derek looked at her a moment, blinking. "Who... who are you?"

She stepped forward. "Lucia. Me and my people are the ones Eden commissioned to help take down Zane, but it looks like we may not be needed."

Derek looked back at Brian, who nodded. Derek looked back at her. "You may still be needed. If something doesn't go as planned, we may still have to fight."

I growled and crossed my arms. "You talk like you've had this grand plan all along."

Brian and Derek didn't respond and avoided my eyes, an action that made the blood within me overheat.

"Don't tell me you planned this?" Old Bob's voice held warning. Brian slowly met his eyes, leveling his jaw.

"How?"

"We weren't able to predict what would happen for sure, but knowing Zane's thirst for power and Eden's impulsivity and need to help the helpless, we took our chances."

I stepped toward them. "You sacrificed her?"

Lucia chuckled. "I thought I was cold."

Derek shook his head. "We sacrificed no one. She'll be fine—"

"If she wins the fight," Old Bob said. "I have to say, Brian, I'm disappointed. I trusted you. You could've just told us the whole plan. We could've helped. Thought of something, anything other than this!"

"It was too risky. If any one of you were taken, then it risked the whole plan getting to Zane." Brian faced Old Bob. "I would never have left you in the dark if this wasn't important. We don't have more than one chance. Zane won't allow it."

I clenched my hands into fists, ready to attack Brian, when I felt a small presence next to me.

Kemp.

Closing my eyes, I steadied my breath. I couldn't teach him this. He had to see me in control. It was an action not missed by Derek. His eyes flicked down to Kemp, then back to mine before he spoke quietly. "She thinks you're dead."

"What?"

"Zane said some things, not sure what exactly, but she came to the conclusion that you're dead."

"You have to tell her I'm alive."

"No."

"No?"

"She has a week to get herself under control. Ready to fight. If I go and tell her before she's supposed to fight that you're alive, it may throw her focus off. Remember, we only have this *one* chance."

"Then tell her now. Today!"

This time I didn't care that Kemp was there. I stepped toward him, holding my chest high, my fists bunched at my sides, but I was pulled back when Old Bob grabbed my arm.

"I can't. I'm not allowed near her. I know I'll see her the day of the fight, but I can't promise I can see her before."

I lunged toward him again, but Old Bob's hand held firm. "He's right. Maybe she'll fight better thinking you're dead."

I raised my eyebrows at him. "It's a lie." My stomach roiled with all the disinformation.

"It's necessary. When she wins, she'll be so happy to see you." Old Bob released my arm slightly.

I growled and looked back at Derek. "The fight's in a week?"

He nodded. "Everyone should attend." His eyes roam over the crowd again. "Be ready for anything."

I grunted. "See you in a week." I turned and pushed through the crowd. I felt Kemp close behind and only relaxed slightly when his small hand filled mine.

~

The week went by painfully slow. I tried to keep busy by working with Kemp and strategizing with the others for any possible situations that may come up. Sleep didn't last more than an hour, and if I did fall into a slumber, I was woken by the image of Eden being killed, her blood painting the white snow red.

Some nights Kemp would also wake from my restless movements. We'd lull each other back to sleep by telling silly stories. It kept both our minds off the loss of our loved ones.

On the fighting day, our group walked quietly in unison. Kemp clutched my hand, and Old Bob stayed close on my other side. Lucia and Raul walked among their people, more curious about what would happen than worried. I hoped they took this seriously; we may need them more than ever.

The wolves, who had kept to the perimeter of the camp in all our preparations, walked as a pack, fanned out among us.

"Remember to try and stay out of sight," Old Bob mumbled.

I swallowed, hating the plan of not telling Eden that I was alive. It left a sour feeling in my stomach, and I'd been unable to eat for two days.

As we entered the city, city folk joined our group while we walked to the arena in the city center. The closer I got, the more tense my body was. My head pounded, and I started to find it more difficult to breathe.

Kemp looked up at me with wide worried eyes. "You OK?"

Looking down at him, I let out a long breath. "Yeah." Giving him a small smile, I said, "I'm just worried you'll be seeing some things that you're far too young for." I gave his hand a small squeeze.

He laughed a little. "I saw both my parents and sister be killed. I think I'll be all right."

I watched him as he looked forward toward the seating area of the arena. His body and features looked like his age of six, but the knowledge in his eyes was much, much older. My heart tightened at the fact that he would never have his young childhood. When all this was over, I'd do my best to give him the childhood he deserved.

Brian led us to a few rows of seating halfway up the inclined rows. He looked at me and motioned for me to sit at the end.

So you can get away when she shows. We don't want her to see you until after.

I stifled a growl but sat. With my legs bouncing, I searched the area for any sign that people were ready to revolt, but my stomach sank when I was met with the faces of scared people. None of them looked willing to fight.

Once most of the people were seated, Zane marched out into the middle of the arena. He wore his signature suit, impeccably clean and ironed as usual, but a look down at his hands made my teeth clench.

Claws.

He really did change himself.

He stopped at a microphone and held up a hand to get the attention of the already-silent crowd.

"Good afternoon!" His voice rang among the people. His elongated fangs peeked out from under his upper lip as he spoke. "Thank you all for coming. We have a very special show today. I've been formally challenged for leadership by none other than Eden."

He paused, looking gravely through the murmuring crowd. Confusion hinted with hope filled the air, and Zane continued, "Yes, yes, I know. It's a shame that I have to kill her so publicly, but I wouldn't want to leave you all with a young, impulsive leader."

A growl filled my chest, and Old Bob squeezed my forearm gently. Letting out a few breaths, I calmed my anger and spoke quietly to no one in particular. "If this turns into an execution, I won't stay hidden."

"It won't be," Brian mumbled, keeping his eyes on Zane.

"Bring her out!" Zane's voice was so loud he almost didn't need the microphone.

My body tensed, and I looked at the snow-covered ground in the split between two sections of seating where Zane had emerged from. Slowly, Eden stepped into view, her head held high with narrowed eyes locked onto Zane. Those eyes held death. Her hands were cuffed together in the front, and I almost laughed at the thought that Zane really thought those could hold her.

She moved confidently into the middle of the arena with four armed guards behind her. Power and vengeance flowed from her in waves. I had never been so proud to know she was mine and I was hers.

Zane was quiet as he watched her approach, glancing at the nervous-looking crowd frequently, watching their reactions. It was his only show of unease. It would be lost on most people, but not me, and I'm sure not Eden.

I felt the familiar presence of the wolves, which had me searching the crowd. They had stayed out of the arena after we entered the city, but I smiled when I spotted Ash's dark coat and gold eyes watching Eden. Behind him were a few of his pack; the rest scattered around the edges of the crowd, careful not to be seen and cause havoc. I recognized their intent glowing eyes in the shadows.

I knew the moment when Eden sensed Ash by the slight twitch at the corner of her mouth.

"All right, Eden. Kill," I whispered, wishing she could hear me.

Chapter 51

Eden

I held my head high as I entered the arena. At least the snow was packed down, showing small patches of dead grass. Movement on it wouldn't be difficult, and hopefully, it would help me kill Zane faster.

Sending my senses out, I felt Ash and his pack almost immediately. They were here, tense and worried, but ready to fight.

I'm all right, Ash.

A rush of relief flooded my senses. He was relieved at my words. My mouth twitched again when I felt it, but I steadied my face and continued forward.

The last week had been agony. Daily, I was brought into the gym to kill more groups of scourge. Zane and Derek never graced me with their presence, but I was told I needed to be the executioner if I didn't want more of my family to be killed. Still numb from Jace's death and knowing my fight with Zane was coming soon, I didn't argue. I ended the lives of the scourge brought to me. For every life I took, I repeated that they were better off dead.

In my spare time, I exercised, reviewed movements Brian and Old Bob had taught me, and mourned Jace. My heart sank at the thought of him.

My broken heart has been fractured too many times in the last year, losing so many that I loved. All because of one man—Zane.

I set my jaw and eyes forward and walked toward his smug face, my butterfly necklace hanging heavy over my heart. I have vowed daily since learning of Jace's death that Zane will die, and today was that day. I will not fail Jace... or Ellie... or Tristan.

Zane held up a hand, and I stopped. The guards around me moved to the edges of the arena, blocking various sections of the crowd. Whether it was to protect them from me or keep me from trying to run, I don't know, but I didn't care. My focus was only on killing.

"Eden," Zane's voice rang through the clear-skied morning. "You've formally challenged me, so it's only honorable that I accept that challenge."

"There is nothing honorable about you." I growled, loud enough for everyone to hear. My top lip twitched to bare my fangs.

He sneered and ignored my words. "But first, you'll show the people who you really are. What you've been doing for me the past few weeks."

I tensed.

A loud shriek echoed behind me, and I spun. A group of a dozen scourge were pulled into the arena. At their center was David.

My heart sank, and I thanked whatever higher power there may be that Jace wasn't here to see his father like this. That he wasn't here to see me kill him.

Zane's voice brought me back to him. "Now, you've been killing them while they are helpless, but I wonder how you'll do if they're loose." He tilted his head, carefully watching my response. I gave him nothing, but the crowd became noticeably more agitated.

I scanned the area around him, but Zane was alone in the center of the arena. Looking back toward the entrance, I saw a few seats right in the front. Derek occupied one, his face tense but unreadable.

What is this? I looked at him.

I knew nothing of it. Just... do your best.

I let out a snarl. Derek knew it was directed at him, but to the crowd, it was an animal about to let loose. Do your best. He didn't think I'd survive. Ash's agitation filled me, but I sent him a few calming words, willing him to stay away.

"Release them," Zane said, quickly stepping behind a few guards. I smiled at his continued fear, even though he was supposedly more powerful now.

The scourge, including David, charged me. Why they only went for me and no one else, I don't know, but I didn't have time to breathe before the first one was in the air coming down at me. Quickly curling my claws, I slashed out, swiping a death wound over its chest. My movements were smooth and fast as I ended scourge after scourge.

After my sixth one, I spun toward my seventh when one grabbed my arm, yanking me back. I hit the ground hard, coughing and dazed at how one got the better of me. A stabbing pain in my shoulder brought a scream out from within me.

I kicked at two scourge before they could pile on the one that had my shoulder between its fangs. Pulling in a deep breath, I grabbed its hair and yanked back, grunting in pain as a chunk of my skin came off, dangling from the scourge's mouth. I shoved it back and hit the other two who charged me again, knocking them all to the ground.

Jumping fast, I spun. My movements were faster and more precise from the adrenaline rush. My shoulder was numb from pain as I took out four more scourge in less than a minute. When I turned to the last group of three, I froze.

David charged me, his gold eye wasn't vibrant like Jace's but a duller yellow, like all the scourge. A sign their old self wasn't there—at least that's what I told myself.

His inky black hair had streaks of white, giving me a glimpse of what Jace's would have looked like if he was able to grow old.

"Eden, move!" Brian's voice echoed through the area. It was the only sound besides the shrieks of the remaining scourge.

I was hit from the side and then the front by David. I hesitated, looking into David's face as he bared his yellow teeth, saliva dripping onto my shirt. But I couldn't make that killing blow.

Piercing pain dug into my side and I screamed, dropping one hand that held David to grab the scourge that had his fangs dug into my side.

I panted and weighed my options.

A snarl radiated around me just before dark fur flew over my head and knocked David from my grasp.

"Ash."

David and Ash fell in a pile of limbs and paws, but Ash quickly gained the upper ground. I grabbed the head of the scourge at my side and snapped its neck and jumped up. Ash had David by the throat, so I turned to the last scourge and charged. Holding an arm to my injured side, with blood seeping between my fingers, I slashed its throat with my good arm.

A deafening shot rang out behind me followed by a small yip.

"No."

My heart pounded in my ears, and I slowly turned. Ash lay on his side. Still.

"No," I whispered again, stepping toward him. "No, no, no."

David got up and moved toward him with a shriek, but I was too fast. I grabbed him by his neck and buried my claws into his windpipe. His eyes widened as he struggled for breath, but I didn't drop my hold until his chest stopped moving and blood dripped from his mouth.

Everything around me was silent. My heart pumped in my ears, drowning out any other sounds around me. I didn't want to turn and see one of the last beings I love dead, but I forced my body to move.

Ash was still. His gold eyes closed. As I approached him, I watched for any sign that he was still alive. I dropped my knees at his side.

"Ash?" My voice broke and I choked on a sob.

Tears wet his dark thick coat as I leaned over him and gave him a small shove. The softness of his thick coat moved between my fingers, and I thought of all the times I stroked his fur in the cabin by the fire or relaxed while fishing in the river. The thought of never feeling this coat again was unbearable.

"Ash!"

My sobs echoed between the rows of silent people. They watched with wide eyes as I clutched my dead wolf, his blood staining the white snow beneath us.

Zane approached me from behind. I sat up but kept him at my back. "Are you finally going to show the people how much honor you have?" My voice held steady despite the grief in my heart.

"He broke the rules—"

I stood and spun so fast he stepped back midsentence with wide his eyes.

"Zane!" My snarl echoed between us. "I formally challenge you, to the *death*."

Zane blinked, momentarily perplexed, then dropped his eyes to my injured shoulder and bleeding side. He smiled and gave me a mocking bow. "I accept your challenge."

Chapter 52

Jace

Kemp pulled his hand from mine and shook it out. I didn't realize I had been clutching it so tightly after Ash was shot. I should've been the one to stop Zane. Eden wouldn't survive this.

Everyone, including me, sat on the edges of their seats. Old Bob kept me from interfering when it looked like Eden may be overwhelmed. I knew I would've been if I had to fight twelve scourge alone.

I kept my eyes from dropping to my father's lifeless body. When I saw him arrive with the rest of the scourge, I didn't have the reaction I expected. I didn't feel the anguish I had felt after hearing what he had become—maybe because I knew he was technically already dead, or maybe it was because I knew he would soon be at peace.

Eden faced Zane with curled claws and a taut body, ignoring the injuries that she obtained. Nothing but disdain, anger, and revenge rippled off her.

Zane showed no fear as he circled her slowly, stopping only to kick dead scourge's bodies to the side, never taking his eyes off Eden. She tracked him, staying at Ash's side. I could see the hesitation of leaving him, but in order to beat Zane, she would have to.

Please, let me talk to her. I watched Brian's face as I spoke to him.

He turned and looked at me with furrowed brows. *No. If she is distracted, that could be the end of her. She needs to focus.*

She has lost almost everyone she loves. She's fighting for revenge now, so she won't care if she wins or loses. She'll let herself die if it also means Zane will go down.

He studied me a moment before looking back at Eden who had taken a few steps away from Ash's body. *I still say no. It's too risky.*

I let a snarl radiate into his head, and he shook his head to clear the sound but didn't respond or look at me.

Zane waited for Eden to make the first move, but she didn't play into it. She patiently tracked him, slowly turning along with him as he worked his way in a circle around her.

"Scared, Zane?" Eden taunted.

He chuckled. "Of you? Never." He took a few more steps, avoiding a large pool of blood that had melted some of the snow. "You're injured."

Eden laughed, looking down at her two wounds. "What, these? They're nothing."

I groaned internally at her response. She would let herself die in order to kill Zane.

"Is she going to win?" Kemp whispered next to me. He wrung his hands together on his lap. I sighed, wishing I hadn't let him come. This wasn't something a child should see.

"Yes."

I couldn't manage to say anything else, even though the fear that she may not win filled me to my core.

Without any indication, Eden charged. She wrapped her arms around Zane's middle, and he went down with a loud umph, but he quickly kicked up his legs to knock her off, then twisted onto his knees.

Eden jumped to her feet before he made it up to standing and kicked him in the jaw. It was so fast I wouldn't have realized what happened if I hadn't seen the blood pouring from Zane's mouth. He touched his jaw and narrowed his eyes at her.

Eden went in again, but this time, Zane ducked and reached up to catch her foot. She pulled quickly, but not before he swung it to the side. She fell, landing on her injured shoulder. Her scream was brief, but I still moved to stand, stopping myself halfway. "She isn't going to last long."

"She's stronger than you think. She's well trained," Old Bob said, but his face was etched with worry as he watched his daughter stumble back to her feet.

"That seems like more than a scratch," Zane said.

"How's the jaw?" Eden asked.

Zane put his hand on his jaw to feel where her foot had landed. He opened and closed his mouth a few times and froze. Bringing his hand to his temple, he squeezed his eyes shut and gave his head a quick shake.

Eden smirked and charged him again. This time Zane braced himself before she hit and was able to flip her onto her back before they landed. Instead of jumping onto her to make a blow, he heeled over into a fit of coughs.

"What's going on?" I asked, quietly.

Brian didn't look at me. "Just wait." Peeling my eyes from the fight, I looked at him only to see his eyes were locked with Derek's.

"Brian, what's going on?" I repeated, this time with a hint of warning.

He didn't respond.

Eden stood, holding her injured arm over her injured side to protect it before charging forward again. Her steps were uneven, and her strength was diminishing. She connected with Zane again, and they both fell onto the blood-covered snow, rolling in a heap of limbs. Their grunts reverberated around the arena.

Zane held up his hands to protect his face, but his coughs picked up, and he continued to touch his head.

"Something's not right," I said.

Brian looked at me finally. "That's because he's infected."

My jaw dropped.

"Don't worry, Jace. It's all part of the plan."

I growled and looked back into the arena where Zane, still coughing and weak, had pinned Eden down by her shoulders. He made sure to put a considerable amount of pressure onto her injured shoulder.

I hated this plan, whatever it was.

Chapter 53

Eden

My scream scratched my throat and pain caused my vision to blur, but I pushed back toward Zane with all my might. He coughed and shook his head frequently. Something was bothering him, and I expected it was from the blow to the head I gave him, but his clammy skin didn't add up. His eyes were rimmed with red, and his breathing sounded raspy.

He picked up a hand and slapped it across my cheek. My head whipped to the side, the sting radiating down my neck.

Focus, Eden. Derek's voice filled me.

Whap!

Zane slapped me again, only this time on the other cheek. My surroundings were a blur. Zane's slaps turned to punches, and my head was jostled from side to side. My face became numb and my vision was bursts of light.

I pushed up onto my elbows, trying to get him off me, but he was too heavy, and the wound on my side made it impossible for me to use my core strength.

Zane stopped and panted over me. Sweat built on his brow, and he coughed again, a deep cough that echoed throughout the arena. I heard murmurs from the crowd of confusion.

"You don't... look too well," I said.

Zane toppled off me onto the blood-covered snow. After pushing him up to a sitting position, I looked over at him, weak and defenseless. I almost felt bad having to kill him.

Almost.

I scanned the crowd, trying to find any familiar faces, but my head was so foggy I couldn't make anyone out. I was able, however, to meet Derek's eyes.

Kill him.

I don't know if I'm strong enough. I pushed myself again but winced from the pain. My adrenaline was wearing off, and the pain from my injuries was too much.

You have to. You're strong.

I swallowed and looked back at Ash's body, tears welling in my eyes, and my heart filled with grief. *No, I can just be with Ash. With all of them.*

No! Derek's voice boomed in my mind, and I sucked in a breath. *Jace is alive.*

I sucked in a breath and snapped my eyes toward him. *What?*
Kill him, Eden. You still have much to live for.

I froze and pushed up onto my hands and knees, stifling the painful grunt that rose within me. *Jace?* I scanned the crowd frantically, searching for him. *Jace?*

Eden, you have to fight. I closed my eyes and let out a sob at Jace's voice in my head. He was alive.

I looked back at Zane who was stumbling to a stand.

Eden, he's infected.

I sucked in a breath at Jace's words, running my eyes over Zane's sweating, clammy skin and red-rimmed eyes. He was infected, but his symptoms shouldn't be this severe. The more I was infected, the less the symptoms came while the side effects grew stronger.

Seeming to read my mind, Derek responded to my thought.

The dose I gave him was much higher than usual. I wanted to make sure he showed something.

I staggered to my feet and squared off with Zane. He watched me through coughs and raspy intakes of breath.

"You must've given me a harder kick than I thought."

I gave him a wry smile. "I don't think so. I think you need to be more careful about who you keep by your side."

He watched me a moment, then stood tall and stretched out his back and neck. His movements were careful, like his range of motion was inhibited.

I curled my claws and readied my body for impact as much as I could and watched his feet dig into the sloppy red snow.

Don't waste time! Do it!

I gritted my teeth. I could just snap his neck or... I glanced down at Ash's body. To make a scourge, I needed dead animal blood, but the thought of using Ash like that was too much. When I met Zane's eyes, he smiled.

"I know what you're thinking, but can you do it?"

I swallowed, my stomach sour and empty. No. I couldn't do it.

Just kill him, Eden. No heroics, remember?

My heart twisted at Jace's words, but I had to prove to the world that Zane was wrong. That he was lying; otherwise, there would always be questions concerning the truth.

I'm sorry. I have to try.

I charged him, but this time instead of hitting him from the middle, I dropped and swiped my leg behind his to knock him over. He fell hard onto a small pile of dead scourge.

I blinked down at him.

No, Eden.

I shook my head, not meeting Derek's eyes. *This may work.*

We don't know that!

I guess we'll find out.

Before Derek could respond, I jumped onto Zane, who was already halfway to standing. I reached my claw deep into the wound of the nearest dead scourge and pulled up a thick slop of blood and something else I didn't want to think about. Pushing down a gag, I pushed it into Zane's stomach, opening a large wound with my claws. He let out a loud scream that changed into a laugh, which eventually transformed into another fit of coughs.

I crawled off him and stood. He watched me with his hand over the new wound on his belly.

"You really... think that'll do anything?" He laughed again and pushed to a stand.

I continued to step backward, keeping my eyes on him. "Well, if it doesn't change you, the wound will probably kill you. Either way, I win."

The crowd watched with tense wide eyes. Everything was silent except Zane's labored breaths and coughs.

I roved my eyes over them again before I spoke. "He has told you that only sinners become scourge." I pointed at Zane, who still laughed and staggered a few steps toward me. I continued, keeping my voice loud and steady, despite my aching wounds. "But that was a lie. The scourge were created from a mistake while creating the vaccine. If dead animal blood is given instead of a live one, then this is what they become." I pointed to the dead scourge that scattered the ground.

The crowd's murmurs grew louder. Zane quieted and narrowed his eyes at me.

"And you think giving me scourge blood will make me like them? You just lost your one chance to prove your point."

A man from the crowd stood and pointed a finger at Zane. "Is what she saying true? You lied to us?" The crowd started to erupt in yells.

Zane didn't give the man a glance, but he did respond. "She lies!" His voice was loud, yet weak. "Look. She did nothing but injure me!" He held up his arms, his left arm a little lower due to the gaping wound I created.

"You don't know that." I looked back at the crowd. "I was there when this was discovered. This man"—I jabbed a single claw at Zane—"infected my best friend, making him a scourge. He's a monster and—"

Zane screamed and hunched over, clutching his belly. His breathing increased to a rapid pant mixed with uncontrollable coughing.

"What's happening to him?" someone yelled from the crowd.

I took a few more steps back, never letting my eyes drop from Zane.

He fell to his knees and let out a pained growl. He rolled his head against his shoulders and let his eyes meet mine. I held his gaze firmly. I don't know how long we stared at each other, but I did know the moment he died behind those eyes, only to be replaced by the dull eyes of a scourge.

His skin dulled to a clammy grey, and he let out a loud deafening shriek.

"Behold"—I held my hand out toward Zane's scourge body— "the sinner!"

The crowd erupted into yells. People stood, making to move from the seats to flee. They pushed past the wary guards who looked to each other unsure of what their commands were now.

Zane's scourge let out another loud screech and charged me. I stood firm and ready, stepping to the side just before he reached me, and grabbed his head, snapping it all the way around. The neck break was only audible to me now that the entire arena was filled with screams.

Zane's body fell.

Dead.

I stared at him a moment, listening to my pounding heart in my ears, waiting for the feeling of elation to hit me, but it never came.

Nothing changed.

Ellie was still dead. Tristan and Ash—all were still dead.

Ash.

I looked back at his body, lying among the red snow. I stumbled toward him and fell to my knees at his side. I didn't know I was crying until my tears wet his thick coat when I looked down at him. I didn't even look at the swarms of scourge that the guards let loose into the field or the battle that erupted between them and my people. Pushing aside the chaos around me, I buried my face in his coat and let the world around me melt away.

Chapter 54

Eden

"You got it!" I smiled down at Kemp as he continued to weed through the garden.

It took us two weeks to get the garden back into shape, and it was finally starting to look like I remembered it. I closed the book of garden notes Ellie had kept, swiping my hand over the rough leather cover. I could almost see her scribing diligently in it after each day.

The spring air was finally warming to early summer, and the cool breeze soothed my warm skin. I could feel the humid air building again for another few rainy days, which I'm sure will help the garden.

"I caught my first fish!" Lillyanne's voice echoed through the trees. She emerged near the boathouse with Tate at her side.

"I wouldn't call it much of a fish." His eyes were fixed on Lillyanne's smiling face, but when he felt my gaze, he quickly turned away, and a rosy tint filled his cheeks.

Jace emerged from the boathouse covered in sawdust from cutting firewood. "Let me have a look." He peered into the bucket of fish Tate dropped near the cleaning stump.

Hovering over the bucket, Lillyanne pointed inside. "There!" She looked up at Jace with twinkling eyes.

I could see the twitch of his cheek before he nodded his head. "Well... it *is* a fish."

I smiled and stepped up to look as Lillyanne beamed at me. "Here, Eden. That's the one."

I followed her slender finger to the smallest sunfish I had ever seen. It was about the length of three minnows, and it didn't have much meat on it. I smiled back at her warmly.

"That's great, Lillyanne."

She gave Tate a playful elbow jab. "See." Tate chuckled as he pulled out a large fish from the bucket and slammed it onto the tree stump to clean.

Jace's hand slid over my shoulders, and I leaned into him, breathing in his scent of sawdust and sweat. I pulled Jace away toward the garden where Kemp continued to work diligently.

"He seems to be enjoying the garden." Jace's deep voice soothed me. All the tension I had from the past year slowly uncoiled from within me.

"Yeah." I watched Kemp as he sat back for a moment of rest, swiping a dirt-covered hand over his brow that left a smear of mud down his face.

"I think it's good for him. Keeps his mind busy."

Jace looked down at me, his eyes warm on my cheek. "For you too."

Before I could respond, a small yipping and growling emerged from the trees, and my heart jumped. Quickly pulling away from Jace, I jogged toward the tree edge and dropped to my knees.

"Come here."

Small dark balls of fur flew from the thick brush and tackled me. The feeling of rough, warm tongues and slight nips pulled a giggle from my chest. Yes, a giggle.

"Rascal!" Kemp yelled, running to the pups. He picked up the small dark wolf pup from my chest and buried his face in his fur. Rascal's tail waved so fast it was almost a blur as he kissed Kemp.

Sitting up, I smiled at the light grey female wolf that emerged behind the five pups. Her rare green eyes twinkled at the sight of her litter so happy. "Hey, Emmy." She dipped her head just slightly enough for me to know she acknowledged my greeting.

The ache for Ash still lingered in my chest, but the day Emmy came to the cabin and led me to the cave where the pups slept, I knew he had left me the best gift. Five of his pups. I could see him in all of them. In the ways their ears twitched at every sound, in their similar gold eyes, the brown undertones of their dark coats, and the way all of them smiled at the sight of humans. They may be wolves, but they loved human companionship.

Tate and Lillyanne finished cleaning the fish, Jace built the fire inside the cabin, and Kemp and I brought in some vegetables from the garden. Emmy and her pups followed us inside. She liked to curl up in Ash's old favorite spot near the fire. I'm sure she could still smell him on the blanket I left there; I know I could when I curled up there late at night after the others were asleep. His scent was slowly fading, but I still recognized it enough for it to bring me comfort.

I heard the footsteps approach the cabin long before they met the creaky wood of the porch stairs. They were hard and clipped, bringing the tightness back into my shoulders.

"Brian's here."

The screech of the porch door had Emmy's ears twitching, and the pups running toward Brian as he stepped into the kitchen. Smiling, he bent down to pet them.

"You're just in time for dinner." Lillyanne grabbed another plate and fork.

"Thank you, but I won't be staying long." Brian stood. He looked right at me, the skin around his eyes tightening "Can we talk?"

I pursed my lips and felt Jace's presence emerge beside me. I hadn't spoken to Brian or Derek since I left the city months ago. The feeling of betrayal still boiled deep within, but I gave him a curt nod.

"Outside."

His chest dropped slightly, letting me know he had been holding his breath.

"Wait! We want to hear who won the election too," Lillyanne squealed. Tate stepped to her side and gently grabbed her hand. She furrowed her brows when he gently pulled her to him, but he just shook his head slightly.

I took Jace's hand and led him outside after Brian. I might need him to hold me back if I lost my temper.

"So?" I asked.

"Robert won."

I let out a long breath and smiled. Old Bob did it. "He'll be a good leader. How is Derek taking it?"

"He accepts it, and I think deep down he knew it would happen. Robert is going to assign him a leadership position. Now with almost an equal number of humans and Chimera, we'll need a representative." He smiled, trying to lighten the mood, but I kept my eyes on the green grass around us, avoiding his poignant stare.

"And the scourge?" I asked quietly, fighting the bile at the memory of killing so many. After I'd killed Zane, Reverend Peters had instructed the guards to let all the scourge loose. They almost managed to win, but because of Lucia's people, we were able to kill half and blockade the other half within the arena to be taken care of later. We still lost forty-four people, so it wasn't much of a victory in my book.

Brian pursed his lips. "There are none left." He paused a moment before adding. "It was done quickly and humanely."

Not sure how humane you could be when having to kill, but at least, they weren't suffering anymore. I nodded and dropped my eyes again.

"Have you heard from Lucia?" Jace asked.

"Not since Robert was elected, but we sent word to her. I'm sure she'll be relieved. She was concerned about having a peaceful relationship with her bordering lands."

The tension between my shoulders had almost disappeared. Before the election, we had agreed to a border line with Lucia and to conditions of her leadership role. Much to our surprise, when she moved back south, the people didn't fight her. She was the more peaceful one between her and Izan. After this election, it was decided that northern borders would be created, and the people who had followed Zane south could move back north and conduct their own election. This way there would be three lands. It was our measly way to try and restart what was left of the world.

"We had told her we'd visit this winter. A good way to get out of the cold weather," I said, trying to break the formality of our conversation. I met Brian's eyes, and he visibly relaxed. He hated the tension between us as much as I did. We may not have known each other that long, but we had been through hell together, and he had trained me.

"Yes. I'm sure it is."

Jace squeezed my shoulder. "Brian, why don't you stay for dinner? I'm sure you're hungry after your journey, and Lillyanne will be excited to show you the first fish she's ever caught."

I snorted, and Brian's face lit up a little watching us. The longing for what we had etched in his eyes. He nodded. "Thank you."

We sat around the table full of charred fish, potatoes, and carrots. Laughter and quiet chatter filled the room. Kemp, always staying close to Jace, grinned at me just before he dropped a piece of fish to the pups, who all congregated around his feet. I shook my head with a chuckle.

After my belly was full, I sat back and watched the conversation flow freely. Lillyanne and Tate had been chipper at the news of Old Bob winning the election. I watched as Lillyanne leaned closer to Tate, her shoulder slightly nestled into his side. My heart fluttered at the happiness in his eyes when he looked at her. They complemented each other perfectly.

"You all right?" Jace whispered into my ear.

I looked at him. His one blue eye was as vibrant as his gold one as they searched mine. Thinking back, I realized it had been almost a year ago that I met him, lying beaten on the boathouse floor with long shaggy hair. I never dreamed that he'd become everything to me. My soulmate.

I smiled and brought my hand up to his dark hair, soft and thick under my fingers, pushed my hands through his hair, and met his forehead to mine.

"Yes. Everything is perfect."

Thank you

I hope you enjoyed reading the rest of Eden and Jace's story as much as I enjoyed writing it. Thank you for taking the time to read my novel. In a world filled with amazing stories, I am honored you picked up my book to enjoy.

Authors wouldn't exist without readers, so thank you for making me an author.

Since the best social proof a book can receive are reviews, I would greatly appreciate your review of Chimera.

You can follow me on Instagram at writer_cjsingh, Facebook at World of C. J. Singh and of course my website worldofcjsingh. com.

Acknowledgments

There are so many people to thank for the development of this novel. First, my grandmother, Elizabeth Harri. She was my first reader and always had positive things to say about my six-year-old writing.

Thank you to my friends, Melissa Williams and Katie Ginivan. You both helped me so much in the creation and flow of this story. It wouldn't be what it is today without your help.

Anna Lynch, thank you, thank you, thank you. You are the world building and creation guru. I know I blew your phone up constantly with what ifs and questions, but your expert suggestions helped make this book what it is.

Thank you again to Katie Chambers at Beacon Point LLC for your expert editing. You not only edited my work, but you made me a better writer with all your help and insight. I will be forever thankful.

Thank you to Robin J. Samuels at Shadowcat editing for your amazing proofreading. Your sharp eye and dedication helped polish my book, making it the best it could be.

Thank you to my parents who always kept my path open so I could be whatever I wanted. To my brother, you will get a signed first edition. Don't worry.

To my husband, thank you for continuing to support me on my writing journey. Now you get to read your fifth book!

To my daughters, you have thrown my life upside down with both your wild spirits, but I wouldn't have it any other way. I love you both to the moon and back.

Last, but not least. Thank you to my dog, GCH CH Chrisan Playing for the Ashes, 'Ash' You are my inspiration for Ash in the book. If it wasn't for you, the seed of Eden's story would not have bloomed on our walk in the woods. Thank you, buddy.

About the Author

At a young age, C. J. Singh was enraptured with books and the art of storytelling. She would write little stores about animals for her grandma to read. As she got older, she enjoyed reading fantasy, romance, and thrillers in between studying for tests for her master's in education. Longing for a real-life adventure outside the pages of these books, she traveled around the world, learning about other cultures and ways of life. To date, she has been to twelve countries. While out on one of her adventures—walking her dog, Ash, in the woods—she got the idea to write about a girl living in the woods with her pet, Ash. She tested out her ideas by telling short made-up bedtime stories to her daughter. Eventually, she decided to embark on one of her greatest adventures: writing this book. She may have just been destined to be an author; after all, she shares a birthday with her favorite author, Beatrix Potter—how cool is that?

Made in the USA
Las Vegas, NV
05 September 2022

54723854R00240